THE ADVENTURES OF

Pinocchio

When old Geppetto carved himself a little puppet out of a piece of wood, he never realized that Pinocchio, as he named the puppet, would be almost a real boy—and every bit as mischievous. In this famous Italian story of childhood, Pinocchio's fantastic adventures on land and sea have made the hero puppet an all-time favorite with children everywhere.

THE ADVENTURES OF
Pinocchio

BY C. COLLODI (CARLO LORENZINI)

TRANSLATED BY M. A. MURRAY

ILLUSTRATIONS BY MARIANO LEONE

COMPANION LIBRARY

Grosset & Dunlap
PUBLISHERS
NEW YORK

Contents

CHAPTER   **PAGE**

1. How it came to pass that Master Cherry, the carpenter, found a piece of wood that laughed and cried like a child.   9
2. Master Cherry makes a present of the piece of wood to his friend Geppetto, who takes it to make for himself a wonderful puppet, that shall know how to dance and to fence and to leap like an acrobat.   12
3. Geppetto having returned home begins at once to make a puppet, to which he gives the name of Pinocchio. The first tricks played by the puppet.   16
4. The story of Pinocchio and the Talking Cricket, from which we see that naughty boys cannot endure to be corrected by those who know more than they do. . . .   22
5. Pinocchio is hungry and searches for an egg to make himself an omelet; but just at the most interesting moment the omelet flies out of the window.   25

CONTENTS

CHAPTER   PAGE

6. Pinocchio falls asleep with his feet on the brazier, and wakes in the morning to find them burnt off.   28

7. Geppetto returns home and gives Pinocchio the breakfast that the poor man had brought for himself.   30

8. Geppetto makes Pinocchio new feet and sells his own coat to buy him a spelling book.   .   34

9. Pinocchio sells his spelling book that he may go and see a puppet show.   37

10. The puppets recognize their brother Pinocchio and receive him with delight; but at that moment their master Fire-Eater makes his appearance and Pinocchio is in danger of coming to a bad end.   40

11. Fire-Eater sneezes and pardons Pinocchio, who then saves the life of his friend Harlequin.   44

12. The showman, Fire-Eater, makes Pinocchio a present of five gold pieces to take home to his father, Geppetto, but Pinocchio instead allows himself to be taken in by the Fox and the Cat, and goes with them.   48

13. The Inn of the Red Crawfish.   54

14. Pinocchio, because he would not heed the good counsels of the Talking Cricket, falls among assassins.   58

15. The assassins pursue Pinocchio; and having overtaken him hang him to a branch of the Big Oak.   62

16. The beautiful child with blue hair has the puppet taken down; has him put to bed and calls in three doctors to know if he is alive or dead.   65

CONTENTS

CHAPTER   PAGE

17. Pinocchio eats the sugar, but will not take his medicine; when, however, he sees the grave-diggers, who have arrived to carry him away, he takes it. He then tells a lie, and as a punishment his nose grows longer. . . .   70

18. Pinocchio meets again the Fox and the Cat, and goes with them to bury his money in the Field of Miracles.   76

19. Pinocchio is robbed of his money, and as a punishment he is sent to prison for four months.   81

20. Liberated from prison, he starts to return to the Fairy's house, but on the road he meets with a horrible Serpent, and afterwards he is caught in a trap.   85

21. Pinocchio is taken by a peasant, who obliges him to fill the place of his watchdog in the poultry yard.   89

22. Pinocchio discovers the robbers, and as a reward for his fidelity is set at liberty. . .   92

23. Pinocchio mourns the death of the beautiful child with the blue hair. He then meets with a Pigeon who flies with him to the seashore, and there he throws himself into the water to go to the assistance of his father, Geppetto. .   97

24. Pinocchio arrives at the Island of the Industrious Bees and finds the Fairy again. . .   103

25. Pinocchio promises the Fairy to be good and studious, for he is quite sick of being a puppet and wishes to become an exemplary boy. .   109

26. Pinocchio accompanies his schoolfellows to the seashore to see the terrible Dogfish. . .   113

27. Great fight between Pinocchio and his companions. One of them is wounded, and

CONTENTS

CHAPTER		PAGE
	Pinocchio is arrested by the gendarmes.	117
28.	Pinocchio is in danger of being fried in a frying pan like a fish.	124
29.	He returns to the Fairy's house. She promises him that the following day he shall cease to be a puppet and shall become a boy. Grand breakfast of coffee and milk to celebrate this great event.	130
30.	Pinocchio, instead of becoming a boy, starts secretly with his friend Candlewick for the Land of Boobies.	138
31.	After five months' residence in the land of Cocagne, Pinocchio, to his great astonishment, grows a beautiful pair of donkey's ears, and he becomes a little donkey, tail and all.	144
32.	Pinocchio gets donkey's ears; and then he becomes a real little donkey and begins to bray.	152
33.	Pinocchio, having become a genuine little donkey, is taken to be sold, and is bought by the director of a company of buffoons to be taught to dance and to jump through hoops, but one evening he lames himself, and then he is bought by a man who wishes to make a drum of his skin.	158
34.	Pinocchio, having been thrown into the sea, is eaten by the fish and becomes a puppet as he was before. While he is swimming away to save his life he is swallowed by the terrible Dogfish.	167
35.	Pinocchio finds in the body of the Dogfish ... whom does he find? Read this chapter and you will know.	175
36.	Pinocchio at last ceases to be a puppet and becomes a boy.	181

I

How it came to pass that MASTER CHERRY *the carpenter found a piece of wood that laughed and cried like a child*

THERE WAS once upon a time . . .

"A king!" my little readers will instantly exclaim.

No, children you are wrong. There was once upon a time a piece of wood.

This wood was not valuable: it was only a common log like those that are burnt in winter in the stoves and fireplaces to make a cheerful blaze and warm the rooms.

I cannot say how it came about, but the fact is that one fine day this piece of wood was lying in the shop of an old carpenter of the name of Master Antonio. He was, however, called by everybody Master Cherry, on account of the end of his nose, which was always as red and polished as a ripe cherry.

No sooner had Master Cherry set eyes on the piece of wood than his face beamed with delight; and, rubbing his hands together with satisfaction, he said softly to himself:

"This wood has come at the right moment; it will just do to make the leg of a little table."

Having said this he immediately took a sharp ax with which to remove the bark and the rough surface. Just, however, as he was going to give the first stroke, he remained with his arm suspended in the air, for he heard a very small voice saying imploringly, "Do not strike me so hard!"

Picture to yourselves the astonishment of good old Master Cherry!

He turned his terrified eyes all round the room to try and discover where the little voice could possibly have come from, but he saw nobody! He looked under the bench—nobody; he looked into a cupboard that was always shut—nobody; he looked into a basket of shavings and sawdust—nobody; he even opened the door of the shop and gave a glance into the street—and still nobody. Who, then, could it be?

"I see how it is," he said, laughing and scratching his wig. "Evidently that little voice was all my imagination. Let us set to work again."

And taking up the ax he struck a tremendous blow on the piece of wood.

"Oh! oh! You have hurt me!" cried the same little voice dolefully.

This time Master Cherry was petrified. His eyes started out of his head with fright, his mouth remained open, and his tongue hung out almost to the end of his chin, like a mask on a fountain. As soon as he had recovered the use of his speech, he began to say, stuttering and trembling with fear:

"But where on earth can that little voice have come from that said Oh! oh!? Here there is certainly no living soul. Is it possible that this piece of wood can have learnt to cry and to lament like a child? I cannot believe it. This piece of wood, here it is; a log for fuel like all the others, and thrown on the fire it would about suffice to boil a saucepan of beans. . . . How then? Can anyone be hidden inside it? If anyone is hidden inside, so much the worse for him. I will settle him at once."

So saying, he seized the poor piece of wood and commenced beating it without mercy against the walls of the room.

Then he stopped to listen if he could hear any little voice lamenting. He waited two minutes—nothing; five minutes—nothing; ten minutes—still nothing!

"I see how it is," he then said, forcing himself to laugh and pushing up his wig. "Evidently the little voice that said Oh! oh! was all my imagination! Let us set to work again."

Nevertheless, he was very frightened, so he tried to sing to give himself a little courage.

Putting the ax aside he took his plane, to plane and polish the bit of wood; but while he was running it up and down he heard the same little voice say, laughing:

"Have done! You are tickling me all over!"

This time poor Master Cherry fell down as if he had been struck by lightning. When he at last opened his eyes he found himself seated on the floor.

His face was quite changed, even the end of his nose, instead of being crimson, as it was nearly always, had become blue from fright.

2

MASTER CHERRY *makes a present of the piece of wood to his friend* GEPPETTO, *who takes it to make for himself a wonderful puppet, that shall know how to dance, and to fence, and to leap like an acrobat*

AT THAT MOMENT someone knocked at the door.

"Come in," said the carpenter, without having the strength to rise to his feet.

A lively little old man immediately walked into the shop. His name was Geppetto, but when the boys of the neighborhood wished to put him in a passion they called him by the nickname of Polendina,* because his yellow wig greatly resembled a pudding made of Indian corn.

Geppetto was very fiery. Woe to him who called him Polendina! He became furious, and there was no holding him.

* In Italian, pudding of Indian corn.

"Good day, Master Antonio," said Geppetto. "What are you doing there on the floor?"

"I am teaching the alphabet to the ants."

"Much good may that do you."

"What has brought you to me, neighbor Geppetto?"

"My legs. But to say the truth, Master Antonio, I am come to ask a favor of you."

"Here I am, ready to serve you," replied the carpenter, getting on to his knees.

"This morning an idea came into my head."

"Let us hear it."

"I thought I would make a beautiful wooden puppet; but a wonderful puppet that should know how to dance, to fence, and to leap like an acrobat. With this puppet I would travel about the world to earn a piece of bread and a glass of wine. What do you think of it?"

"Bravo, Polendina!" exclaimed the same little voice, and it was impossible to say where it came from.

Hearing himself called Polendina, Geppetto became as red as a turkey cock from rage, and turning to the carpenter he said in a fury:

"Why do you insult me?"

"Who insults you?"

"You called me Polendina!"

"It was not I!"

"Would you have it, then, that it was I? It was you, I say!"

"No!"

"Yes!"

"No!"

"Yes!"

And becoming more and more angry, from words they came to blows, and flying at each other they bit, and fought, and scratched manfully.

When the fight was over, Master Antonio was in possession of Geppetto's yellow wig, and Geppetto discovered that the gray wig belonging to the carpenter had remained between his teeth.

"Give me back my wig," screamed Master Antonio.

"And you, return me mine, and let us make friends."

The two old men, having each recovered his own wig, shook hands and swore that they would remain friends to the end of their lives.

"Well, then, neighbor Geppetto," said the carpenter, to prove that peace was made, "what is the favor that you wish of me?"

"I want a little wood to make my puppet; will you give me some?"

Master Antonio was delighted and he immediately went to the bench and fetched the piece of wood that had caused him so much fear. But just as he was going to give it to his friend the piece of wood gave a shake, and wriggling violently out of his hands struck with all of its force against the dried-up shins of poor Geppetto.

"Ah! Is that the courteous way in which you make your presents, Master Antonio? You have almost lamed me!"

"I swear to you that it was not I!"

"Then you would have it that it was I?"

"The wood is entirely to blame!"

"I know that it was the wood; but it was you that hit my legs with it!"

"I did not hit you with it!"

"Liar!"

"Geppetto, don't insult me or I will call you Polendina!"

"Ass!"

"Polendina!"

"Donkey!"

"Polendina!"

"Baboon!"

"Polendina!"

On hearing himself called Polendina for the third time Geppetto, blind with rage, fell upon the carpenter and they fought desperately.

When the battle was over, Master Antonio had two more scratches on his nose, and his adversary had two buttons too little on his waistcoat. Their accounts being thus squared, they shook hands and swore to remain good friends for the rest of their lives.

Geppetto carried off his fine piece of wood and, thanking Master Antonio, returned limping to his house.

3

GEPPETTO, *having returned home, begins at once to make a puppet, to which he gives the name of* PINOCCHIO. *The first tricks played by the puppet*

GEPPETTO LIVED in a small ground-floor room that was lighted only from the staircase. The furniture could not have been simpler—a bad chair, a poor bed, and a broken-down table. At the end of the room there was a fireplace with a lighted fire; but the fire was painted, and by the fire was a painted saucepan that was boiling cheerfully, and sending out a cloud of smoke that looked exactly like real smoke.

As soon as he reached home Geppetto took his tools and set to work to cut out and model his puppet.

"What name shall I give him?" he said to himself. "I think I will call him Pinocchio. It is a name that will bring him luck. I once knew a whole family so called. There was Pinocchio the father, Pinocchia the mother, and Pinocchi the children, and all of them did well. The richest of them was a beggar."

Having found a name for his puppet he began to work in good earnest, and he first made his hair, then his forehead, and then his eyes.

The eyes being finished, imagine his astonishment when he perceived that they moved and looked fixedly at him.

Geppetto, seeing himself stared at by those two wooden eyes, took it almost in bad part, and said in an angry voice:

"Wicked wooden eyes, why do you look at me?"

No one answered.

He then proceeded to carve the nose; but no sooner had he made it than it began to grow. And it grew, and grew, and grew, until in a few minutes it had become an immense nose that seemed as if it would never end.

Poor Geppetto tired himself out with cutting it off; but the more he cut and shortened it, the longer did that impertinent nose become!

The mouth was not even completed when it began to laugh and deride him.

"Stop laughing!" said Geppetto, provoked; but he might as well have spoken to the wall.

"Stop laughing, I say!" he roared in a threatening tone.

The mouth then ceased laughing, but put out its tongue as far as it would go.

Geppetto, not to spoil his handiwork, pretended not to see, and continued his labors. After the mouth he fashioned the chin, then the throat, then the shoulders, the stomach, the arms and the hands.

The hands were scarcely finished when Geppetto felt his wig snatched from his head. He turned round, and what did he see? He saw his yellow wig in the puppet's hand.

"Pinocchio! Give me back my wig instantly!"

"Pinocchio! Give me back my wig instantly!"

But Pinocchio, instead of returning it, put it on his own head, and was in consequence nearly smothered.

Geppetto at this insolent and derisive behavior felt sadder and more melancholy than he had ever been in his life before; and turning to Pinocchio he said to him:

"You young rascal! You are not yet completed, and you are already beginning to show want of respect to your father! That is bad, my boy, very bad!"

And he dried a tear.

The legs and the feet remained to be done.

When Geppetto had finished the feet he received a kick on the point of his nose.

"I deserve it!" he said to himself. "I should have thought of it sooner! Now it is too late!"

He then took the puppet under the arms and placed him on the floor to teach him to walk.

Pinocchio's legs were stiff and he could not move, but Geppetto led him by the hand and showed him how to put one foot before the other.

When his legs became flexible Pinocchio began to walk by himself and to run about the room; until, having gone out of the house door, he jumped into the street and escaped.

Poor Geppetto rushed after him but was not able to overtake him, for that rascal Pinocchio leapt in front of him like a hare, and knocking his wooden feet together against the pavement made as much clatter as twenty pairs of peasants' clogs.

"Stop him! Stop him!" shouted Geppetto; but the people in the street, seeing a wooden puppet running like a race horse, stood still in astonishment to look at it, and laughed, and laughed, and laughed, until it beats description.

At last, as good luck would have it, a carabineer

arrived who, hearing the uproar, imagined that a colt had escaped from his master. Planting himself courageously with his legs apart in the middle of the road, he waited with the determined purpose of stopping him, and thus preventing the chance of worse disasters.

When Pinocchio, still at some distance, saw the carabineer barricading the whole street, he endeavored to take him by surprise and to pass between his legs. But he failed sadly.

The carabineer without disturbing himself in the least caught him cleverly by the nose—it was an immense nose of ridiculous proportions that seemed made on purpose to be laid hold of by carabineers—and consigned him to Geppetto. Wishing to punish him, Geppetto intended to pull his ears at once. But imagine his feelings when he could not succeed in finding them. And do you know the reason? It was that, in his hurry to model him, he had forgotten to make them.

He then took him by the collar, and as he was leading him away he said to him, shaking his head threateningly:

"We will go home at once, and as soon as we arrive we will regulate our accounts, never doubt it."

At this announcement Pinocchio threw himself on the ground and would not take another step. In the meanwhile a crowd of idlers and inquisitive people began to assemble and to make a ring around them.

Some of them said one thing, some another.

"Poor puppet," said several, "he is right not to wish to return home! Who knows how Geppetto, that bad old man, will beat him!"

And the others added maliciously:

"Geppetto seems a good man, but with boys he is a regular tyrant! If that poor puppet is left in his hands he is quite capable of tearing him in pieces!"

It ended in so much being said and done that the

carabineer at last set Pinocchio at liberty and conducted Geppetto to prison. The poor man, not being ready with words to defend himself, cried like a calf, and as he was being led away to prison sobbed out:

"Wretched boy! And to think how I have labored to make him a well-conducted puppet! But it serves me right! I should have thought of it sooner!"

What happened afterward is a story that really is past all belief, but I will relate it to you in the following chapters.

4

The story of PINOCCHIO *and the* TALKING CRICKET, *from which we see that naughty boys cannot endure to be corrected by those who know more than they do*

WELL, THEN, CHILDREN, I must tell you that while poor Geppetto was being taken to prison for no fault of his, that imp Pinocchio, finding himself free from the clutches of the carabineer, ran off as fast as his legs could carry him. That he might reach home the quicker he rushed across the fields, and in his mad hurry he jumped high banks, thorn hedges, and ditches full of water, exactly as a kid or a leveret would have done if pursued by hunters.

Having arrived at the house he found the street door ajar. He pushed it open, went in, and having secured the latch, threw himself on the ground and gave a great sigh of satisfaction.

But his satisfaction did not last long, for he heard someone in the room who was saying:

"Cri-cri-cri!"

"Who calls me?" said Pinocchio in a fright.

"It is I!"

Pinocchio turned around and saw a big cricket crawling slowly up the wall.

"Tell me, Cricket, who may you be?"

"I am the Talking Cricket, and I have lived in this room a hundred years and more."

"Now, however, this room is mine," said the puppet, "and if you would do me a pleasure go away at once, without even turning round."

"I will not go," answered the Cricket, "until I have told you a great truth."

"Tell it me, then, and be quick about it."

"Woe to those boys who rebel against their parents, and run away capriciously from home. They will never come to any good in the world, and sooner or later they will repent bitterly."

"Sing away, Cricket, as you please, and as long as you please. For me, I have made up my mind to run away tomorrow at daybreak, because if I remain I shall not escape the fate of all other boys. I shall be sent to school and shall be made to study either by love or by force. To tell you in confidence, I have no wish to learn; it is much more amusing to run after butterflies, or to climb trees and to take the birds out of their nests."

"Poor little goose! But do you not know that in that way you will grow up a perfect donkey, and that everyone will make game of you?"

"Hold your tongue, you wicked ill-omened croaker!" shouted Pinocchio.

But the Cricket, who was patient and philosophical, instead of becoming angry at this impertinence, continued in the same tone:

"But if you do not wish to go to school, why not at least learn a trade, if only to enable you to earn honestly a piece of bread!"

"Do you want me to tell you?" replied Pinocchio, who was beginning to lose patience. "Among all the trades in the world there is only one that really takes my fancy."

"And that trade—what is it?"

"It is to eat, drink, sleep, and amuse myself, and to lead a vagabond life from morning to night."

"As a rule," said the Talking Cricket with the same composure, "all those who follow that trade end almost always either in a hospital or in prison."

"Take care, you wicked ill-omened croaker! Woe to you if I fly into a passion!"

"Poor Pinocchio! I really pity you!"

"Why do you pity me?"

"Because you are a puppet and, what is worse, because you have a wooden head."

At these last words Pinocchio jumped up in a rage, and snatching a wooden hammer from the bench he threw it at the Talking Cricket.

Perhaps he never meant to hit him; but unfortunately it struck him exactly on the head, so that the poor Cricket had scarcely breath to cry Cri-cri-cri, and then he remained dried up and flattened against the wall.

5

PINOCCHIO *is hungry and searches for an egg to make himself an omelet; but just at the most interesting moment the omelet flies out of the window*

NIGHT WAS COMING ON, and Pinocchio, remembering that he had eaten nothing all day, began to feel a gnawing in his stomach that very much resembled appetite.

But appetite with boys travels quickly, and in fact after a few minutes his appetite had become hunger, and in no time his hunger became ravenous—a hunger that was really quite insupportable.

Poor Pinocchio ran quickly to the fireplace where a saucepan was boiling, and was going to take off the lid to see what was in it, but the saucepan was only painted on the wall. You can imagine his feelings. His nose, which was already long, became longer by at least three fingers.

He then began to run about the room, searching in the drawers and in every imaginable place, in hope of finding a bit of bread. If it was only a bit of dry bread, a crust, a bone left by a dog, a little moldy pudding of Indian corn, a fishbone, a cherry stone—in fact anything that he could gnaw. But he could find nothing, nothing at all, absolutely nothing.

And in the meanwhile his hunger grew and grew; and poor Pinocchio had no other relief than yawning, and his yawns were so tremendous that sometimes his mouth almost reached the place where his ears should have been. And after he had yawned he spluttered, and felt as if he were going to faint.

Then he began to cry desperately, and he said:

"The Talking Cricket was right. I did wrong to rebel against my papa and to run away from home. If my papa were here I should not now be dying of yawning! Oh, what a dreadful illness hunger is!"

Just then he thought he saw something in the dust heap—something round and white that looked like a hen's egg. To give a spring and seize hold of it was the affair of a moment. It was indeed an egg.

Pinocchio's joy beats description; it can only be imagined. Almost believing it must be a dream, he kept turning the egg over in his hands, feeling it and kissing it. And as he kissed it he said:

"And now, how shall I cook it? Shall I make an omelet? . . . No, it would be better to cook it in a saucer! . . . Or would it not be more savory to fry it in the frying pan? Or shall I simply boil it? No, the quickest way of all is to cook it in a saucer: I am in such a hurry to eat it!"

Without loss of time he placed an earthenware saucer on a brazier full of red-hot embers. Into the saucer, instead of oil or butter, he poured a little water; and when the water began to smoke, tac! he broke the eggshell over it that the contents might drop in. But instead of the white and the yolk, a little chicken popped out very gay and polite. Making a beautiful curtsy it said to him:

"A thousand thanks, Master Pinocchio, for saving me the trouble of breaking the shell. Adieu until we meet again. Keep well, and my best compliments to all at home!"

Thus saying, it spread its wings, darted through the open window, and flying away was lost to sight.

The poor puppet stood as if he had been bewitched, with his eyes fixed, his mouth open, and the eggshell in his hand. Recovering, however, from his first stupefaction, he began to cry and scream, and to stamp his feet on the floor in desperation, and amidst his sobs, he said:

"Ah, indeed the Talking Cricket was right. If I had not run away from home, and if my papa were here, I should not now be dying of hunger! Oh, what a dreadful illness hunger is!"

And as his stomach cried out more than ever and he did not know how to quiet it, he thought he would leave the house and make an excursion in the neighborhood in hope of finding some charitable person who would give him a piece of bread.

6

PINOCCHIO *falls asleep with his feet on the brazier, and wakes in the morning to find them burnt off*

IT WAS a wild and stormy winter's night. The thunder was tremendous and the lightning so vivid that the sky seemed on fire. A bitter blusterous wind whistled angrily, and raising clouds of dust swept over the country, causing the trees to creak and groan as it passed.

Pinocchio had a great fear of thunder, but hunger was stronger than fear. He therefore closed the house door and made a rush for the village, which he reached in a hundred bounds, with his tongue hanging out and panting for breath, like a dog after game.

But he found it all dark and deserted. The shops were closed, the windows shut, and there was not so much as a dog in the street. It seemed the land of the dead.

Pinocchio, urged by desperation and hunger, laid hold of the bell of a house and began to peal it with all his might, saying to himself:

"That will bring somebody."

And so it did. A little old man appeared at a window with a nightcap on his head, and called to him angrily:

"What do you want at such an hour?"

"Would you be kind enough to give me a little bread?"

"Wait there, I will be back directly," said the little old man, thinking he had to do with one of those rascally boys who amuse themselves at night by ringing the house bells to rouse respectable people who are sleeping quietly.

After half a minute the window was again opened, and the voice of the same little old man shouted to Pinocchio:

"Come underneath and hold out your cap."

Pinocchio had no cap; but as he stood under the window, an enormous basin of water was poured down on him, watering him from head to foot as if he had been a pot of dried-up geraniums.

He returned home like a wet chicken quite exhausted with fatigue and hunger; and having no longer strength to stand, he sat down and rested his damp muddy feet on a brazier full of burning embers.

And then he fell asleep; and while he slept his feet, which were wooden, took fire, and little by little they burnt away and became cinders.

Pinocchio continued to sleep and to snore as if his feet belonged to someone else. At last about daybreak he awoke because someone was knocking at the door.

"Who is there?" he asked, yawning and rubbing his eyes.

"It is I!" answered a voice.

And the voice was Geppetto's voice.

7

GEPPETTO *returns home and he gives* PINOCCHIO *the breakfast that the poor man had brought for himself*

POOR PINOCCHIO, whose eyes were still half shut from sleep, had not as yet discovered that his feet were burnt off. The moment, therefore, that he heard his father's voice he slipped off his stool to run and open the door; but after stumbling two or three times he fell his whole length on the floor.

And the noise he made in falling was as if a sack of wooden ladles had been thrown from a fifth story.

"Open the door!" shouted Geppetto from the street.

"Dear papa, I cannot," answered the puppet, crying and rolling about on the ground.

"Why cannot you?"

"Because my feet have been eaten."

"And who has eaten your feet?"

"The cat," said Pinocchio, seeing the cat, who was amusing herself by making some shavings dance with her forepaws.

"Open the door, I tell you!" repeated Geppetto. "If you don't, when I get into the house you shall have the cat from me!"

"I cannot stand up, believe me. Oh, poor me, poor me! I shall have to walk on my knees for the rest of my life!"

Geppetto, believing that all this lamentation was only another of the puppet's tricks, thought of a means of putting an end to it, and climbing up the wall he got in at the window.

He was very angry, and at first he did nothing but scold; but when he saw his Pinocchio lying on the ground and really without feet he was quite overcome. He took him in his arms and began to kiss and caress him and to say a thousand endearing things to him, and as the big tears ran down his cheeks, he said, sobbing:

"My little Pinocchio! How did you manage to burn your feet?"

"I don't know, papa, but believe me it has been an infernal night that I shall remember as long as I live. It thundered and lightened, and I was very hungry, and then the Talking Cricket said to me: 'It serves you right; you have been wicked and you deserve it,' and I said to him: 'Take care, Cricket!' . . . and he said: 'You are a puppet and you have a wooden head,' and I threw the handle of a hammer at him, and he died, but the fault was his, for I didn't wish to kill him, and the proof of it is that I put an earthenware saucer on a brazier of burning embers, but a chicken flew out and said: 'Adieu until we meet again, and many compliments to all at home': and I got still more hungry, for which reason that little old man in a nightcap opening the window said to me, 'Come underneath and hold out your hat,' and poured a basinful of water on my head, because asking for a little bread isn't a disgrace, is it? And I returned home at once, and because I was always very hungry I put my feet on the brazier to dry them, and then you returned, and I found they were burnt off, and I am always hungry, but I have no longer any feet! Ih! Ih! Ih! Ih! . . ." And poor Pinocchio began to cry and roar so loudly that he was heard five miles off.

Geppetto, who from all this jumbled account had only understood one thing, which was that the puppet was dying of hunger, drew from his pocket three pears, and giving them to him said:

"These three pears were intended for my breakfast; but I will give them to you willingly. Eat them, and I hope they will do you good."

"If you wish me to eat them, be kind enough to peel them for me."

"Peel them?" said Geppetto, astonished. "I should never have thought, my boy, that you were so dainty and fastidious. This is bad! In this world we should accustom ourselves from childhood to like and to eat everything, for there is no saying to what we may be brought. There are so many chances! . . ."

"You are no doubt right," interrupted Pinocchio, "but I will never eat fruit that has not been peeled. I cannot bear rind."

So that good Geppetto fetched a knife, and arming himself with patience peeled the three pears, and put the rind on a corner of the table.

Having eaten the first pear in two mouthfuls, Pinocchio was about to throw away the core; but Geppetto caught hold of his arm and said to him:

"Do not throw it away; in this world everything may be of use."

"But core I am determined I will not eat," shouted the puppet, turning upon him like a viper.

"Who knows! There are so many chances! . . ." repeated Geppetto without losing his temper.

And so the three cores, instead of being thrown out of the window, were placed on the corner of the table together with the three rinds.

Having eaten, or rather having devoured the three pears, Pinocchio yawned tremendously, and then said in a fretful tone:

"I am as hungry as ever!"

"But, my boy, I have nothing more to give you!"

"Nothing, really nothing?"

"I have only the rind and the cores of the three pears."

"One must have patience!" said Pinocchio. "If there is nothing else I will eat a rind."

And he began to chew it. At first he made a wry face; but then one after another he quickly disposed of the rinds; and after the rinds even the cores, and when he had eaten up everything he clapped his hands on his sides in his satisfaction, and said joyfully:

"Ah! Now I feel comfortable."

"You see now," observed Geppetto, "that I was right when I said to you that it did not do to accustom ourselves to be too particular or too dainty in our tastes. We can never know, my dear boy, what may happen to us. There are so many chances! . . ."

8

GEPPETTO *makes* PINOCCHIO *new feet, and sells his own coat to buy him a spelling book*

NO SOONER HAD the puppet appeased his hunger than he began to cry and to grumble because he wanted a pair of new feet.

But Geppetto, to punish him for his naughtiness, allowed him to cry and to despair for half the day. He then said to him:

"Why should I make you new feet? To enable you, perhaps, to escape again from home?"

"I promise you," said the puppet, sobbing, "that for the future I will be good."

"All boys," replied Geppetto, "when they are bent upon obtaining something, say the same thing."

"I promise you that I will go to school, and that I will study and earn a good character."

"All boys, when they are bent on obtaining something, repeat the same story."

"But I am not like other boys! I am better than all of them and I will always speak the truth. I promise you, papa, that I will learn a trade, and that I will be the consolation and the staff of your old age."

Geppetto, although he put on a severe face, had his eyes full of tears and his heart big with sorrow at seeing his poor Pinocchio in such a pitiable state. He did not say another word, but taking his tools and two small pieces of well-seasoned wood he set to work with great diligence.

In less than an hour the feet were finished: two little feet—swift, well-knit, and nervous. They might have been modeled by an artist of genius.

Geppetto then said to the puppet:

"Shut your eyes and go to sleep!"

And Pinocchio shut his eyes and pretended to be asleep.

And while he pretended to sleep, Geppetto, with a little glue which he had melted in an eggshell, fastened his feet in their place, and it was so well done that not even a trace could be seen of where they were joined.

No sooner had the puppet discovered that he had feet than he jumped down from the table on which he was lying, and began to spring and to cut a thousand capers about the room, as if he had gone mad with the greatness of his delight.

"To reward you for what you have done for me," said Pinocchio to his father, "I will go to school at once."

"Good boy."

"But to go to school I shall want some clothes."

Geppetto, who was poor, and who had not so much as a farthing in his pocket, then made him a little jacket of flowered paper, a pair of shoes from the bark of a tree, and a cap of a crumb of bread.

Pinocchio ran immediately to look at himself in a crock of water, and he was so pleased with his appearance that he said, strutting about like a peacock:

"I look quite like a gentleman!"

"Yes, indeed," answered Geppetto, "for bear in mind that it is not fine clothes that make the gentleman, but rather clean clothes."

"By the bye," added the puppet, "to go to school I am still in want—indeed I am without the best thing, and the most important."

"And what is it?"

"I have no spelling book."

"You are right; but what shall we do to get one?"

"It is quite easy. We have only to go to the book-seller's and buy it."

"And the money?"

"I have got none."

"No more have I," added the good old man very sadly.

And Pinocchio, although he was a very merry boy, became sad also; because poverty, when it is real poverty, is understood by everybody—even by boys.

"Well, patience!" exclaimed Geppetto, all at once rising to his feet, and putting on his old fustian coat, all patched and darned, he ran out of the house.

He returned shortly, holding in his hand a spelling book for Pinocchio, but the old coat was gone. The poor man was in his shirt sleeves, and out of doors it was snowing.

"And the coat, papa?"

"I have sold it."

"Why did you sell it?"

"Because I found it too hot."

Pinocchio understood this answer in an instant, and unable to restrain the impulse of his good heart he sprang up, and throwing his arms around Geppetto's neck he began kissing him again and again.

9

PINOCCHIO *sells his spelling book that he may go and see a puppet show*

AS SOON as it had done snowing Pinocchio set out for school with his fine spelling book under his arm. As he went along he began to imagine a thousand things in his little brain, and to build a thousand castles in the air, one more beautiful than the other.

And talking to himself he said:

"Today at school I will learn to read at once; then tomorrow I will begin to write, and the day after tomorrow to cipher. Then with my acquirements I will earn a great deal of money, and with the first money I have in my pocket I will immediately buy for my papa a beautiful new cloth coat. But what am I saying? Cloth, indeed! It shall be all made of gold and silver, and it shall have diamond buttons. That poor man really deserves it; for to buy me books and have me taught he has remained in his shirt sleeves. . . . And in this cold! It is only fathers who are capable of such sacrifices! . . ."

While he was saying this with great emotion he thought that he heard music in the distance that sounded like fifes and the beating of a big drum: fi-fi-fi, fi-fi-fi, zum, zum, zum, zum.

He stopped and listened. The sounds came from the end of a cross street which led to a little village on the seashore.

"What can that music be? What a pity that I have to go to school, or else . . ."

And he remained irresolute. It was, however, necessary to come to a decision. Should he go to school? Or should he go after the fifes?

"Today I will go and hear the fifes, and tomorrow I will go to school," finally decided the young scapegrace, shrugging his shoulders.

The more he ran the nearer came the sounds of the fifes and the beating of the big drum: fi-fi-fi, zum, zum, zum, zum.

At last he found himself in the middle of a square quite full of people, who were all crowding round a building made of wood and canvas, and painted a thousand colors.

"What is that building?" asked Pinocchio, turning to a little boy who belonged to the place.

"Read the placard—it is all written—and then you will know."

"I would read it willingly, but it so happens that today I don't know how to read."

"Bravo, blockhead! Then I will read it to you. The writing on that placard in those letters red as fire is:

'GREAT PUPPET THEATER.' "

"Has the play begun long?"
"It is beginning now."
"How much does it cost to go in?"
"Twopence."

Pinocchio, who was in a fever of curiosity, lost all control of himself, and without any shame he said to the little boy to whom he was talking:

"Would you lend me twopence until tomorrow?"

"I would lend them to you willingly," said the other, taking him off, "but it so happens that today I cannot give them to you."

"I will sell you my jacket for twopence," the puppet then said to him.

"What do you think that I could do with a jacket of flowered paper? If there was rain and it got wet, it would be impossible to get it off my back."

"Will you buy my shoes?"

"They would only be of use to light the fire."

"How much will you give me for my cap?"

"That would be a wonderful acquisition indeed! A cap of bread crumb! There would be a risk of the mice coming to eat it while it was on my head."

Pinocchio was on thorns. He was on the point of making another offer, but he had not the courage. He hesitated, felt irresolute and remorseful. At last he said:

"Will you give me twopence for this new spelling book?"

"I am a boy and I don't buy from boys," replied his little interlocutor, who had much more sense than he had.

"I will buy the spelling book for twopence," called out a hawker of old clothes, who had been listening to the conversation.

And the book was sold there and then. And to think that poor Geppetto had remained at home trembling with cold in his shirt sleeves, that he might buy his son a spelling book.

IO

The puppets recognize their broth-er PINOCCHIO, *and receive him with delight; but at that moment their master* FIRE-EATER *makes his appearance and* PINOCCHIO *is in danger of coming to a bad end*

WHEN PINOCCHIO came into the little puppet theater, an incident occurred that almost produced a revolution. I must tell you that the curtain was drawn up, and the play had already begun.

On the stage Harlequin and Punchinello were as usual quarreling with each other, and threatening every moment to come to blows.

The audience, all attention, laughed till they were ill as they listened to the bickerings of these two puppets, who gesticulated and abused each other so naturally that they might have been two reasonable beings, and two persons of the world.

All at once Harlequin stopped short, and turning to the public he pointed with his hand to someone far down in the pit, and exclaimed in a dramatic tone:

"Gods of the firmament! Do I dream, or am I awake? But surely that is Pinocchio!"

"It is indeed Pinocchio!" cried Punchinello.

"It is indeed himself!" screamed Miss Rose, peeping from behind the scenes.

"It is Pinocchio! It is Pinocchio!" shouted all the puppets in chorus, leaping from all sides on to the stage. "It is Pinocchio! It is our brother Pinocchio! Long live Pinocchio!"

"Pinocchio, come up here to me," cried Harlequin, "and throw yourself into the arms of your wooden brothers!"

At this affectionate invitation Pinocchio made a leap from the end of the pit into the reserved seats; another leap landed him on the head of the leader of the orchestra, and he then sprang upon the stage.

The embraces, the hugs, the friendly pinches, and the demonstrations of warm brotherly affection that Pinocchio received from the excited crowd of actors and actresses of the puppet dramatic company beat description.

The sight was doubtless a moving one, but the public in the pit, finding that the play was stopped, became impatient and began to shout: "We will have the play —go on with the play!"

It was all breath thrown away. The puppets, instead of continuing the recital, redoubled their noise and outcries, and putting Pinocchio on their shoulders they carried him in triumph before the footlights.

At that moment out came the showman. He was very big, and so ugly that the sight of him was enough to frighten anyone. His beard was as black as ink, and so long that it reached from his chin to the ground. I need

At that moment, out came the showman

only say that he trod upon it when he walked. His mouth was as big as an oven, and his eyes were like two lanterns of red glass with lights burning inside them. He carried a large whip made of snakes' and foxes' tails twisted together, which he cracked constantly.

At his unexpected appearance there was a profound silence: no one dared to breathe. A fly might have been heard in the stillness. The poor puppets of both sexes trembled like so many leaves.

"Why have you come to raise a disturbance in my theater?" asked the showman of Pinocchio, in the gruff voice of a hobgoblin suffering from a severe cold in the head.

"Believe me, honored sir, that it was not my fault! . . ."

"That is enough! Tonight we will settle our accounts."

As soon as the play was over, the showman went into the kitchen where a fine sheep, preparing for his supper, was turning slowly on the spit in front of the fire. As there was not enough wood to finish roasting and browning it, he called Harlequin and Punchinello, and said to them:

"Bring that puppet here: you will find him hanging on a nail. It seems to me that he is made of very dry wood, and I am sure that if he were thrown on the fire he would make a beautiful blaze for the roast."

At first Harlequin and Punchinello hesitated; but, appalled by a severe glance from their master, they obeyed. In a short time they returned to the kitchen carrying poor Pinocchio, who was wriggling like an eel taken out of water, and screaming desperately:

"Papa, papa, save me! I will not die, I will not die! . . ."

II

FIRE-EATER *sneezes and pardons* PINOCCHIO, *who then saves the life of his friend* HARLEQUIN

THE SHOWMAN Fire-eater—for that was his name—looked, I must say, a terrible man, especially with his black beard that covered his chest and legs like an apron. On the whole, however, he had not a bad heart. In proof of this, when he saw poor Pinocchio brought before him, struggling and screaming "I will not die, I will not die!" he was quite moved and felt very sorry for him. He tried to hold out, but after a little he could stand it no longer and he sneezed violently. When he heard the sneeze, Harlequin, who up to that moment had been in the deepest affliction, and bowed down like a weeping willow, became quite cheerful, and leaning toward Pinocchio he whispered to him softly:

"Good news, brother. The showman has sneezed, and that is a sign that he pities you, and consequently you are saved."

For you must know that while most men, when they feel compassion for somebody, either weep or at least pretend to dry their eyes, Fire-eater, on the contrary, whenever he was really overcome, had the habit of sneezing.

After he had sneezed, the showman, still acting the ruffian, shouted to Pinocchio:

"Have done crying! Your lamentations have given me a pain in my stomach. . . . I feel a spasm, that almost . . . Etci! etci!" and he sneezed again twice.

"Bless you!" said Pinocchio.

"Thank you! And your papa and your mamma, are they still alive?" asked Fire-eater.

"Papa, yes; my mamma I have never known."

"Who can say what a sorrow it would be for your poor old father if I were to have you thrown among those burning coals! Poor old man! I compassionate him! . . . Etci! etci! etci!" and he sneezed again three times.

"Bless you!" said Pinocchio.

"Thank you! All the same, some compassion is due to me, for as you see I have no more wood with which to finish roasting my mutton, and to tell you the truth, under the circumstances you would have been of great use to me! However, I have had pity on you, so I must have patience. Instead of you I will burn under the spit one of the puppets belonging to my company. Ho there, gendarmes!"

At this call two wooden gendarmes immediately appeared. They were very long and very thin, and had on cocked hats, and held unsheathed swords in their hands.

The showman said to them in a hoarse voice:

"Take Harlequin, bind him securely, and then throw him on the fire to burn. I am determined that my mutton shall be well roasted."

Only imagine that poor Harlequin! His terror was so great that his legs bent under him and he fell with his face on the ground.

At this agonizing sight Pinocchio, weeping bitterly, threw himself at the showman's feet, and bathing his long beard with his tears he began to say in a supplicating voice:

"Have pity, Sir Fire-eater! . . ."

"Here there are no sirs," the showman answered severely.

"Have pity, Sir Knight! . . ."

"Here there are no knights!"

"Have pity, Commander! . . ."

"Here there are no commanders!"

"Have pity, Excellence! . . ."

Upon hearing himself called Excellence the showman began to smile, and became at once kinder and more tractable. Turning to Pinocchio, he asked:

"Well, what do you want from me?"

"I implore you to pardon poor Harlequin."

"For him there can be no pardon. As I have spared you, he must be put on the fire, for I am determined that my mutton shall be well roasted."

"In that case," cried Pinocchio proudly, rising and throwing away his cap of bread crumb—"in that case I know my duty. Come on, gendarmes! Bind me and throw me among the flames. No, it is not just that poor Harlequin, my true friend, should die for me!"

These words, pronounced in a loud heroic voice, made all the puppets who were present cry. Even the gendarmes, although they were made of wood, wept like two newly born lambs.

Fire-eater at first remained as hard and unmoved as ice, but little by little he began to melt and to sneeze. And having sneezed four or five times, the showman opened his arms affectionately and said to Pinocchio:

"You are a good, brave boy! Come here and give me a kiss."

Pinocchio ran at once, and climbing like a squirrel up

the showman's beard he deposited a hearty kiss on the point of his nose.

"Then the pardon is granted?" asked poor Harlequin in a faint voice that was scarcely audible.

"The pardon is granted!" answered Fire-eater; he then added, sighing and shaking his head:

"I must have patience!   Tonight I shall have to resign myself to eat the mutton half raw; but another time woe to him who chances! . . ."

At the news of the pardon the puppets all ran to the stage, and having lighted the lamps and chandeliers as if for a full-dress performance, they began to leap and to dance merrily.   At dawn they were still dancing.

12

The showman, FIRE-EATER, *makes* PINOCCHIO *a present of five gold pieces to take home to his father,* GEPPETTO, *but* PINOCCHIO *instead allows himself to be taken in by the* FOX *and the* CAT, *and goes with them*

THE FOLLOWING DAY Fire-eater called Pinocchio on one side and asked him:

"What is your father's name?"

"Geppetto."

"And what trade does he follow?"

"He is a beggar."

"Does he gain much?"

"Gain much? Why, he has never a penny in his pocket. Only think, to buy a spelling book for me to go to school he was obliged to sell the only coat he had to wear—a coat that, between patches and darns, was not fit to be seen."

"Poor devil! I feel almost sorry for him! Here are five gold pieces. Go at once and take them to him with my compliments."

You can easily understand that Pinocchio thanked the showman a thousand times. He embraced all the puppets of the company one by one, even to the gendarmes, and beside himself with delight set out to return home.

But he had not gone far when he met on the road a Fox lame of one foot and a Cat blind of both eyes, who were going along helping each other like good companions in misfortune. The Fox, who was lame, walked leaning on the Cat, and the Cat, who was blind, was guided by the Fox.

"Good day, Pinocchio," said the Fox, accosting him politely.

"How do you come to know my name?" asked the puppet.

"I know your father well."

"Where did you see him?"

"I saw him yesterday at the door of his house."

"And what was he doing?"

"He was in his shirt sleeves and shivering with cold."

"Poor papa! But that is over; for the future he shall shiver no more!"

"Why?"

"Because I have become a gentleman."

"A gentleman—you!" said the Fox, and he began to laugh rudely and scornfully. The Cat also began to laugh, but to conceal it she combed her whiskers.

"There is little to laugh at," cried Pinocchio angrily. "I am really sorry to make your mouth water, but if you know anything about it, you can see that these here are five gold pieces."

And he pulled out the money that Fire-eater had made him a present of.

At the sympathetic ring of the money the Fox, with

an involuntary movement, stretched out the paw that seemed crippled, and the Cat opened wide two eyes that looked like two green lanterns. It is true that she shut them again, and so quickly that Pinocchio observed nothing.

"And now," asked the Fox, "what are you going to do with all that money?"

"First of all," answered the puppet, "I intend to buy a new coat for my papa, made of gold and silver, and with diamond buttons; and then I will buy a spelling book for myself."

"For yourself?"

"Yes, indeed: for I wish to go to school to study in earnest."

"Look at me!" said the Fox. "Through my foolish passion for study I have lost a leg."

"Look at me!" said the Cat. "Through my foolish passion for study I have lost the sight of both my eyes."

At that moment a white Blackbird, that was perched on the hedge by the road, began his usual song, and said:

"Pinocchio, don't listen to the advice of bad companions: if you do you will repent it!"

Poor Blackbird! If only he had not spoken! The Cat, with a great leap, sprang upon him, and without even giving him time to say Oh! ate him in a mouthful, feathers and all.

Having eaten him and cleaned her mouth she shut her eyes again and feigned blindness as before.

"Poor Blackbird!" said Pinocchio to the Cat. "Why did you treat him so badly?"

"I did it to give him a lesson. He will learn another time not to meddle in other people's conversation."

They had gone almost halfway when the Fox, halting suddenly, said to the puppet:

"Would you like to double your money?"

"In what way?"

"Would you like to make out of your five miserable sovereigns, a hundred, a thousand, two thousand?"

"I should think so! But in what way?"

"The way is easy enough. Instead of returning home you must go with us."

"And where do you wish to take me?"

"To the Land of the Owls."

Pinocchio reflected a moment, and then he said resolutely:

"No, I will not go. I am already close to the house, and I will return home to my papa who is waiting for me. Who can tell how often the poor old man must have sighed yesterday when I did not come back! I have indeed been a bad son, and the Talking Cricket was right when he said: 'Disobedient boys never come to any good in the world.' I have found it to my cost, for many misfortunes have happened to me. Even yesterday in Fire-eater's house I ran the risk . . . Oh, it makes me shudder only to think of it!"

"Well, then," said the Fox, "you are quite decided to go home? Go then, and so much the worse for you."

"So much the worse for you!" repeated the Cat.

"Think well of it, Pinocchio, for you are giving a kick to fortune."

"To fortune!" repeated the Cat.

"Between today and tomorrow your five sovereigns would have become two thousand."

"Two thousand!" repeated the Cat.

"But how is it possible that they could have become so many?" asked Pinocchio, remaining with his mouth open from astonishment.

"I will explain it to you at once," said the Fox. "You must know that in the Land of the Owls there is a sacred field called by everybody the Field of Miracles. In this

"Would you like to double your money?"

field you must dig a little hole, and you put into it, we will say, one gold sovereign. You then cover up the hole with a little earth: you must water it with two pails of water from the fountain, then sprinkle it with two pinches of salt, and when night comes you can go quietly to bed. In the meanwhile, during the night, the gold piece will grow and flower, and in the morning when you get up and return to the field, what do you find? You find a beautiful tree laden with as many gold sovereigns as a fine ear of corn has grains in the month of June."

"So that," said Pinocchio, more and more bewildered, "supposing I buried my five sovereigns in that field, how many should I find there the following morning?"

"That is an exceedingly easy calculation," replied the Fox, "a calculation that you can make on the ends of your fingers. Put that every sovereign gives you an increase of five hundred: multiply five hundred by five, and the following morning will find you with two thousand five hundred shining gold pieces in your pocket."

"Oh, how delightful!" cried Pinocchio, dancing for joy. "As soon as ever I have obtained those sovereigns, I will keep two thousand for myself, and the other five hundred I will make a present of to you two."

"A present to us?" cried the Fox with indignation and appearing much offended. "What are you dreaming of?"

"What are you dreaming of?" repeated the Cat.

"We do not work," said the Fox, "for dirty interest: we work solely to enrich others."

"Others!" repeated the Cat.

"What good people!" thought Pinocchio to himself; and forgetting there and then his papa, the new coat, the spelling book, and all his good resolutions, he said to the Fox and the Cat:

"Let us be off at once. I will go with you."

13

The inn of the RED CRAWFISH

THEY WALKED, and walked, and walked, until at last, toward evening, they arrived dead tired at the inn of the Red Crawfish.

"Let us stop here a little," said the Fox, "that we may have something to eat and rest ourselves for an hour or two. We will start again at midnight so as to arrive at the Field of Miracles by dawn tomorrow morning."

Having gone into the inn they all three sat down to table: but none of them had any appetite.

The Cat, who was suffering from indigestion and feeling seriously indisposed, could only eat thirty-five mullet with tomato sauce, and four portions of tripe with Parmesan cheese; and because she thought the tripe was not seasoned enough, she asked three times for the butter and grated cheese!

The Fox would also willingly have picked a little, but as his doctor had ordered him a strict diet, he was forced to content himself simply with a hare dressed with a sweet and sour sauce, and garnished lightly with fat chickens and early pullets. After the hare he sent for a dish made of partridges, rabbits, frogs, lizards, and other delicacies; he could not touch anything else. He had such a disgust to food, he said, that he could put nothing to his lips.

The one who ate the least was Pinocchio. He asked for some walnuts and a hunch of bread, and left everything on his plate. The poor boy, whose thoughts were continually fixed on the Field of Miracles, had got in anticipation an indigestion of gold pieces.

When they had supped, the Fox said to the host:

"Give us two good rooms, one for Mr. Pinocchio, and the other for me and my companion. We will snatch a little sleep before we leave. Remember, however, that at midnight we wish to be called to continue our journey."

"Yes, gentlemen," answered the host, and he winked at the Fox and the Cat, as much as to say: "I know what you are up to. We understand one another!"

No sooner had Pinocchio got into bed than he fell asleep at once and began to dream. And he dreamt that he was in the middle of a field, and the field was full of shrubs covered with clusters of gold sovereigns, and as they swung in the wind they went zin, zin, zin, almost as if they would say: "Let who will, come and take us." But when Pinocchio was at the most interesting moment, that is, just as he was stretching out his hand to pick handfuls of those beautiful gold pieces and to put them in his pocket, he was suddenly awakened by three violent blows on the door of his room.

It was the host who had come to tell him that midnight had struck.

"Are my companions ready?" asked the puppet.

"Ready! Why, they left two hours ago."

"Why were they in such a hurry?"

"Because the Cat had received a message to say that her eldest kitten was ill with chilblains on his feet, and was in danger of death."

"Did they pay for the supper?"

"What are you thinking of? They are much too well educated to dream of offering such an insult to a gentleman like you."

"What a pity! It is an insult that would have given me so much pleasure!" said Pinocchio, scratching his head. He then asked:

"And where did my good friends say they would wait for me?"

"At the Field of Miracles, tomorrow morning at daybreak."

Pinocchio paid a sovereign for his supper and that of his companions, and then left.

Outside the inn it was so pitch dark that he had almost to grope his way, for it was impossible to see a hand's breadth in front of him. In the adjacent country not a leaf moved. Only some night birds flying across the road from one hedge to the other brushed Pinocchio's nose with their wings as they passed, which caused him so much terror that, springing back, he shouted, "Who goes there?" and the echo in the surrounding hills repeated in the distance: "Who goes there? Who goes there? Who goes there?"

As he was walking along he saw a little insect shining dimly on the trunk of a tree, like a night light in a lamp of transparent china.

"Who are you?" asked Pinocchio.

"I am the ghost of the Talking Cricket," answered the insect in a low voice, so weak and faint that it seemed to come from the other world.

"What do you want with me?" said the puppet.

"I want to give you some advice. Go back, and take the four sovereigns that you have left to your poor father, who is weeping and in despair because you have not returned to him."

"By tomorrow my papa will be a gentleman, for these four sovereigns will have become two thousand."

"Don't trust, my boy, those who promise to make you rich in a day. Usually they are either mad or rogues! Give ear to me, and go back."

"On the contrary, I am determined to go on."

"The hour is late!"

"I am determined to go on."

"The night is dark!"

"I am determined to go on."

"The road is dangerous!"

"I am determined to go on."

"Remember that boys who are bent on following their caprices, and will have their own way, sooner or later repent it."

"Always the same stories. Good night, Cricket."

"Good night, Pinocchio, and may Heaven preserve you from dangers and from assassins."

No sooner had he said these words than the Talking Cricket vanished suddenly like a light that has been blown out, and the road became darker than ever.

14

"REALLY," said the puppet to himself as he resumed his journey, "how unfortunate we poor boys are. Everybody scolds us, everybody admonishes us, everybody gives us good advice. To let them talk, they would all take it into their heads to be our fathers and our masters —all: even the Talking Cricket. See now; because I don't choose to listen to that tiresome cricket, who knows, according to him, how many misfortunes are to happen to me! I am even to meet with assassins! That is, however, of little consequence, for I don't believe in assassins—I have never believed in them. For me, I think that assassins have been invented purposely by papas to frighten boys who want to go out at night. Besides, supposing I was to come across them here in the road, do you imagine they would frighten me? Not the least in the world. I should go to meet them and cry: 'Gentlemen assassins, what do you want with me? Remember that with me there is no joking. Therefore go about your business and be quiet!' At this speech, said in a determined tone, those poor assassins—I think I see them—would run away like the wind. If, however, they were so badly educated as not to run away, why, then, I would run away myself, and there would be an end of it."

But Pinocchio had not time to finish his reasoning, for at that moment he thought that he heard a slight rustle of leaves behind him.

He turned to look, and saw in the gloom two evil-looking black figures completely enveloped in charcoal sacks. They were running after him on tiptoe, and making great leaps like two phantoms.

"Here they are in reality!" he said to himself, and not knowing where to hide his gold pieces he put them in his mouth precisely under his tongue.

Then he tried to escape. But he had not gone a step when he felt himself seized by the arm, and heard two horrid sepulchral voices saying to him:

"Your money or your life!"

Pinocchio, not being able to answer in words, owing to the money that was in his mouth, made a thousand low bows and a thousand pantomimes. He tried thus to make the two muffled figures, whose eyes were only visible through the holes in their sacks, understand that he was a poor puppet, and that he had not as much as a false farthing in his pocket.

"Come now! Less nonsense and out with the money!" cried the two brigands threateningly.

And the puppet made a gesture with his hands to signify "I have got none."

"Deliver up your money or you are dead," said the taller of the brigands.

"Dead!" repeated the other.

"And after we have killed you, we will also kill your father."

"Also your father!"

"No, no, no, not my poor papa!" cried Pinocchio in a despairing tone; and as he said it, the sovereigns clinked in his mouth.

"Ah! You rascal! Then you have hidden your money under your tongue! Spit it out at once!"

But Pinocchio was obdurate.

"Ah! You pretend to be deaf, do you? Wait a moment, leave it to us to find a means to make you spit it out."

And one of them seized the puppet by the end of his nose, and the other took him by the chin, and began to pull them brutally, the one up and the other down, to constrain him to open his mouth. But it was all to no purpose. Pinocchio's mouth seemed to be nailed and riveted together.

Then the shorter assassin drew out an ugly knife and tried to force it between his lips like a lever or chisel. But Pinocchio, as quick as lightning, caught his hand with his teeth, and with one bite bit it clean off and spat it out. Imagine his astonishment when instead of a hand he perceived that he had spat a cat's paw to the ground.

Encouraged by this first victory he used his nails to such purpose that he succeeded in liberating himself from his assailants, and jumping the hedge by the roadside he began to fly across the country. The assassins ran after him like two dogs chasing a hare: and the one who had lost a paw ran on one leg, and no one ever knew how he managed it.

After a race of some miles Pinocchio could do no more. Giving himself up for lost he climbed the trunk of a very high pine tree and seated himself in the topmost branches. The assassins attempted to climb after him, but when they had reached halfway up the trunk they slid down again, and arrived on the ground with the skin grazed from their hands and knees.

But they were not to be beaten by so little: collecting a quantity of dry wood they piled it beneath the pine and set fire to it. In less time than it takes to tell, the pine began to burn and to flame like a candle blown by the wind. Pinocchio, seeing that the flames were mounting higher every instant, and not wishing to end his life like a roasted pigeon, made a stupendous leap from the top of the tree and started afresh across the fields and vineyards. The assassins followed him, and kept behind him without once giving in.

The day began to break and they were still pursuing him. Suddenly Pinocchio found his way barred by a wide deep ditch full of dirty water the color of coffee. What was he to do? "One! two! three!" cried the puppet, and making a rush he sprang to the other side. The assassins also jumped, but not having measured the distance properly, splash, splash! they fell into the very middle of the ditch. Pinocchio, who heard the plunge and the splashing of the water, shouted out, laughing, and without stopping:

"A fine bath to you, gentlemen assassins."

And he felt convinced that they were drowned, when, turning to look, he perceived that on the contrary they were both running after him, still enveloped in their sacks, with the water dripping from them as if they had been two hollow baskets.

15

The assassins pursue PINOCCHIO; *and having overtaken him hang him to a branch of the Big Oak*

AT THIS SIGHT the puppet's courage failed him, and he was on the point of throwing himself on the ground and giving himself over for lost. Turning, however, his eyes in every direction, he saw at some distance, standing out amidst the dark green of the trees, a small house as white as snow.

"If I had only breath to reach that house," he said to himself, "perhaps I should be saved."

And without delaying an instant, he recommenced running for his life through the wood, and the assassins after him.

At last, after a desperate race of nearly two hours, he arrived quite breathless at the door of the house, and knocked. No one answered.

He knocked again with great violence, for he heard the sound of steps approaching him, and the heavy panting of his persecutors. The same silence.

Seeing that knocking was uselsss he began in desperation to kick and pommel the door with all his might. The window then opened and a beautiful Child appeared at it. She had blue hair and a face as white as a waxen image; her eyes were closed and her hands were crossed on her breast. Without moving her lips in the least, she said in a voice that seemed to come from the other world:

"In this house there is no one. They are all dead."

"Then at least open the door for me yourself," shouted Pinocchio, crying and imploring.

"I am dead also."

"Dead? Then what are you doing there at the window?"

"I am waiting for the bier to come to carry me away."

Having said this she immediately disappeared, and the window was closed again without the slightest noise.

"Oh, beautiful Child with blue hair," cried Pinocchio, "open the door for pity's sake! Have compassion on a poor boy pursued by assas . . ."

But he could not finish the word, for he felt himself seized by the collar, and the same two horrible voices said to him threateningly:

"You shall not escape from us again!"

The puppet, seeing death staring him in the face, was taken with such a violent fit of trembling that the joints of his wooden legs began to creak, and the sovereigns hidden under his tongue to clink.

"Now then," demanded the assassins, "will you open your mouth, yes or no? Ah; no answer? . . . Leave it to us: this time we will force you to open it!"

And drawing out two long horrid knives as sharp as razors, clash! they attempted to stab him twice.

But the puppet, luckily for him, was made of very hard wood; the knives therefore broke into a thousand pieces, and the assassins were left with the handles in their hands, staring at each other.

"I see what we must do," said one of them.   "He must be hung; let us hang him!"

"Let us hang him!" repeated the other.

Without loss of time they tied his arms behind him, passed a running noose round his throat, and then hung him to the branch of a tree called the Big Oak.

They then sat down on the grass and waited for his last struggle.   But at the end of three hours the puppet's eyes were still open, his mouth closed, and he was kicking more than ever.

Losing patience, they turned to Pinocchio and said in a bantering tone:

"Good-by till tomorrow.   Let us hope that when we return you will be polite enough to allow yourself to be found quite dead, and with your mouth wide open."

And they walked off.

In the meantime a tempestuous northerly wind began to blow and roar angrily, and it beat the poor puppet as he hung, from side to side, making him swing violently like the clatter of a bell ringing for a wedding.   And the swinging gave him atrocious spasms, and the running noose, becoming still tighter round his throat, took away his breath.

Little by little his eyes began to grow dim, but although he felt that death was near he still continued to hope that some charitable person would come to his assistance before it was too late.   But when, after waiting and waiting, he found that no one came, absolutely no one, then he remembered his poor father, and thinking he was dying, he stammered out:

"Oh, papa, papa!   If only you were here!"

His breath failed him and he could say no more.   He shut his eyes, opened his mouth, stretched his legs, gave a long shudder, and hung stiff and insensible.

16

The beautiful CHILD *with blue hair has the puppet taken down; has him put to bed and calls in three doctors to know if he is alive or dead*

WHILE POOR PINOCCHIO, suspended to a branch of the Big Oak, was apparently more dead than alive, the beautiful Child with blue hair came again to the window. When she saw the unhappy puppet hanging by his throat, and dancing up and down in the gusts of the north wind, she was moved by compassion. Striking her hands together she made three little claps.

At this signal there came a sound of the sweep of wings flying rapidly, and a large Falcon flew onto the window sill.

"What are your orders, gracious Fairy?" he asked, inclining his beak in sign of reverence—for I must tell you that the Child with blue hair was no more and no less than a beautiful Fairy, who for more than a thousand years had lived in the wood.

"Do you see that puppet dangling from a branch of the Big Oak?"

"I see him."

"Very well. Fly there at once: with your strong beak break the knot that keeps him suspended in the air, and lay him gently on the grass at the foot of the tree."

The Falcon flew away, and after two minutes he returned, saying:

"I have done as you commanded."

"And how did you find him?"

"To see him he appeared dead, but he cannot really be quite dead, for I had no sooner loosened the running noose that tightened his throat than, giving a sigh, he muttered in a faint voice: 'Now I feel better!' . . ."

The Fairy, then striking her hands together, made two little claps, and a magnificent Poodle appeared, walking upright on his hind legs exactly as if he had been a man.

He was in the full-dress livery of a coachman. On his head he had a three-cornered cap braided with gold, his curly white wig came down onto his shoulders, he had a chocolate-colored waistcoat with diamond buttons, and two large pockets to contain the bones that his mistress gave him at dinner. He had besides a pair of short crimson velvet breeches, silk stockings, cut-down shoes, and hanging behind him a species of umbrella case made of blue satin, to put his tail into when the weather was rainy.

"Be quick, Medoro, like a good dog!" said the Fairy to the Poodle. "Have the most beautiful carriage in my coach house put to, and take the road to the wood. When you come to the Big Oak you will find a poor puppet stretched on the grass half dead. Pick him up gently, and lay him flat on the cushions of the carriage and bring him here to me. Have you understood?"

The Poodle, to show that he had understood, shook the case of blue satin three or four times, and ran off like a race horse.

Shortly afterward a beautiful little carriage came out of the coach house. The cushions were stuffed with canary feathers, and it was lined in the inside with whipped cream, custard, and Savoy biscuits. The little carriage was drawn by a hundred pairs of white mice, and the Poodle, seated on the coach box, cracked his whip from side to side like a driver when he is afraid that he is behind time.

A quarter of an hour had not passed when the carriage returned. The Fairy, who was waiting at the door of the house, took the poor puppet in her arms, and carried him into a little room that was wainscoted with mother-of-pearl, and sent at once to summon the most famous doctors in the neighborhood.

The doctors came immediately one after another: namely, a Crow, an Owl, and a Talking Cricket.

"I wish to know from you gentlemen," said the Fairy, turning to the three doctors who were assembled round Pinocchio's bed—"I wish to know from you gentlemen, if this unfortunate puppet is alive or dead!"

At this request the Crow, advancing first, felt Pinocchio's pulse; he then felt his nose, and then the little toe of his foot: and having done this carefully, he pronounced solemnly the following words:

"To my belief the puppet is already quite dead; but if unfortunately he should not be dead, then it would be a sign that he is still alive!"

"I regret," said the Owl, "to be obliged to contradict the Crow, my illustrious friend and colleague; but in my opinion the puppet is still alive: but if unfortunately he should not be alive, then it would be a sign that he is dead indeed!"

"To my belief, the puppet is already dead."

"And you—have you nothing to say?" asked the Fairy of the Talking Cricket.

"In my opinion the wisest thing a prudent doctor can do, when he does not know what he is talking about, is to be silent. For the rest, that puppet there has a face that is not new to me. I have known him for some time! . . ."

Pinocchio, who up to that moment had lain immovable, like a real piece of wood, was seized with a fit of convulsive trembling that shook the whole bed.

"That puppet there," continued the Talking Cricket, "is a confirmed rogue."

Pinocchio opened his eyes, but shut them again immediately.

"He is a ragamuffin, a do-nothing, a vagabond."

Pinocchio hid his face beneath the clothes.

"That puppet there is a disobedient son who will make his poor father die of a broken heart!"

At that instant a suffocated sound of sobs and crying was heard in the room. Imagine everybody's astonishment when, having raised the sheets a little, it was discovered that the sounds came from Pinocchio.

"When the dead person cries, it is a sign that he is on the road to get well," said the Crow solemnly.

"I grieve to contradict my illustrious friend and colleague," added the Owl, "but for me, when the dead person cries, it is a sign that he is sorry to die."

17

PINOCCHIO *eats the sugar, but will not take his medicine; when, however, he sees the gravediggers, who have arrived to carry him away, he takes it. He then tells a lie, and as a punishment his nose grows longer*

AS SOON as the three doctors had left the room the Fairy approached Pinocchio, and having touched his forehead she perceived that he was in a high fever that was not to be trifled with.

She therefore dissolved a certain white powder in half a tumbler of water, and offering it to the puppet she said to him lovingly:

"Drink it, and in a few days you will be cured."

Pinocchio looked at the tumbler, made a wry face, and then asked in a plaintive voice:

"Is it sweet or bitter?"

"It is bitter, but it will do you good."

"If it is bitter, I will not take it."

"Listen to me: drink it."

"I don't like anything bitter."

"Drink it, and when you have drunk it I will give you a lump of sugar to take away the taste."

"Where is the lump of sugar?"

"Here it is," said the Fairy, taking a piece from a gold sugar basin.

"Give me first the lump of sugar, and then I will drink that bad bitter water."

"Do you promise me?"

"Yes."

The Fairy gave him the sugar, and Pinocchio having crunched it up and swallowed it in a second, said, licking his lips:

"It would be a fine thing if sugar were medicine! I would take it every day."

"Now keep your promise and drink these few drops of water, which will restore you to health."

Pinocchio took the tumbler unwillingly in his hand and put the point of his nose to it: he then approached it to his lips: he then again put his nose to it, and at last said:

"It is too bitter, too bitter! I cannot drink it."

"How can you tell that, when you have not even tasted it?"

"I can imagine it! I know it from the smell. I want first another lump of sugar . . . and then I will drink it!"

The Fairy then, with all the patience of a good mamma, put another lump of sugar in his mouth, and then again presented the tumbler to him.

"I cannot drink it so!" said the puppet, making a thousand grimaces.

"Why?"

"Because that pillow that is down there on my feet bothers me."

The Fairy removed the pillow.

"It is useless. Even so I cannot drink it."

"What is the matter now?"

"The door of the room, which is half open, bothers me."

The Fairy went and closed the door.

"In short," cried Pinocchio, bursting into tears, "I will not drink that bitter water—no, no, no!"

"My boy, you will repent it."

"I don't care."

"Your illness is serious."

"I don't care."

"The fever in a few hours will carry you into the other world."

"I don't care."

"Are you not afraid of death?"

"I am not in the least afraid! I would rather die than drink that bitter medicine."

At that moment the door of the room flew open, and four rabbits as black as ink entered carrying on their shoulders a little bier.

"What do you want with me?" cried Pinocchio, sitting up in bed in a great fright.

"We are come to take you," said the biggest rabbit.

"To take me? . . . But I am not yet dead!"

"No, **not** yet: but you have only a few minutes to live, as you **have** refused the medicine that would have cured you **of** the fever."

"Oh, Fairy, Fairy!" the puppet then began to scream. "Give me the tumbler at once . . . be quick, for pity's sake, for I will not die—no . . . I will not die. . . ."

And taking the tumbler in both hands he emptied it at a draught.

"We must have patience!" said the rabbits. "This time we have made our journey in vain." And taking the little bier again on their shoulders they left the room, grumbling and murmuring between their teeth.

In fact, a few minutes afterward Pinocchio jumped down from the bed quite well: because you must know that wooden puppets have the privilege of being seldom ill and of being cured very quickly.

The Fairy, seeing him running and rushing about the room as gay and as lively as a young cock, said to him:

"Then my medicine has really done you good?"

"Good, I should think so! It has restored me to life!"

"Then why on earth did you require so much persuasion to take it?"

"Because, you see, we boys are all like that! We are more afraid of medicine than of the illness."

"Disgraceful! Boys ought to know that a good remedy taken in time may save them from a serious illness, and perhaps even from death."

"Oh, but another time I shall not require so much persuasion. I shall remember those black rabbits with the bier on their shoulders . . . and then I shall immediately take the tumbler in my hand, and down it will go!"

"Now come here to me, and tell me how it came about that you fell into the hands of those assassins."

"It came about that the showman Fire-eater gave me some gold pieces and said to me: 'Go, and take them to your father!' and instead I met on the road a Fox and a Cat, two very respectable persons, who said to me: 'Would you like those pieces of gold to become a thousand or two? Come with us and we will take you to the Field of Miracles,' and I said: 'Let us go.' And they said: 'Let us stop at the inn of the Red Crawfish,' and before midnight they left. And when I awoke I found that they were no longer there, because they had gone away. Then I began to travel by night, for you cannot imagine how dark it was; and on that account I met on the road two assassins in charcoal sacks who said to me: 'Out with your money,' and I said to them: 'I have got none,' because I had hidden the four gold pieces in my mouth, and one of the assassins tried to put his hand in my mouth, and I bit his hand off and spat it out, but instead of a hand I spat out a cat's paw. And the assassins ran after me, and I ran, and ran, until at last they caught me, and tied me by the neck to a tree in this wood, and said to me: 'Tomorrow we shall return here, and then you will be dead with your mouth open, and we shall be able to carry off the pieces of gold that you have hidden under your tongue."

"And the four pieces—where have you put them?" asked the Fairy.

"I have lost them!" said Pinocchio; but he was telling a lie, for he had them in his pocket.

He had scarcely told the lie when his nose, which was already long, grew at once two fingers longer.

"And where did you lose them?"

"In the wood near here."

At this second lie his nose went on growing.

"If you have lost them in the wood near here," said the Fairy, "we will look for them, and we shall find them: because everything that is lost in that wood is always found."

"Ah! Now I remember all about it," replied the puppet, getting quite confused. "I didn't lose the four gold pieces, I swallowed them inadvertently while I was drinking your medicine."

At this third lie his nose grew to such an extraordinary length that poor Pinocchio could not move in any direction. If he turned to one side he struck his nose against the bed or the windowpanes, if he turned to the other he struck it against the walls or the door, if he raised his head a little he ran the risk of sticking it into one of the Fairy's eyes.

And the Fairy looked at him and laughed.

"What are you laughing at?" asked the puppet, very confused and anxious at finding his nose growing so prodigiously.

"I am laughing at the lie you have told."

"And how can you possibly know that I have told a lie?"

"Lies, my dear boy, are found out immediately, because they are of two sorts. There are lies that have short legs, and lies that have long noses. Your lie, as it happens, is one of those that have a long nose."

Pinocchio, not knowing where to hide himself for shame, tried to run out of the room; but he did not succeed, for his nose had increased so much that it could no longer pass through the door.

18

PINOCCHIO *meets again the* FOX *and the* CAT, *and goes with them to bury his money in the* FIELD OF MIRACLES

THE FAIRY, as you can imagine, allowed the puppet to cry and to roar for a good half hour over his nose, which could no longer pass through the door of the room. This she did to give him a severe lesson, and to correct him of the disgraceful fault of telling lies—the most disgraceful fault that a boy can have. But when she saw him quite disfigured, and his eyes swollen out of his head from weeping, she felt full of compassion for him. She therefore beat her hands together, and at that signal a thousand large birds called Woodpeckers flew in at the window. They immediately perched on Pinocchio's nose, and began to peck at it with such zeal that in a few minutes his enormous and ridiculous nose was reduced to its usual dimensions.

"What a good Fairy you are," said the puppet, drying his eyes, "and how much I love you!"

"I love you also," answered the Fairy, "and if you will remain with me, you shall be my little brother and I will be your good little sister."

"I would remain willingly . . . but my poor papa?"

"I have thought of everything. I have already let your father know, and he will be here tonight."

"Really?" shouted Pinocchio, jumping for joy. "Then, little Fairy, if you consent, I should like to go and meet him. I am so anxious to give a kiss to that poor old man, who has suffered so much on my account, that I am counting the minutes."

"Go, then, but be careful not to lose yourself. Take the road through the wood and I am sure that you will meet him."

Pinocchio set out; and as soon as he was in the wood he began to run like a kid. But when he had reached a certain spot, almost in front of the Big Oak, he stopped, because he thought that he heard people among the bushes. In fact, two persons came out onto the road. Can you guess who they were? . . . His two traveling companions, the Fox and the Cat, with whom he had supped at the inn of the Red Crawfish.

"Why, here is our dear Pinocchio!" cried the Fox, kissing and embracing him. "How come you to be here?"

"How come you to be here?" repeated the Cat.

"It is a long story," answered the puppet, "which I will tell you when I have time. But do you know that the other night, when you left me alone at the inn, I met with assassins on the road."

"Assassins! . . . Oh, poor Pinocchio! And what did they want?"

"They wanted to rob me of my gold pieces."

"Villains!" said the Fox.

"Infamous villains!" repeated the Cat.

"But I ran away from them," continued the puppet,

"and they followed me. And at last they overtook me and hung me to a branch of that oak tree."

And Pinocchio pointed to the Big Oak, which was two steps from them.

"Is it possible to hear of anything more dreadful?" said the Fox. "In what a world we are condemned to live! Where can respectable people like us find a safe refuge?"

While they were thus talking Pinocchio observed that the Cat was lame of her front right leg, for in fact she had lost her paw with all its claws. He therefore asked her:

"What have you done with your paw?"

The Cat tried to answer but became confused. Therefore the Fox said immediately:

"My friend is too modest, and that is why she doesn't speak. I will answer for her. I must tell you that an hour ago we met an old wolf on the road, almost fainting from want of food, who asked alms of us. Not having so much as a fishbone to give him, what did my friend, who has really the heart of a Caesar, do? She bit off one of her forepaws, and threw it to that poor beast that he might appease his hunger."

And the Fox, in relating this, dried a tear.

Pinocchio also was touched, and approaching the Cat he whispered into her ear:

"If all cats resembled you, how fortunate the mice would be!"

"And now, what are you doing here?" asked the Fox of the puppet.

"I am waiting for my papa, whom I expect to arrive any moment."

"And your gold pieces?"

"I have got them in my pocket, all but one that I spent at the inn of the Red Crawfish."

"And to think that, instead of four pieces, by tomorrow they might become one or two thousand! Why do you not listen to my advice? Why will you not go and bury them in the Field of Miracles?"

"Today it is impossible: I will go another day."

"Another day will be too late!" said the Fox.

"Why?"

"Because the field has been bought by a gentleman, and after tomorrow no one will be allowed to bury money there."

"How far off is the Field of Miracles?"

"Not two miles. Will you come with us? In half an hour you will be there. You can bury your money at once, and in a few minutes you will collect two thousand, and this evening you will return with your pockets full. Will you come with us?"

Pinocchio thought of the good Fairy, old Geppetto, and the warnings of the Talking Cricket, and he hesitated a little before answering. He ended, however, by doing as all boys do who have not a grain of sense and who have no heart—he ended by giving his head a little shake, and saying to the Fox and the Cat:

"Let us go: I will come with you."

And they went.

After having walked half the day they reached a town that was called "Trap for Blockheads." As soon as Pinocchio entered this town, he saw that the streets were crowded with dogs who had lost their coats and who were yawning from hunger, shorn sheep trembling with cold, cocks without combs or crests who were begging for a grain of Indian corn, large butterflies who could no longer fly because they had sold their beautiful colored wings, peacocks who had no tails and were ashamed to be seen, and pheasants who went scratching about in a subdued fashion, mourning for their brilliant gold and silver feathers gone forever.

In the midst of this crowd of beggars and shamefaced

creatures, some lordly carriage passed from time to time containing a Fox, or a thieving Magpie, or some other ravenous bird of prey.

"And where is the Field of Miracles?" asked Pinocchio.

"It is here, not two steps from us."

They crossed the town, and having gone beyond the walls they came to a solitary field which to look at resembled all other fields.

"We are arrived," said the Fox to the puppet. "Now stoop down and dig with your hands a little hole in the ground and put your gold pieces into it."

Pinocchio obeyed. He dug a hole, put into it the four gold pieces that he had left, and then filled up the hole with a little earth.

"Now, then," said the Fox, "go to that canal close to us, fetch a can of water, and water the ground where you have sowed them."

Pinocchio went to the canal, and as he had no can he took off one of his old shoes, and filling it with water he watered the ground over the hole.

He then asked:

"Is there anything else to be done?"

"Nothing else," answered the Fox. "We can now go away. You can return in about twenty minutes, and you will find a shrub already pushing through the ground, with its branches quite loaded with money."

The poor puppet, beside himself with joy, thanked the Fox and the Cat a thousand times, and promised them a beautiful present.

"We wish for no presents," answered the two rascals. "It is enough for us to have taught you the way to enrich yourself without undergoing hard work, and we are as happy as folk out for a holiday."

Thus saying they took leave of Pinocchio, and, wishing him a good harvest, went about their business.

19

PINOCCHIO *is robbed of his money, and as a punishment he is sent to prison for four months*

THE PUPPET RETURNED to the town and began to count the minutes one by one; and when he thought that it must be time he took the road leading to the Field of Miracles.

And as he walked along with hurried steps his heart beat fast tic, tac, tic, tac, like a drawing-room clock when it is really going well. Meanwhile he was thinking to himself:

"And if instead of a thousand gold pieces, I was to find on the branches of the tree two thousand? And instead of two thousand supposing I found five thousand? And instead of five thousand that I found a hundred thousand? Oh, what a fine gentleman I should then become! . . . I would have a beautiful palace, a thousand little wooden horses and a thousand stables to amuse myself with, a cellar full of currant wine and sweet syrups, and a library quite full of candies, tarts, plum cakes, macaroons, and biscuits with cream."

While he was building these castles in the air he had arrived in the neighborhood of the field, and he stopped to look if by chance he could perceive a tree with its branches laden with money: but he saw nothing. He advanced another hundred steps—nothing: he entered the field . . . he went right up to the little hole where he had buried his sovereigns—and nothing. He then became very thoughtful, and forgetting the rules of society and good manners he took his hands out of his pockets and gave his head a long scratch.

At that moment he heard an explosion of laughter close to him, and looking up he saw a large Parrot perched on a tree, who was preening the few feathers he had left.

"Why are you laughing?" asked Pinocchio in an angry voice.

"I am laughing because in preening my feathers I tickled myself under my wings."

The puppet did not answer, but went to the canal and, filling the same old shoe full of water, he proceeded to water the earth afresh that covered his gold pieces.

While he was thus occupied another laugh, and still more impertinent than the first, rang out in the silence of that solitary place.

"Once for all," shouted Pinocchio in a rage, "may I know, you ill-educated Parrot, what you are laughing at?"

"I am laughing at those simpletons who believe in all the foolish things that are told them, and who allow themselves to be entrapped by those who are more cunning than they are."

"Are you perhaps speaking of me?"

"Yes, I am speaking of you, poor Pinocchio—of you who are simple enough to believe that money can be sown and gathered in fields in the same way as beans and gourds. I also believed it once, and today I am suffering for it. Today—but it is too late—I have learned at last that to put a few pennies honestly together it is necessary to know how to earn them, either by the work of our own hands or by the cleverness of our own brains."

"I don't understand you," said the puppet, who was already trembling with fear.

"Have patience! I will explain myself better," rejoined the Parrot. "You must know, then, that while you were in the town the Fox and the Cat returned to the field: they took the buried money and then fled like the wind. And now he that catches them will be clever."

Pinocchio remained with his mouth open, and not choosing to believe the Parrot's words he began with his hands and nails to dig up the earth that he had watered. And he dug, and dug, and dug, and made such a deep hole that a rick of straw might have stood upright in it: but the money was no longer there.

He rushed back to the town in a state of desperation and went at once to the Courts of Justice to denounce the two knaves who had robbed him to the judge.

The judge was a big ape of the gorilla tribe—an old ape respectable for his age, his white beard, but especially for his gold spectacles without glasses that he was always obliged to wear, on account of an inflammation of the eyes that had tormented him for many years.

Pinocchio related in the presence of the judge all the particulars of the infamous fraud of which he had been the victim. He gave the names, the surnames, and other details, of the two rascals, and ended by demanding justice.

The judge listened with great benignity; took a lively interest in the story; was much touched and moved; and when the puppet had nothing further to say, he stretched out his hand and rang a bell.

At this summons two mastiffs immediately appeared dressed as gendarmes. The judge then, pointing to Pinocchio, said to them:

"That poor devil has been robbed of four gold pieces; take him up, and put him immediately into prison."

The puppet was petrified on hearing this unexpected sentence, and tried to protest; but the gendarmes, to avoid losing time, stopped his mouth, and carried him off to the lockup.

And there he remained for four months—four long months—and he would have remained longer still if a fortunate chance had not released him. For I must tell you that the young Emperor who reigned over the town of Trap for Blockheads, having won a splendid victory over his enemies, ordered great public rejoicings. There were illuminations, fireworks, horse races, and velocipede races, and as a further sign of triumph he commanded that the prisons should be opened and all the prisoners liberated.

"If the others are to be let out of prison, I will go also," said Pinocchio to the jailer.

"No, not you," said the jailer, "because you do not belong to the fortunate class."

"I beg your pardon," replied Pinocchio, "I am also a criminal."

"In that case you are perfectly right," said the jailer; and taking off his hat and bowing to him respectfully he opened the prison doors and let him escape.

20

Liberated from prison, he starts to return to the FAIRY'S *house, but on the road he meets with a horrible* SERPENT, *and afterwards he is caught in a trap*

YOU CAN IMAGINE Pinocchio's joy when he found himself free. Without stopping to take breath he immediately left the town and took the road that led to the Fairy's house.

On account of the rainy weather the road had become a marsh into which he sank knee-deep. But the puppet would not give in. Tormented by the desire of seeing his father and his little sister with blue hair again he ran and leapt like a greyhound, and as he ran he was splashed with mud from head to foot. And he said to himself as he went along: "How many misfortunes have happened to me . . . and I deserved them; for I am an obstinate, passionate puppet. . . . I am always bent upon having my own way, without listening to those who wish me well, and who have a thousand times more sense than I have! . . . But from this time forth I am determined to change and to become orderly and obedient. . . . For at last I have seen that disobedient boys come to no good and gain nothing. And will papa have waited for me? Shall I find him at the Fairy's house! Poor man, it is so long since I last saw him: I am dying to embrace him, and to cover him with kisses! And will the Fairy forgive me my bad conduct to her? . . . To think of all the kindness and loving care I received from her . . . to think that if I am now alive I owe it to her! . . . Would it be possible to find a more ungrateful boy, or one with less heart than I have! . . ."

While he was saying this he stopped suddenly, frightened to death, and made four steps backwards.

What had he seen? . . .

He had seen an immense Serpent stretched across the road. Its skin was green, it had red eyes, and a pointed tail that was smoking like a chimney.

It would be impossible to imagine the puppet's terror. He walked away to a safe distance, and sitting down on a heap of stones waited until the Serpent should have gone about its business and had left the road clear.

He waited an hour; two hours; three hours; but the Serpent was always there, and even from a distance he could see the red light of his fiery eyes and the column of smoke that ascended from the end of his tail.

At last Pinocchio, trying to feel courageous, approached to within a few steps, and said to the Serpent in a little soft, insinuating voice:

"Excuse me, Sir Serpent, but would you be so good as to move a little to one side, just enough to allow me to pass?"

He might as well have spoken to the wall. Nobody moved.

He began again in the same soft voice:

"You must know, Sir Serpent, that I am on my way

He fell so awkwardly that his head stuck in the mud

home, where my father is waiting for me, and it is such a long time since I saw him last! . . . Will you therefore allow me to continue my road?"

He waited for a sign in answer to this request, but there was none: in fact the Serpent, who up to that moment had been sprightly and full of life, became motionless and almost rigid. He shut his eyes and his tail ceased smoking.

"Can he really be dead?" said Pinocchio, rubbing his hands with delight; and he determined to jump over him and reach the other side of the road. But just as he was going to leap, the Serpent raised himself suddenly on end, like a spring set in motion; and the puppet, drawing back, in his terror caught his feet and fell to the ground.

And he fell so awkwardly that his head stuck in the mud and his legs went into the air.

At the sight of the puppet kicking violently with his head in the mud the Serpent went into convulsions of laughter, and he laughed, and laughed, and laughed, until from the violence of his laughter he broke a blood vessel in his chest and died. And that time he was really dead.

Pinocchio then set off running in hope that he should reach the Fairy's house before dark. But before long he began to suffer so dreadfully from hunger that he could not bear it, and he jumped into a field by the wayside intending to pick some bunches of muscatel grapes. Oh, that he had never done it!

He had scarcely reached the vines when crac! . . . his legs were caught between two cutting iron bars, and he became so giddy with pain that stars of every color danced before his eyes.

The poor puppet had been taken in a trap put there to capture some big polecats who were the scourge of the poultry yards in the neighborhood.

21

PINOCCHIO *is taken by a peasant, who obliges him to fill the place of his watchdog in the poultry yard*

PINOCCHIO, as you can imagine, began to cry and scream: but his tears and groans were useless, for there was not a house to be seen, and not a living soul passed down the road. At last night came on.

Partly from the pain of the trap that cut his legs, and a little from fear at finding himself alone in the dark in the midst of the fields, the puppet was on the point of fainting. Just at that moment he saw a Firefly flitting over his head. He called to it and said:

"Oh, little Firefly, will you have pity on me and liberate me from this torture?"

"Poor boy!" said the Firefly, stopping and looking at him with compassion. "But how could your legs have been caught by those sharp irons?"

"I came into the field to pick two bunches of these muscatel grapes, and. . . ."

"But were the grapes yours?"

"No."

"Then who taught you to carry off other people's property?"

"I was so hungry."

"Hunger, my boy, is not a good reason for appropriating what does not belong to us."

"That is true, that is true!" said Pinocchio, crying. "I will never do it again."

At this moment their conversation was interrupted by a slight sound of approaching footsteps. It was the owner of the field coming on tiptoe to see if one of the polecats that ate his chickens during the night had been caught in his trap.

His astonishment was great when, having brought out his lantern from under his coat, he perceived that instead of a polecat a boy had been taken.

"Ah, little thief," said the angry peasant, "then it is you who carry off my chickens?"

"No, it is not I; indeed it is not!" cried Pinocchio, sobbing. "I only came into the field to take two bunches of grapes!"

"He who steals grapes is quite capable of stealing chickens. Leave it to me, I will give you a lesson that you will not forget in a hurry."

Opening the trap he seized the puppet by the collar, and carried him to his house as if he had been a young lamb.

When he reached the yard in front of the house he threw him roughly on the ground, and putting his foot on his neck he said to him:

"It is late, and I want to go to bed; we will settle our accounts tomorrow. In the meanwhile, as the dog who kept guard at night died today, you shall take his place at once. You shall be my watchdog."

And taking a great collar covered with brass knobs he

strapped it tightly round Pinocchio's throat that he might not be able to draw his head out of it. A heavy chain attached to the collar was fastened to the wall.

"If it should rain tonight," he then said to him, "you can go and lie down in the kennel; the straw that has served as a bed for my poor dog for the last four years is still there. If, unfortunately, robbers should come, remember to keep your ears pricked and to bark."

After giving him this last injunction the man went into the house, shut the door, and put up the chain.

Poor Pinocchio remained lying on the ground more dead than alive from the effects of cold, hunger, and fear. From time to time he put his hands angrily to the collar that tightened his throat and said, crying:

"It serves me right! Decidedly it serves me right! I was determined to be a vagabond and a good-for-nothing. I would listen to bad companions, and that is why I always meet with misfortunes. If I had been a good little boy as so many are; if I had been willing to learn and to work; if I had remained at home with my poor papa, I should not now be in the midst of the fields and obliged to be the watchdog to a peasant's house. Oh, if I could be born again! But now it is too late, and I must have patience!"

Relieved by this little outburst, which came straight from his heart, he went into the dog kennel and fell asleep.

22

PINOCCHIO *discovers the robbers,
and as a reward for his fidelity
is set at liberty*

HE HAD BEEN sleeping heavily for about two hours
when, toward midnight, he was roused by a whispering
of strange voices that seemed to come from the court-
yard. Putting the point of his nose out of the kennel he
saw four little beasts with dark fur, that looked like cats,
standing consulting together. But they were not cats;
they were polecats—carnivorous little animals, especially greedy for eggs and young chickens. One of the
polecats, leaving his companions, came to the opening
of the kennel and said in a low voice:

"Good evening, Melampo."

"My name is not Melampo," answered the puppet.

"Oh! Then, who are you?"

"I am Pinocchio."

"And what are you doing here?"

"I am acting as watchdog."

"Then where is Melampo? Where is the old dog who
lived in this kennel?"

"I am Pinocchio"

"He died this morning."

"Is he dead? Poor beast! He was so good. But judging you by your face I should say that you were also a good dog."

"I beg your pardon, I am not a dog."

"Not a dog? Then, what are you?"

"I am a puppet."

"And you are acting as watchdog?"

"That is only too true—as a punishment."

"Well, then, I will offer you the same conditions that we made with the deceased Melampo, and I am sure you will be satisfied with them."

"What are these conditions?"

"One night in every week you are to permit us to visit this poultry yard as we have hitherto done, and to carry off eight chickens. Of these chickens seven are to be eaten by us, and one we will give to you, on the express understanding, however, that you pretend to be asleep, and that it never enters your head to bark and to wake the peasant."

"Did Melampo act in this manner?" asked Pinocchio.

"Certainly, and we were always on the best terms with him. Sleep quietly, and rest assured that before we go we will leave by the kennel a beautiful chicken ready plucked for your breakfast tomorrow. Have we understood each other clearly?"

"Only too clearly! . . ." answered Pinocchio, and he shook his head threateningly as much as to say: "You shall hear of this shortly!"

The four polecats, thinking themselves safe, repaired to the poultry yard, which was close to the kennel, and having opened the wooden gate with their teeth and claws, they slipped in one by one. But they had only just passed through when they heard the gate shut behind them with great violence.

It was Pinocchio who had shut it; and for greater

security he put a large stone against it to keep it closed.

He then began to bark, and he barked exactly like a watchdog: bow-wow, bow-wow.

Hearing the barking the peasant jumped out of bed, and taking his gun he came to the window and asked:

"What is the matter?"

"There are robbers!" answered Pinocchio.

"Where are they?"

"In the poultry yard."

"I will come down directly."

In fact, in less time than it takes to say Amen, the peasant came down. He rushed into the poultry yard, caught the polecats, and having put them into a sack, he said to them in a tone of great satisfaction:

"At last you have fallen into my hands! I might punish you, but I am not so cruel. I will content myself instead by carrying you in the morning to the innkeeper of the neighboring village, who will skin and cook you as hares with a sweet and sour sauce. It is an honor that you don't deserve, but generous people like me don't consider such trifles!"

He then approached Pinocchio and began to caress him, and among other things he asked him:

"How did you manage to discover the four thieves? To think that Melampo, my faithful Melampo, never found out anything!"

The puppet might then have told him the whole story; he might have informed him of the disgraceful conditions that had been made between the dog and the polecats; but he remembered that the dog was dead, and he thought to himself:

"What is the good of accusing the dead? . . . The dead are dead, and the best thing to be done is to leave them in peace!"

"When the thieves got into the yard were you asleep or awake?" the peasant went on to ask him.

"I was asleep," answered Pinocchio, "but the polecats woke me with their chatter, and one of them came to the kennel and said to me: 'If you promise not to bark, and not to wake the master, we will make you a present of a fine chicken ready plucked!' To think that they should have the audacity to make such a proposal to me! For although I am a puppet, possessing perhaps nearly all the faults in the world, there is one that I certainly will never be guilty of, that of making terms with, and sharing the gains of, dishonest people!"

"Well said, my boy!" cried the peasant, slapping him on the shoulder. "Such sentiments do you honor: and as a proof of my gratitude I will at once set you at liberty, and you may return home."

And he removed the dog collar.

23

PINOCCHIO *mourns the death of the beautiful* CHILD *with the blue hair. He then meets with a* PIGEON *who flies with him to the seashore, and there he throws himself into the water to go to the assistance of his father,* GEPPETTO

AS SOON as Pinocchio was released from the heavy and humiliating weight of the dog collar he started across the fields, and never stopped until he had reached the highroad that led to the Fairy's house. There he turned and looked down into the plain beneath. He could see distinctly with his naked eye the wood where he had been so unfortunate as to meet with the Fox and the Cat; he could see among the trees the top of the Big Oak to which he had been hung; but although he looked in every direction, the little house belonging to the beautiful Child with the blue hair was nowhere visible.

Seized with a sad presentiment he began to run with all the strength he had left, and in a few minutes he reached the field where the little white house had once stood.   But the little white house was no longer there. He saw instead a marble stone, on which were engraved these sad words:

> **HERE LIES**
> **THE CHILD WITH THE BLUE HAIR**
> **WHO DIED FROM SORROW**
> **BECAUSE SHE WAS ABANDONED BY HER**
> **LITTLE BROTHER PINOCCHIO**

I leave you to imagine the puppet's feelings when he had with difficulty spelled out this epitaph.   He fell with his face on the ground and, covering the tombstone with a thousand kisses, burst into an agony of tears.   He cried all night, and when morning came he was still crying although he had no tears left, and his sobs and lamentations were so acute and heartbreaking that they roused the echoes in the surrounding hills.

And as he wept he said:

"Oh, little Fairy, why did you die?   Why did not I die instead of you, I who am so wicked, while you were so good? . . .   And my papa?   Where can he be?   Oh, little Fairy, tell me where I can find him, for I want to remain with him always and never to leave him again, never again! . . .   Oh, little Fairy, tell me that it is not true that you are dead! . . .   If you really love me . . . if you really love your little brother, come to life again . . . come to life as you were before! . . .   Does it not grieve you to see me alone and abandoned by everybody? . . .   If assassins come they will hang me again to the branch of a tree . . . and then I should die

indeed. What do you imagine that I can do here alone
in the world? Now that I have lost you and my papa,
who will give me food? Where shall I go to sleep at
night? Who will make me a new jacket? Oh, it would
be better, a hundred times better, that I should die also!
Yes, I want to die . . . ih! ih! ih!"

And in his despair he tried to tear his hair; but his hair
being made of wood, he could not even have the satisfaction of sticking his fingers into it.

Just then a large Pigeon flew over his head, and
stopping with distended wings called down to him from
a great height:

"Tell me, child, what are you doing there?"

"Don't you see? I am crying!" said Pinocchio, raising
his head toward the voice and rubbing his eyes with his
jacket.

"Tell me," continued the Pigeon, "among your companions, do you happen to know a puppet who is called
Pinocchio?"

"Pinocchio? Did you say Pinocchio?" repeated the
puppet, jumping quickly to his feet. "I am Pinocchio!"

The Pigeon at this answer descended rapidly to the
ground. He was larger than a turkey.

"Do you also know Geppetto?" he asked.

"Do I know him! He is my poor papa! Has he
perhaps spoken to you of me? Will you take me to him?
Is he still alive? Answer me for pity's sake: is he still
alive?"

"I left him three days ago on the seashore."

"What was he doing?"

"He was building a little boat for himself, to cross the
ocean. For more than three months that poor man has
been going all round the world looking for you. Not
having succeeded in finding you, he has now taken it
into his head to go to the distant countries of the new
world in search of you."

"How far is it from here to the shore?" asked Pinocchio breathlessly.

"More than six hundred miles."

"Six hundred miles? Oh, beautiful Pigeon, what a fine thing it would be to have your wings! . . ."

"If you wish to go, I will carry you there."

"How?"

"Astride on my back. Do you weigh much?"

"I weigh next to nothing. I am as light as a feather."

And without waiting for more, Pinocchio jumped at once on the Pigeon's back, and putting a leg on each side of him as men do on horseback, he exclaimed joyfully:

"Gallop, gallop, my little horse, for I am anxious to arrive quickly!"

The Pigeon took flight, and in a few minutes had soared so high that they almost touched the clouds. Finding himself at such an immense height the puppet had the curiosity to turn and look down; but his head spun round, and he became so frightened that to save himself from the danger of falling he wound his arms tightly round the neck of his feathered steed.

They flew all day. Toward evening the Pigeon said:

"I am very thirsty!"

"And I am very hungry!" rejoined Pinocchio.

"Let us stop at that dovecot for a few minutes, and then we will continue our journey that we may reach the seashore by dawn tomorrow."

They went into a deserted dovecot, where they found nothing but a basin of water and a basket of vetch.

The puppet had never in his life been able to eat vetch: according to him, it made him sick and revolted him. That evening, however, he ate to repletion, and when he had nearly emptied the basket he turned to the Pigeon and said to him:

"I never could have believed that vetch was so good!"

"Be assured, my boy," replied the Pigeon, "that when hunger is real, and there is nothing else to eat, even vetch becomes delicious. Hunger knows neither caprice nor greediness."

Having quickly finished their little meal they recommenced their journey and flew away. The following morning they reached the seashore.

The Pigeon placed Pinocchio on the ground, and not wishing to be troubled with thanks for having done a good action, flew quickly away and disappeared.

The shore was crowded with people who were looking out to sea, shouting and gesticulating.

"What has happened?" asked Pinocchio of an old woman.

"A poor father who has lost his son has gone away in a boat to search for him on the other side of the water, and today the sea is tempestuous and the little boat is in danger of sinking."

"Where is the little boat?"

"It is out there in a line with my finger," said the old woman, pointing to a little boat which, seen at that distance, looked like a nutshell with a very little man in it.

Pinocchio fixed his eyes on it, and after looking attentively he gave a piercing scream, crying:

"It is my papa! It is my papa!"

The boat meanwhile, beaten by the fury of the waves, at one moment disappeared in the trough of the sea, and the next came again to the surface. Pinocchio, standing on the top of a high rock, kept calling to his father by name, and making every kind of signal to him with his hands, his handkerchief, and his cap.

And although he was so far off, Geppetto appeared to recognize his son, for he also took off his cap and waved it, and tried by gestures to make him understand that he would have returned if it had been possible, but that the sea was so tempestuous that he could not use his oars or approach the shore.

Suddenly a tremendous wave rose and the boat disappeared. They waited, hoping it would come again to the surface, but it was seen no more.

"Poor man!" said the fishermen who were assembled on the shore, and murmuring a prayer they turned to go home.

Just then they heard a desperate cry, and looking back they saw a little boy who exclaimed, as he jumped from a rock into the sea:

"I will save my papa!"

Pinocchio, being made of wood, floated easily and he swam like a fish. At one moment they saw him disappear under the water, carried down by the fury of the waves; and next he reappeared struggling with a leg or an arm. At last they lost sight of him, and he was seen no more.

"Poor boy!" said the fishermen who were collected on the shore, and murmuring a prayer they returned home.

24

PINOCCHIO *arrives at the* ISLAND OF THE INDUSTRIOUS BEES *and* *finds the* FAIRY *again*

PINOCCHIO, hoping to be in time to help his father, swam the whole night.

And what a horrible night it was! The rain came down in torrents, it hailed, the thunder was frightful, and the flashes of lightning made it as light as day.

Toward morning he saw a long strip of land not far off. It was an island in the midst of the sea.

He tried his utmost to reach the shore: but it was all in vain. The waves, racing and tumbling over each other, knocked him about as if he had been a stick or a wisp of straw. At last, fortunately for him, a billow rolled up with such fury and impetuosity that he was lifted up and thrown violently far onto the sands.

He fell with such force that, as he struck the ground, his ribs and all his joints cracked, but he comforted himself, saying:

"This time also I have made a wonderful escape!"

Little by little the sky cleared, the sun shone out in all his splendor, and the sea became as quiet and as smooth as oil.

The puppet put his clothes in the sun to dry, and began to look in every direction in hope of seeing on the vast expanse of water a little boat with a little man in it. But although he looked and looked, he could see nothing but the sky, and the sea, and the sail of some ship, but so far away that it seemed no bigger than a fly.

"If I only knew what this island was called!" he said to himself. "If I only knew whether it was inhabited by civilized people—I mean by people who haven't the bad habit of hanging boys to the branches of the trees. But who can I ask? Who, if there is nobody? . . ."

This idea of finding himself alone, alone, all alone, in the midst of this great uninhabited country, made him so melancholy that he was just beginning to cry. But at that moment, at a short distance from the shore, he saw a big fish swimming by; it was going quietly on its own business with its head out of the water.

Not knowing its name the puppet called to it in a loud voice to make himself heard:

"Eh, Sir Fish, will you permit me a word with you?"

"Two if you like," answered the fish, who was a Dolphin, and so polite that few like him are to be found in any sea in the world.

"Will you be kind enough to tell me if there are villages in this island where it would be possible to obtain something to eat, without running the danger of being eaten?"

"Certainly there are," replied the Dolphin. "Indeed, you will find one at a short distance from here."

"And what road must I take to go there?"

"You must take that path to your left and follow your nose. You cannot make a mistake."

"Will you tell me another thing? You who swim about the sea all day and all night, have you by chance met a little boat with my papa in it?"

"And who is your papa?"

"He is the best papa in the world, while it would be difficult to find a worse son than I am."

"During the terrible storm last night," answered the Dolphin, "the little boat must have gone to the bottom."

"And my papa?"

"He must have been swallowed by the terrible Dogfish who for some days past has been spreading devastation and ruin in our waters."

"Is this Dogfish very big?" asked Pinocchio, who was already beginning to quake with fear.

"Big! . . ." replied the Dolphin. "That you may form some idea of his size, I need only tell you that he is bigger than a five-storied house, and that his mouth is so enormous and so deep that a railway train with its smoking engine could pass easily down his throat."

"Mercy upon us!" exclaimed the terrified puppet; and putting on his clothes with the greatest haste he said to the Dolphin:

"Good-by, Sir Fish: excuse the trouble I have given you, and many thanks for your politeness."

He then took the path that had been pointed out to him and began to walk fast—so fast, indeed, that he was almost running. And at the slightest noise he turned to look behind him, fearing that he might see the terrible Dogfish with a railway train in its mouth following him.

After a walk of half an hour he reached a little village called the "Village of the Industrious Bees." The road was alive with people running here and there to attend to their business: all were at work, all had something to do. You could not have found an idler or a vagabond, not even if you had searched for him with a lighted lamp.

"Ah," said that lazy Pinocchio at once, "I see that this village will never suit me! I wasn't born to work!"

In the meanwhile he was tormented by hunger, for he had eaten nothing for twenty-four hours—not even vetch. What was he to do?

There were only two ways by which he could obtain food—either by asking for a little work, or by begging for a halfpenny or for a mouthful of bread.

He was ashamed to beg, for his father had always preached to him that no one had a right to beg except the aged and the infirm. The really poor in this world, deserving of compassion and assistance, are only those who from age or sickness are no longer able to earn their own bread with the labor of their hands. It is the duty of everyone else to work; and if they will not work, so much the worse for them if they suffer from hunger.

At that moment a man came down the road, tired and panting for breath. He was dragging along, with fatigue and difficulty, two carts full of charcoal.

Pinocchio, judging by his face that he was a kind man, approached him, and casting down his eyes with shame he said to him in a low voice:

"Would you have the charity to give me a halfpenny, for I am dying of hunger?"

"You shall have not only a halfpenny," said the man, "but I will give you twopence, provided that you help me to drag home these two carts of charcoal."

"I am surprised at you!" answered the puppet in a tone of offense. "Let me tell you that I am not accustomed to do the work of a donkey: I have never drawn a cart!"

"So much the better for you," answered the man. "Then, my boy, if you are really dying of hunger, eat two fine slices of your pride, and be careful not to get indigestion."

A few minutes afterward a mason passed down the road carrying on his shoulders a basket of lime.

"Would you have the charity, good man, to give a halfpenny to a poor boy who is yawning for want of food?"

"Willingly," answered the man. "Come with me and

carry the lime, and instead of a halfpenny I will give you five."

"But the lime is heavy," objected Pinocchio, "and I don't want to tire myself."

"If you don't want to tire yourself, then, my boy, amuse yourself with yawning, and much good may it do you."

In less than half an hour twenty other people went by; and Pinocchio asked charity of them all, but they all answered:

"Are you not ashamed to beg? Instead of idling about the roads, go and look for a little work and learn to earn your bread."

At last a nice little woman carrying two cans of water came by.

"Will you let me drink a little water out of your can?" asked Pinocchio, who was burning with thirst.

"Drink, my boy, if you wish it!" said the little woman, setting down the two cans.

Pinocchio drank like a fish, and as he dried his mouth he mumbled:

"I have quenched my thirst. If I could only appease my hunger! . . ."

The good woman, hearing these words, said at once:

"If you help me to carry home these two cans of water, I will give you a fine piece of bread."

Pinocchio looked at the can and answered neither yes nor no.

"And besides the bread you shall have a nice dish of cauliflower dressed with oil and vinegar," added the good woman.

Pinocchio gave another look at the can, and answered neither yes nor no.

"And after the caluiflower I will give you a beautiful bonbon full of syrup."

The temptation of this last dainty was so great that

Pinocchio could resist no longer, and with an air of decision he said:

"I must have patience! I will carry the can to your house."

The can was heavy, and the puppet, not being strong enough to carry it in his hand, had to resign himself to carry it on his head.

When they reached the house the good little woman made Pinocchio sit down at a small table already laid and she placed before him the bread, the cauliflower, and the bonbon.

Pinocchio did not eat, he devoured. His stomach was like an apartment that had been left empty and uninhabited for five months.

When his ravenous hunger was somewhat appeased he raised his head to thank his benefactress; but he had no sooner looked at her than he gave a prolonged Oh-h-! of astonishment, and continued staring at her, with wide-open eyes, his fork in the air, and his mouth full of bread and cauliflower, as if he had been bewitched.

"What has surprised you so much?" asked the good woman, laughing.

"It is . . ." answered the puppet, "it is . . . it is . . . that you are like . . . that you remind me . . . yes, yes, yes, the same voice . . . the same eyes . . . the same hair . . . yes, yes, yes . . . you also have blue hair . . . as she had . . . Oh, little Fairy! . . . Tell me that it is you, really you! . . . Do not make me cry any more! If you knew . . . I have cried so much, I have suffered so much. . . ."

And throwing himself at her feet on the floor, Pinocchio embraced the knees of the mysterious little woman and began to cry bitterly.

25

PINOCCHIO *promises the* FAIRY *to be good and studious, for he is quite sick of being a puppet and wishes to become an exemplary boy*

AT FIRST the good little woman maintained that she was not the little Fairy with blue hair; but seeing that she was found out, and not wishing to continue the comedy any longer, she ended by making herself known, and she said to Pinocchio:

"You little rogue! How did you ever discover who I was?"

"It was my great affection for you that told me."

"Do you remember? You left me a child, and now that you have found me again I am a woman—a woman almost old enough to be your mamma."

"I am delighted at that, for now, instead of calling you little sister, I will call you mamma. I have wished for such a long time to have a mamma like other boys! . . . But how did you manage to grow so fast?"

"That is a secret."

"Teach it to me, for I should also like to grow. Don't you see? I always remain no bigger than a ninepin."

"But you cannot grow," replied the Fairy.

"Why?"

"Because puppets never grow. They are born puppets, live puppets, and die puppets."

"Oh, I am sick of being a puppet!" cried Pinocchio, giving himself a slap. "It is time that I became a man."

"And you will become one, if you know how to deserve it."

"Not really? And what can I do to deserve it?"

"A very easy thing: by learning to be a good boy."

"And you think I am not?"

"You are quite the contrary. Good boys are obedient, and you . . ."

"And I never obey."

"Good boys like to learn and to work, and you . . ."

"And I instead lead an idle vagabond life the year through."

"Good boys always speak the truth . . ."

"And I always tell lies."

"Good boys go willingly to school . . ."

"And school gives me pain all over my body. But from today I will change my life."

"Do you promise me?"

"I promise you. I will become a good little boy, and I will be the consolation of my papa. . . . Where is my poor papa at this moment?"

"I do not know."

"Shall I ever have the happiness of seeing him again and kissing him?"

"I think so; indeed, I am sure of it."

At his answer Pinocchio was so delighted that he took the Fairy's hands and began to kiss them with such fervor that he seemed beside himself.   Then raising his face and looking at her lovingly, he asked:

"Tell me, little mamma: then it was not true that you were dead?"

"It seems not," said the Fairy, smiling.

"If you only knew the sorrow I felt and the tightening of my throat when I read 'Here lies . . .'"

"I know it, and it is on that account that I have forgiven you.   I saw from the sincerity of your grief that you had a good heart; and when boys have good hearts, even if they are scamps and have bad habits, there is always something to hope for: that is, there is always hope that they will turn to better ways.   That is why I came to look for you here.   I will be your mamma."

"Oh, how delightful!" shouted Pinocchio, jumping for joy.

"You must obey me and do everything that I bid you."

"Willingly, willingly, willingly!"

"Tomorrow," rejoined the Fairy, "you will begin to go to school."

Pinocchio became at once a little less joyful.

"Then you must choose an art, or a trade, according to your own wishes."

Pinocchio became very grave.

"What are you muttering between your teeth?" asked the Fairy in an angry voice.

"I was saying," moaned the puppet in a low voice, "that it seemed to me too late for me to go to school now. . . ."

"No, sir.   Keep it in mind that it is never too late to learn and to instruct ourselves."

"But I do not wish to follow either an art or a trade."

"Why?"

"Because it tires me to work."

"My boy," said the Fairy, "those who talk in that way

end almost always either in prison or in the hospital. Let me tell you that every man, whether he is born rich or poor, is obliged to do something in this world—to occupy himelf, to work. Woe to those who lead slothful lives. Sloth is a dreadful illness and must be cured at once, in childhood. If not, when we are old it can never be cured."

Pinocchio was touched by these words, and lifting his head quickly he said to the Fairy:

"I will study, I will work, I will do all that you tell me, for indeed I have become weary of being a puppet, and I wish at any price to become a boy. You promised me that I should, did you not?"

"I did promise you, and it now depends upon yourself."

26

PINOCCHIO *accompanies his schoolfellows to the seashore to see the terrible* DOGFISH

THE FOLLOWING DAY Pinocchio went to the government school.

Imagine the delight of all the little rogues when they saw a puppet walk into their school! They set up a roar of laughter that never ended. They played all sorts of tricks on him. One boy carried off his cap, another pulled his jacket behind; one tried to give him a pair of inky mustachios just under his nose, and another attempted to tie strings to his feet and hands to make him dance.

For a short time Pinocchio pretended not to care and got on as well as he could; but at last, losing all patience, he turned to those who were teasing him most and making game of him, and said to them, looking very angry:

"Beware, boys: I am not come here to be your buffoon. I respect others, and I intend to be respected."

"Well said, boaster!   You have spoken like a book!" howled the young rascals, convulsed with mad laughter; and one of them, more impertinent than the others, stretched out his hand intending to seize the puppet by the end of his nose.

But he was not in time, for Pinocchio stuck his leg out from under the table and gave him a great kick on his shins.

"Oh, what hard feet!" roared the boy, rubbing the bruise that the puppet had given him.

"And what elbows! . . . Even harder than his feet!" said another, who for his rude tricks had received a blow in the stomach.

But nevertheless the kick and the blow acquired at once for Pinocchio the sympathy and the esteem of all the boys in the school.   They all made friends with him and liked him heartily.

And even the master praised him, for he found him attentive, studious and intelligent—always the first to come to school, and the last to leave when school was over.

But he had one fault: he made too many friends; and among them were several young rascals well known for their dislike to study and love of mischief.

The master warned him every day, and even the good Fairy never failed to tell him, and to repeat constantly:

"Take care, Pinocchio!   Those bad schoolfellows of yours will end sooner or later by making you lose all love of study, and perhaps even they may bring upon you some great misfortune."

"There is no fear of that!" answered the puppet, shrugging his shoulders and touching his forehead as much as to say: "There is so much sense here!"

Now it happened that one fine day, as he was on his way to school, he met several of his usual companions who, coming up to him, asked:

"Have you heard the great news?"

"No."

"In the sea near here a Dogfish has appeared as big as a mountain."

"Not really? Can it be the same Dogfish that was there when my poor papa was drowned?"

"We are going to the shore to see him. Will you come with us?"

"No; I am going to school."

"What matters school? We can go to school tomorrow. Whether we have a lesson more or a lesson less, we shall always remain the same donkeys."

"But what will the master say?"

"The master may say what he likes. He is paid on purpose to grumble all day."

"And my mamma?"

"Mammas know nothing," answered those bad little boys.

"Do you know what I will do?" said Pinocchio. "I have reasons for wishing to see the Dogfish, but I will go and see him when school is over."

"Poor donkey!" exclaimed one of the number. "Do you suppose that a fish of that size will wait your convenience? As soon as he is tired of being here he will start for another place, and then it will be too late."

"How long does it take from here to the shore?" asked the puppet.

"We can be there and back in an hour."

"Then away!" shouted Pinocchio. "And he who runs fastest is the best!"

Having thus given the signal to start, the boys, with their books and copybooks under their arms, rushed off across the fields, and Pinocchio was always the first—he seemed to have wings to his feet.

From time to time he turned to jeer at his companions,

who were some distance behind, and seeing them panting for breath, covered with dust and their tongues hanging out of their mouths, he laughed heartily.   The unfortunate boy little knew what terrors and horrible disasters he was going to meet with!

27

Great fight between PINOCCHIO
*and his companions. One of them
is wounded, and* PINOCCHIO *is
arrested by the gendarmes*

WHEN HE ARRIVED on the shore Pinocchio looked
out to sea; but he saw no Dogfish. The sea was as
smooth as a great crystal mirror.

"Where is the Dogfish?" he asked, turning to his
companions.

"He must have gone to have his breakfast," said one of
them, laughing.

"Or he has thrown himself on to his bed to have a little
nap," added another, laughing still louder.

From their absurd answers and silly laughter Pinocchio perceived that his companions had been making a
fool of him, in inducing him to believe a tale with no
truth in it. Taking it very badly, he said to them
angrily:

"And now may I ask what fun you could find in
deceiving me with the story of the Dogfish?"

"Oh, it was great fun!" answered the little rascals in chorus.

"And in what did it consist?"

"In making you miss school, and persuading you to come with us. Are you not ashamed of being always so punctual and so diligent with your lessons? Are you not ashamed of studying so hard?"

"And if I study hard what concern is it of yours?"

"It concerns us excessively, because it makes us appear in a bad light to the master."

"Why?"

"Because boys who study make those who, like us, have no wish to learn seem worse by comparison. And that is too bad. We too have our pride!"

"Then what must I do to please you?"

"You must follow our example and hate school, lessons, and the master—our three greatest enemies."

"And if I wish to continue my studies?"

"In that case we will have nothing more to do with you, and at the first opportunity we will make you pay for it."

"Really," said the puppet, shaking his head, "you make me inclined to laugh."

"Eh, Pinocchio!" shouted the biggest of the boys, confronting him. "None of your superior airs: don't come here to crow over us! . . . For if you are not afraid of us, we are not afraid of you. Remember that you are one against seven of us."

"Seven, like the seven deadly sins," said Pinocchio, with a shout of laughter.

"Listen to him! He has insulted us all! He called us the seven deadly sins!"

"Pinocchio! beg pardon . . . or it will be the worse for you!"

"Cuckoo!" sang the puppet, putting his forefinger to the end of his nose scoffingly.

"Pinocchio!   It will end badly!"

"Cuckoo!"

"You will get as many blows as a donkey!"

"Cuckoo!"

"You will return home with a broken nose!"

"Cuckoo!"

"Ah, you shall have the cuckoo from me!" said the most courageous of the boys. "Take that to begin with, and keep it for your supper tonight."

And so saying he gave him a blow on the head with his fist.

But it was give-and-take; for the puppet, as was to be expected, immediately returned the blow, and the fight in a moment became general and desperate.

Pinocchio, although he was one alone, defended himself like a hero. He used his feet, which were of the hardest wood, to such purpose that he kept his enemies at a respectful distance. Wherever they touched they left a bruise by way of reminder.

The boys, becoming furious at not being able to measure themselves hand to hand with the puppet, had recourse to other weapons. Loosening their satchels they commenced throwing their schoolbooks at him—grammars, dictionaries, spelling books, geography books, and other scholastic works. But Pinocchio was quick and had sharp eyes, and always managed to duck in time, so that the books passed over his head and all fell into the sea.

Imagine the astonishment of the fish! Thinking that the books were something to eat, they all arrived in shoals, but having tasted a page or two, or a frontispiece, they spat it quickly out and made a wry face that seemed to say: "It isn't food for us; we are accustomed to something much better!"

The battle meantime had become fiercer than ever, when a big Crab, who had come out of the water and had climbed slowly up on the shore, called out in a hoarse voice that sounded like a trumpet with a bad cold:

"Have done with that, you young ruffians, for you are nothing else! These hand-to-hand fights between boys seldom finish well. Some disaster is sure to happen!"

Poor Crab! He might as well have preached to the wind. Even that young rascal Pinocchio, turning around, looked at him mockingly and said rudely:

"Hold your tongue, you tiresome Crab! You had better suck some licorice lozenges to cure that cold in your throat. Or better still, go to bed and try to get a reaction!"

Just then the boys, who had no more books of their own to throw, spied at a little distance the satchel that belonged to Pinocchio, and took possession of it in less time than it takes to tell.

Among the books there was one bound in strong cardboard with the back and points of parchment. It was a Treatise on Arithmetic. I leave you to imagine if it was big or not!

One of the boys seized this volume, and aiming at Pinocchio's head threw it at him with all the force he could muster. But instead of hitting the puppet it struck one of his companions on the temple, who, turning as white as a sheet, said only:

"Oh, mother, help! . . . I am dying!" and fell his whole length on the sand. Thinking he was dead, the terrified boys ran off as hard as their legs could carry them, and in a few minutes they were out of sight.

But Pinocchio remained. Although from grief and fright he was more dead than alive, nevertheless he ran and soaked his handkerchief in the sea and began to bathe the temples of his poor schoolfellow. Crying bitterly in his despair he kept calling him by name and saying to him:

"Eugene! . . . my poor Eugene! . . . open your eyes and look at me! . . . Why do you not answer? I did not do it, indeed it was not I that hurt you so! Believe me, it was not! Open your eyes, Eugene. . . . If you keep your eyes shut I shall die too. . . . Oh! what shall I do? How shall I ever return home? How can I ever have the courage to go back to my good mamma? What will become of me? . . . Where can I fly to? . . . Oh, how much better it would have been, a thousand times better, if I had only gone to school! . . . Why did I listen to my companions? They have been my ruin. The master said to me, and my mamma repeated it often: 'Beware of bad companions!' But I am obstinate . . . a willful fool. . . . I let them talk and then I always take my own way! And I have to suffer for it. . . . And so, ever since I have been in the world, I have never had a happy quarter of an hour. Oh, dear, what will become of me, what will become of me, what will become of me? . . ."

And Pinocchio began to cry and sob, and to strike his head with his fists, and to call poor Eugene by his name. Suddenly he heard the sound of approaching footsteps.

He turned and saw two carabineers.

"What are you doing there lying on the ground?" they asked Pinocchio.

"I am helping my schoolfellow."

"Has he been hurt?"

"So it seems."

"Hurt indeed!" said one of the carabineers, stooping down and examining Eugene closely.

"This boy has been wounded in the temple. Who wounded him?"

"Not I," stammered the puppet breathlessly.

"If it was not you, then who was it?"

"Not I," repeated Pinocchio.

"And with what was he wounded?"

"With this book." And the puppet picked up from the ground the Treatise on Arithmetic, bound in cardboard and parchment, and showed it to the carabineer.

"And to whom does this belong?"

"To me."

"That is enough: nothing more is wanted. Get up and come with us at once."

"But I am innocent!"

"Come along with us!"

"But I am innocent."

"Come along with us!"

Before they left, the carabineers called some fishermen, who were passing at that moment near the shore in their boat, and said to them:

"We give this boy who has been wounded in the head into your charge. Carry him to your house and nurse him. Tomorrow we will come and see him."

They then turned to Pinocchio, and having placed him between them they said to him in a commanding voice:

"Forward!   And walk quickly, or it will be the worse for you."

Without requiring it to be repeated, the puppet set out along the road leading to the village. But the poor little devil hardly knew where he was. He thought he must be dreaming, and what a dreadful dream! He was beside himself. He saw double; his legs shook; his tongue clung to the roof of his mouth, and he could not utter a word. And yet in the midst of his stupefaction and apathy his heart was pierced by a cruel thorn—the thought that he would have to pass under the windows of the good Fairy's house between the carabineers. He would rather have died.

They had already reached the village when a gust of wind blew Pinocchio's cap off his head and carried it ten yards off.

"Will you permit me," said the puppet to the carabineers, "to go and get my cap?"

"Go, then; but be quick about it."

The puppet went and picked up his cap . . . but instead of putting it on his head he took it between his teeth and began to run as hard as he could toward the seashore.

The carabineers, thinking it would be difficult to overtake him, sent after him a large mastiff who had won the first prizes at all the dog races. Pinocchio ran, but the dog ran faster. The people came to their windows and crowded into the street in their anxiety to see the end of the desperate race. But they could not satisfy their curiosity, for Pinocchio and the dog raised such clouds of dust that in a few minutes nothing could be seen of either of them.

28

PINOCCHIO *is in danger of being fried in a frying pan like a fish*

THERE CAME a moment in this desperate race—a terrible moment when Pinocchio thought himself lost: for you must know that Alidoro—for so the mastiff was called—had run so swiftly that he had nearly come up with him.

The puppet could hear the panting of the dreadful beast close behind him; there was not a hand's breadth between them, he could even feel the dog's hot breath.

Fortunately the shore was close and the sea but a few steps off.

As soon as he reached the sands the puppet made a wonderful leap—a frog could have done no better—and plunged into the water.

Alidoro, on the contrary, wished to stop himself; but carried away by the impetus of the race he also went into the sea. The unfortunate dog could not swim, but he made great efforts to keep himself afloat with his paws; but the more he struggled the farther he sank head downward under the water.

When he rose to the surface again his eyes were rolling with terror, and he barked out:

"I am drowning! I am drowning!"

"Drown!" shouted Pinocchio from a distance, seeing himself safe from all danger.

"Help me, dear Pinocchio! . . . Save me from death!"

At that agonizing cry the puppet, who had in reality an excellent heart, was moved with compassion, and turning to the dog he said:

"But if I save your life, will you promise to give me no further annoyance, and not to run after me?"

"I promise! I promise! Be quick, for pity's sake, for if you delay another half minute I shall be dead."

Pinocchio hesitated; but remembering that his father had often told him that a good action is never lost, he swam to Alidoro, and taking hold of his tail with both hands brought him safe and sound on to the dry sand of the beach.

The poor dog could not stand. He had drunk, against his will, so much salt water that he was like a balloon. The puppet, however, not wishing to trust him too far, thought it more prudent to jump again into the water. When he had swum some distance from the shore he called out to the friend he had rescued:

"Good-by, Alidoro; a good journey to you, and take my compliments to all at home."

"Good-by, Pinocchio," answered the dog. "A thousand thanks for having saved my life. You have done me a great service, and in this world what is given is returned. If an occasion offers I shall not forget it."

Pinocchio swam on, keeping always near the land. At last he thought that he had reached a safe place. Giving a look along the shore, he saw among the rocks a kind of cave from which a cloud of smoke was ascending.

"In that cave," he said to himself, "there must be a fire. So much the better. I will go and dry and warm myself, and then? . . . And then we shall see."

Having taken the resolution, he approached the rocks; but as he was going to climb up, he felt something under the water that rose higher and higher and carried him into the air. He tried to escape, but it was too late, for to his extreme surprise he found himself enclosed in a great net, together with a swarm of fish of every size and shape, who were flapping and struggling like so many despairing souls.

At the same moment a fisherman came out of the cave; he was so ugly, so horribly ugly, that he looked like a sea monster. Instead of hair his head was covered with a thick bush of green grass, his skin was green, his eyes were green, his long beard that came down to the ground was also green. He had the appearance of an immense lizard standing on its hind paws.

When the fisherman had drawn his net out of the sea, he exclaimed with great satisfaction:

"Thank Heaven! Again today I shall have a splendid feast of fish!"

"What a mercy that I am not a fish!" said Pinocchio to himself, regaining a little courage.

The net full of fish was carried into the cave, which was dark and smoky. In the middle of the cave a large frying pan full of oil was frying, and sending out a smell of mushrooms that was suffocating.

"Now we will see what fish we have taken!" said the green fisherman; and putting into the net an enormous hand, so out of all proportion that it looked like a baker's shovel, he pulled out a handful of mullet.

"These mullet are good!" he said, looking at them and smelling them complacently. And after he had smelt them he threw them into a pan without water.

He repeated the same operation many times; and as he drew out the fish, his mouth watered and he said, chuckling to himself:

"What good whiting! . . .

"What exquisite sardines! . . .

"These soles are delicious! . . .

"And these crabs excellent! . . .

"What dear little anchovies! . . ."

I need not tell you that the whiting, the sardines, the soles, the crabs, and the anchovies were all thrown promiscuously into the pan to keep company with the mullet.

The last to remain in the net was Pinocchio.

No sooner had the fisherman taken him out than he opened his big green eyes with astonishment, and cried, half frightened:

"What species of fish is this? I never remember eating this kind of fish!"

And he looked at him again attentively, and having examined him well all over, he ended by saying:

"I know: he must be a crawfish."

Pinocchio, mortified at being mistaken for a crawfish, said in an angry voice:

"A crawfish indeed! Do you take me for a crawfish? What treatment! Let me tell you that I am a puppet."

"A puppet?" replied the fisherman. "To tell the truth, a puppet is quite a new fish for me. All the better! I shall eat you with greater pleasure."

"Eat me! But will you understand that I am not a fish? Do you not hear that I talk and reason as you do?"

"That is quite true," said the fisherman. "And as I see that you are a fish possessed of the talent of talking and reasoning as I do, I will treat you with all the attention that is your due."

"And this attention? . . ."

"In token of my friendship and particular regard, I will leave you the choice of how you would like to be cooked. Would you like to be fried in the frying pan, or would you prefer to be stewed with tomato sauce?"

"Do you take me for a crawfish?"

"To tell the truth," answered Pinocchio, "if I am to choose, I should prefer to be set at liberty and to return home."

"You are joking! Do you imagine that I would lose the opportunity of tasting such a rare fish? It is not every day, I assure you, that a puppet fish is caught in these waters. Leave it to me. I will fry you in the frying pan with the other fish, and you will be quite satisfied. It is always consolation to be fried in company."

At this speech the unhappy Pinocchio began to cry and scream and to implore for mercy; and he said, sobbing: "How much better it would have been if I had gone to school! . . . I would listen to my companions and now I am paying for it! Ih! . . . Ih! . . . Ih! . . ."

And he wriggled like an eel, and made indescribable efforts to slip out of the clutches of the green fisherman. But it was useless: the fisherman took a long strip of rush, and having bound his hands and feet as if he had been a sausage, he threw him into the pan with the other fish.

He then fetched a wooden bowl full of flour and began to flour them each in turn, and as soon as they were ready he threw them into the frying pan.

The first to dance in the boiling oil were the poor whiting; the crabs followed, then the sardines, then the soles, then the anchovies, and at last it was Pinocchio's turn. Seeing himself so near death, and such a horrible death, he was so frightened, and trembled so violently, that he had neither voice nor breath left for further entreaties.

But the poor boy implored with his eyes! The green fisherman, however, without caring in the least, plunged him five or six times in the flour, until he was white from head to foot, and looked like a puppet made of plaster.

He then took him by the head, and . . .

29

He returns to the FAIRY'S *house. She promises him that the following day he shall cease to be a puppet and shall become a boy. Grand breakfast of coffee and milk to celebrate this great event*

JUST AS THE FISHERMAN WAS on the point of throwing Pinocchio into the frying pan a large dog entered the cave, enticed there by the strong and savory odor of fried fish.

"Get out!" shouted the fisherman threateningly, holding the floured puppet in his hand.

But the poor dog, who was as hungry as a wolf, whined and wagged his tail as much as to say:

"Give me a mouthful of fish and I will leave you in peace."

"Get out, I tell you!" repeated the fisherman, and he stretched out his leg to give him a kick.

But the dog, who, when he was really hungry, would not stand trifling, turned upon him, growling and showing his terrible tusks.

At that moment a little feeble voice was heard in the cave saying entreatingly:

"Save me, Alidoro! If you do not save me I shall be fried!"

The dog recognized Pinocchio's voice, and to his extreme surprise perceived that it proceeded from the floured bundle that the fisherman held in his hand.

So what do you think he did? He made a spring, seized the bundle in his mouth, and holding it gently between his teeth he rushed out of the cave and was gone like a flash of lightning.

The fisherman, furious at seeing a fish he was so anxious to eat snatched from him, ran after the dog; but he had not gone many steps when he was taken with a fit of coughing and had to give up the chase.

Alidoro, when he had reached the path that led to the village, stopped, and put his friend Pinocchio gently on to the ground.

"How much I have to thank you for!" said the puppet.

"There is no necessity," replied the dog. "You saved me and I have now returned it. You know that we must all help each other in this world."

"But how did you happen to come to the cave?"

"I was lying on the shore more dead than alive when the wind brought to me the smell of fried fish. The smell excited my appetite, and I followed it up. If I had arrived a second later . . ."

"Do not mention it!" groaned Pinocchio, who was still trembling with fright. "Do not mention it! If you had arrived a second later I should by this time have been fried, eaten, and digested. Brrr! . . . It makes me shudder only to think of it!"

Alidoro, laughing, extended his right paw to the puppet, who shook it heartily in token of great friendship, and they then separated.

The dog took the road home; and Pinocchio, left alone, went to a cottage not far off, and said to a little old man who was warming himself in the sun:

"Tell me, good man, do you know anything of a poor boy called Eugene who was wounded in the head?"

"The boy was brought by some fishermen to this cottage, and now . . ."

"And now he is dead!" interrupted Pinocchio with great sorrow.

"No, he is alive, and has returned to his home."

"Not really? Not really?" cried the puppet, dancing with delight. "Then the wound was not serious?"

"It might have been very serious and even fatal," answered the little old man, "for they threw a thick book bound in cardboard at his head."

"And who threw it at him?"

"One of his schoolfellows, a certain Pinocchio."

"And who is this Pinocchio?" asked the puppet, pretending ignorance.

"They say that he is a bad boy, a vagabond, a regular good-for-nothing."

"Calumnies! All calumnies!"

"Do you know this Pinocchio?"

"By sight!" answered the puppet.

"And what is your opinion of him?" asked the little man.

"He seems to me to be a very good boy, anxious to learn, and obedient and affectionate to his father and family."

While the puppet was firing off all these lies, he touched his nose and perceived that it had lengthened more than a hand. Very much alarmed, he began to cry out:

"Don't believe, good man, what I have been telling you. I know Pinocchio very well, and I can assure you that he is really a very bad boy, disobedient and idle, who instead of going to school runs off with his companions to amuse himself."

He had hardly finished speaking when his nose became shorter and returned to the same size that it was before.

"And why are you all covered with white?" asked the old man suddenly.

"I will tell you. . . . Without observing it, I rubbed myself against a wall which had been freshly whitewashed," answered the puppet, ashamed to confess that he had been floured like a fish prepared for the frying pan.

"And what have you done with your jacket, your trousers, and your cap?"

"I met with robbers who took them from me. Tell me, good old man, could you perhaps give me some clothes to return home in?"

"My boy, as to clothes, I have nothing but a little sack in which I keep beans. If you wish it, take it; there it is."

Pinocchio did not wait to be told twice. He took the sack at once, and with a pair of scissors he cut a hole at the end and at each side, and put it on like a shirt. And with this slight clothing he set off for the village.

But as he went he did not feel at all comfortable—so little so, indeed, that for a step forward he took another backwards, and he said, talking to himself:

"How shall I ever present myself to my good little Fairy? What will she say when she sees me? Will she forgive me this second escapade? I bet that she will not forgive me! Oh, I am sure that she will not forgive me! . . . And it serves me right, for I am a rascal. I am always promising to correct myself, and I never keep my word!"

When he reached the village it was night and very dark. A storm had come on, and as the rain was coming down in torrents he went straight to the Fairy's house, resolved to knock at the door, and hoping to be let in.

But when he was there his courage failed him, and instead of knocking he ran away some twenty paces. He returned to the door a second time, but could not make up his mind; he came back a third time, still he dared not; the fourth time he laid hold of the knocker and, trembling, gave a little knock.

He waited and waited. At last, after half an hour had passed, a window on the top floor was opened—the house was four stories high—and Pinocchio saw a big Snail with a lighted candle on her head looking out. She called to him:

"Who is there at this hour?"

"Is the Fairy at home?" asked the puppet.

"The Fairy is asleep and must not be awakened; but who are you?"

"It is I!"

"Who is I?"

"Pinocchio."

"And who is Pinocchio?"

"The puppet who lives in the Fairy's house."

"Ah, I understand!" said the Snail. "Wait for me there. I will come down and open the door directly."

"Be quick, for pity's sake, for I am dying of cold."

"My boy, I am a snail, and snails are never in a hurry."

An hour passed, and then two, and the door was not opened. Pinocchio, who was wet through, and trembling from cold and fear, at last took courage and knocked again, and this time he knocked louder.

At this second knock a window on the lower story opened, and the same Snail appeared at it.

"Beautiful little Snail," cried Pinocchio from the street, "I have been waiting for two hours! And two hours on such a bad night seem longer than two years. Be quick, for pity's sake."

"My boy," answered the calm, phlegmatic little animal—"my boy, I am a snail, and snails are never in a hurry." And the window was shut again.

Shortly afterward midnight struck; then one o'clock, then two o'clock, and the door remained still closed.

Pinocchio at last, losing all patience, seized the knocker in a rage, intending to give a blow that would resound through the house. But the knocker, which was iron, turned suddenly into an eel, and slipping out of his hands disappeared in the stream of water that ran down the middle of the street.

"Ah! Is that It?" shouted Pinocchio, blind with rage. "Since the knocker has disappeared, I will kick instead with all my might."

And drawing a little back he gave a tremendous kick against the house door. The blow was indeed so violent that his foot went through the wood and stuck; and when he tried to draw it back again it was trouble thrown away, for it remained fixed like a nail that has been hammered down.

Think of poor Pinocchio! He was obliged to spend the remainder of the night with one foot on the ground and the other in the air.

The following morning at daybreak the door was at last opened. That clever little Snail had taken only nine hours to come down from the fourth story to the house door. It is evident that her exertions must have been great.

"What are you doing with your foot stuck in the door?" she asked the puppet, laughing.

"It was an accident. Do try, beautiful Snail, and see if you cannot release me from this torture."

"My boy, that is the work of a carpenter, and I have never been a carpenter."

"Beg the Fairy for me!"

"The Fairy is asleep and must not be awakened."

"But what do you suppose that I can do all day nailed to this door?"

"Amuse yourself by counting the ants that pass down the street."

"Bring me at least something to eat, for I am quite exhausted."

"At once," said the Snail.

In fact, after three hours and a half she returned to Pinocchio carrying a silver tray on her head. The tray contained a loaf of bread, a roast chicken, and four ripe apricots.

"Here is the breakfast that the Fairy has sent you," said the Snail.

The puppet felt very much comforted at the sight of these good things. But when he began to eat them, what was his dismay at making the discovery that the bread was plaster, the chicken cardboard, and the four appricots painted alabaster.

He wanted to cry. In his desperation he tried to throw away the tray and all that was on it; but instead, either from grief or exhaustion, he fainted away.

When he came to himself he found that he was lying on a sofa, and the Fairy was beside him.

"I will pardon you once more," the Fairy said, "but woe to you if you behave badly a third time!"

Pinocchio promised and swore that he would study, and that for the future he would always conduct himself well.

And he kept his word for the remainder of the year. Indeed, at the examinations before the holidays, he had the honor of being the first in the school, and his behavior in general was so satisfactory and praiseworthy that the Fairy was very much pleased, and said to him:

"Tomorrow your wish shall be gratified."

"And that is?"

"Tomorrow you shall cease to be a wooden puppet, and you shall become a boy."

No one who had not witnessed it could ever imagine Pinocchio's joy at this long-sighed-for good fortune. All his schoolfellows were to be invited for the following day to a grand breakfast at the Fairy's house, that they might celebrate together the great event. The Fairy had prepared two hundred cups of coffee and milk, and four hundred rolls cut and buttered on each side. The day promised to be most happy and delightful, but . . .

Unfortunately, in the lives of puppets there is always a "but" that spoils everything.

30

PINOCCHIO, *instead of becoming a boy, starts secretly with his friend* CANDLEWICK *for the* LAND OF BOOBIES

PINOCCHIO, as was natural, asked the Fairy's permission to go round the town to make the invitations; and the Fairy said to him:

"Go if you like and invite your companions for the breakfast tomorrow, but remember to return home before dark. Have you understood?"

"I promise to be back in an hour," answered the puppet.

"Take care, Pinocchio! Boys are always very ready to promise; but generally they are little given to keep their word."

"But I am not like other boys. When I say a thing, I do it."

"We shall see. If you are disobedient, so much the worse for you."

"Why?"

"Because boys who do not listen to the advice of those who know more than they do always meet with some misfortune or other."

"I have experienced that," said Pinocchio. "But I shall never make that mistake again."

"We shall see if that is true."

Without saying more the puppet took leave of his good Fairy, who was like a mamma to him, and went out of the house singing and dancing.

In less than an hour all his friends were invited. Some accepted at once heartily; others at first required pressing; but when they heard that the rolls to be eaten with the coffee were to be buttered on both sides, they ended by saying:

"We will come also, to do you a pleasure."

Now I must tell you that among Pinocchio's friends and schoolfellows there was one that he greatly preferred and was very fond of. This boy's name was Romeo; but he always went by the nickname of Candlewick, because he was so thin, straight, and bright like the new wick of a little night light.

Candlewick was the laziest and the naughtiest boy in the school; but Pinocchio was devoted to him. He had indeed gone at once to his house to invite him to the breakfast, but he had not found him. He returned a second time, but Candlewick was not there. He went a third time, but it was in vain. Where could he search for him? He looked everywhere, and at last he saw him hiding in the porch of a peasant's cottage.

"What are you doing there?" asked Pinocchio, coming up to him.

"I am waiting for midnight, to start . . ."

"Why, where are you going?"

"Very far, very far, very far away."

"And I have been three times to your house to look for you."

"What did you want with me?"

"Do you not know the great event? Have you not heard of my good fortune?"

"What is it?"

"Tomorrow I cease to be a puppet, and I become a boy like you, and like all the other boys."

"Much good may it do you."

"Tomorrow, therefore, I expect you to breakfast at my house."

"But I tell you I am going away tonight . . ."

"At what o'clock?"

"In a short time."

"And where are you going?"

"I am going to live in a country . . . the most delightful country in the world: a real land of Cocagne!"

"And how is it called?"

"It is called the 'Land of Boobies.' Why do you not come too?"

"I? No, never!"

"You are wrong, Pinocchio. Believe me, if you do not come you will repent it. Where could you find a better country for us boys? There are no schools there: there are no masters: there are no books. In that delightful land nobody ever studies. On Thursday there is never school; and every week consists of six Thursdays and one Sunday. Only think, the autumn holidays begin on the first of January and finish on the last day of December. That is the country for me! That is what all civilized countries should be like!"

"But how are the days spent in the Land of Boobies?"

"They are spent in play and amusement from morning till night. When night comes you go to bed, and recommence the same life in the morning. What do you think of it?"

"Hum! . . ." said Pinocchio; and he shook his head slightly as much as to say, "That is a life that I also would willingly lead."

"Well, will you go with me? Yes or no? Resolve quickly."

"No, no, no, and again no. I promised my good Fairy to become a well-conducted boy, and I will keep my word. And as I see that the sun is setting I must leave you at once and run away. Good-by, and a pleasant journey to you."

"Where are you rushing off to in such a hurry?"

"Home. My good Fairy wishes me to be back before dark."

"Wait another two minutes."

"It will make me too late."

"Only two minutes."

"And if the Fairy scolds me?"

"Let her scold. When she has scolded well, she will hold her tongue," said that rascal Candlewick.

"And what are you going to do? Are you going alone or with companions?"

"Alone? We will be more than a hundred boys."

"And do you make the journey on foot?"

"A coach will pass by shortly which is to take me to that happy country."

"What would I not give for the coach to pass by now!"

"Why?"

"That I might see you all start together."

"Stay here a little longer and you will see us."

"No, no, I must go home."

"Wait another two minutes."

"I have already delayed too long. The Fairy will be anxious about me."

"Poor Fairy! Is she afraid that the bats will eat you?"

"But now," continued Pinocchio, "are you really certain that there are no schools in that country?"

"Not even the shadow of one."

"And no masters either?"

"Not one."

"And no one is ever made to study?"

"Never, never, never!"

"What a delightful country!" said Pinocchio, his mouth watering. "What a delightful country! I have never been there, but I can quite imagine it . . ."

"Why will you not come also?"

"It is useless to tempt me. I promised my good Fairy to become a sensible boy, and I will not break my word."

"Good-by, then, and give my compliments to all the boys at the gymnasiums, and also to those of the lyceums, if you meet them in the street."

"Good-by, Candlewick. A pleasant journey to you, amuse yourself, and think sometimes of your friends."

Thus saying the puppet made two steps to go, but then stopped, and turning to his friend he inquired:

"But are you quite certain that in that country all the weeks consist of six Thursdays and one Sunday?"

"Most certain."

"But do you know for certain that the holidays begin on the first of January and finish on the last day of December?"

"Assuredly."

"What a delightful country!" repeated Pinocchio, looking enchanted. Then, with a resolute air, he added in a great hurry:

"This time really good-by, and a pleasant journey to you."

"Good-by."

"When do you start?"

"Shortly."

"What a pity! If really it wanted only an hour to the time of your start, I should be almost tempted to wait."

"And the Fairy?"

"It is already late. . . . If I return home an hour sooner or an hour later it will be all the same."

"Poor Pinocchio! And if the Fairy scolds you?"

"I must have patience! I will let her scold. When she has scolded well, she will hold her tongue."

In the meantime night had come on and it was quite dark. Suddenly they saw in the distance a small light moving . . . and they heard a noise of talking, and the sound of a trumpet, but so small and feeble that it resembled the hum of a mosquito.

"Here it is!" shouted Candlewick, jumping to his feet.

"What is it?" asked Pinocchio in a whisper.

"It is the coach coming to take me. Now will you come, yes or no?"

"But is it really true," asked the puppet, "that in that country boys are never obliged to study?"

"Never, never, never!"

"What a delightful country! . . . What a delightful country! . . . What a delightful country!"

3I

After five months' residence in the land of COCAGNE, PINOCCHIO, *to his great astonishment, grows a beautiful pair of donkey's ears, and he becomes a little donkey, tail and all*

AT LAST THE COACH ARRIVED; and it arrived without making the slightest noise, for its wheels were bound round with tow and rags. It was drawn by twelve pairs of donkeys, all the same size but of different colors.

Some were gray, some white, some brindled like pepper and salt, and others had large stripes of yellow and blue.

But the most extraordinary thing was this: the twelve pairs, that is, the twenty-four donkeys, instead of being shod like other beasts of burden, had on their feet men's boots made of white kid.

And the coachman? . . .

Picture to yourself a little man broader than he was long, flabby and greasy like a lump of butter, with a small round face like an orange, a little mouth that was always laughing, and a soft caressing voice like a cat when she is trying to insinuate herself into the good graces of the mistress of the house.

All the boys, as soon as they saw him, fell in love with him and vied with each other in taking places in his coach to be conducted to the true land of Cocagne, known on the geographical map by the seducing name of the Land of Boobies.

The coach was in fact quite full of boys between eight and twelve years old, heaped one upon another like herrings in a barrel. They were uncomfortable, packed close together, and could hardly breathe: but nobody said Oh!—nobody grumbled. The consolation of knowing that in a few hours they would reach a country where there were no books, no schools, and no masters made them so happy and resigned that they felt neither fatigue nor inconvenience, neither hunger, nor thirst, nor want of sleep.

As soon as the coach had drawn up, the little man turned to Candlewick, and with a thousand smirks and grimaces said to him, smiling:

"Tell me, my fine boy, would you also like to go to that fortunate country?"

"I certainly wish to go."

"But I must warn you, my dear child, that there is not a place left in the coach. You can see for yourself that it is quite full."

"No matter," replied Candlewick. "If there is no place inside, I will manage to sit on the springs."

And giving a leap he seated himself astride of the springs.

"And you, my love," said the little man, turning in a flattering manner to Pinocchio, "what do you intend to do? Are you coming with us, or are you going to remain behind?"

"I remain behind," answered Pinocchio. "I am going home. I intend to study and to earn a good character at school, as all well-conducted boys do."

"Much good may it do you!"

"Pinocchio!" called out Candlewick. "Listen to me: come with us and we shall have such fun."

"No, no, no!"

"Come with us, and we shall have such fun," cried four other voices from the inside of the coach.

"Come with us, and we shall have such fun," shouted in chorus, a hundred voices from the inside of the coach.

"But if I come with you, what will my good Fairy say?" said the puppet, who was beginning to yield.

"Do not trouble your head with melancholy thoughts. Consider only that we are going to a country where we shall be at liberty to run riot from morning till night."

Pinocchio did not answer; but he sighed; he sighed
again; he sighed for the third time, and he said finally:
"Make a little room for me, for I am coming too."
"The places are all full," replied the little man, "but to

show you how welcome you are, you shall have my seat on the box."

"And you?"

"Oh, I will go on foot."

"No, indeed, I could not allow that. I would rather mount one of these donkeys," cried Pinocchio.

Approaching the right-hand donkey of the first pair he attempted to mount him, but the animal turned on him, and giving him a great blow in the stomach rolled him over with his legs in the air.

You can imagine the impertinent and immoderate laughter of all the boys who witnessed this scene.

But the little man did not laugh. He approached the rebellious donkey and, pretending to give him a kiss, bit off half of his ear.

Pinocchio in the meantime had got up from the ground in a fury, and with a spring he seated himself on the poor animal's back. And he sprang so well that the boys stopped laughing and began to shout: "Hurrah, Pinocchio!" And they clapped their hands and applauded him as if they would never finish.

But the donkey suddenly kicked up its hind legs, and backing violently threw the poor puppet into the middle of the road onto a heap of stones.

The roars of laughter recommenced; but the little man, instead of laughing, felt such affection for the restive ass that he kissed him again, and as he did so he bit half of his other ear clean off. He then said to the puppet:

"Mount him now without fear. That little donkey had got some whim into his head; but I whispered two little words into his ears which have, I hope, made him gentle and reasonable."

Pinocchio mounted, and the coach started. While the donkeys were galloping and the coach was rattling over the stones of the highroad, the puppet thought that he heard a low voice that was scarcely intelligible saying to him:

"Poor fool! You would follow your own way, but you will repent it!"

Pinocchio, feeling almost frightened, looked from side to side to try and discover where these words could come from; but he saw nobody. The donkeys galloped, the coach rattled, the boys inside slept, Candlewick snored like a dormouse, and the little man seated on the box sang between his teeth:

> "During the night all sleep,
> But I sleep never . . ."

After they had gone another mile, Pinocchio heard the same little low voice saying to him:

"Bear it in mind, simpleton! Boys who refuse to study, and turn their backs upon books, schools, and masters, to pass their time in play and amusements, sooner or later come to a bad end . . . I know it by experience . . . and I can tell you. A day will come when you will weep as I am weeping now . . . but then it will be too late!"

On hearing these words whispered very softly, the puppet, more frightened than ever, sprang down from the back of his donkey and went and took hold of his mouth.

Imagine his surprise when he found that the donkey was crying . . . and he was crying like a boy!

"Eh, Sir Coachman," cried Pinocchio to the little man, "here is an extraordinary thing! This donkey is crying."

"Let him cry; he will laugh when he is a bridegroom."

"But have you by chance taught him to talk?"

"No; but he spent three years in a company of learned dogs, and he learnt to mutter a few words."

"Poor beast!"

"Come, come," said the little man, "don't let us waste time in seeing a donkey cry. Mount him and let us go on: the night is cold and the road is long."

Pinocchio obeyed without another word. In the morning about daybreak they arrived safely in the Land of Boobies.

It was a country unlike any other country in the world. The population was composed entirely of boys. The oldest were fourteen, and the youngest scarcely eight years old. In the streets there was such merriment, noise, and shouting that it was enough to turn anybody's head. There were troops of boys everywhere. Some were playing with nuts, some with battledores, some with balls. Some rode velocipedes, others wooden horses. A party were playing at hide and seek, a few were chasing each other. Boys dressed in straw were eating lighted tow; some were reciting, some singing, some leaping. Some were amusing themselves with walking on their hands with their feet in the air; others were trundling hoops, or strutting about dressed as generals, wearing leaf helmets and commanding a squadron of cardboard soldiers. Some were laughing, some shouting, some were calling out; others clapped their hands, or whistled, or clucked like a hen who has just laid an egg. To sum it all up, it was such a pandemonium, such a bedlam, such an uproar, that not to be deafened it would have been necessary to stuff one's ears with cotton wool. In every square, canvas theaters had been erected, and they were crowded with boys from morning till evening. On the walls of the houses there were inscriptions written in charcoal: "Long live playthings, we will have no more schools, down with arithmetic"; and similar other fine sentiments all in bad spelling.

Pinocchio, Candlewick, and the other boys who had

made the journey with the little man had scarcely set foot in the town before they were in the thick of the tumult, and I need not tell you that in a few minutes they had made acquaintance with everybody. Where could happier or more contented boys be found?

In the midst of continual games and every variety of amusement, the hours, the days, and the weeks passed like lightning.

"Oh, what a delightful life!" said Pinocchio, whenever by chance he met Candlewick.

"See, then, if I was not right?" replied the other. "And to think that you did not want to come! To think that you had taken it into your head to return home to your Fairy, and to lose your time in studying! . . . If you are this moment free from the bother of books and school, you must acknowledge that you owe it to me, to my advice and to my persuasions. It is only friends who know how to render such great services."

"It is true, Candlewick! If I am now a really happy boy, it is all your doing. But do you know what the master used to say when he talked to me of you? He always said to me: 'Do not associate with that rascal Candlewick, for he is a bad companion, and will only lead you into mischief!'"

"Poor master!" replied the other, shaking his head. "I know only too well that he disliked me, and amused himself by calumniating me; but I am generous and I forgive him!"

"Noble soul!" said Pinocchio, embracing his friend affectionately and kissing him between the eyes.

This delightful life had gone on for five months. The days had been entirely spent in play and amusement, without a thought of books or school, when one morning Pinocchio awoke to a most disagreeable surprise that put him into a very bad humor.

32

PINOCCHIO gets donkey's ears; and then he becomes a real little donkey and begins to bray

---

WHAT WAS THIS SURPRISE?

I will tell you, my dear little readers. The surprise was that Pinocchio when he awoke scratched his head; and in scratching his head he discovered . . . Can you guess in the least what he discovered?

He discovered to his great astonishment that his ears had grown more than a hand.

You know that the puppet from his birth had such very small ears that they were not visible to the naked eye. You can imagine, then, what he felt when he found that during the night his ears had become so long that they seemed like two brooms.

He went at once in search of a glass that he might look at himself, but not being able to find one he filled the basin of his washing stand with water, and he saw reflected what he certainly would never have wished to see. He saw his head embellished with a magnificent pair of donkey's ears!

Only think of poor Pinocchio's sorrow, shame, and despair!

He began to cry and roar, and he beat his head against the wall; but the more he cried the longer his ears grew: they grew, and grew, and became hairy toward the points.

At the sound of his loud outcries a beautiful little Marmot that lived on the first floor came into the room. Seeing the puppet in such grief, she asked earnestly:

"What has happened to you, my dear fellow lodger?"

"I am ill, my dear little Marmot, very ill . . . and of an illness that frightens me. Do you understand counting a pulse?"

"A little."

"Then feel and see if by chance I have fever."

The little Marmot raised her right forepaw; and after having felt Pinocchio's pulse she said to him, sighing:

"My friend, I am grieved to be obliged to give you bad news!"

"What is it?"

"You have got a very bad fever!"

"What fever is it?"

"It is donkey fever."

"That is a fever that I do not understand," said the puppet, but he understood it only too well.

"Then I will explain it to you," said the Marmot. "You must know that in two or three hours you will be no longer a puppet, or a boy . . ."

"Then what shall I be?"

"In two or three hours you will become really and truly a little donkey, like those that draw carts and carry cabbages and salad to market."

"Oh, unfortunate that I am! Unfortunate that I am!" cried Pinocchio, seizing his two ears with his hands, and pulling them and tearing them furiously as if they had been someone else's ears.

"My dear boy," said the Marmot, by way of consoling him, "what can you do to prevent it? It is destiny. It is written in the decrees of wisdom that all boys who are lazy, and who take a dislike to books, to schools, and to masters, and who pass their time in amusement, games, and diversions, must end sooner or later by becoming transformed into so many little donkeys."

"But is it really so?" asked the puppet, sobbing.

"It is indeed only too true! And tears are now useless. You should have thought of it sooner!"

"But it was not my fault: believe me, little Marmot, the fault was all Candlewick's!"

"And who is this Candlewick?"

"One of my schoolfellows. I wanted to return home: I wanted to be obedient. I wished to study and earn a good character . . . but Candlewick said to me: 'Why should you bother yourself by studying? Why should you go to school? . . . Come with us instead to the Land of Boobies: there we shall none of us have to learn; there we shall amuse ourselves from morning to night, and we shall always be merry.'"

"And why did you follow the advice of that false friend—of that bad companion?"

"Why? . . . Because, my dear little Marmot, I am a puppet with no sense . . . and with no heart. Ah, if I had had the least heart I should never have left that good Fairy who loved me like a mamma, and who had done so much for me! . . . And I should be no longer a puppet . . . for I should by this time have become a little boy like so many others. But if I meet Candlewick, woe to him! He shall hear what I think of him!"

And he turned to go out. But when he reached the door he remembered his donkey's ears, and feeling ashamed to show them in public, what do you think he did? He took a big cotton cap, and putting it on his head he pulled it well down over the point of his nose.

He then set out, and went everywhere in search of Candlewick. He looked for him in the streets, in the squares, in the little theaters, in every possible place; but he could not find him. He inquired for him of everybody he met, but no one had seen him.

He then went to seek him at his house; and having reached the door, he knocked.

"Who is there?" asked Candlewick from within.

"It is I!" answered the puppet.

"Wait a moment and I will let you in."

After half an hour the door was opened, and imagine Pinocchio's feelings when upon going into the room he saw his friend Candlewick with a big cotton cap on his head which came down over his nose.

At the sight of the cap Pinocchio felt almost consoled, and thought to himself:

"Has my friend got the same illness that I have? Is he also suffering from donkey fever?"

And pretending to have observed nothing, he asked him, smiling:

"How are you, my dear Candlewick?"

"Very well; as well as a mouse in a Parmesan cheese."

"Are you saying that seriously?"

"Why should I tell you a lie?"

"Excuse me; but why, then, do you keep that cotton cap on your head which covers up your ears?"

"The doctor ordered me to wear it because I have hurt this knee. And you, dear puppet, why have you got on that cotton cap pulled down over your nose?"

"The doctor prescribed it because I have grazed my foot."

"Oh, poor Pinocchio!"

"Oh, poor Candlewick!"

After these words a long silence followed, during

which the two friends did nothing but look mockingly at each other.

At last the puppet said in a soft mellifluous voice to his companion:

"Satisfy my curiosity, my dear Candlewick: have you ever suffered from disease of the ears?"

"Never! . . . And you?"

"Never! Only since this morning one of my ears aches."

"Mine is also paining me."

"You also? . . . And which of your ears hurts you?"

"Both of them. And you?"

"Both of them. Can we have got the same illness?"

"I fear so."

"Will you do me a kindness, Candlewick?"

"Willingly! With all my heart."

"Will you let me see your ears?"

"Why not? But first, my dear Pinocchio, I should like to see yours."

"No: you must be first."

"No, dear: first you and then I!"

"Well," said the puppet, "let us come to an agreement like good friends."

"Let us hear it."

"We will both take off our caps at the same moment. Do you agree?"

"I agree."

"Then, attention!"

And Pinocchio began to count in a loud voice:

"One! Two! Three!"

At the word Three! the two boys took off their caps and threw them into the air.

And then a scene followed that would seem incredible if it was not true. That is, when Pinocchio and Candlewick discovered that they were both struck with the same misfortune, instead of feeling full of mortifica-

tion and grief, they began to prick their ungainly ears
and to make a thousand antics, and they ended by going
into bursts of laughter.

And they laughed, and laughed, and laughed, until
they had to hold themselves together. But in the midst
of their merriment, Candlewick suddenly stopped, staggered, and changing color, said to his friend:

"Help, help, Pinocchio!"

"What is the matter with you?"

"Alas, I cannot any longer stand upright."

"No more can I," exclaimed Pinocchio, tottering and
beginning to cry.

And while they were talking they both doubled up
and began to run around the room on their hands and
feet. And as they ran, their hands became hoofs, their
faces lengthened into muzzles, and their backs became
covered with a light-gray hairy coat sprinkled with
black.

But do you know what was the worst moment for
these two wretched boys? The worst and the most
humiliating moment was when their tails grew. Van-
quished by shame and sorrow, they wept and lamented
their fate.

Oh, if they had but been wiser! But instead of sighs
and lamentations they could only bray like asses; and
they both brayed loudly and said in chorus: "J-a, j-a,
j-a."

While this was going on someone knocked at the door,
and a voice on the outside said:

"Open the door! I am the little man, I am the
coachman who brought you to this country. Open at
once, or it will be the worse for you!"

33

PINOCCHIO, *having become a gen-uine little donkey, is taken to be sold, and is bought by the director of a company of buffoons to be taught to dance, and to jump through hoops, but one evening he lames himself, and then he is bought by a man who wishes to make a drum of his skin*

FINDING THAT THE DOOR remained shut, the little man burst it open with a violent kick, and coming into the room he said to Pinocchio and Candlewick with his usual little laugh:

"Well done, boys! You brayed well, and I recognized you by your voices. That is why I am here."

At these words the two little donkeys were quite stupefied, and stood with their heads down, their ears lowered, and their tails between their legs.

At first the little man stroked and caressed them; then taking out a currycomb he currycombed them well. And when by this process he had polished them till they shone like two mirrors, he put a halter round their necks and led them to the market place, in hope of selling them and making a good profit.

And indeed buyers were not wanting. Candlewick was bought by a peasant whose donkey had died the previous day. Pinocchio was sold to the director of a company of buffoons and tightrope dancers, who bought him that he might teach him to leap and to dance with the other animals belonging to the company.

And now, my little readers, you will have understood the fine trade that little man pursued. The wicked little monster, who had a face all milk and honey, made frequent journeys round the world with his coach. As he went along he collected, with promises and flattery, all the idle boys who had taken an aversion to books and school. As soon as his coach was full he conducted them to the Land of Boobies, that they might pass their time in games, in uproar, and in amusement. When these poor deluded boys, from continual play and no study, had become so many little donkeys, he took possession of them with great delight and satisfaction and carried them off to the fairs and markets to be sold. And in this way he had in a few years made heaps of money and had become a millionaire.

What became of Candlewick I do not know; but I do know that Pinocchio from the very first day had to endure a very hard, laborious life.

When he was put into his stall, his master filled the manger with straw; but Pinocchio, having tried a mouthful, spat it out again.

Then his master, grumbling, filled the manger with hay; but neither did the hay please him.

"Ah!" exclaimed his master in a passion. "Does not hay please you either? Leave it to me, my fine donkey; if you are so full of caprices, I will find a way to cure you!"

And by way of correcting him he struck his legs with his whip.

Pinocchio began to cry and to bray with pain, and he said, braying:

"J-a, j-a, I cannot digest straw!"

"Then eat hay!" said his master, who understood perfectly the asinine dialect.

"J-a, j-a, hay gives me a pain in my stomach."

"Do you mean to pretend that a little donkey like you must be kept on breasts of chickens, and capons in jelly?" asked his master, getting more and more angry, and whipping him again.

At this second whipping Pinocchio prudently held his tongue and said nothing more.

The stable was then shut and Pinocchio was left alone. He had not eaten for many hours, and he began to yawn from hunger. And when he yawned he opened a mouth that seemed as wide as an oven.

At last, finding nothing else in the manger, he resigned himself, and chewed a little hay; and after he had chewed it well, he shut his eyes and swallowed it.

"This hay is not bad," he said to himself, "but how much better it would have been if I had gone on with my studies! Instead of hay I might now be eating a hunch of new bread and a fine slice of sausage. But I must have patience! . . ."

The next morning when he woke he looked in the manger for a little more hay; but he found none, for he had eaten it all during the night.

Then he took a mouthful of chopped straw; but while he was chewing it he had to acknowledge that the taste of chopped straw did not in the least resemble a savory dish of macaroni or rice.

"But I must have patience!" he repeated as he went on chewing. "May my example serve at least as a warning to all disobedient boys who do not want to study."

"Patience, indeed!" shouted his master, coming at that moment into the stable. "Do you think, my little donkey, that I bought you only to give you food and drink? I bought you to make you work, and that you might earn money for me. Up, then, at once! You must come with me into the circus, and there I will teach you to jump through hoops, to go through frames of paper head foremost, to dance waltzes and polkas, and to stand upright on your hind legs."

Poor Pinocchio, either by love or by force, had to learn all these fine things. But it took him three months before he had learnt them, and he got many a whipping that nearly took off his skin.

At last a day came when his master was able to announce that he would give a really extraordinary representation. The many-colored placards stuck on the street corners were thus worded:

GREAT FULL-DRESS REPRESENTATION

TONIGHT
WILL TAKE PLACE THE USUAL FEATS
AND SURPRISING PERFORMANCES
EXECUTED BY ALL THE ARTISTES
AND BY ALL THE HORSES OF THE COMPANY
AND MOREOVER
THE FAMOUS
LITTLE DONKEY PINOCCHIO
CALLED
THE STAR OF THE DANCE
WILL MAKE HIS FIRST APPEARANCE

THE THEATER WILL BE BRILLIANTLY ILLUMINATED

On that evening, as you may imagine, an hour before

the play was to begin the theater was crammed.

There was not a place to be had either in the pit or in the stalls, or in the boxes even, by paying its weight in gold.

The benches round the circus were crowded with children and with boys of all ages, who were in a fever of impatience to see the famous little donkey Pinocchio.

When the first part of the performance was over, the director of the company, dressed in a black coat, white shorts, and big leather boots that came above his knees, presented himself to the public, and after making a profound bow he began with much solemnity the following ridiculous speech:

"Respectable public, ladies and gentlemen! The humble undersigned being a passer-by in this illustrious city, I have wished to procure for myself the honor, not to say the pleasure, of presenting to this intelligent and distinguished audience a celebrated little donkey, who has already had the honor of dancing in the presence of his Majesty the Emperor of all the principal courts of Europe.

"And thanking you, I beg of you to help us with your inspiring presence and to be indulgent to us."

This speech was received with much laughter and applause; but the applause redoubled and became tumultuous when the little donkey Pinocchio made his appearance in the middle of the circus. He was decked out for the occasion. He had a new bridle of polished leather with brass buckles and studs, and two white camellias in his ears. His mane was divided and curled, and each curl was tied with bows of colored ribbon. He had a girth of gold and silver round his body, and his tail was plaited with amaranth and blue velvet ribbons. He was, in fact, a little donkey to fall in love with!

The director, in presenting him to the public, added these few words:

"My respectable auditors! I am not here to tell you falsehoods of the great difficulties that I have overcome in understanding and subjugating this mammifer, while he was grazing at liberty among the mountains in the plains of the torrid zone. I beg you will observe the wild rolling of his eyes. Every means having been tried in vain to tame him, and to accustom him to the life of domestic quadrupeds, I was often forced to have recourse to the convincing argument of the whip. But all my goodness to him, instead of gaining his affections, has, on the contrary, increased his viciousness. However, following the system of Gall, I discovered in his cranium a bony cartilage, that the Faculty of Medicine in Paris has itself recognized as the regenerating bulb of the hair, and of dance. For this reason I have not only taught him to dance, but also to jump through hoops and through frames covered with paper. Admire him, and then pass your opinion on him! But before taking my leave of you, permit me, ladies and gentlemen, to invite you to the daily performance that will take place tomorrow evening; but in the apotheosis that the weather should threaten rain, the performance will be postponed till tomorrow morning at eleven antemeridian of postmeridian."

Here the director made another profound bow; and then turning to Pinocchio, he said:

"Courage, Pinocchio! Before you begin your feats make your bow to this distinguished audience—ladies, gentlemen, and children."

Pinocchio obeyed, and bent both his knees till they touched the ground, and remained kneeling until the director, cracking his whip, shouted to him:

"At a foot's pace!"

Then the little donkey raised himself on his four legs and began to walk round the theater, keeping at a foot's pace.

After a little the director cried:

"Trot!" and Pinocchio, obeying the order, changed to a trot.

"Gallop!" and Pinocchio broke into a gallop.

"Full gallop!" and Pinocchio went full gallop. But while he was going full speed like a race horse, the director, raising his arm in the air, fired off a pistol.

At the shot the little donkey, pretending to be wounded, fell his whole length in the circus, as if he were really dying.

As he got up from the ground amid an outburst of applause, shouts, and clapping of hands, he naturally raised his head and looked up . . . and he saw in one of the boxes a beautiful lady who wore round her neck a thick gold chain from which hung a medallion. On the medallion was painted the portrait of a puppet.

"That is my portrait! . . . That lady is the Fairy!" said Pinocchio to himself, recognizing her immediately; and overcome with delight he tried to cry:

"Oh, my little Fairy! Oh, my little Fairy!"

But instead of these words a bray came from his throat, so sonorous and so prolonged that all the spectators laughed, and more especially all the children who were in the theater.

Then the director, to teach him a lesson, and to make him understand that it is not good manners to bray before the public, gave him a blow on his nose with the handle of his whip.

The poor little donkey put his tongue out an inch, and licked his nose for at least five minutes, thinking perhaps that it would ease the pain he felt.

But what was his despair when, looking up a second time, he saw that the box was empty and that the Fairy had disappeared!

He thought he was going to die: his eyes filled with tears and he began to weep. Nobody, however, noticed it, and least of all the director who, cracking his whip, shouted:

"Courage, Pinocchio! Now let the audience see how gracefully you can jump through the hoops."

Pinocchio tried two or three times, but each time that he came in front of the hoop, instead of going through it, he found it easier to go under it. At last he made a leap and went through it; but his right leg unfortunately caught in the hoop, and that caused him to fall to the ground doubled up in a heap on the other side.

When he got up he was lame, and it was only with great difficulty that he managed to return to the stable.

"Bring out Pinocchio! We want the little donkey! Bring out the little donkey!" shouted all the boys in the theater, touched and sorry for the sad accident.

But the little donkey was seen no more that evening.

The following morning the veterinary, that is, the doctor of animals, paid him a visit, and declared that he would remain lame for life.

The director then said to the stableboy:

"What do you suppose I can do with a lame donkey? He would eat food without earning it. Take him to the market and sell him."

When they reached the market a purchaser was found at once. He asked the stableboy:

"How much do you want for that lame donkey?"

"Twenty francs."

"I will give you twenty pence. Don't suppose that I am buying him to make use of; I am buying him solely for his skin. I see that his skin is very hard, and I intend to make a drum with it for the band of my village."

I leave it to my readers to imagine poor Pinocchio's feelings when he heard that he was destined to become a drum!

As soon as the purchaser had paid his twenty pence he conducted the little donkey to the seashore. He then put a stone round his neck, and tying a rope, the end of which he held in his hand, round his leg, he gave him a sudden push and threw him into the water.

Pinocchio, weighed down by the stone, went at once to the bottom; and his owner, keeping tight hold of the cord, sat down quietly on a piece of rock to wait until the little donkey was drowned, intending then to skin him.

34

PINOCCHIO, *having been thrown into the sea, is eaten by the fish and becomes a puppet as he was before. While he is swimming away to save his life he is swallowed by the terrible* DOGFISH

AFTER PINOCCHIO HAD BEEN fifty minutes under the water, his purchaser said aloud to himself:

"My poor little lame donkey must by this time be quite drowned. I will therefore pull him out of the water, and I will make a fine drum of his skin."

And he began to haul in the rope that he had tied to the donkey's leg; and he hauled, and hauled, and hauled, until at last . . . what do you think appeared above the water? Instead of a little dead donkey he saw a live puppet, who was wriggling like an eel.

Seeing this wooden puppet, the poor man thought he

was dreaming, and, struck dumb with astonishment, he remained with his mouth open and his eyes starting out of his head.

Having somewhat recovered from his first stupefaction, he asked in a quavering voice:

"And the little donkey that I threw into the sea? What has become of him?"

"I am the little donkey!" said Pinocchio, laughing.

"You?"

"I."

"Ah, you young scamp! Do you dare to make game of me?"

"To make game of you? Quite the contrary, my dear master; I am speaking seriously."

"But how can you, who, but a short time ago, were a little donkey, have become a wooden puppet, only from having been left in the water?"

"It must have been the effect of sea water. The sea makes extraordinary changes."

"Beware, puppet, beware! . . . Don't imagine that you can amuse yourself at my expense. Woe to you, if I lose patience!"

"Well, master, do you wish to know the true story? If you will set my leg free I will tell it you."

The good man, who was curious to hear the true story, immediately untied the knot that kept him bound; and Pinocchio, finding himself free as a bird in the air, commenced as follows:

"You must know that I was once a puppet as I am now, and I was on the point of becoming a boy like the many that there are in the world. But instead, induced by my dislike to study and the advice of bad companions, I ran away from home . . . and one fine day when I awoke I found myself changed into a donkey with long ears . . . and a long tail! What a disgrace it was to me!—a disgrace, dear master, that the blessed

St. Anthony would not inflict even upon you! Taken to the market to be sold, I was bought by the director of an equestrian company, who took it into his head to make a famous dancer of me, and a famous leaper through hoops. But one night during a performance I had a bad fall in the circus and lamed both my legs. Then the director, not knowing what to do with a lame donkey, sent me to be sold, and you were the purchaser!"

"Only too true! And I paid twenty pence for you. And now who will give me back my poor pennies?"

"And why did you buy me? You bought me to make a drum of my skin! . . . A drum!"

"Only too true! And now where shall I find another skin?"

"Don't despair, master. There are such a number of little donkeys in the world!"

"Tell me, you impertinent rascal, does your story end here?"

"No," answered the puppet. "I have another two words to say and then I shall have finished. After you had bought me you brought me to this place to kill me; but then, yielding to a feeling of compassion, you preferred to tie a stone round my neck and to throw me into the sea. This humane feeling does you great honor, and I shall always be grateful to you for it. But nevertheless, dear master, this time you made your calculations without considering the Fairy!"

"And who is this Fairy?"

"She is my mamma, and she resembles all other good mammas who care for their children, and who never lose sight of them, but help them lovingly, even when, on account of their foolishness and evil conduct, they deserve to be abandoned and left to themselves. Well, then, the good Fairy, as soon as she saw that I was in danger of drowning, sent immediately an immense shoal of fish, who, believing me really to be a little dead donkey, began to eat me. And what mouthfuls they took: I should never have thought that fish were greedier than boys! . . . Some ate my ears, some my muzzle, others my neck and mane, some the skin of my legs, some my coat . . . and among them there was a little fish so polite that he even condescended to eat my tail."

"From this time forth," said his purchaser, horrified, "I swear that I will never touch fish. It would be too dreadful to open a mullet, or a fried whiting, and to find inside a donkey's tail!"

"I agree with you," said the puppet, laughing. "However, I must tell you that when the fish had finished eating the donkey's hide that covered me from head to foot, they naturally reached the bone . . . or rather the wood, for as you see I am made of the hardest wood. But after giving a few bites they soon discovered that I was not a morsel for their teeth, and, disgusted with such indigestible food, they went off, some in one direction and some in another, without so much as saying thank you to me. And now, at last, I have told you how it was that when you pulled up the rope you found a live puppet instead of a dead donkey."

"I laugh at your story," cried the man in a rage. "I know only that I spent twenty pence to buy you, and I will have my money back. Shall I tell you what I will do? I will take you back to the market and I will sell you by weight as seasoned wood for lighting fires."

"Sell me if you like; I am content," said Pinocchio.

But as he said it he made a spring and plunged into the water. Swimming gaily away from the shore, he called to his poor owner:

"Good-by, master. If you should be in want of a skin to make a drum, remember me."

And he laughed and went on swimming; and after a while he turned again and shouted louder:

"Good-by, master. If you should be in want of a little well-seasoned wood for lighting the fire, remember me."

In the twinkling of an eye he had swum so far off that he was scarcely visible. All that could be seen of him was a little black speck on the surface of the sea that from time to time lifted its legs out of the water and leapt and capered like a dolphin enjoying himself.

While Pinocchio was swimming, he knew not whither, he saw in the midst of the sea a rock that seemed to be made of white marble, and on the summit there stood a beautiful little goat who bleated lovingly and made signs to him to approach.

But the most singular thing was this: The little goat's hair, instead of being white or black, or a mixture of two colors as is usual with other goats, was blue, and of a very vivid blue, greatly resembling the hair of the beautiful Child.

I leave you to imagine how rapidly poor Pinocchio's heart began to beat. He swam with redoubled strength and energy towards the white rock; and he was already halfway when he saw, rising up out of the water and coming to meet him, the horrible head of a sea monster. His wide-open cavernous mouth and his three rows of enormous teeth would have been terrifying to look at even in a picture.

And do you know what this sea monster was?

This sea monster was neither more nor less than that gigantic Dogfish who has been mentioned many times in this story, and who, for his slaughter and for his insatiable voracity, had been named the "Attila of Fish and Fishermen."

Only think of poor Pinocchio's terror at the sight of the monster. He tried to avoid it, to change his direction; he tried to escape; but that immense wide-open mouth came toward him with the velocity of an arrow.

"Be quick, Pinocchio, for pity's sake," cried the beautiful little goat, bleating.

And Pinocchio swam desperately with his arms, his chest, his legs, and his feet.

"Quick, Pinocchio, the monster is close upon you!"

And Pinocchio swam quicker than ever, and flew on with the rapidity of a ball from a gun. He had nearly reached the rock, and the little goat, leaning over toward the sea, had stretched out her forelegs to help him out of the water . . .

But it was too late! The monster had overtaken him, and drawing in his breath, he sucked in the poor puppet as he would have sucked a hen's egg; and he swallowed him with such violence and avidity that Pinocchio, in falling into the Dogfish's stomach, received such a blow that he remained unconscious for a quarter of an hour afterward.

When he came to himself again after the shock he could not in the least imagine in what world he was. All around him it was quite dark, and the darkness was so black and so profound that it seemed to him that he had fallen head downward into an inkstand full of ink. He listened, but he could hear no noise; only from time to time great gusts of wind blew in his face. At first he could not understand where the wind came from, but at last he discovered that it came out of the monster's lungs. For you must know that the Dogfish suffered very much from asthma, and when he breathed it was exactly as if a north wind was blowing.

Pinocchio at first tried to keep up his courage; but when he had one proof after another that he was really shut up in the body of this sea monster he began to cry and scream and to sob out:

"Help! Help! Oh, how unfortunate I am! Will nobody come to save me?"

"Who do you think could save you, unhappy wretch?"

said a voice in the dark that sounded like a guitar out of tune.

"Who is speaking?" asked Pinocchio, frozen with terror.

"It is I! I am a poor Tunny who was swallowed by the Dogfish at the same time that you were. And what fish are you?"

"I have nothing in common with fish. I am a puppet."

"Then if you are not a fish, why did you let yourself be swallowed by the monster?"

"I didn't let myself be swallowed: it was the monster swallowed me! And now, what are we to do here in the dark?"

"Resign ourselves and wait until the Dogfish has digested us both."

"But I do not want to be digested!" howled Pinocchio, beginning to cry again.

"Neither do I want to be digested," added the Tunny; "but I am enough of a philosopher to console myself by thinking that when one is born a Tunny it is more dignified to die in the water than in oil."

"That is all nonsense!" cried Pinocchio.

"It is my opinion," replied the Tunny, "and opinions, so say the political Tunnies, ought to be respected."

"To sum it all up . . . I want to get away from here . . . I want to escape."

"Escape if you are able!"

"Is this Dogfish who has swallowed us very big?" asked the puppet.

"Big! Why, only imagine, his body is two miles long without counting his tail."

While they were holding this conversation in the dark, Pinocchio thought that he saw a light a long way off. "What is that little light I see in the distance?" he asked.

"It is most likely some companion in misfortune who is waiting like us to be digested."

"I will go and find him. Do you not think that it may by chance be some old fish who perhaps could show us how to escape?"

"I hope it may be so with all my heart, dear puppet."

"Good-by, Tunny."

"Good-by, puppet, and good fortune attend you."

"Where shall we meet again?"

"Who can say? . . . It is better not even to think of it!"

35

PINOCCHIO *finds in the body of* the DOGFISH ... *whom does he find? Read this chapter and you will know*

PINOCCHIO, having taken leave of his friend the Tunny, began to grope his way in the dark through the body of the Dogfish, taking a step at a time in the direction of the light that he saw shining dimly at a great distance.

The farther he advanced the brighter became the light; and he walked and walked until at last he reached it: and when he reached it . . . what did he find? I will give you a thousand guesses. He found a little table spread out, and on it a lighted candle stuck into a green glass bottle, and seated at the table was a little old man. He was eating some live fish, and they were so very much alive that while he was eating them they sometimes even jumped out of his mouth.

At this sight Pinocchio was filled with such great and unexpected joy that he became almost delirious. He wanted to laugh, he wanted to cry, he wanted to say a thousand things, and instead he could only stammer out a few confused and broken words. At last he succeeded in uttering a cry of joy, and opening his arms he threw them around the little old man's neck, and began to shout:

"Oh, my dear papa! I have found you at last! I will never leave you more, never more, never more!"

"Then my eyes tell me true?" said the little old man, rubbing his eyes. "Then you are really my dear Pinocchio?"

"Yes, yes, I am Pinocchio, really Pinocchio! And you have quite forgiven me, have you not? Oh, my dear papa, how good you are . . . and to think that I, on the contrary . . . Oh, but if you only knew what misfortunes have been poured on my head, and all that has befallen me! Only imagine, the day that you, poor dear papa, sold your coat to buy me a spelling book that I might go to school, I escaped to see the puppet show, and the showman wanted to put me on the fire that I might roast his mutton, and it was he who afterwards gave me five gold pieces to take them to you, but I met the Fox and the Cat, who took me to the inn of the Red Crawfish, where they ate like wolves, and I left by myself in the middle of the night, and I encountered assassins who ran after me, and I ran away, and they followed, and I ran, and they always followed me, and I ran, until they hung me to a branch of a Big Oak, and the beautiful Child with blue hair sent a little carriage to fetch me, and the doctors when they had seen me said immediately: 'If he is not dead, it is proof that he is still alive'—and then by chance I told a lie, and my nose began to grow until I could no longer get through the door of the room, for which reason I went with the Fox and the Cat to bury the four gold pieces, for one I had spent at the inn, and the Parrot began to laugh, and instead of two thousand gold pieces I found none left, for which reason the judge when he heard that I had been robbed had me immediately put in prison to content the robbers, and then when I was coming away I saw a beautiful bunch of grapes in a field, and I was caught in a trap, and the peasant, who was quite right, put a dog collar round my neck that I might guard the poultry yard, and acknowledging my innocence let me go, and the Serpent with the smoking tail began to laugh and broke a blood vessel in his chest, and so I returned to the house of the beautiful Child who was dead, and the Pigeon, seeing that I was crying, said to me, 'I have seen your father who was building a little boat to go in search of you,' and I said to him, 'Oh, if I also had wings!' and he said to me, 'Do you want to go to your father?' and I said, 'Without doubt! But who will take me to him?' and he said to me, 'I will take you,' and I said to him, 'How?' and he said to me, 'Get on my back,' and so we flew all night, and then in the morning all the fishermen who were looking out to sea said to me, 'There is a poor man in a boat who is on the point of being drowned,' and I recognized you at once, even at that distance, for my heart told me, and I made signs to you to return to land . . ."

"I also recognized you," said Geppetto, "and I would willingly have returned to the shore: but what was I to do? The sea was tremendous, and a great wave upset my boat. Then a horrible Dogfish who was near, as soon as he saw me in the water, came toward me, and putting out his tongue took hold of me, and swallowed me as if I had been a little Bologna tart."

"And how long have you been shut up here?" asked Pinocchio.

"Since that day—it must be nearly two years ago: two years, my dear Pinocchio, that have seemed like two centuries!"

"And how have you managed to live? And where did

you get the candle? And the matches to light it? Who gave them to you?"

"Stop, and I will tell you everything. You must know, then, that in the same storm in which my boat was upset a merchant vessel foundered. The sailors were all saved, but the vessel went to the bottom, and the Dogfish, who had that day an excellent appetite, after he had swallowed me, swallowed also the vessel . . ."

"How?"

"He swallowed it in one mouthful, and the only thing that he spat out was the mainmast, that had stuck between his teeth like a fishbone. Fortunately for me the vessel was laden with preserved meat in tins, biscuits, bottles of wine, dried raisins, cheese, coffee, sugar, candles, and boxes of wax matches. With this providential supply I have been able to live for two years. But I have arrived at the end of my resources; there is nothing left in the larder, and this candle that you see burning is the last that remains . . ."

"And after that?"

"After that, dear boy, we shall remain in the dark."

"Then, dear little papa," said Pinocchio, "there is no time to lose. We must think of escaping."

"Of escaping? . . . And how?"

"We must escape through the mouth of the Dogfish, throw ourselves into the sea and swim away."

"You talk well: but, dear Pinocchio, I don't know how to swim."

"What does that matter? I am a good swimmer, and you can get on my shoulders and I will carry you safely to shore."

"All illusions, my boy!" replied Geppetto, shaking his head, with a melancholy smile. "Do you suppose it possible that a puppet like you, scarcely a meter high, could have the strength to swim with me on his shoulders!"

*The Dogfish was sleeping so profoundly that even
a cannonade would have failed to wake him*

"Try it and you will see!"

Without another word Pinocchio took the candle in his hand, and going in front to light the way, he said to his father:

"Follow me, and don't be afraid."

And they walked for some time and traversed the body and the stomach of the Dogfish. But when they arrived at the point where the monster's big throat began, they thought it better to stop to give a good look around and to choose the best moment for escaping.

Now I must tell you that the Dogfish, being very old, and suffering from asthma and palpitation of the heart, was obliged to sleep with his mouth open. Pinocchio, therefore, having approached the entrance to his throat and, looking up, could see beyond the enormous gaping mouth a large piece of starry sky and beautiful moonlight.

"This is the moment to escape," he whispered, turning to his father. "The Dogfish is sleeping like a dormouse, the sea is calm, and it is as light as day. Follow me, dear papa, and in a short time we shall be in safety."

They immediately climbed up the throat of the sea monster, and having reached his immense mouth they began to walk on tiptoe down his tongue.

Before taking the final leap the puppet said to his father:

"Get on my shoulders and put your arms tight around my neck. I will take care of the rest."

As soon as Geppetto was firmly settled on his son's shoulders, Pinocchio, feeling sure of himself, threw himself into the water and began to swim. The sea was as smooth as oil, the moon shone brilliantly, and the Dogfish was sleeping so profoundly that even a cannonade would have failed to wake him.

36

PINOCCHIO *at last ceases to be a puppet and becomes a boy*

WHILE PINOCCHIO WAS SWIMMING quickly toward the shore he discovered that his father, who was on his shoulders with his legs in the water, was trembling as violently as if the poor man had got an attack of ague fever.

Was he trembling from cold or from fear? Perhaps a little from both the one and the other. But Pinocchio, thinking that it was from fear, said to comfort him:

"Courage, papa! In a few minutes we shall be safely on shore."

"But where is this blessed shore?" asked the little old man, becoming still more frightened, and screwing up his eyes as tailors do when they wish to thread a needle. "I have been looking in every direction and I see nothing but the sky and the sea."

"But I see the shore as well," said the puppet. "You must know that I am like a cat: I see better by night than by day."

Poor Pinocchio was making a pretense of being in good spirits, but in reality . . . in reality he was beginning to feel discouraged; his strength was failing, he was gasping and panting for breath . . . he could do no more, and the shore was still far off.

He swam until he had no breath left; then he turned his head to Geppetto and said in broken words:

"Papa . . . help me . . . I am dying!"

The father and son were on the point of drowning when they heard a voice like a guitar out of tune saying:

"Who is it that is dying?"

"It is I, and my poor father!"

"I know that voice! You are Pinocchio!"

"Precisely; and you?"

"I am the Tunny, your prison companion in the body of the Dogfish."

"And how did you manage to escape?"

"I followed your example. You showed me the road, and I escaped after you."

"Tunny, you have arrived at the right moment! I implore you to help us, or we are lost."

"Willingly and with all my heart. You must, both of you, take hold of my tail and allow me to guide you. I will take you on shore in four minutes."

Geppetto and Pinocchio, as I need not tell you, accepted the offer at once; but instead of holding on by his tail they thought it would be more comfortable to get on the Tunny's back.

Having reached the shore, Pinocchio sprang first on land that he might help his father to do the same. He then turned to the Tunny, and said to him in a voice full of emotion:

"My friend, you have saved my papa's life. I can find no words with which to thank you properly. Permit me at least to give you a kiss as a sign of my eternal gratitude!"

The Tunny put his head out of the water, and Pinocchio, kneeling on the ground, kissed him tenderly on the mouth. At this spontaneous proof of warm affection, the poor Tunny, who was not accustomed to it, felt extremely touched, and ashamed to let himself be seen crying like a child, he plunged under the water and disappeared.

By this time the day had dawned. Pinocchio, then offering his arm to Geppetto, who had scarcely breath to stand, said to him:

"Lean on my arm, dear papa, and let us go. We will walk very slowly like the ants, and when we are tired we can rest by the wayside."

"And where shall we go?" asked Geppetto.

"In search of some house or cottage, where they will give us for charity a mouthful of bread, and a little straw to serve as a bed."

They had not gone a hundred yards when they saw by the roadside two villainous-looking individuals begging.

They were the Cat and the Fox, but they were scarcely recognizable. Fancy! The Cat had so long feigned blindness that she had become blind in reality; and the Fox, old, mangy, and with one side paralyzed, had not even his tail left. That sneaking thief, having fallen into the most squalid misery, one fine day had found himself obliged to sell his beautiful tail to a traveling peddler, who bought it to drive away flies.

"Oh, Pinocchio!" cried the Fox. "Give a little in charity to two poor infirm people."

"Infirm people," repeated the Cat.

"Begone, impostors!" answered the puppet. "You took me in once, but you will never catch me again."

"Believe me, Pinocchio, we are now poor and unfortunate indeed!"

"If you are poor, you deserve it. Recollect the proverb: 'Stolen money never fructifies.' Begone, impostors!"

And thus saying, Pinocchio and Geppetto went their way in peace. When they had gone another hundred yards they saw, at the end of a path in the middle of the fields, a nice little straw hut with a roof of tiles and bricks.

"That hut must be inhabited by someone," said Pinocchio. "Let us go and knock at the door."

They went and knocked.

"Who is there?" said a little voice from within.

"We are a poor father and son without bread and without a roof," answered the puppet.

"Turn the key and the door will open," said the same little voice.

Pinocchio turned the key and the door opened. They went in and looked here, there, and everywhere, but could see no one.

"Oh, where is the master of the house?" said Pinocchio, much surprised.

"Here I am up here!"

The father and son looked immediately up to the ceiling, and there on a beam they saw the Talking Cricket.

"Oh, my dear little Cricket!" said Pinocchio, bowing politely to him.

"Ah! Now you call me your 'dear little Cricket.' But do you remember the time when you threw the handle of a hammer at me, to drive me from your house?"

"You are right, Cricket! Drive me away also . . . throw the handle of a hammer at me; but have pity on my poor papa . . ."

"I will have pity on both father and son, but I wished to remind you of the ill treatment I received from you, to teach you that in this world, when it is possible, we should show courtesy to everybody, if we wish it to be extended to us in our hour of need."

"You are right, Cricket, you are right, and I will bear

in mind the lesson you have given me.   But tell me how you managed to buy this beautiful hut."

"This hut was given to me yesterday by a goat whose wool was of a beautiful blue color."

"And where has the goat gone?" asked Pinocchio, with lively curiosity.

"I do not know."

"And when will it come back?"

"It will never come back.   It went away yesterday in great grief and, bleating, it seemed to say: 'Poor Pinocchio . . . I shall never see him more . . . by this time the Dogfish must have devoured him!'"

"Did it really say that? . . . Then it was she! . . . It was she! . . . It was my dear little Fairy!" exclaimed Pinocchio, crying and sobbing.

When he had cried for some time he dried his eyes, and prepared a comfortable bed of straw for Geppetto to lie down upon.   Then he asked the Cricket:

"Tell me, little Cricket, where can I find a tumbler of milk for my poor papa?"

"Three fields off from here there lives a gardener called Giangio who keeps cows.   Go to him and you will get the milk you are in want of."

Pinocchio ran all the way to Giangio's house; and the gardener asked him:

"How much milk do you want?"

"I want a tumblerful."

"A tumbler of milk costs a halfpenny.   Begin by giving me the halfpenny."

"I have not even a farthing," replied Pinocchio, grieved and mortified.

"That is bad, puppet," answered the gardener.   "If you have not even a farthing, I have not even a drop of milk."

"I must have patience!" said Pinocchio, and he turned to go.

"Wait a little," said Giangio. "We can come to an arrangement together. Will you undertake to turn the pumping machine?"

"What is the pumping machine?"

"It is a wooden pole which serves to draw up the water from the cistern to water the vegetables."

"You can try me . . ."

"Well, then, if you will draw a hundred buckets of water, I will give you in compensation a tumbler of milk."

"It is a bargain."

Giangio then led Pinocchio to the kitchen garden and taught him how to turn the pumping machine. Pinocchio immediately began to work; but before he had drawn up the hundred buckets of water the perspiration was pouring from his head to his feet. Never before had he undergone such fatigue.

"Up till now," said the gardener, "the labor of turning the pumping machine was performed by my little donkey, but the poor animal is dying."

"Will you take me to see him?" said Pinocchio.

"Willingly."

When Pinocchio went into the stable he saw a beautiful little donkey stretched on the straw, worn out from hunger and overwork. After looking at him earnestly he said to himself, much troubled:

"I am sure I know this little donkey! His face is not new to me."

And bending over him he asked him in asinine language:

"Who are you?"

At this question the little donkey opened his dying eyes, and answered in broken words in the same language: "I am . . . Can . . . dle . . . wick . . ."

And, having again closed his eyes, he expired.

"Oh, poor Candlewick!" said Pinocchio in a low voice;

and taking a handful of straw he dried a tear that was rolling down his face.

"Do you grieve for a donkey that cost you nothing?" said the gardener. "What must it be to me who bought him for ready money?"

"I must tell you . . . he was my friend!"

"Your friend?"

"One of my schoolfellows!"

"How?" shouted Giangio, laughing loudly. "How? Had you donkeys for schoolfellows? . . . I can imagine what wonderful studies you must have made!"

The puppet, who felt much mortified at these words, did not answer; but taking his tumbler of milk, still quite warm, he returned to the hut.

And from that day for more than five months he continued to get up at daybreak every morning to go and turn the pumping machine, to earn the tumbler of milk that was of such benefit to his father in his bad state of health. Nor was he satisfied with this; for, during the time that he had over, he learned to make hampers and baskets of rushes, and with the money he obtained by selling them he was able with great economy to provide for all the daily expenses. Among other things he constructed an elegant little wheel chair, in which he could take his father out on fine days to breathe a mouthful of fresh air.

By his industry, ingenuity, and his anxiety to work and to overcome difficulties, he not only succeeded in maintaining his father, who continued infirm, in comfort, but he also contrived to put aside forty pence to buy himself a new coat.

One morning he said to his father:

"I am going to the neighboring market to buy myself a jacket, a cap, and a pair of shoes. When I return," he added, laughing, "I shall be so well dressed that you will take me for a fine gentleman."

And leaving the house he began to run merrily and happily along. All at once he heard himself called by name, and turning around he saw a big Snail crawling out from the hedge.

"Do you not know me?" asked the Snail.

"It seems to me . . . and yet I am not sure . . ."

"Do you not remember the Snail who was lady's maid to the Fairy with blue hair? Do you not remember the time when I came downstairs to let you in, and you were caught by your foot which you had stuck through the house door?"

"I remember it all!" shouted Pinocchio. "Tell me quickly, my beautiful little Snail, where have you left my good Fairy? What is she doing? Has she forgiven me? Does she still remember me? Does she still wish me well? Is she far from here? Can I go and see her?"

To all these rapid, breathless questions the Snail replied in her usual phlegmatic manner:

"My dear Pinocchio, the poor Fairy is lying in bed at the hospital!"

"At the hospital?"

"It is only too true. Overtaken by a thousand misfortunes, she has fallen seriously ill, and she has not even enough to buy herself a mouthful of bread."

"Is it really so? Oh, what sorrow you have given me! Oh, poor Fairy, poor Fairy, poor Fairy! . . . If I had a million I would run and carry it to her . . . but I have only forty pence . . . Here they are: I was going to buy a new coat. Take them, Snail, and carry them at once to my good Fairy."

"And your new coat?"

"What matters my new coat? I would sell even these rags that I have got on to be able to help her. Go, Snail, and be quick; and in two days return to this place, for I hope I shall then be able to give you some more money.

Up to this time I have worked to maintain my papa; from today I will work five hours more that I may also maintain my good mamma. Good-by, Snail, I shall expect you in two days."

The Snail, contrary to her usual habits, began to run like a lizard in a hot August sun.

That evening Pinocchio, instead of going to bed at ten o'clock, sat up till midnight had struck; and instead of making eight baskets of rushes he made sixteen.

Then he went to bed and fell asleep. And while he slept he thought that he saw the Fairy smiling and beautiful, who, after having kissed him, said to him:

"Well done, Pinocchio! To reward you for your good heart I will forgive you for all that is past. Boys who minister tenderly to their parents, and assist them in their misery and infirmities, are deserving of great praise and affection, even if they cannot be cited as examples of obedience and good behavior. Try and do better in the future and you will be happy."

At this moment his dream ended, and Pinocchio opened his eyes and awoke.

But imagine his astonishment when upon awakening he discovered that he was no longer a wooden puppet, but that he had become instead a boy, like all other boys. He gave a glance round and saw that the straw walls of the hut had disappeared, and that he was in a pretty little room furnished and arranged with a simplicity that was almost elegance. Jumping out of bed he found a new suit of clothes ready for him, a new cap, and a pair of new leather boots that fitted him beautifully.

He was hardly dressed when he naturally put his hands in his pockets, and pulled out a little ivory purse on which these words were written: "The Fairy with blue hair returns the forty pence to her dear Pinocchio, and thanks him for his good heart." He opened the

*He was greeted instead by the image of a bright,
intelligent boy*

purse, and instead of forty copper pennies he saw forty shining gold pieces fresh from the mint.

He then went and looked at himself in the glass, and he thought he was someone else. For he no longer saw the usual reflection of a wooden puppet; he was greeted instead by the image of a bright, intelligent boy with chestnut hair, blue eyes, and looking as happy and joyful as if it were the Easter holidays.

In the midst of all these wonders succeeding each other Pinoccio felt quite bewildered, and he could not tell if he was really awake or if he was dreaming with his eyes open.

"Where can my papa be!" he exclaimed suddenly, and going into the next room he found old Geppetto quite well, lively, and in good humor, just as he had been formerly. He had already resumed his trade of wood carving, and he was designing a rich and beautiful frame of leaves, flowers, and the heads of animals.

"Satisfy my curiosity, dear papa," said Pinocchio, throwing his arms around his neck and covering him with kisses. "How can this sudden change be accounted for?"

"This sudden change in our home is all your doing," answered Geppetto.

"How my doing?"

"Because when boys who have behaved badly turn over a new leaf and become good, they have the power of bringing contentment and happiness to their families."

"And where has the old wooden Pinocchio hidden himself?"

"There he is," answered Geppetto, and he pointed to a big puppet, leaning against a chair, with its head on one side, its arms dangling, and its legs so crossed and bent that it was really a miracle that it remained standing.

Pinocchio turned and looked at it; and after he had

looked at it for a short time, he said to himself with great complacency:

"How ridiculous I was when I was a puppet! And how glad I am that I have become a well-behaved little boy!"

THE STORY OF

King Arthur

AND HIS KNIGHTS

Down through the centuries the stories of King Arthur and his Knights of the Round Table have come to us as fresh and exciting today as when they were first told around the campfires and in the courts of long-gone kings.

What boy or girl can fail to be thrilled by the story of how young Arthur won his birthright back when he alone could pull the great sword from the block of stone? Who can forget how Merlin, the man of magic, saved King Arthur's life as he battled with the Sable Knight?

These great stories of daring and chivalry are a thrilling experience in reading that no youngster should miss.

They shouted and drave their horses together

THE STORY OF

King Arthur

AND HIS KNIGHTS

BY HOWARD PYLE

ILLUSTRATIONS BY SERGIO LEONE

COMPANION LIBRARY

Grosset & Dunlap

PUBLISHERS

NEW YORK

Foreword

AFTER several years of contemplation and of thought upon the matter herein contained, it has at last come about, by the Grace of God, that I have been able to write this work with such pleasure of spirit that, if it gives to you but a part of the joy that it hath afforded me, I shall be very well content with what I have done.

For when, in pursuing this history, I have come to consider the high nobility of spirit that moved these excellent men to act as they did, I have felt that they have afforded such a perfect example of courage and humility that anyone might do exceedingly well to follow after their manner of behavior in such measure as he is able to do.

For I believe that King Arthur was the most honorable, gentle Knight who ever lived in all the world. And those who were his fellows of the Round Table—taking him as their looking-glass of chivalry—made, altogether, such a company of noble knights that it is hardly to be supposed that their like will ever be seen again in this world. Wherefore it is that I have had such extraordinary pleasure in beholding how those famous knights behaved whenever circumstances called upon them to perform their endeavor.

So in the year of grace one thousand nine hundred and two I began to write this history of King Arthur and his Knights of the Round Table and, if I am able so to do, I shall endeavor, with love of that task, to finish the same at some other time in another book and to the satisfaction of whosoever may care to read the story thereof.

Contents

FOREWORD

PROLOGUE

THE BOOK OF KING ARTHUR

PART   I. The Winning of Kinghood 19

PART II. The Winning of a Sword 51

PART III. The Winning of a Queen 89

THE BOOK OF THREE WORTHIES

PART   I. The Story of Merlin 169

PART II. The Story of Sir Pellias 211

PART III. The Story of Sir Gawaine 287

Illustrations

They shouted and drave their horses together   FRONTISPIECE

The hand held a sword of marvellous workmanship . . 79

"Keep this," she said, "for it is of very potent magic" . . 219

THE BOOK OF
King Arthur

Prologue

$\mathfrak{I}$N ancient days there lived a very noble King, named Uther-Pendragon, and he became Overlord of all of Britain. This King was very greatly aided unto the achievement of the Pendragonship of the realm by the help of two men, who rendered him great assistance in all that he did. The one of these men was a certain very powerful enchanter and some-time prophet known to men as Merlin the Wise; and he gave very good counsel unto Uther-Pendragon. The other man was an excellent noble and renowned knight, hight Ulfius (who was thought by many to be the greatest leader in war of any man then alive); and he gave Uther-Pendragon aid and advice in battle. So, with the help of Merlin and Sir Ulfius, Uther-Pendragon was able to overcome all of his enemies and to become King of the entire realm.

After Uther-Pendragon had ruled his kingdom for a number of years he took to wife a certain beautiful and gentle lady, hight Igraine. This noble dame was the window of Gerlois, the Duke of Tintegal; by which prince she had two daughters —one of whom was named Margaise and the other Morgana le Fay. And Morgana le Fay was a famous sorceress. These daughters the Queen brought with her to the Court of Uther-Pendragon after she had married that puissant King, and

there Margaise was wedded to King Urien of Gore, and
Morgana le Fay was wedded to King Lot of Orkney.

Now after awhile Uther-Pendragon and Queen Igraine had a
son born unto them, and he was very beautiful and of great size
and strength of bone. And whilst the child still lay wrapped in
his swaddling clothes and lying in a cradle of gold and
ultramarine, Merlin came to Uther-Pendragon with a spirit of
prophecy strong upon him (for such was often the case with
him), and, speaking in that spirit of prophecy, he said, "Lord, it
is given unto me to foresee that thou shalt shortly fall sick of
a fever and that thou shalt maybe die of a violent sweat that will
follow thereon. Now, should such a dolorous thing befall us
all, this young child (who is, certes, the hope of all this realm)
will be in very great danger of his life; for many enemies will
assuredly rise up with design to seize upon him for the sake of
his inheritance, and either he will be slain or else he will be held
in captivity from which he shall hardly hope to escape.
Wherefore, I do beseech thee, Lord, that thou wilt permit Sir
Ulfius and myself to presently convey the child away unto
some place of safe refuge, where he may be hidden in secret
until he groweth to manhood and is able to guard himself from
such dangers as may threaten him."

When Merlin had made an end of speaking thus, Uther-
Pendragon made reply with a very steadfast countenance in this
wise: "Merlin, so far as my death is concerned—when my time
cometh to die I believe God will give me grace to meet my end
with entire cheerfulness; for, certes, my lot is in that wise no
different from that of any other man who hath been born of
woman. But touching the matter of this young child, if thy
prophecy be true, then his danger is very great, and it would be
well that he should be conveyed hence to some place of safe
harborage as thou dost advise. Wherefore, I pray thee to
perform thy will in this affair, bearing in thy heart the
consideration that the child is the most precious inheritance
which I shall leave unto this land."

All this, as was said, Uther-Pendragon spake with great
calmness and equanimity of spirit. And Merlin did as he had
advised, and he and Sir Ulfius conveyed the child away by
night, and no one but they wist whither the babe had been

taken. And shortly afterward Uther-Pendragon was seized with the sickness as Merlin had foretold, and he died exactly as Merlin had feared that he would die; wherefore it was very well that the child had been taken to a place of safety.

And after Uther-Pendragon had departed from this life, it was likewise as Merlin had feared, for all the realm fell into great disorder. For each lesser king contended against his fellow for overlordship, and wicked knights and barons harried the highways as they listed and there levied toll with great cruelty upon helpless wayfarers. For some such travellers they took prisoners and held for ransom, whiles others they slew because they had no ransom to pay. So it was a very common sight to see a dead man lying by the roadside, if you should venture to make a journey upon some business or other. Thus it befell that, after awhile, all that dolorous land groaned with the trouble that lay upon it.

Thus there passed nearly eighteen years in such great affliction, and then one day the Archbishop of Canterbury summoned Merlin to him and bespake him in this wise: "Merlin, men say that thou art the wisest man in all the world. Canst thou not find some means to heal the distractions of this woeful realm? Bend thou thy wisdom to this matter and choose thou a king who shall be a fit overlord for us, so that we may enjoy happiness of life once more as we did in the days of Uther-Pendragon."

Then Merlin lifted up his countenance upon the Archbishop, and spake in this wise: "My lord, the spirit of prophecy that lieth upon me sometimes moveth me now to say that I do perceive that this country is soon to have a king who shall be wiser and greater and more worthy of praise than was even Uther-Pendragon. And he shall bring order and peace where is now disorder and war. Moreover, I may tell you that this King shall be of Uther-Pendragon's own full blood-royal."

To this the Archbishop said: "What thou tellest me, Merlin, is a wonderfully strange thing. But in this spirit of prophecy canst thou not foretell when this King is to come? And canst thou tell how we shall know him when he appeareth amongst us? For many lesser kings there are who would fain be overlord of this land, and many such there are who deem themselves fit to rule over all the others. How then shall we know the real King from those who may proclaim themselves to be the rightful king?"

"My lord Archbishop," quoth Merlin, "if I have thy leave for to exert my magic I shall set an adventure which, if any man achieve it, all the world shall straightway know that he is the rightful King and overlord of this realm." And to this the Archbishop said, "Merlin, I bid thee do whatsoever may seem to thee to be right in this affair." And Merlin said, "I will do so."

So Merlin caused by magic that a huge marble stone, four square, should suddenly appear in an open place before the cathedral door. And upon this block of marble he caused it to be that there should stand an anvil and into the anvil he caused it that there should be thrust a great naked sword midway deep of the blade. And this sword was the most wonderful that any man had ever seen, for the blade was of blue steel and extraordinarily bright and glistering. And the hilt was of gold, chased and carved with marvellous cunning, and inlaid with a great number of precious stones, so that it shone with wonderful brightness in the sunlight. And about the sword were written these words in letters of gold:—

Whoso Pulleth Out this Sword from the Anvil That same is Rightwise King-Born of England.

So a great many people came and gazed upon that sword and marvelled at it exceedingly, for its like had never before been beheld upon the earth.

Then, when Merlin had accomplished this miracle, he bade the Archbishop to call together all the chief people of that land upon Christmastide; and he bade the Archbishop to command that every man should make assay to draw out the sword, for that he who should succeed in drawing it forth out of the anvil should be rightwise King of Britain.

So the Archbishop did according as Merlin said; and this was the marvel of the marble stone and the anvil, of which same anyone may easily read for himself in that book written a very

long while ago by Robert de Boron, which is called Le Roman
de Merlin.

Now when the mandate of the Lord Archbishop went forth,
summoning all the chief people of the land to the assay of that
miracle (for, indeed, it was a miracle to draw forth a
sword-blade out of an anvil of solid iron), all the realm became
immediately cast into a great ferment, so that each man asked
his fellow, "Who shall draw forth that sword, and who shall be
our King?" Some thought it would be King Lot and others
thought it would be King Urien of Gore (these being the
sons-in-law unto Uther-Pendragon); some thought that it
would be King Leodegrance of Camiliard, and others that it
would be King Ryence of North Wales; some thought it would
be this king and others that it would be that king; for all the
world was divided into different parties who thought according
to their liking.

Then, as Christmastide drew nigh, it presently appeared as
though the entire world was wending its way to London
Town, for the highways and the by-ways became filled with
wayfarers—kings and lords and knights and ladies and esquires
and pages and men-at-arms—all betaking their way whither the
assay was to be made of that adventure of the sword and the
anvil. Every inn and castle was filled so full of travellers that it
was a marvel how so many folk could be contained within their
compass, and everywhere were tents and pavilions pitched
along the wayside for the accommodation of those who could
not find shelter within doors.

But when the Archbishop beheld the multitudes that were
assembling, he said to Merlin, "Indeed, Merlin, it would be a
very singular thing if among all these great kings and noble,
honorable lords we should not find some one worthy of being
the King of this realm."

Unto which the Merlin smiled and said, "Marvel not, my
lord, if among all those who appear to be so extraordinarily
worthy there shall not be found one who is worthy; and marvel
not if, among all those who are unknown, there shall arise one
who shall approve himself to be entirely worthy."

And the Archbishop pondered Merlin's words, and so
beginneth this story.

PART I

The Winning of Kinghood

Chapter First

How Sir Kay Did Combat in a Great Tournament at London Town and of How He Brake His Sword. Likewise, How Arthur Found a New Sword for Him.

IT happened that among those worthies who were summoned unto London Town by the mandate of the Archbishop as above recounted, there was a certain knight, very honorable and of high estate, by name Sir Ector of Bonmaison—surnamed the Trustworthy Knight, because of the fidelity with which he kept the counsel of those who confided in him, and because he always performed unto all men, whether of high or low degree, that which he promised to undertake, without defalcation as to the same. So this noble and excellent knight was held in great regard by all those who knew him; for not only was he thus honorable in conduct but he was, besides, of very high estate, being possessed of seven castles in Wales and in the adjoining country north thereof, and likewise of certain fruitful tracts of land with villages appertaining thereunto, and also of sundry forests of great extent, both in the north country and the west. This very noble knight had two sons; the elder of these was Sir Kay, a young knight of great valor and promise, and already well renowned in the Courts of Chivalry because of several very honorable deeds of worthy achievement in arms which he had performed; the other was a young lad of eighteen years of age, by name Arthur, who at that time was serving with good repute as Sir Kay's esquire-at-arms.

Now when Sir Ector of Bonmaison received by messenger the mandate of the Archbishop, he immediately summoned these two sons unto him and bade them to prepare straightway for to go with him to London Town, and they did so. And in the same manner he bade a great number of retainers and esquires and pages for to make them ready, and they likewise did so. Thus, with a very considerable array at arms and with great show of circumstance, Sir Ector of Bonmaison betook his way unto London Town in obedience to the commands of the Archbishop.

So, when he had come thither he took up his inn in a certain field where many other noble knights and puissant lords had already established themselves, and there he set up a very fair pavilion of green silk, and erected his banner emblazoned with the device of his house; to wit, a gryphon, black, upon a field of green.

And upon this field were a great multitude of other pavilions of many different colors, and over above each pavilion was the pennant and the banner of that puissant lord to whom the pavilion belonged. Wherefore, because of the multitude of these pennants and banners the sky was at places well-nigh hidden with the gaudy colors of the fluttering flags.

Among the great lords who had come thither in pursuance to the Archbishop's summons were many very famous kings and queens and noblemen of high degree. For there was King Lot of Orkney, who had taken to wife a step-daughter of Uther-Pendragon, and there was King Uriens of Gore, who had taken to wife another step-daughter of that great king, and there was King Ban, and King Bors, and King Ryance, and King Leodegrance and many others of like degree, for there were no less than twelve kings and seven dukes, so that, what with their court of lords and ladies and esquires and pages in attendance, the town of London had hardly ever seen the like before that day.

Now the Archbishop of Canterbury, having in mind the extraordinary state of the occasion that had brought so many kings and dukes and high lords unto that adventure of the sword and the anvil, had commanded that there should be a very stately and noble tournament proclaimed. Likewise he commanded that this contest at arms should be held in a certain field nigh to the great cathedral, three days before that assay should be made of the sword and the anvil (which same was to be undertaken, as aforesaid, upon Christmas day). To this tournament were bidden all knights who were of sufficient birth, condition, and quality for to fit them to take part therein. Accordingly, very many exalted knights made application for admission, and that in such numbers that three heralds were kept very busy looking into their pretensions unto the right of battle. For these heralds examined the escutcheons and the rolls of lineage of all applicants with great care and circumspection.

Now when Sir Kay received news of this tournament he went to where his father was, and when he stood before his face he spake in this wise: "Sire, being thy son and of such very high condition both as to birth and estate as I have inherited from thee, I find that I have an extraordinary desire to imperil my body in this tourney. Accordingly, if so be I may approve my quality as to knighthood before this college of heralds, it will maybe be to thy great honor and credit, and to the honor and credit of our house if I should undertake this adventure. Wherefore I do crave thy leave to do as I have a mind."

Unto these Sir Ector made reply: "My son, thou hast my leave for to enter this honorable contest, and I do hope that God will give thee a great deal of strength, and likewise such grace of spirit that thou mayst achieve honor to thyself and credit to us who are of thy blood."

So Sir Kay departed with very great joy and immediately went to that congress of heralds and submitted his pretensions unto them. And, after they had duly examined into his claims to knighthood, they entered his name as a knight-contestant according to his desire; and at this Sir Kay was filled with great content and joy of heart.

So, when his name had been enrolled upon the list of combatants, Sir Kay chose his young brother Arthur for to be his esquire-at-arms and to carry his spear and pennant before him into the field of battle, and Arthur was also made exceedingly glad because of the honor that had befallen him and his brother.

Now, the day having arrived when this tourney was to be held, a very huge concourse of people gathered together to witness that noble and courtly assault at arms. For at that time London was, as aforesaid, extraordinarily full of nobility and knighthood, wherefore it was reckoned that not less than twenty thousand lords and ladies (besides those twelve kings and their courts and seven dukes and their courts) were assembled in the lists circumadjacent to the field of battle for to witness the performance of those chosen knights. And those noble people sat so close together, and so filled the seats and benches assigned to them, that it appeared as though an entirely solid wall of human souls surrounded that meadow where the battle was to be fought. And, indeed, any knight might well be moved to do his uttermost upon such a great occasion with the eyes of so many beautiful dames and noble lords gazing upon his performances. Wherefore the hearts of all the knights attendant were greatly expanded with emulation to overturn their enemies into the dust.

In the centre of this wonderful court of lords and ladies there was erected the stall and the throne of the lord Archbishop himself. Above the throne was a canopy of purple cloth emblazoned with silver lilies, and the throne itself was hung all about with purple cloth of velvet, embroidered, alternately, with the figure of St. George in gold, and with silver crosses of St. George surrounded by golden halos. Here the lord Archbishop himself sat in great estate and pomp, being surrounded by a very exalted court of clerks of high degree and also of knights of honorable estate, so that all that centre of the field glistered with the splendor of gold and silver embroidery, and was made beautiful by various colors of rich apparel and bright with fine armor of excellent workmanship. And, indeed, such was the stateliness of all these circumstances that very few who were there had ever seen so noble a preparation for battle as that which they then beheld.

Now, when all that great assembly were in their places and everything had been prepared in due wise, an herald came and stood forth before the enstalled throne of the Archbishop and blew a very strong, loud blast upon a trumpet. At that signal the turnpikes of the lists were immediately opened and two parties of knights-contestant entered therein—the one party at the northern extremity of the meadow of battle and the other party at the southern extremity thereof. Then immediately all that lone field was a-glitter with the bright-shining splendor of the sunlight upon polished armor and accoutrements. So these two parties took up their station, each at such a place as had been assigned unto them—the one to the north and the other to the south.

Now the party with which Sir Kay had cast his lot was at the north of the field, and that company was fourscore and thirteen in number; and the other party stood at the south end of the field, and that company was fourscore and sixteen in number. But though the party with whom Sir Kay had attached himself numbered less by three than the other party, yet was it the stronger by some degree because that there were a number of knights of great strength and renown in that company. Indeed it may be here mentioned that two of those knights afterward became companions in very good credit of the round table—to wit: Sir Mador de la Porte, and Sir Bedevere—which latter was the last who saw King Arthur alive upon this earth.

So, when all was prepared according to the ordination of the tournament, and when those knights-contestant had made themselves ready in all ways that were necessary, and when they had dressed their spears and their shields in such a manner as befitted knights about to enter serious battle, the herald set his trumpet to his lips a second time and blew upon it with might and main. Then, having sounded this blast, he waited for a while and then he blew upon the trumpet again.

And, upon that blast, each of those parties of knights quitted its station and rushed forth in great tumult against the other party, and that with such noise and fury that the whole earth groaned beneath the feet of the war-horses, and trembled and shook as with an earthquake.

So those two companies met, the one against the other, in the midst of the field, and the roar of breaking lances was so terrible that those who heard it were astonished and appalled at the sound. For several fair dames swooned away with terror of the noise, and others shrieked aloud; for not only was there that great uproar, but the air was altogether filled with the splinters of ash wood that flew about.

In that famous assault threescore and ten very noble and honorable knights were overthrown, many of them being trampled beneath the hoofs of the horses; wherefore, when the two companies withdrew in retreat each to his station the ground was beheld to be covered all over with broken fragments of lances and with cantels of armor, and many knights were seen to be wofully lying in the midst of all that wreck. And some of these champions strove to arise and could not, while others lay altogether quiet as though in death. To these ran divers esquires and pages in great numbers, and lifted up the fallen men and bare them away to places of safe harborage. And likewise attendants ran and gathered up the cantels of armor and the broken spears, and bare them away to the barriers, so that, by and by, the field was altogether cleared.

Then all those who gazed down upon that meadow gave loud acclaim with great joyousness of heart, for such a noble and glorious contest at arms in friendly assay had hardly ever been beheld in all that realm before.

Now turn we unto Sir Kay; for in this assault he had conducted himself with such credit that no knight who was there had done better than he, and maybe no one had done so well as he. For, though two opponents at once had directed their spears against him, yet he had successfully resisted their assault. And one of those two he smote so violently in the midst of his defences that he had lifted that assailant entirely over the crupper of the horse which he rode, and had flung him down to the distance of half a spear's length behind his steed, so that the fallen knight had rolled thrice over in the dust ere he ceased to fall.

And when those of Sir Kay's party who were nigh to him beheld what he did, they gave him loud and vehement acclaim, and that in such measure that Sir Kay was wonderfully well satisfied and pleased at heart.

And, indeed, it is to be said that at that time there was hardly any knight in all the world who was so excellent in deeds of arms as Sir Kay. And though there afterward came knights of much greater renown and of more glorious achievement (as shall be hereinafter recorded in good season), yet at that time Sir Kay was reckoned by many to be one of the most wonderfully puissant knights (whether errant or in battle) in all of that realm.

So was that course of the combat run to the great pleasure and satisfaction of all who beheld it, and more especially of Sir Kay and his friends. And after it had been completed the two parties in array returned each to its assigned station once more.

And when they had come there, each knight delivered up his spear unto his esquire. For the assault which was next to be made was to be undertaken with swords, wherefore all lances and other weapons were to be put away; such being the order of that courteous and gentle bout at arms.

Accordingly, when the herald again blew upon his trumpet, each knight drew his weapon with such readiness for battle that there was a great splendor of blades all flashing in the air at once. And when the herald blew a second time each party pushed forward to the contest with great nobleness of heart and eagerness of spirit, every knight being moved with intent to engage his oppugnant with all the might and main that lay in him.

Then immediately began so fierce a battle that if those knights had been very enemies of long standing instead of friendly contestants, the blows which they delivered the one upon the other could not have been more vehement as to strength or more astonishing to gaze upon.

And in this affair likewise Sir Kay approved himself to be so extraordinary a champion that his like was nowhere to be seen in all that field; for he violently smote down five knights, the one after the other, ere he was stayed in his advance.

Wherefore, beholding him to be doing work of such a sort, several of the knights of the other party endeavored to come at him with intent to meet him in his advance.

Amongst these was a certain knight, hight Sir Balamorgineas, who was so huge of frame that he rode head and shoulders above any other knight. And he was possessed of such extraordinary strength that it was believed that he could successfully withstand the assault of three ordinary knights at one time. Wherefore when this knight beheld the work that Sir Kay did, he cried out to him, "Ho! ho! Sir Knight of the black gryphon, turn thou hitherward and do a battle with me!"

Now when Sir Kay beheld Sir Balamorgineas to be minded to come against him in that wise—very threateningly and minded to do him battle—he turned him toward his enemy with great cheerfulness of spirit. For at that time Sir Kay was very full of youthful fire and reckoned nothing of assaulting any enemy who might demand battle of him.

(So it was at that time. But it after befell, when he became Seneschal, and when other and mightier knights appeared at the court of the King, that he would sometimes avoid an encounter with such a knight as Sir Launcelot, or Sir Pellias, or Sir Marhaus, or Sir Gawaine, if he might do so with credit to his honor.)

So, being very full of the spirit of youth, he turned him with great lustiness of heart, altogether inflamed with the eagerness and fury of battle. And he cried out in a great voice, "Very well, I will do battle with thee, and I will cast thee down like thy fellows!" And therewith he smote with wonderful fierceness at Sir Balamorgineas, and that with all his might. And Sir Balamorgineas received the stroke upon his helmet and was altogether bewildered by the fury thereof, for he had never felt its like before that time. Wherefore his brains swam so light that it was necessary for him to hold to the horn of his saddle to save himself from falling.

But it was a great pity for Sir Kay that, with the fierceness of the blow, his sword-blade snapped short at the haft, flying so high in the air that it appeared to overtop the turrets of the cathedral in its flight. Yet so it happened, and thus it befell that

Sir Kay was left without any weapon. Yet it was thought that, because of that stroke, he had Sir Balamorgineas entirely at his mercy, and that if he could have struck another blow with his sword he might easily have overcome him.

But as it was, Sir Balamorgineas presently so far recovered himself that he perceived his enemy to be altogether at his mercy; wherefore, being filled beyond measure with rage because of the blow he had received, he pushed against Sir Kay with intent to smite him down in a violent assault.

In this pass it would maybe have gone very ill with Sir Kay but that three of his companions in arms, perceiving the extreme peril in which he lay, thrust in betwixt him and Sir Balamorgineas with intent to take upon themselves the assault of that knight and so to save Sir Kay from overthrow. This they did with such success that Sir Kay was able to push out from the press and to escape to the barriers without suffering any further harm at the hands of his enemies.

Now when he reached the barrier, his esquire, young Arthur, came running to him with a goblet of spiced wine. And Sir Kay opened the umbril of his helmet for to drink, for he was athirst beyond measure. And, lo! his face was all covered over with blood and sweat, and he was so a-drought with battle that his tongue clave to the roof of his mouth and he could not speak. But when he had drunk of the draught that Arthur gave him, his tongue was loosened and he cried out to the young man in a loud and violent voice: "Ho! ho! Brother, get me another sword for to do battle, for I am assuredly winning for our house much glory this day!" And Arthur said, "Where shall I get thee a sword?" And Kay said, "Make haste unto our father's pavilion and fetch me thence another sword, for this which I have is broken." And Arthur said, "I will do so with all speed," and thereupon he set hand to the barrier and leaped over it into the alleyway beyond. And he ran down the alleyway with all the speed that he was able with intent to fulfil that task which his brother had bidden him to undertake; and with like speed he ran to that pavilion that his father had set up in the meadows.

But when he came to the pavilion of Sir Ector he found no one there, for all the attendants had betaken themselves unto the tournament. And neither could he find any sword fit for his brother's handling, wherefore he was put to a great pass to know what to do in that matter.

In this extremity he bethought him of that sword that stood thrust into the anvil before the cathedral, and it appeared to him that such a sword as that would suit his brother's purposes very well. Wherefore he said to himself, "I will go thither and get that sword if I am able to do so, for it will assuredly do very well for my brother for to finish his battle withal." Whereupon he ran with all speed to the cathedral. And when he had come there he discovered that no one was there upon guard at the block of marble, as had heretofore been the case, for all who had been upon guard had betaken themselves unto the contest of arms that was toward. And the anvil and the sword stood where he could reach them. So, there being no one to stay young Arthur, he leaped up upon the block of marble and laid his hands unto the hilt of the sword. And he bent his body and drew upon the sword very strongly, and, lo! it came forth from the anvil with wonderful smoothness and ease, and he held the sword in his hand, and it was his.

And when he had got the sword in that way, he wrapped it in his cloak so that no one might see it (for it shone with an exceeding brightness and splendor) and he leaped down from the block of marble stone and hastened with it unto the field of battle.

Now when Arthur had entered into that meadow once more, he found Sir Kay awaiting his coming with great impatience of spirit. And when Sir Kay saw him he cried out, very vehemently, "Hast thou got a sword?" And Arthur said, "Yea, I have one here." Thereupon he opened his cloak and showed Sir Kay what sword it was he had brought.

Now when Sir Kay beheld the sword he immediately knew it, and he wist not what to think or what to say, wherefore he stood for a while, like one turned into a stone, looking upon that sword. Then in awhile he said, in a very strange voice "Where got ye that sword?" And Arthur looked upon his brother and he beheld that his countenance was greatly disturbed, and that his face was altogether as white as wax. And he said, "Brother, what ails thee that thou lookest so strangely?

I will tell the entire truth. I could find no sword in our father's pavilion, wherefore I bethought me of that sword that stood in the anvil upon the marble cube before the cathedral. So I went thither and made assay for to draw it forth, and it came forth with wonderful ease. So, when I had drawn it out, I wrapped it in my cloak and brought it hither unto thee as thou beholdest."

Then Sir Kay turned his thoughts inward and communed with himself in this wise, "Lo! my brother Arthur is as yet hardly more than a child. And he is, moreover, exceedingly innocent. Therefore he knoweth not what he hath done in this nor what the doing thereof signifieth. Now, since he hath achieved this weapon, why should I not myself lay claim to that achievement, and so obtain the glory which it signifieth." Whereupon he presently aroused himself, and he said to Arthur, "Give the sword and the cloak to me," and Arthur did as his brother commanded. And when he had done so Sir Kay said to him, "Tell no man of this but keep it privy in thine own heart. Meantime go thou to our father where he sits at the lists and bid him come straightway unto the pavilion where we have taken up our inn."

And Arthur did as Sir Kay commanded him, greatly possessed with wonder that his brother should be so disturbed in spirit as he had appeared to be. For he wist not what he had done in drawing out that sword from the anvil, nor did he know of what great things should arise from that little thing, for so it is in this world that a man sometimes approves himself to be worthy of such a great trust as that, and yet, in lowliness of spirit, he is yet altogether unaware that he is worthy thereof. And so it was with young Arthur at that time.

Chapter Second

*How Arthur Twice Performed the Miracle
of the Sword Before Sir Ector and of How
His Birthright Was Discovered Unto Him.*

So Arthur made haste to that part of the lists where Sir
Ector sat with the people of his household. And he stood
before his father and said, "Sire, my brother Kay hath sent me
hitherward for to bid thee come straightway unto the pavilion
where we have taken up our inn. And, truly, I think
something very extraordinary hath befallen, for my brother
Kay hath such a countenance as I never saw him wear."
Then Sir Ector marvelled very greatly what it was that
should cause Sir Kay to quit that battle and to summon him at
such a time, wherefore he arose from where he sat and went
with Arthur. And they went to the pavilion, and when he had
come there, behold! Sir Kay was standing in the midst of the
pavilion. And Sir Ector saw that his face was as white as ashes
of wood and that his eyes shone with a wonderful brightness.
And Sir Ector said, "My son, what ails thee?" whereunto Sir
Kay made reply, "Sire, here is a very wonderful matter."
Therewith he took his father by the hand and brought him to
the table that stood in the pavilion. And upon the table there
lay a cloak and there was *something* within the cloak. Then Sir
Kay opened the cloak and, lo! there lay the sword of the anvil,

and the hilt thereof and the blade thereof glistered with exceeding splendor.

And Sir Ector immediately knew that sword and whence it came. Wherefore he was filled with such astonishment that he wist not what to do. And for a while his tongue refused to speak, and after a while he found speech and cried out aloud in a great voice, "What is this that mine eyes behold!"

To this Sir Kay made reply, "Sire. I have that sword which stood a while since embedded in the anvil that stands upon the cube of marble stone before the great cathedral. Wherefore I demand that thou tellest me what this may foretend?"

Then Sir Ector said, "How came you by that sword?"

And for a while Sir Kay was silent, but after a while he said, "Sire, I brake my sword in that battle which of late I fought, whereupon I found me this sword in its stead."

Then Sir Ector was altogether bemazed and knew not whether to believe what his ears heard. And after a while he said, "If so be that thou didst draw forth this sword from the anvil, then it must also be that thou art rightwise King of Britain, for so the saying of the sword proclaimeth. But if thou didst indeed draw it forth from the anvil, then it will be that thou shalt as easily be able for to thrust it back again into that place from whence thou didst take it."

At this a great trouble of spirit fell upon Sir Kay, and he cried out in a very loud voice, "Who may do such a thing as that, and who could perform so great a miracle as to thrust a sword into solid iron." Whereunto Sir Ector made reply. "Such a miracle is no greater than the miracle that thou hast performed in drawing it out from its embedment. For who ever heard that a man could draw forth a sword from a place and yet would not thrust it back whence he drew it?"

Then Sir Kay wist not what to say to his father, and he greatly feared that he should not be able to perform that miracle. But, nevertheless, he took what comfort to himself he was able, saying, "If my young brother Arthur was able to perform this miracle why should I not do a miracle of a like sort, for, assuredly, I am not less worthy than he. Wherefore if he drew the sword forth with such ease, it may be that I with equal ease shall be able to thrust it back into its place again."

Accordingly he took such comfort to himself in these thoughts as he was able.

So he wrapped the sword in the cloak again, and when he had done so he and Sir Ector went forth from the pavilion and betook their way unto where was the marble stone and the anvil before the cathedral. And Arthur went with his father

and his brother and they forebade him not. And when they had come to that place where the sword had been, Sir Kay mounted upon the cube of marble stone and beheld the face of the anvil. And lo! the face of the anvil was altogether smooth and without a scratch or scar of any sort. And Sir Kay said to himself, "What is this my father would have me do! What man is there in life who could thrust a sword-blade into a solid anvil of iron?" But, ne'theless, he could not withdraw from that impossible undertaking, but was constrained to assay that miracle, wherefore he set the point of the sword to the iron and bore upon it with all his strength. But it was impossible for him to accomplish that thing, and though he endeavored with all his might with the sword against the face of the anvil, yet did he not pierce the iron even to the breadth of a hair.

So, after he had thus assayed for a great while, he at last ceased what he did and came down from where he stood. And he said to his father, "Sire, no man in life may perform that miracle."

Unto this Sir Ector made reply, "How is it possible then that thou couldst have drawn out that sword as thou sayst and yet cannot put it back again?"

Then young Arthur lifted up his voice and said, "My father, have I thy leave to speak?" And Sir Ector said, "Speak, my son." And Arthur said, "I would that I might assay to handle that sword." Whereunto Sir Ector replied, "By what authority wouldst thou handle that sword?" And Arthur said, "Because it was I who drew that sword forth from the anvil for my brother. Wherefore, as thou sayest, to draw it forth is not more difficult than to thrust it back again. So I believe that I shall be able to set it back into the iron whence I drew it."

Then Sir Ector gazed upon young Arthur in such a strange manner that Arthur wist not why he looked at him in that wise. Wherefore he cried out, "Sire, why dost thou gaze so strangely upon me? Has thou anger against me?" Whereunto Sir Ector made reply, "In the sight of God, my son, I have no anger against thee." Then he said, "If thou hast a desire to handle the sword, thou mayst assuredly make assay of that miracle."

So Arthur took the sword from his brother Kay and he leaped up upon the marble stone. And he set the point of the sword upon the anvil and bare very strongly upon it and lo! the sword penetrated very smoothly into the centre of the anvil until it stood midway deep therein, and there it stood fast. And after he had performed that miracle he drew the sword forth again very swiftly and easily, and then thrust it back again once more as he had done before.

But when Sir Ector beheld what Arthur did, he cried out in a voice of exceeding loudness, "Lord! Lord! what is the miracle mine eyes behold!" And when Arthur came down from the cube of marble stone, Sir Ector kneeled down before him and set his hands together, palm to palm.

But when Arthur beheld what his father did, he cried out aloud like one in a great measure of pain; and he said, "My father! my father! why dost thou kneel down to me?"

To him Sir Ector made reply, "I am not thy father, and now it is made manifest that thou art assuredly of very exalted race and that the blood of kings flows in thy veins, else thou couldst not have handled that sword as thou hast done."

Then Arthur fell a-weeping beyond all measure and he cried out as with great agony of spirit, "Father! Father! What is this thou sayest? I beseech thee to arise and not to kneel unto me."

So Sir Ector arose from his knees and stood before the face of Arthur, and he said, "Arthur, why dost thou weep?" And Arthur said, "Because I am afeard."

Now all this while Sir Kay had stood near by and he could neither move nor speak, but stood like one entranced, and he said to himself, "What is this? Is my brother a King?"

Then Sir Ector spake, saying, "Arthur, the time hath come for thee to know thyself, for the true circumstances of thy life have, heretofore, been altogether hidden from thee.

"Now I do confess everything to thee in this wise: that eighteen year ago there came to me a certain man very wise and high in favor with Uther-Pendragon and that man was the Enchanter Merlin. And Merlin showed me the signet ring of Uther-Pendragon and he commanded me by virtue of that ring that I should be at a certain assigned place at a particular time which he nominated; and the place which he assigned was the postern gate of Uther-Pendragon's castle; and the time which he named was midnight of that very day.

"And he bade me tell no man aught concerning those things which he communicated to me, and so I kept his counsel as he desired me to do.

"So I went to that postern gate at midnight as Merlin had commanded, and at that place there came unto me Merlin and another man, and the other man was Sir Ulfius, who was the chief knight of Uther-Pendragon's household. And I tell thee that these two worthies stood nigher unto Uther-Pendragon than any other men in all of the world.

"Now when those two came unto me, I perceived that Merlin bare in his arms a certain thing wrapped in a scarlet mantle of fine texture. And he opened the folds of the mantle and, lo! I beheld a child not long born and wrapped in swaddling clothes. And I saw the child in the light of a lanthorn which Sir Ulfius bare, and I perceived that he was very fair of face and large of bone—and thou wert that child.

"Then Merlin commanded me in this wise: that I was to take that child and that I should rear him as mine own; and he said that the child was to be called by the name of Arthur; and he said that no one in all the world was to know otherwise than that the child was mine own. And I told Merlin that I would do as he would have me, whereupon I took the child and bare it away with me. And I proclaimed that the child was mine own, and all over the world believed my words, wherefore no one ever knew otherwise than that thou wert mine own son. And that lady who was my wife, when she died she took that secret with her unto Paradise, and since then until now no one in all the world knew aught of this matter but I and those two aforementioned worthies.

"Nor have I until now ever know aught of who was thy father; but now I do suspect who he was and that thou hast in thy veins very high and kingly blood. And I do have in mind that perhaps thy father was Uther-Pendragon himself. For who but the son of Uther-Pendragon could have drawn forth that sword from out of the anvil as thou hast done?"

Then, when Arthur heard that saying of his father's, he cried out in very loud and vehement voice, "Woe! Woe! Woe!"— saying that word three times. And Sir Ector said, "Arthur, why art thou woful?" And Arthur said, "Because I have lost my father, for I would rather have my father than be a King!"

Now as these things passed, there came unto that place two men, very tall and of a wonderfully noble and haughty appearance. And when these two men had come nigh to where they were, Arthur and Sir Ector and Sir Kay perceived that one of them was the Enchanter Merlin and that the other was Sir Ulfius—for those two men were very famous and well known unto all the world. And when those two had come to where were the three, Merlin spake, saying, "What cheer?" And Sir Ector made answer, "Here is cheer of a very wonderful sort; for, behold, Merlin! this is that child that thou didst bring unto me eighteen years ago, and, lo! thou seest he hath grown unto manhood."

Then Merlin said, "Sir Ector, I know very well who is this youth, for I have kept diligent watch over him for all this time. And I know that in him lieth the hope of Britain. Moreover, I tell thee that even to-day within the surface of an enchanted looking-glass I have beheld all that he hath done since the morning; and I know how he drew forth the sword from the anvil, and how he thrust it back again; and I know how he drew it forth and thrust it back a second time. And I know all that thou hast been saying unto him this while; wherefore I also do now avouch that thou hast told him the very truth. And lo! the spirit of prophecy is upon me and I do foresee into the future that thou, Arthur, shall become the greatest and most famous King that ever lived in Britain; and I do foresee that many knights of extraordinary excellence shall gather about thee and that men shall tell of their marvellous deeds as long as this land shall continue, and I do foresee that through these knights thy reign shall be full of splendor and glory; and I do foresee that the most marvellous adventure of the Holy Grail shall be achieved by three of the knights of thy Court, and that to thy lasting renown, who shall be the King under whose reign the holy cup shall be achieved. All these things I foresee; and, lo! the time is now at hand when the glory of thy House shall again be made manifest unto the world, and all the people of this land shall rejoice in thee and thy kinghood. Wherefore, Sir Ector, for these three days to come, I do charge it upon thee that thou do guard this young man as the apple of thine eye, for in him doth lie the hope and salvation of all this realm."

Then Sir Ector lifted up his voice and cried unto Arthur, "A boon! a boon!" And Arthur said, "Alas! how is this? Dost thou, my father, ask a boon of me who may have all in the world that is mine to give? Ask what thou wilt and it is thine!" Then Sir Ector said, "I do beseech this of thee: that when thou art King thy brother Kay may be Seneschal of all this realm." And Arthur said, "It shall be as thou dost ask." And he said, "As for thee, it shall be still better with thee, for thou shalt be my father unto the end!" Whereupon so saying, he took Sir Ector's head into his hands and he kissed Sir Ector upon the forehead and upon the cheeks, and so sealed his plighted word.

But all this while Sir Kay had stood like unto one struck by thunder, and he wist not whether to be uplifted unto the skies or to be cast down into the depths, that his young brother should thus have been passed by him and exalted unto that extraordinary altitude of fortune. Wherefore he stood like to one bereft of life and motion.

And let it here be said that Arthur fulfilled all that he had thus promised to his father—for, in after times, he made Sir Kay his Seneschal, and Sir Ector was to him a father until the day of his death, which same befell five years from that time.

Thus I have told you how the royalty of Arthur was first discovered. And now, if you will listen, ye shall hear how it was confirmed before all the world.

Chapter Third

*How Several Kings and High Dukes
Assayed to Draw the Sword Out of the
Anvil and How They Failed.   Likewise
How Arthur Made the Assay and
Succeeded Therein.*

So when the morning of Christmas day had come, many thousands of folk of all qualities, both gentle and simple, gathered together in front of the cathedral for to behold the assay of that sword.

Now there had been a canopy of embroidered cloth of divers colors spread above the sword and the anvil, and a platform had been built around about the cube of marble stone.   And nigh unto that place there had been a throne for the Archbishop established; for the Archbishop was to overlook that assay and to see that every circumstance was fulfilled with due equity and circumspection.

So, when the morning was half gone by, the Archbishop himself came with great pomp of estate and took his seat upon the high throne that had been placed for him, and all his court of clerks and knights gathered about him, so that he presented a very proud and excellent appearance of courtliness.

Now unto that assay there had gathered nineteen kings and sixteen dukes, and each of these was of such noble and exalted estate that he entertained high hopes that he would that day be approved before the world to be the right king and overlord of all Britain. Wherefore after the Archbishop had established himself upon his throne, there came several of these and made demand that he should straightway put that matter to the test. So the Archbishop commanded his herald for to sound a trumpet, and to bid all who had the right to make assay of the sword to come unto that adventure, and the herald did according as the Archbishop ordered.

And when the herald had sounded his trumpet there immediately appeared the first of those kings to make trial of the sword, and he who came was King Lot of Orkney and the Isles. With King Lot there came eleven knights and five esquires, so that he appeared in very noble estate before the eyes of all. And when King Lot had arrived at that place, he mounted the platform. And first he saluted the Archbishop, and then he laid his hands to the pommel of the sword in the sight of all. And he bent his body and drew upon the sword with great strength, but he could not move the blade in the anvil even so much as the breadth of a hair, for it stood as fast as the iron in which it was planted. And after that first assay he tried three times more, but still he was altogether unable to move the blade in the iron. Then, after that he had thus four times made assay, he ceased his endeavor and came down from that place. And he was filled with great anger and indignation that he had not succeeded in his endeavor.

And after King Lot there came his brother-in-law, King Urien of Gore, and he also made assay in the same wise as King Lot had done. But neither did he succeed any better than that other king. And after King Urien there came King Fion of Scotland, and after King Fion there came King Mark of Cornwall, and after King Mark there came King Ryence of North Wales, and after King Ryence there came King Leodegrance of Cameliard, and after him came all those other kings and dukes before numerated, and not one of all these was able to move the blade. And some of these high and mighty lords were filled with anger and indignation that they had not succeeded, and others were ashamed that they had failed in that undertaking before the eyes of all those who looked upon them.

But whether they were angry or whether they were ashamed it in no wise helped their case.

Now when all the kings and dukes had thus failed in that adventure, the people who were there were very much astonished, and they said to one another, "How is this? If all those kings and dukes of very exalted estate have failed to achieve that adventure, who then may hope to succeed? For here have been all those who were most worthy of that high honor, and all have tried to draw that sword and all have failed. Who then is there now to come after these who may hope to succeed?"

And, likewise, those kings and dukes spoke together in the same manner. And by and by there came six of the most worthy—to wit, King Lot, King Urien, King Pellinore, King Ban, King Ryence, and Duke Clarence of Northumberland— and these stood before the throne of the Archbishop and spake to him in this wise: "Sir, here have all the kings and dukes of this realm striven before you for to draw forth that sword, and lo! not one of all those who have undertaken that thing hath succeeded in his undertaking. What, then, may we understand but that the enchanter Merlin hath set this adventure for to bring shame and discredit upon all of us who are here, and upon you, who are the head of the church in this realm? For who in all the world may hope to draw forth a sword-blade out from a bed of solid iron? Behold! it is beyond the power of any man. Is it not then plain to be seen that Merlin hath made a mock of us all? Now, therefore, lest all this great congregation should have been called here in vain, we do beseech you of your wisdom that you presently choose the one from among the kings here gathered, who may be best fitted to be overlord of this realm. And when ye shall have chosen him, we will promise to obey him in all things whatsoever he may ordain. Verily, such a choice as that will be better worth while than to spend time in this foolish task of striving to draw forth a sword out of an anvil which no man in all the world may draw forth."

Then was the Archbishop much troubled in spirit, for he said to himself, "Can it be sooth that Merlin hath deceived me, and hath made a mock of me and of all these kings and lordly folk?

Surely this cannot be. For Merlin is passing wise, and he would not make a mock of all the realm for the sake of so sorry a jest as this would be. Certes he hath some intent in this of which we know naught, being of less wisdom than he—wherefore I will be patient for a while longer." Accordingly, having communed thus within himself, he spake aloud in this wise to those seven high lords: "Messires," he said, "I have yet faith that Merlin hath not deceived us, wherefore I pray your patience for one little while longer. For if, in the time a man may count five hundred twice over, no one cometh forward to perform this task, then will I, at your behest, proceed to choose one from amongst you and will proclaim him King and Overlord of all." For the Archbishop had faith that Merlin was about to immediately declare a king before them all.

Now leave we these and turn we unto Arthur and his father and brother.

For Merlin had bidden those three to abide in their pavilion until such time as he thought would be fit for them to come out thence. And that time being now come, Merlin and Sir Ulfius went to the pavilion of Sir Ector, and Merlin said, "Arthur, arise and come forth, for now the hour is come for thee to assay before the whole world that miracle which thou didst of late execute in privacy." So Arthur did as Merlin bade him to do, and he came forth from the pavilion with his father and his brother, and, lo! he was like one who walked in a dream.

So they five went down from thence toward the cathedral and unto that place of assay. And when they had come to the congregation there assembled, the people made way for them, greatly marvelling and saying to one another, "Who are these with the Enchanter Merlin and Sir Ulfius, and whence come they? For all the world knew Merlin and Sir Ulfius, and they wist that here was something very extraordinary about to happen. And Arthur was clad all in flame-colored raiment embroidered with threads of silver, so that others of the people said, "Certes, that youth is very fair for to look upon; now who may he be?"

But Merlin said no word to any man, but he brought Arthur through the press unto that place where the Archbishop sat;

and the press made way for him so that he was not stayed in his going. And when the Archbishop beheld Merlin come thus with those others, he arose and said, "Merlin, who are these whom thou bringest unto us, and what is their business here?" And Merlin said, "Lord, here is one come to make the assay of yonder sword." And the Archbishop said, "Which one is he?" and Merlin said, "This is he," and he laid his hand upon Arthur.

Then the Archbishop looked upon Arthur and he beheld that the youth was very comely of face, wherefore his heart went out unto Arthur and he loved him a very great deal. And the Archbishop said, "Merlin, by what right doth this young man come hither?" And Merlin made reply, "Lord, he cometh hither by the best right that there is in the world; for he who standeth before thee clad in red is the true son of Uther-Pendragon and of his lawful wife, Queen Igraine."

Then the Archbishop cried out aloud in great amazement and those who stood nigh and who heard what Merlin said were so astonished that they wist not what to think. And the Archbishop said, "Merlin, what is this that thou tellest me? For who, until now, in all the world hath ever heard that Uther-Pendragon had a son?"

Unto this Merlin made reply: "No one hath ever known of such a thing until now, only a very few. For it was in this wise: When this child was born the spirit of prophecy lay upon me and I foresaw that Uther-Pendragon would die before a very great while. Wherefore I feared that the enemies of the King would lay violent hands upon the young child for the sake of his inheritance. So, at the King's behest, I and another took the young child from his mother and gave him unto a third, and that man received the kingly child and maintained him ever since as his own son. And as to the truth of these things there are others here who may attest the verity of them—for he was with me when the young child was taken from his mother was Sir Ulfius, and he to whom he was entrusted was Sir Ector of Bonmaison—and those two witnesses, who are without any reproach, will avouch to the verity of that which I have asserted, for here they stand before thee to certify unto what I have said."

And Sir Ulfius and Sir Ector said, "All that Merlin hath spoken is true, and thereunto we do pledge our most faithful and sacred word of honor."

Then the Archbishop said, "Who is there may doubt the word of such honorable witnesses?" And he looked upon Arthur and smiled upon him.

Then Arthur said, "Have I then thy leave, Lord, to handle yonder sword?" And the Archbishop said, "Thou hast my leave, and may the grace of God go with thee to do thy endeavor."

Thereupon Arthur went to the cube of marble stone and he laid his hands upon the haft of the sword that was thrust into the anvil. And he bent his body and drew very strongly and, lo! the sword came forth with great ease and very smoothly. And when he had got the sword into his hands, he swung it about his head so that it flashed like lightning. And after he had swung it thus thrice about his head, he set the point thereof against the face of the anvil and bore upon it very strongly, and, behold! the sword slid very smoothly back again into that place where it had aforetime stood; and when it was there, midway deep, it stood fast where it was. And thus did Arthur successfully accomplish that marvellous miracle of the sword in the eyes of all the world.

Now when the people who were congregated at that place beheld this miracle performed before their faces, they lifted up their voices all together, and shouted so vehemently and with so huge a tumult of outcry that it was as though the whole earth rocked and trembled with the sound of their shouting.

And whiles they so shouted Arthur took hold of the sword again and drew it forth and swung it again, and again drave it back into the anvil. And when he had done that he drew it forth a third time and did the same thing as before. Thus it was that all those who were there beheld that miracle performed three times over.

And all the kings and dukes who were there were filled with great amazement, and they wist not what to think or to say when they beheld one who was little more than a boy perform that undertaking in which the best of them had failed. And some of them, seeing that miracle, were willing to acknowledge

Arthur because of it, but others would not acknowledge him. These withdrew themselves and stood aloof; and as they stood thus apart, they said among themselves: "What is this and who can accredit such a thing that a beardless boy should be set before us all and should be made King and overlord of this great realm for to govern us. Nay! nay! we will have none of him for our King." And others said, "Is it not apparent that Merlin and Sir Ulfius are thus exalting this unknown boy so that they may elevate themselves along with him?" Thus these discontented kings spake among themselves, and of all of them the most bitter were King Lot and King Urien, who were brothers by marriage with Arthur.

Now when the Archbishop perceived the discontent of these kings and dukes, he said to them, "How now, Messires! Are ye not satisfied?" And they said, "We are not satisfied." And the Archbishop said, "What would ye have?" And they said, "We would have another sort of king for Britain than a beardless boy of whom no one knoweth and of whose birthright there are only three men to attest." And the Archbishop said, "What of that? Hath he not performed the miracle that ye yourselves assayed and failed to perform?"

But these high and mighty lords would not be satisfied, but with angry and averted faces they went away from that place.

But others of these kings and dukes came and saluted Arthur and paid him court, giving him joy of that which he had achieved; and the chiefest of those who came thus unto him in friendliness was King Leodegrance of Cameliard. And all the multitude acknowledged him and crowded around that place shouting so that it sounded like to the noise of thunder.

Now all this while Sir Ector and Sir Kay had stood upon one side. And they were greatly weighed down by sorrow; for it appeared to them that Arthur had, of a sudden, been uplifted so far from their estate that they might never hope to approach him more. For now he was of kingly consequence and they but common knights. And, after awhile, Arthur beheld them where they stood with downcast looks, whereupon he straightway went to them and took first one and then the other by the hand and kissed each upon the cheek. Thereupon they were again very glad at being thus uplifted unto him.

And when Arthur departed from that place, great crowds of people followed after him so that the streets were altogether filled with the press of people. And the multitude continually gave him loud acclaim as the chosen King of England, and those who were nearest to him sought to touch the hem of his garments; wherefore the heart of Arthur was exceedingly uplifted with great joy and gladness, so that his soul took wing and flew like a bird into the sky.

Thus Arthur achieved the adventure of the sword that day and entered into his birthright of royalty. Wherefore, may God grant His Grace unto you all that ye too may likewise succeed in your undertakings. For any man may be a king in that life in which he is placed if so be he may draw forth the sword of success from out of the iron of circumstance. Wherefore when your time of assay cometh, I do hope it may be with you as it was with Arthur that day, and that ye too may achieve success with entire satisfaction unto yourself and to your great glory and perfect happiness. Amen.

Conclusion

Now after these things had happened there was much talk among men and great confusion and tumult. For while some of the kings and nearly all the multitude said, "Lo! here is a king come to us, as it were, from out of Heaven for to bring peace unto our distracted land," yet other kings (and they were of greater number) said, "Who is this beardless boy who cometh with a claim to be High King of Britain? Who ever heard of him before? We will have none of him except upon further trial and upon greater avouchment." So, for the sake of peace, the Archbishop ordained that another assay of the sword should be made at Candlemas; and here again all those who endeavored to draw forth the sword failed thereat, but Arthur drew it forth several times, very easily, in the sight of all. And after that a third trial was made at Easter and after that a fourth trial was made at Pentecost. And at all these trials Arthur repeatedly drew out the sword from the anvil, and no one but he could draw it forth.

And, after that fourth trial, sundry of the kings and many of the lesser barons and knights and all of the commons cried out that these were trials enough, and that Arthur had assuredly approved himself to be rightwise King; wherefore they demanded that he should be made King indeed so that he might rule over them. For it had come to pass that whithersoever Arthur went great crowds followed after him hailing him as the true son of Uther-Pendragon, and rightwise overlord of Britain. Wherefore, the Archbishop (seeing how the people

loved Arthur and how greatly they desired him for their King)
ordained that he should be anointed and crowned unto royal
estate; and so it was done at the great Cathedral. And some say
that that Cathedral was St. Paul's and some say that it was
not.

But when Arthur had thus been crowned, all those who were
opposed unto his Kingship withdrew themselves in great anger,
and immediately set about to prepare war against him. But the
people were with Arthur and joined with him, and so also did
several Kings and many of the lesser barons and knights. And,
with the advice of Merlin, Arthur made friends and allies of
sundry other kings and they and he fought two great wars with
his enemies and won both of these wars. And in the second
war was fought a very famous battle nigh to the Forest of
Bedegraine (wherefore it was called the Battle of Bedegraine),
and in that battle Arthur overthrew his enemies so entirely that
it was not possible for them ever to hope to unite in war against
him again.

And of King Lot, his brother-in-law, King Arthur brought
two of his sons to Court for to dwell there and to serve as
hostages of peace thereafter. And these two were Gawaine
and Geharris and they became, after awhile, very famous and
accomplished knights. And of King Urien, his other brother-
in-law, Arthur brought unto Court his one son, Ewaine, for to
hold as an hostage of peace; and he also became in time a very
famous and accomplished knight. And because of these
hostages there was peace thereafter betwixt those three kingly
brothers for all time. And a certain very famous king and
knight hight King Pellinore (who was one of his enemies)
Arthur drove out of his possessions and away from the
habitations of men and into the forest. And King Ryence
(who was another of his enemies) he drave into the mountains
of North Wales. And other kings who were his enemies he
subjugated to his will, so that all the land was at such peace that
it had not enjoyed the like since the days of Uther-Pendragon.

And King Arthur made Sir Kay his Seneschal as he had
promised to do; and he made Sir Ulfius his Chamberlain; and
Merlin he made his Counsellor; and Sir Bodwain of Britain he
made his Constable. And these men were all of such a sort as

greatly enhanced the glory and renown of his reign and established him upon his throne with entire security.

Now when the reign of King Arthur became thus entirely established, and when the renown of his greatness began to be known in the world, many men of noble souls and of large spirit and of high knightly prowess—knights who desired above all things to achieve glory at arms in Courts of Chivalry—perceived that great credit and exaltation of estate were likely to be won under such a king. So it fell out that, from all parts, by little and little, there began to gather together such a Court of noble, honorable knights about King Arthur as men never beheld before that time, and shall haply never behold again.

For even to this day the history of these good knights is known to the greater part of mankind. Yea; the names of many kings and emperors have passed away and have been forgotten, but the names of Sir Galahad, and of Sir Launcelot of the Lake, and of Sir Tristram of Lyonesse, and of Sir Percival of Gales, and of Sir Gawaine, and of Sir Ewaine, and of Sir Bors de Ganis, and of many others of that noble household of worthy brotherhood, is still remembered by men. Wherefore, I think that it is very likely that so long as words shall be written, the performances of these worthies shall be remembered.

So in this history yet to be written, I have set it for my task to inform him who reads this book of many of these adventures, telling him, besides, such several circumstances as I do not believe are known unto everybody. And by and by, when I shall tell of the establishment of the Round Table, I shall set forth a tabulated list of a number of those worthies who at this time assembled at the Court of Arthur as men chosen to found that order of the Round Table, and who, for that reason, were entitled "The Ancient and Honorable Companions of the Round Table."

For though this entire history chiefly concerneth King Arthur, yet the glory of these great honorable knights was his glory, and his glory was their glory, wherefore one cannot tell of the glory of King Arthur without also telling of the glory of those noble gentlemen aforesaid.

PART II

The Winning of a Sword

Chapter First

How There Came a Certain Wounded Knight Unto the Court of King Arthur, How a Young Knight of the King's Court Sought to Avenge Him and Failed and How the King Thereupon Took That Assay Upon Himself.

Now it fell upon a certain pleasant time in the Springtide season that King Arthur and his Court were making a royal progression through that part of Britain which lieth close to the Forests of the Usk. At that time the weather was exceedingly warm, and so the King and Court made pause within the forest under the trees in the cool and pleasant shade that the place afforded, and there the King rested for a while upon a couch of rushes spread with scarlet cloth.

And the knights then present at that Court were, Sir Gawaine, and Sir Ewaine, and Sir Kay, and Sir Pellias, and Sir Bedevere, and Sir Caradoc, and Sir Geraint, and Sir Bodwin of Britain and Sir Constantine of Cornwall, and Sir Brandiles and

Sir Mador de la Porte, and there was not to be found anywhere in the world a company of such noble and exalted knights as these.

Now as the King lay drowsing and as these worthies sat holding cheerful converse together at that place, there came, of a sudden, a considerable bustle and stir upon the outskirts of the Court, and presently there appeared a very sad and woful sight. For there came thitherward a knight, sore wounded, and upheld upon his horse by a goldenhaired page, clad in an apparel of white and azure. And, likewise, the knight's apparel and the trappings of his horse were of white and azure, and upon his shield he bore the emblazonment of a single lily flower of silver upon a ground of pure azure.

But the knight was in a very woful plight. For his face was as pale as wax and hung down upon his breast. And his eyes were glazed and saw naught that passed around him, and his fair apparel of white and blue was all red with the blood of life that ran from a great wound in his side. And, as they came upon their way, the young page lamented in such wise that it wrung the heart for to hear him.

Now, as these approached, King Arthur aroused cried out, "Alas! what doleful spectacle is that which I behold? Now hasten, ye my lords, and bring succor to yonder knight; and do thou, Sir Kay, go quickly and bring that fair young page hither that we may presently hear from his lips what mishap hath befallen his lord."

So certain of those knights hastened at the King's bidding and gave all succor to the wounded knight, and conveyed him to King Arthur's own pavilion, which had been pitched at a little distance. And when he had come there the King's chirurgeon presently attended upon him—albeit his wounds were of such a sort he might not hope to live for a very long while.

Meantime, Sir Kay brought that fair young page before the King, where he sat, and the King thought that he had hardly ever seen a more beautiful countenance. And the King said, "I prithee tell me, Sir Page, who is thy master, and how came he in such a sad and pitiable condition as that which we have just now beheld."

"That will I so, Lord," said the youth. "Know that my

master is entitled Sir Myles of the White Fountain, and that he cometh from the country north of where we are and at a considerable distance from this. In that country he is the Lord of seven castles and several noble estates, wherefore, as thou mayst see, he is of considerable consequence. A fortnight ago (being doubtless moved thereunto by the lustiness of the Springtime), he set forth with only me for his esquire, for he had a mind to seek adventure in such manner as beseemed a good knight who would be errant. And we had several adventures, and in all of them my lord was entirely successful; for he overcame six knights at various places and sent them all to his castle for to attest his valor unto his lady.

"At last, this morning, coming to a certain place situated at a considerable distance from this, we came upon a fair castle of the forest, which stood in a valley surrounded by open spaces of level lawn, bedight with many flowers of divers sorts. There we beheld three fair damsels who tossed a golden ball from one to another, and the damsels were clad all in flame-colored satin, and their hair was of the color of gold. And as we drew nigh to them they stinted their play, and she who was the chief of those damsel called out to my lord, demanding of him whither he went and what was his errand.

"To her my lord made answer that he was errant and in search of adventure, and upon this, the three damsels laughed, and she who had first spoken said, 'An thou art in search of adventure, Sir Knight, happily I may be able to help thee to one that shall satisfy thee to thy heart's content.'

"Unto this my master made reply, 'I prithee, fair damsel, tell me what that adventure may be so that I may presently assay it.'

"Thereupon this lady bade my master to take a certain path, and to follow the same for the distance of a league or a little more, and that he would then come to a bridge of stone that crossed a violent stream, and she assured him that there he might find adventure enough for to satisfy any man.

"So my master and I wended thitherward as that damoiselle had directed, and, by and by, we came unto the bridge whereof she had spoken. And, lo! beyond the bridge was a lonesome castle with a tall straight tower, and before the castle was a wide and level lawn of well-trimmed grass. And immediately beyond the bridge was an apple-tree hung over with a multitude of shields. And midway upon the bridge was a single shield, entirely of black; and beside it hung a hammer of brass; and beneath the shield was written these words in letters of red:

Whoso Smiteth This Shield Doeth So At His Peril.

"Now, my master, Sir Myles, when he read those words went straightway to that shield and, seizing the hammer that hung beside it, he smote upon it a blow so that it rang like thunder.

"Thereupon, as in answer, the portcullis of the castle was let fall, and there immediately came forth a knight, clad all from head to foot in sable armor. And his apparel and the trappings of his horse and all the appointments thereof were likewise entirely of sable.

"Now when that Sable Knight perceived my master he came riding swiftly across the meadow and so to the other end of the bridge. And when he had come there he drew rein and saluted my master and cried out, 'Sir Knight, I demand of thee why thou didst smite that shield. Now let me tell thee, because of thy boldness, I shall take away from thee thine own shield, and shall hang it upon yonder apple-tree, where thou beholdest all those other shields to be hanging.' Unto this my master made reply. 'That thou shalt not do unless thou mayst overcome me, as knight to knight.' And thereupon, immediately, he dressed his shield and put himself into array for an assault at arms.

"So my master and this Sable Knight, having made themselves ready for that encounter, presently drave together with might and main. And they met in the middle of the course, where my master's spear burst into splinters. But the spear of the Sable Knight held and it pierced through Sir Myles, his shield, and it penetrated his side, so that both he and his horse were overthrown violently into the dust; he being wounded so grievously that he could not arise again from the ground whereon he lay.

"Then the Sable Knight took my master's shield and hung it up in the branches of the apple-tree where the other shields were hanging, and, thereupon, without paying further heed to my master, or inquiring as to his hurt, he rode away into his castle again, whereof the portcullis was immediately closed behind him.

"So, after that he had gone, I got my master to his horse with great labor, and straightway took him thence, not knowing where I might find harborage for him, until I came to this place. And that, my lord King, is the true story of how my master came by that mortal hurt which he hath suffered."

"Ha! By the glory of Paradise!" cried King Arthur, "I do consider it great shame that in my Kingdom and so near to my Court strangers should be so discourteously treated as Sir Myles hath been served. For it is certainly a discourtesy for to leave a fallen knight upon the ground, without tarrying to inquire as to his hurt how grievous it may be. And still more discourteous is it for to take away the shield of a fallen knight who hath done good battle."

And so did all the knights of the King's Court exclaim against the discourtesy of that Sable Knight.

Then there came forth a certain esquire attendant upon the King's person, by name Griflet, who was much beloved by his Royal Master, and he kneeled before the King and cried out in a loud voice: "I crave a boon of thee, my lord King! and do beseech thee that thou wilt grant it unto me!"

Then King Arthur uplifted his countenance upon the youth as he knelt before him and he said, "Ask, Griflet, and thy boon shall be granted unto thee."

Thereupon Griflet said, "It is this that I would ask—I crave that thou wilt make me straightway knight, and that thou wilt let me go forth and endeavor to punish this unkindly knight, by overthrowing him, and so redeeming those shields which he hath hung upon that apple-tree."

Then was King Arthur much troubled in his spirit, for Griflet was as yet only an esquire and altogether untried in arms. So he said, "Behold, thou art yet too young to have to do with so potent a knight as this sable champion must be, who has thus overthrown so many knights without himself suffering any mishap. I prithee, dear Griflet, consider and ask some other boon."

But young Griflet only cried the more, "A boon! A boon! and thou hast granted it unto me."

Thereupon King Arthur said, "Thou shalt have thy boon, though my heart much misgiveth me that thou wilt suffer great ill and misfortune from this adventure."

So that night Griflet kept watch upon his armor in a chapel of the forest, and, in the morning, having received the Sacrament, he was created a knight by the hand of King Arthur—and it was not possible for any knight to have greater honor than that. Then King Arthur fastened the golden spurs to Sir Griflet's heels with his own hand.

So Griflet was made a knight, and having mounted his charger, he rode straightway upon his adventure, much rejoicing and singing for pure pleasure.

And it was at this time that Sir Myles died of his hurt, for it is often so that death and misfortune befall some, whiles others laugh and sing for hope and joy, as though such grievous things as sorrow and death could never happen in their world.

Now that afternoon King Arthur sat waiting with great anxiety for word of that young knight, but there was no word until toward evening, when there came hurrying to him certain of his attendants, proclaiming that Sir Griflet was returning, but without his shield, and in such guise that it seemed as though a great misfortune had befallen him. And straightway thereafter came Sir Griflet himself, sustained upon his horse on the one hand by Sir Constantine and upon the other by Sir Brandiles. And, lo! Sir Griflet's head hung down upon his breast, and his fair new armor was all broken and stained with blood and dust. And so woful was he of appearance that King Arthur's heart was contracted with sorrow to behold that young knight in so pitiable a condition.

So, at King Arthur's bidding, they conducted Sir Griflet to the Royal Pavilion, and there they laid him down upon a soft couch. Then the King's chirurgeon searched his wounds and found that the head of a spear and a part of the shaft thereof were still piercing Sir Griflet's side, so that he was in most woful and grievous pain.

And when King Arthur beheld in what a parlous state Sir Griflet lay he cried out, "Alas! my dear young knight, what hath happened thee to bring thee unto such a woful condition as this which I behold?"

Then Sir Griflet, speaking in a very weak voice, told King Arthur how he had fared. And he said that he had proceeded through the forest, until he had discovered the three beautiful damsels whereof the page of Sir Myles had spoke. And he said that these damsels had directed him as to the manner in which he should pursue his adventure. And he said that he had found the bridge whereon hung the shield and the brazen mall, and that he had there beheld the apple-tree hung full of shields; and he said that he smote the shield of the Sable Knight with the brazen mall, and that the Sable Knight had thereupon come riding out against him. And he said that this knight did not appear of a mind to fight with him; instead, he cried out to him with a great deal of nobleness that he was too young and too untried in arms to have to do with a seasoned knight; wherefore he advised Sir Griflet to withdraw him from that adventure ere it was too late. But, notwithstanding this advice, Sir Griflet would not withdraw but declared that he would certainly have to do with that other knight in sable. Now at the very first onset Sir Griflet's spear had burst into pieces, but the spear of the Sable Knight had held and had pierced through Sir Griflet's shield and into his side, causing him this grievous wound whereof he suffered. And Sir Griflet said that the Sable Knight had then, most courteously, uplifted him upon his horse again (albeit he had kept Sir Griflet's shield and had hung it upon the tree with those others that hung there) and had then directed him upon his way, so that he had made shift to ride thither, though with great pain and dole.

Then was King Arthur very wode and greatly disturbed in his mind, for indeed he loved Sir Griflet exceedingly well. Wherefore he declared that he himself would now go forth for to punish that Sable Knight, and for to humble him with his own hand. And, though the knights of his Court strove to dissuade him, yet he declared that he with his own hand would accomplish that proud knight's humiliation, and that he would undertake the adventure, with God His Grace, the next day.

Now, as soon as the birds first began to chirp and the east to brighten with the coming of the daylight, King Arthur summoned his two esquires, and, having with their aid donned his armor and mounted a milk-white war-horse, he presently took his departure upon that adventure which he had determined upon.

And, indeed it is a very pleasant thing for to ride forth in the dawning of a Springtime day. For then the little birds do sing their sweetest song, all joining in one joyous medley, whereof one may scarce tell one note from another, so multitudinous is that pretty roundelay; then do the growing things of the earth smell the sweetest in the freshness of the early daytime—the fair flowers, the shrubs, and the blossoms upon the trees; then doth the dew bespangle all the sward as with an incredible multitude of jewels of various colors; then is all the world sweet and clean and new, as though it had been fresh created for him who came to roam abroad so early in the morning.

So King Arthur's heart expanded with great joy, and he chanted a quaint song as he rode through the forest upon the quest of that knightly adventure.

So, about noon-tide, he came to that part of the forest lands whereof he had heard those several times before. For of a sudden, he discovered before him a wide and gently sloping valley, a-down which ran a stream as bright as silver. And, lo! the valley was strewn all over with an infinite multitude of fair and fragrant flowers of divers sorts. And in the midst of the valley there stood a comely castle, with tall red roofs and many bright windows, so that it seemed to King Arthur that it was a very fine castle indeed. And upon a smooth green lawn he perceived those three damoiselles clad in flame-colored satin of whom the page of Sir Myles and Sir Griflet had spoken. And they played at ball with a golden ball, and the hair of each was of the hue of gold, and it seemed to King Arthur, as he drew nigh, that they were the most beautiful damoiselles that he had ever beheld in all of his life.

Now as King Arthur came unto them the three ceased tossing the ball, and she who was the fairest of all damoiselles demanded of him whither he went and upon what errand he was bound.

Then King Arthur made reply: "Ha! fair lady! Whither should a belted knight ride upon such a day as this, and upon what business, other than the search of adventure such as beseemeth a knight of a proper strength of heart and frame who would be errant?"

Then the three damoiselles smiled upon the King, for he was exceedingly comely of face and they liked him very well. "Alas, Sir Knight!" said she who had before spoken, "I prithee be in no such haste to undertake a dangerous adventure, but rather tarry with us for a day or two or three, for to feast and make merry with us. For surely good cheer doth greatly enlarge the heart, and we would fain enjoy the company of so gallant a knight as thou appearest to be. Yonder castle is ours and all this gay valley is ours, and those who have visited it are pleased, because of its joyousness, to call it the Valley of Delight. So tarry with us for a little and be not in such haste to go forward."

"Nay," said King Arthur, "I may not tarry with ye, fair ladies, for I am bent upon an adventure of which ye may wot right well, when I tell ye that I seek that Sable Knight, who hath overcome so many other knights and hath taken away their shields. So I do pray ye of your grace for to tell me where I may find him."

"Grace of Heaven!" cried she who spake for the others, "this is certainly a sorry adventure which ye seek, Sir Knight! For already, in these two days, have two knights assayed with that knight, and both have fallen into great pain and disregard. Ne'theless, an thou wilt undertake this peril, yet shalt thou not go until thou hast eaten and refreshed thyself." So saying, she lifted a little ivory whistle that hung from her neck by a chain of gold, and blew upon it very shrilly.

In answer to this summons there came forth from the castle three fair young pages, clad all in flame-colored raiment, bearing among them a silver table covered with a white napkin. And after them came five other pages of the same appearance, bearing flagons of white wine and red, dried fruits and comfits and manchets of white fair bread.

Then King Arthur descended from his war-horse with great gladness, for he was both hungry and athirst, and, seating himself at the table with the damsels beside him, he ate with great enjoyment, discoursing pleasantly the while with those fair ladies, who listened to him with great cheerfulness of spirit. Yet he told them not who he was, though they greatly marvelled who might be the noble warrior who had come thus into that place.

So, having satisfied his hunger and his thirst, King Arthur mounted his steed again, and the three damsels conducted him across the valley a little way—he riding upon his horse and they walking beside him. So, by and by, he perceived where was a dark pathway that led into the farther side of the forest land; and when he had come thither the lady who had addressed him before said to him, "Yonder is the way that thou must take an thou wouldst enter upon this adventure. So fare thee well, and may good hap go with thee, for, certes, thou art the Knight most pleasant of address who hath come hitherward for this long time."

Thereupon King Arthur, having saluted those ladies right courteously, rode away with very great joy of that pleasant adventure through which he had thus passed.

Now when King Arthur had gone some ways he came, by and by, to a certain place where charcoal burners plied their trade. For here were many mounds of earth, all a-smoke with the smouldering logs within, whilst all the air was filled with the smell of the dampened fires.

As the King approached this spot, he presently beheld that something was toward that was sadly amiss. For, in the open clearing, he beheld three sooty fellows with long knives in their hands, who pursued one old man, whose beard was as white as snow. And he beheld that the reverend old man, who was clad richly in black, and whose horse stood at a little distance, was running hither and thither, as though to escape from those wicked men, and he appeared to be very hard pressed and in great danger of his life.

"Pardee!" quoth the young King to himself, "here, certes, is one in sore need of succor." Whereupon he cried out in a great voice, "Hold, villains! What would you be at!" and therewith set spurs to his horse and dropped his spear into rest and drove down upon them with a noise like to thunder for loudness.

But when the three wicked fellows beheld the armed Knight thus thundering down upon them, they straightway dropped their knives and, with loud outcries of fear, ran away hither and thither until they had escaped into the thickets of the forest, where one upon a horse might not hope to pursue them.

Whereupon, having driven away those wicked fellows, King Arthur rode up to him whom he had succored, thinking to offer him condolence. And behold! when he had come nigh to him, he perceived that the old man was the Enchanter Merlin. Yet whence he had so suddenly come, who had only a little while before been at the King's Court at Carleon, and what he did in that place, the King could in no wise understand. Wherefore he bespoke the Enchanter in this wise, "Ha! Merlin, it seemeth to me that I have saved thy life. For, surely, thou hadst not escaped from the hands of those wicked men had I not happened to come hitherward at this time."

"Dost thou think so, Lord?" said Merlin. "Now let me tell thee that I did maybe appear to be in danger, yet I might have saved myself very easily had I been of a mind to do so. But, as thou sawst me in this seeming peril, so may thou know that a real peril, far greater than this, lieth before thee, and there will be no errant knight to succor thee from it. Wherefore, I pray thee, Lord, for to take me with thee upon this adventure that thou art set upon, for I do tell thee that thou shalt certainly suffer great dole and pain therein."

"Merlin," said King Arthur, "even an I were to face my death, yet would I not turn back from this adventure. But touching the advice thou givest me, meseems it will be very well to take thee with me if such peril lieth before me as thou sayest."

And Merlin said, "Yea, it would be very well for thee to do so."

So Merlin mounted upon his palfrey, and King Arthur and he betook their way from that place in pursuit of that adventure which the King had undertaken to perform.

Chapter Second

How King Arthur Fought With the Sable Knight and How He Was Sorely Wounded. Likewise How Merlin Brought Him Safe Away From the Field of Battle.

So King Arthur and Merlin rode together through the forest for a considerable while, until they perceived that they must be approaching nigh to the place where dwelt the Sable Knight whom the King sought so diligently. For the forest, which had till then been altogether a wilderness, very deep and mossy, began to show an aspect more thin and open, as though a dwelling-place of mankind was close at hand.

And, after a little, they beheld before them a violent stream of water, that rushed through a dark and dismal glen. And, likewise, they perceived that across this stream of water there was a bridge of stone, and that upon the other side of the bridge there was a smooth and level lawn of green grass, whereon Knights-contestants might joust very well. And beyond this lawn they beheld a tall and forbidding castle, with smooth walls and a straight tower; and this castle was built upon the rocks so that it appeared to be altogether a part of the stone. So they wist that this must be the castle whereof the page and Sir Griflet had spoken.

For, midway upon the bridge, they beheld that there hung a sable shield and a brass mall exactly as the page and Sir Griflet had said; and that upon the farther side of the stream was an apple-tree, amid the leaves of which hung a very great many shields of various devices, exactly as those two had reported: and they beheld that some of those shields were clean and fair, and that some were foul and stained with blood, and that some were smooth and unbroken, and that some were cleft as though by battle of knight with knight. And all those shields were the shields of different knights whom the Sable Knight, who dwelt within the castle, had overthrown in combat with his own hand.

"Splendor of Paradise!" quoth King Arthur, "that must, indeed, be a right valiant knight who, with his own single strength, hath overthrown and cast down so many other knights. For, indeed, Merlin, there must be an hundred shields hanging in yonder tree!"

Unto this Merlin made reply, "And thou, Lord, mayst be very happy an thy shield, too, hangeth not there ere the sun goeth down this even-tide."

"That," said King Arthur, with a very steadfast countenance, "shall be as God willeth. For, certes, I have a greater mind than ever for to try my power against yonder knight. For, consider, what especial honor would fall to me should I overcome so valiant a warrior as this same Sable Champion appeareth to be, seeing that he hath been victorious over so many other good knights."

Thereupon, having so spoken his mind, King Arthur immediately pushed forward his horse and so, coming upon the bridge, he clearly read that challenge writ in letters of red beneath the shield:

Whoso Smiteth This Shield
Doeth So At His Peril.

Upon reading these words, the King seized the brazen mall, and smote that shield so violent a blow that the sound thereof echoed back from the smooth walls of the castle, and from the rocks whereon it stood, and from the skirts of the forest around about, as though twelve other shields had been struck in those several places.

And in answer to that sound, the portcullis of the castle was immediately let fall, and there issued forth a knight, very huge of frame, and clad all in sable armor. And, likewise, all of his apparel and all the trappings of his horse were entirely of sable, so that he presented a most grim and forbidding aspect. And this Sable Knight came across that level meadow of smooth grass with a very stately and honorable gait; for neither did he ride in haste, nor did he ride slowly, but with great pride and haughtiness of mien, as became a champion who, haply, had never yet been overcome in battle. So, reaching the bridge-head, he drew rein and saluted King Arthur with great dignity, and also right haughtily. "Ha! Sir Knight!" quoth he, "why didst thou, having read those words yonder inscribed, smite upon my shield? Now I do tell thee that, for thy discourtesy, I shall presently take thy shield away from thee, and shall hang it up upon yonder apple-tree where thou beholdest all those other shields to be hanging. Wherefore, either deliver thou thy shield unto me without more ado or else prepare for to defend it with thy person—in the which event thou shalt certainly suffer great pain and discomfort to thy body."

"Gramercy for the choice thou grantest me," said King Arthur. "But as for taking away my shield—I do believe that that shall be as Heaven willeth, and not as thou willest. Know, thou unkind knight, that I have come hither for no other purpose than to do battle with thee and so to endeavor for to redeem with my person all those shields that hang yonder upon that apple-tree. So make thou ready straightway that I may have to do with thee, maybe to thy great disadvantage."

"That will I so," replied the Sable Knight. And thereupon he turned his horse's head and, riding back a certain distance across the level lawn, he took stand in such place as appeared to him to be convenient. And so did King Arthur ride forth also upon that lawn, and take his station.

Then each knight dressed his spear and his shield for the encounter, and, having thus made ready for the assault, each shouted to his war-horse and drave his spurs deep into its flank.

Then those two noble steeds rushed forth like lightning, coursing across the ground with such violent speed that the earth trembled and shook beneath them, an it were by cause of an earthquake. So those two knights met fairly in the midst of the centre of the field, crashing together like a thunderbolt. And so violently did they smite the one against the other that the spears burst into splinters, even unto the guard and the truncheon thereof, and the horses of the riders staggered back from the onset, so that only because of the extraordinary address of the knights-rider did they recover from falling before that shock of meeting.

But, with great spirit, these two knights uplifted each his horse with his own spirit, and so completed his course in safety.

And indeed King Arthur was very much amazed that he had not overthrown his opponent, for, at that time, as aforesaid, he was considered to be the very best knight and the one best approved in deeds of arms that lived in all of Britain. Wherefore he marvelled at the power and the address of that knight against whom he had driven, that he had not been overthrown by the greatness of the blow that had been delivered against his defences. So, when they met again in the midst of the field, King Arthur gave that knight greeting, and bespoke him with great courtesy, addressing him in this wise: "Sir Knight, I know not who thou art, but I do pledge my knightly word that thou art the most potent knight that ever I have met in all of my life. Now I do bid thee get down straightway from thy horse, and let us two fight this battle with sword and upon foot, for it were pity to let it end in this way."

"Not so," qouth the Sable Knight—"not so, nor until one of us twain be overthrown will I so contest this battle upon foot." And upon this he shouted, "Ho! Ho!" in a very loud voice, and straightway thereupon the gateway of the castle opened and there came running forth two tall esquires clad all in black, pied with crimson. And each of these esquires bare in his hand a great spear of ash-wood, new and well-seasoned, and never yet strained in battle.

So King Arthur chose one of these spears and the Sable Knight took the other, and thereupon each returned to that station wherefrom he had before essayed the encounter.

Then once again each knight rushed his steed to the assault, and once again did each smite so fairly in the midst of the defence of the other that the spears were splintered, so that only the guard and the truncheon thereof remained in the grasp of the knight who held it.

Then, as before, King Arthur would have fought the battle out with swords and upon foot, but again the Sable Knight would not have it so, but called aloud upon those within the castle, whereupon there immediately came forth two other esquires with fresh, new spears of ash-wood. So each knight again took him a spear, and having armed himself therewith, chose each his station upon that fair, level lawn of grass.

And now, for the third time, having thus prepared themselves thereof assault, those two excellent knights hurled themselves together in furious assault. And now, as twice before, did King Arthur strike the Sable Knight so fairly in the centre of his defence that the spear which he held was burst into splinters. But this time, the spear of the Sable Knight did not so break in that manner, but held; and so violent was the blow that he delivered upon King Arthur's shield that he pierced through the centre of it. Then the girths of the King's saddle burst apart by that great, powerful blow, and both he and his steed were cast violently backward. So King Arthur might have been overcast, had he not voided his saddle with extraordinary skill and knightly address, wherefore, though his horse was overthrown, he himself still held his footing and did not fall into the dust. Ne'theless, so violent was the blow that he received that, for a little space, he was altogether bereft of his senses so that everything whirled around before his eyes.

But when his sight returned to him he was filled with an anger so vehement that it appeared to him as though all the blood in his heart rushed into his brains so that he saw naught but red, as of blood, before his eyes. And when this also had passed he perceived the Sable Knight that he sat his horse at no great distance. Then immediately King Arthur ran to him and catching the bridle-rein of his horse, he cried out aloud unto that Sable Knight with great violence: "Come down, thou black knight! and fight me upon foot and with thy sword."

"That will I not do," said the Sable Knight, "for, lo! I have overthrown thee. Wherefore deliver thou to me thy shield, that I may hang it upon yonder apple-tree, and go thy way as others have done before thee."

"That will I not!" cried King Arthur, with exceeding passion, "neither will I yield myself nor go hence until either thou or I have altogether conquered the other." Thereupon he thrust the horse of the Sable Knight backward by the bridle-rein so vehemently, that the other was constrained to void his saddle to save himself from being overthrown.

And now each knight was as entirely furious as the other, wherefore, each drew his sword and dressed his shield, and thereupon rushed together like two wild bulls in battle. They foined, they smote, they traced, they parried, they struck again and again, and the sound of their blows, crashing and clashing the one upon the other, filled the entire surrounding space with an extraordinary uproar. Nor may any man altogether conceive of the entire fury of that encounter, for, because of the violence of the blows which the one delivered upon the other, whole cantels of armor were hewn from their bodies and many deep and grievous wounds were given and received, so that the armor to each was altogether stained with red because of the blood that flowed down upon it.

At last King Arthur, waxing, as it were, entirely mad, struck so fierce a blow that no armor could have withstood that stroke had it fallen fairly upon it. But it befell with that stroke that his sword broke at the hilt and the blade thereof flew into three several pieces into the air. Yet was the stroke so wonderfully fierce that the Sable Knight groaned, and staggered, and ran about in a circle as though he had gone blind and knew not whither to direct his steps.

But presently he recovered himself again, and perceiving King Arthur standing near by, and not knowing that his enemy had now no sword for to defend himself withal, he cast aside his shield and took his own sword into both hands, and therewith smote so dolorous a stroke that he clave through King Arthur's shield and through his helmet and even to the bone of his brain-pan.

Then King Arthur thought that he had received his death-wound, for his brains swam like water, his thighs trembled exceedingly, and he sank down to his knees, whilst the blood and sweat, commingled together in the darkness of his helmet, flowed down into his eyes in a lather and blinded him. Thereupon, seeing him thus grievously hurt, the Sable Knight called upon him with great vehemence for to yield himself and to surrender his shield, because he was now too sorely wounded for to fight any more.

But King Arthur would not yield himself, but catching the other by the sword-belt, he lifted himself to his feet. Then, being in a manner recovered from his amazement, he embraced

the other with both arms, and placing his knee behind the thigh of the Sable Knight, he cast him backward down upon the ground so violently that the sound of the fall was astounding to hear. And with that fall the Sable Knight was, awhile, entirely bereft of consciousness. Then King Arthur straightway unlaced the helm of the Sable Knight and so beheld his face, and he knew him in spite of the blood that still ran down his own countenance in great quantities, and he knew that knight was King Pellinore, aforenamed in this history, who had twice warred against King Arthur. (It hath already been said how King Arthur had driven that other king from the habitations of men and into the forests, so that now he dwelt in this poor gloomy castle whence he waged war against all the knights who came unto that place.)

Now when King Arthur beheld whom it was against whom he had done battle, he cried out aloud, "Ha! Pellinore, is it then thou? Now yield thee to me, for thou art entirely at my mercy." And upon this he drew his misericordia and set the point thereof at King Pellinore's throat.

But by now King Pellinore had greatly recovered from his fall, and perceiving that the blood was flowing down in great measure from out his enemy's helmet, he wist that that other

must have been very sorely wounded by the blow which he had just now received. Wherefore he catched King Arthur's wrist in his hand and directed the point of the dagger away from his own throat so that no great danger threatened therefrom.

And, indeed, what with his sore wound and with the loss of blood, King Arthur was now fallen exceedingly sick and faint, so that it appeared to him that he was nigh to death. Accordingly, it was with no very great ado that King Pellinore suddenly heaved himself up from the ground and so overthrew his enemy that King Arthur was now underneath his knees.

And by this King Pellinore was exceedingly mad with the fury of the sore battle he had fought. For he was so enraged that his eyes were all beshot with blood like those of a wild boar, and a froth, like the champings of a wild boar, stood in the beard about his lips. Wherefore he wrenched the dagger out of his enemy's hand, and immediately began to unlace his helm, with intent to slay him where he lay. But at this moment Merlin came in great haste, crying out, "Stay! stay! Sir Pellinore; what would you be at? Stay your sacrilegious hand! For he who lieth beneath you is none other than Arthur, King of all this realm!"

At this King Pellinore was astonished beyond measure. And for a little he was silent, and then after awhile he cried out in a very loud voice, "Say you so, old man? Then verily your words have doomed this man unto death. For no one in all this world hath ever suffered such ill and such wrongs as I have suffered at his hands. For, lo! he hath taken from me power, and kingship, and honors, and estates, and hath left me only this gloomy, dismal castle of the forest as an abiding-place. Wherefore, seeing that he is thus in my power, he shall now presently die; if for no other reason than because if I now let him go free, he will certainly revenge himself when he shall have recovered from all the ill he hath suffered at my hands."

Then Merlin said, "Not so! He shall not die at thy hands, for I, myself, shall save him." Whereupon he uplifted his staff and smote King Pellinore across the shoulders. Then immediately King Pellinore fell down and lay upon the ground on his face like one who had suddenly gone dead.

Upon this, King Arthur uplifted himself upon his elbow and beheld his enemy lying there as though dead, and he cried out, "Ha! Merlin! what is this that thou hast done? I am very sorry, for I do perceive that thou, by thy arts of magic, hath slain one of the best knights in all the world."

"Not so, my lord King!" said Merlin; "for, in sooth, I tell thee that thou art far nigher to thy death than he. For he is but in sleep and will soon awaken; but thou art in such a case that it would take only a very little for to cause thee to die."

And indeed King Arthur was exceeding sick, even to the heart, with the sore wound he had received, so that it was only with much ado that Merlin could help him up upon his horse. Having done the which and having hung the King's shield upon the horn of his saddle, Merlin straightway conveyed the wounded man thence across the bridge, and, leading the horse by the bridle, so took him away into the forest.

Now I must tell you that there was in that part of the forest a certain hermit so holy that the wild birds of the woodland would come and rest upon his hand whiles he read his breviary; and so sanctified was he in gentleness that the wild does would come even to the door of his hermitage, and there stand whilst he milked them for his refreshment. And this hermit dwelt in that part of the forest so remote from the habitations of man that when he rang the bell for matins or for vespers, there was hardly ever anyone to hear the sound thereof excepting the wild creatures that dwelt thereabout. Yet, ne'theless, to this remote and lonely place royal folk and others of high degree would sometimes come, as though on a pilgrimage, because of the hermit's exceeding saintliness.

So Merlin conveyed King Arthur unto this sanctuary, and, having reached that place, he and the hermit lifted the wounded man down from his saddle—the hermit giving many words of pity and sorrow—and together they conveyed him into the holy man's cell. There they laid him upon a couch of moss and unlaced his armor and searched his wounds and bathed them with pure water and dressed his hurts, for that hermit was a very skillful leech. So for all that day and part of the next, King Arthur lay upon the hermit's pallet like one about to die; for he beheld all things about him as though through thin water, and the breath hung upon his lips and fluttered, and he could not even lift his head from the pallet because of the weakness that lay upon him.

Now upon the afternoon of the second day there fell a great noise and tumult in that part of the forest. For it happened that the Lady Guinevere of Cameliard, together with her Court, both of ladies and of knights, had come upon a pilgrimage to that holy man, the fame of whose saintliness had reached even unto the place where she dwelt. For that lady had a favorite page who was very sick of a fever, and she trusted that the holy man might give her some charm or amulet by the virtue of which he might haply be cured. Wherefore she had come to that place with her entire Court so that all that part of the forest was made gay with fine raiment and the silence thereof was made merry with the sound of talk and laughter and the singing of songs and the chattering of many voices and the neighing of horses. And the Lady Guinevere rode in the midst of her damsels and her Court, and her beauty outshone the beauty of her damsels as the splendor of the morning star outshines that of all the lesser stars that surround it. For then and afterward she was held by all the Courts of Chivalry to be the most beautiful lady in the world.

Now when the Lady Guinevere had come to that place, she perceived the milk-white war-horse of King Arthur where it stood cropping the green grass of the open glade nigh to the hermitage. And likewise she perceived Merlin, where he stood beside the door of the cell. So of him she demanded whose was that noble war-horse that stood browsing upon the grass at that lonely place, and who was it that lay within that cell. And unto her Merlin made answer, "Lady, he who lieth within is a knight, very sorely wounded, so that he is sick nigh unto death!"

"Pity of Heaven!" cried the Lady Guinevere. "What a sad thing is this that thou tellest me! Now I do beseech thee to lead me presently unto that knight that I may behold him. For I have in my Court a very skilful leech, who is well used to the cure of hurts such as knights receive in battle."

So Merlin brought the lady into the cell, and there she beheld King Arthur where he lay stretched upon the pallet. And she wist not who he was. Yet it appeared to her that in all her life she had not beheld so noble appearing a knight as he who lay sorely wounded in that lonely place. And King Arthur cast his looks upward to where she stood beside his bed of pain, surrounded by her maidens, and in the great weakness that lay upon him he wist not whether she whom he beheld was a mortal lady or whether she was not rather some tall straight angel who had descended from one of the Lordly Courts of Paradise for to visit him in his pain and distresses. And the Lady Guinevere was filled with a great pity at beholding King Arthur's sorrowful estate. Wherefore she called to her that skilful leech who was with her Court. And she bade him bring a certain alabaster box of exceedingly precious balsam. And she commanded him for to search that knight's wounds and to anoint them with the balsam, so that he might be healed of his hurts with all despatch.

So that wise and skilful leech did according to the Lady Guinevere's commands, and immediately King Arthur felt entire ease of all his aches and great content of spirit. And when the Lady and her Court had departed, he found himself much uplifted in heart, and three days thereafter he was entirely healed and was as well and strong and lusty as ever he had been in all of his life.

And this was the first time that King Arthur ever beheld that beautiful lady, the Lady Guinevere of Cameliard, and from that time forth he never forgot her, but she was almost always present in his thoughts. Wherefore, when he was recovered he said thus to himself: "I will forget that I am a king and I will cherish the thought of this lady and will serve her faithfully as a good knight may serve his chosen dame."

And so he did, as ye shall hear later in this book.

Chapter Third

How King Arthur Found a Noble Sword In a Very Wonderful Manner. And How He Again Fought With It and Won That Battle.

N ow, as soon as King Arthur had, by means of that extraordinary balsam, been thus healed of those grievous wounds which he had received in his battle with King Pellinore, he found himself to be moved by a most vehement desire to meet his enemy again for to try issue of battle with him once more, and so recover the credit which he had lost in that combat. Now, upon the morning of the fourth day, being entirely cured, and having broken his fast, he walked for refreshment beside the skirts of the forest, listening the while to the cheerful sound of the wood-birds singing their matins, all with might and main. And Merlin walked beside him, and King Arthur spake his mind to Merlin concerning his intent to engage once more in knightly contest with King Pellinore. And he said, "Merlin, it doth vex me very sorely for to have come off so ill in my late encounter with King Pellinore. Certes, he is the very best knight in all the world whom I have ever yet encountered. Ne'theless, it might have fared differently with me had I not broken my sword, and so left myself altogether defenceless in that respect. Howsoever that may be, I am of a mind for to assay this adventure once more, and so will I do as immediately as may be."

Thereunto Merlin made reply, "Thou art, assuredly, a very brave man to have so much appetite for battle, seeing how nigh thou camest unto thy death not even four days ago. Yet how mayst thou hope to undertake this adventure without due preparation? For, lo! thou hast no sword, nor hast thou a spear, nor hast thou even thy misericordia for to do battle withal. How then mayst thou hope for to assay this adventure?"

And King Arthur said, "That I know not, nevertheless I will presently seek for some weapon as soon as may be. For, even an I have no better weapon than an oaken cudgel, yet would I assay this battle again with so poor a tool as that."

"Ha! Lord," said Merlin, "I do perceive that thou art altogether fixed in thy purpose for to renew this quarrel. Wherefore, I will not seek to stay thee therefrom, but will do all that in me lies for to aid thee in thy desires. Now to this end I must tell thee that in one part of this forest (which is, indeed, a very strange place) there is a certain woodland sometimes called Arroy, and other times called the Forest of Adventure. For no knight ever entereth therein but some adventure befalleth him. And close to Arroy is a land of enchantment which has several times been seen. And that is a very wonderful land, for there is in it a wide and considerable lake, which is also of enchantment. And in the centre of that lake there hath for some time been seen the appearance as of a woman's arm—exceedingly beautiful and clad in white samite, and the hand of this arm holdeth a sword of such exceeding excellence and beauty that no eye hath ever beheld its like. And the name of this sword is Excalibur—it being so named by those who have beheld it because of its marvellous brightness and beauty. For it hath come to pass that several knights have already seen that sword and have endeavored to obtain it for their own, but, heretofore, no one hath been able to touch it, and many have lost their lives in that adventure. For when any man draweth near unto it, either he sinks into the lake, or else the arm disappeareth entirely, or else it is withdrawn beneath the lake; wherefore no man hath ever been able to obtain the possession of that sword. Now I am able to conduct thee unto that Lake of Enchantment, and there thou mayst see Excalibur with thine own eyes. Then when thou hast seen him thou mayst, haply, have the desire to obtain him; which, an thou art able to do, thou wilt have a sword very fitted for to do battle with."

"Merlin," quoth the King, "this is a very strange thing which thou tellest me. Now I am desirous beyond measure for to attempt to obtain this sword for mine own, wherefore I do beseech thee to lead me with all despatch to this enchanted lake whereof thou tellest me." And Merlin said, "I will do so."

So that morning King Arthur and Merlin took leave of that holy hermit (the King having kneeled in the grass to receive his benediction), and so, departing from that place, they entered the deeper forest once more, betaking their way to that part which was known as Arroy.

And after awhile they came to Arroy, and it was about noon-tide. And when they had entered into those woodlands they came to a certain little open place, and in that place they beheld a white doe with a golden collar about its neck. And King Arthur said, "Look, Merlin, yonder is a wonderful sight." And Merlin said, "Let us follow that doe." And upon this the doe turned and they followed it. And by and by in following it they came to an opening in the trees where was a little lawn of sweet soft grass. Here they beheld a bower and before the bower was a table spread with a fair snow-white cloth, and set with refreshments of white bread, wine, and meats of several sorts. And at the door of this bower there stood a page, clad all in green, and his hair was as black as ebony, and his eyes as black as jet and exceeding bright. And when this page beheld King Arthur and Merlin, he gave them greeting, and welcomed the King very pleasantly saying, "Ha! King Arthur, thou art welcome to this place. Now I prithee dismount and refresh thyself before going farther."

Then was King Arthur a-doubt as to whether there might not be some enchantment in this for to work him an ill, for he was astonished that that page in the deep forest should know him so well. But Merlin bade him have good cheer, and he said,

"Indeed, Lord, thou mayst freely partake of that refreshment which, I may tell thee, was prepared especially for thee. Moreover in this thou mayst foretell a very happy issue unto this adventure."

So King Arthur sat down to the table with great comfort of heart (for he was an hungered) and that page and another like unto him ministered unto his needs, serving him all the food upon silver plates, and all the wine in golden goblets as he was used to being served in his own court—only that those things were much more cunningly wrought and fashioned, and were more beautiful than the table furniture of the King's court.

Then, after he had eaten his fill and had washed his hands from a silver basin which the first page offered to him, and had wiped his hands upon a fine linen napkin which the other page brought unto him, and after Merlin had also refreshed himself, they went their way, greatly rejoicing at this pleasant adventure, which, it seemed to the King, could not but betoken a very good issue to his undertaking.

Now about the middle of the afternoon King Arthur and Merlin came, of a sudden, out from the forest and upon a fair and level plain, bedight all over with such a number of flowers that no man could conceive of their quantity nor of the beauty thereof.

And this was a very wonderful land, for, lo! all the air appeared as it were to be as of gold—so bright was it and so singularly radiant. And here and there upon that plain were sundry trees all in blossom; and the fragrance of the blossoms was so sweet that the King had never smelt any fragrance like to it. And in the branches of those trees were a multitude of birds of many colors, and the melody of their singing ravished the heart of the hearer. And midway in the plain was a lake of water as bright as silver, and all around the borders of the lake were incredible numbers of lilies and of daffodils. Yet, although this place was so exceedingly fair, there was, nevertheless, nowhere about it a single sign of human life of any sort, but it appeared altogether as lonely as the hollow sky upon a day of summer. So, because of all the marvellous beauty of this place, and because of its strangeness and its entire solitude, King

Arthur perceived that he must have come into a land of powerful enchantment where, happily, dwelt a fairy of very exalted quality; wherefore his spirit was enwrapped in a manner of fear, as he pushed his great milk-white war-horse through that long fair grass, all bedight with flowers, and he wist not what strange things were about to befall him.

So when he had come unto the margin of the lake he beheld there the miracle that Merlin had told him of aforetime. For, lo! in the midst of the expanse of water there was the appearance of a fair and beautiful arm, as of a woman, clad all in white samite. And the arm was encircled with several bracelets of wrought gold; and the hand held a sword of marvellous workmanship aloft in the air above the surface of the water; and neither the arm nor the sword moved so much as a hair's-breadth, but were motionless like to a carven image upon the surface of the lake. And, behold! the sun of that strange land shone down upon the hilt of the sword, and it was of pure gold beset with jewels of several sorts, so that the hilt of the sword and the bracelets that encircled the arm glistered in the midst of the lake like to some singular star of exceeding splendor. And King Arthur sat upon his war-horse and gazed from a distance at the arm and the sword, and he greatly marvelled thereat; yet he wist not how he might come at that sword, for the lake was wonderfully wide and deep, wherefore he knew not how he might come thereunto for to make it his own. And as he sat pondering this thing within himself, he was suddenly aware of a strange lady, who approached him through those tall flowers that bloomed along the margin of the lake. And when he perceived her coming toward him he quickly dismounted from his war-horse and he went forward for to meet her with the bridle-rein over his arm. And when he had come nigh to her, he perceived that she was extraordinarily beautiful, and that her face was like wax for clearness, and that her eyes were perfectly black, and that they were as bright and glistening as though they were two jewels set in ivory. And he perceived that her hair was like silk and as black as it was possible to be, and so long that it reached unto the ground as she walked. And the lady was clad all in green—only that a fine cord of crimson and gold was interwoven into the plaits of her

The hand held a sword of marvellous workmanship

hair. And around her neck there hung a very beautiful necklace of several strands of opal stones and emeralds, set in cunningly wrought gold; and around her wrists were bracelets of the like sort—of opal stones and emeralds set into gold. So when King Arthur beheld her wonderful appearance, that it was like to an ivory statue of exceeding beauty clad all in green, he immediately kneeled before her in the midst of all those flowers as he said, "Lady, I do certainly perceive that thou art no mortal damoiselle, but that thou art Fay. Also that this place, because of its extraordinary beauty, can be no other than some land of Faerie into which I have entered."

And the Lady replied, "King Arthur, thou sayest soothly, for I am indeed Faerie. Moreover, I may tell thee that my name is Nymue, and that I am the chiefest of those Ladies of the Lake of whom thou mayst have heard people speak. Also thou art to know that what thou beholdest yonder as a wide lake is, in truth, a plain like unto this, all bedight with flowers. And likewise thou art to know that in the midst of that plain there standeth a castle of white marble and of ultramarine illuminated with gold. But, lest mortal eyes should behold our dwelling-place, my sisters and I have caused it to be that this appearance as of a lake should extend all over that castle so that it is entirely hidden from sight. Nor may any mortal man cross that lake, saving in one way—otherwise he shall certainly perish therein."

"Lady," said King Arthur, "that which thou tellest me causes me to wonder a very great deal. And, indeed, I am afraid that in coming hitherward I have been doing amiss for to intrude upon the solitude of your dwelling-place."

"Nay, not so, King Arthur," said the Lady of the Lake, "for, in truth, thou art very welcome hereunto. Moreover, I may tell thee that I have a greater friendliness for thee and those noble knights of thy court than thou canst easily wot of. But I do beseech thee of thy courtesy for to tell me what it is that brings thee to our land?"

"Lady," quoth the King, "I will tell thee the entire truth. I fought of late a battle with a certain sable knight, in the which I was sorely and grievously wounded, and wherein I burst my spear and snapped my sword and lost even my misericordia, so that I had not a single thing left me by way of a weapon. In this extremity Merlin, here, told me of Excalibur, and of how he is continually upheld by an arm in the midst of this magical lake. So I came hither and, behold, I find it even as he hath said. Now, Lady, an it be possible, I would fain achieve that excellent sword, that, by means of it I might fight my battle to its entire end."

"Ha! my lord King," said the Lady of the Lake, "that sword is no easy thing for to achieve, and, moreover, I may tell thee that several knights have lost their lives by attempting that which thou hast a mind to do. For, in sooth, no man may win yonder sword unless he be without fear and without reproach."

"Alas, Lady!" quoth King Arthur, "that is indeed a sad saying for me. For, though I may not lack in knightly courage, yet, in truth, there be many things wherewith I do reproach myself withal. Ne'theless, I would fain attempt this thing, even an it be to my great endangerment. Wherefore, I prithee tell me how I may best undertake this adventure."

"King Arthur," said the Lady of the Lake, "I will do what I may to aid thee in thy wishes in this matter." Whereupon she lifted a single emerald that hung by a small chain of gold at her girdle and, lo! the emerald was cunningly carved into the form of a whistle. And she set the whistle to her lips and blew upon it very shrilly. Then straightway there appeared upon the water, a great way off, a certain thing that shone very brightly. And this drew near with great speed, and as it came nigh, behold! it was a boat all of carven brass. And the prow of the boat was carved into the form of a head of a beautiful woman, and upon either side were wings like the wings of a swan. And the boat moved upon the water like a swan—very swiftly—so that long lines, like to silver threads, stretched far away behind, across the face of the water, which otherwise was like unto glass for smoothness. And when the brazen boat had reached the bank it rested there and moved no more.

Then the Lady of the Lake bade King Arthur to enter the boat, and so he entered it. And immediately he had done so, the boat moved away from the bank as swiftly as it had come thither. And Merlin and the Lady of the Lake stood upon the margin of the water, and gazed after King Arthur.

And King Arthur beheld that the boat floated swiftly across the lake to where was the arm uplifting the sword, and that the arm and the sword moved not but remained where they were.

Then King Arthur reached forth and took the sword in his hand, and immediately the arm disappeared beneath the water, and King Arthur held the sword and the scabbard thereof and the belt thereof in his hand and, lo! they were his own.

Then verily his heart swelled with joy an it would burst within his bosom, for Excalibur was an hundred times more beautiful than he had thought possible. Wherefore his heart was nigh breaking for pure joy at having obtained that magic sword.

Then the brazen boat bore him very quickly back to the land again and he stepped ashore where stood the Lady of the Lake and Merlin. And when he stood upon the shore, he gave the Lady great thanks beyond measure for all that she had done for to aid him in his great undertaking; and she gave him cheerful and pleasing words in reply.

Then King Arthur saluted the lady, as became him, and, having mounted his war-horse, and Merlin having mounted his palfrey, they rode away thence upon their business—the King's heart still greatly expanded with pure delight at having for his own that beautiful sword—the most beautiful and the most famous sword in all the world.

That night King Arthur and Merlin abided with the holy hermit at the forest sanctuary, and when the next morning had come (the King having bathed himself in the ice-cold forest fountain, and being exceedingly refreshed thereby) they took their departure, offering thanks to that saintly man for the harborage he had given them.

Anon, about noon-tide, they reached the valley of the Sable Knight, and there were all things appointed exactly as when King Arthur had been there before: to wit, that gloomy castle, the lawn of smooth grass, the apple-tree covered over with shields, and the bridge whereon hung that single shield of sable.

"Now, Merlin," quoth King Arthur, "I do this time most

strictly forbid thee for to interfere in this quarrel. Nor shalt thou, under pain of my displeasure, exert any of thy arts of magic in my behalf. So hearken thou to what I say, and heed it with all possible diligence."

Thereupon, straightway, the King rode forth upon the bridge and, seizing the brazen mall, he smote upon the sable shield with all his might and main. Immediately the portcullis of the castle was let fall as afore told, and, in the same manner as that other time, the Sable Knight rode forth therefrom, already bedight and equipped for the encounter. So he came to the bridge-head and there King Arthur spake to him in this wise: "Sir Pellinore, we do now know one another entirely well, and each doth judge that he hath cause of quarrel with the other: thou, that I, for mine own reasons as seemed to me to be fit, have taken away from thee thy kingly estate, and have driven thee into this forest solitude: I, that thou has set thyself up here for to do injury and affront to knights and lords and other people of this kingdom of mine. Wherefore, seeing that I am here as an errant Knight, I do challenge thee for to fight with me, man to man, until either thou or I have conquered the other."

Unto this speech King Pellinore bowed his head in obedience, and thereupon he wheeled his horse, and, riding to some little distance, took his place where he had afore stood. And King Arthur also rode to some little distance, and took his station where he had afore stood. At the same time there came forth from the castle one of those tall pages clad all in sable, pied with crimson, and gave to King Arthur a good, stout spear of ash-wood, well seasoned and untried in battle; and when the two Knights were duly prepared, they shouted and drave their horses together, the one smiting the other so fairly in the midst of his defences that the spears shivered in the hand of each, bursting all into small splinters as they had aforetime done.

Then each of these two knights immediately voided his horse with great skill and address, and drew each his sword. And thereupon they fell to at a combat, so furious and so violent, that two wild bulls upon the mountains could not have engaged in a more desperate encounter.

But now, having Excalibur for to aid him in his battle, King

Arthur soon overcame his enemy. For he gave him several wounds and yet received none himself, nor did he shed a single drop of blood in all that fight, though his enemy's armor was in a little while all stained with crimson. And at last King Arthur delivered so vehement a stroke that King Pellinore was entirely benumbed thereby, wherefore his sword and his shield fell down from their defence, his thighs trembled beneath him and he sank unto his knees upon the ground. Then he called upon King Arthur to have mercy, saying, "Spare my life and I will yield myself unto thee."

And King Arthur said, "I will spare thee and I will do more than that. For now that thou hast yielded thyself unto me, lo! I will restore unto thee thy power and estate. For I bear no ill-will toward thee, Pellinore, ne'theless, I can brook no rebels against my power in this realm. For, as God judges me, I do declare that I hold singly in my sight the good of the people of my kingdom. Wherefore, he who is against me is also against them, and he who is against them is also against me. But now that thou hast acknowledged me I will take thee into my favor. Only as a pledge of thy good faith toward me in the future, I shall require it of thee that thou shalt send me as hostage of thy good-will, thy two eldest sons, to wit: Sir Aglaval and Sir Lamorack. Thy young son, Dornar, thou mayest keep with thee for thy comfort."

So those two young knights above mentioned came to the Court of King Arthur, and they became very famous knights, and by and by were made fellows in great honor of the Round Table.

And King Arthur and King Pellinore went together into the castle of King Pellinore, and there King Pellinore's wounds were dressed and he was made comfortable. That night King Arthur abode in the castle of King Pellinore, and when the next morning had come, he and Merlin returned unto the Court of the King, where it awaited him in the forest at that place where he had established it.

Now King Arthur took very great pleasure unto himself as he and Merlin rode together in return through that forest; for it was the leafiest time of all the year, what time the woodlands decked themselves in their best apparel of clear, bright green. Each bosky dell and dingle was full of the perfume of the thickets, and in every tangled depth the small bird sang with all his might and main, and as though he would burst his little throat with the melody of his singing. And the ground beneath the horses' feet was so soft with fragrant moss that the ear could not hear any sound of hoof-beats upon the earth. And the bright yellow sunlight came down through the leaves so that the ground was scattered over with a great multitude of trembling circles as of pure yellow gold. And, anon, that sunlight would fall down upon the armed knight as he rode, so that every little while his armor appeared to catch fire with a great glory, shining like a sudden bright star amid the dark shadows of the woodland.

So it was that King Arthur took great joy in that forest land, for he was without ache or pain of any sort and his heart was very greatly elated with the wonderfulness of the success of that adventure into which he had entered. For in that adventure he had not only won a very bitter enemy into a friend who should be of great usefulness and satisfaction to him, but likewise, he had obtained for himself a sword, the like of which the world had never before beheld. And whenever he would think of that singularly splendid sword which now hung by his side, and whenever he remembered that land of Faëry into which he had wandered, and of that which had befallen him therein, his heart would become so greatly elated with pure joyousness that he hardly knew how to contain himself because of the great delight that filled his entire bosom.

And, indeed, I know of no greater good that I could wish for you in all of your life than to have you enjoy such happiness as cometh to one when he hath done his best endeavor and hath succeeded with great entirety in his undertaking. For then all the world appears to be filled as with a bright shining light, and the body seemeth to become so elated that the feet are uplifted from heaviness and touch the earth very lightly because of the lightness of the spirit within. Wherefore, it is, that if I could have it in my power to give you the very best that the world hath to give, I would wish that you might win your battle as

King Arthur won his battle at that time, and that you might ride homeward in such triumph and joyousness as filled him that day, and that the sunlight might shine around you as it shone around him, and that the breezes might blow and that all the little birds might sing with might and main as they sang for him, and that your heart also might sing its song of rejoicing in the pleasantness of the world in which you live.

Now as they rode thus through the forest together, Merlin said to the King: "Lord, which wouldst thou rather have, Excalibur, or the sheath that holds him?" To which King Arthur replied, "Ten thousand times would I rather have Excalibur than his sheath." "In that thou art wrong, my Lord," said Merlin, "for let me tell thee, that though Excalibur is of so great a temper that he may cut in twain either a feather or a bar of iron, yet is his sheath of such a sort that he who wears it can suffer no wound in battle, neither may he lose a single drop of blood. In witness whereof, thou mayst remember that, in thy late battle with King Pellinore, thou didst suffer no wound, neither didst thou lose any blood."

Then King Arthur directed a countenance of great displeasure upon his companion and he said, "Now, Merlin, I do declare that thou hast taken from me the entire glory of that battle which I have lately fought. For what credit may there be to any knight who fights his enemy by means of enchantment such as thou tellest me of? And, indeed, I am minded to take this glorious sword back to that magic lake and to cast it therein where it belongeth; for I believe that a knight should fight by means of his own strength, and not by means of magic."

"My Lord," said Merlin, "assuredly thou art entirely right in what thou holdest. But thou must bear in mind that thou art not as an ordinary errant knight, but that thou art a King, and that thy life belongeth not unto thee, but unto thy people. Accordingly thou hast no right to imperil it, but shouldst do all that lieth in thy power for to preserve it. Wherefore thou shouldst keep that sword so that it may safeguard thy life."

Then King Arthur meditated that saying for a long while in silence; and when he spake it was in this wise: "Merlin, thou art right in what thou sayest, and, for the sake of my people, I will keep both Excalibur for to fight for them, and likewise his sheath for to preserve my life for their sake. Ne'theless, I will never use him again saving in serious battle." And King Arthur held to that saying, so that thereafter he did no battle in sport excepting with lance and a-horseback.

King Arthur kept Excalibur as the chiefest treasure of all his possessions. For he said to himself, "Such a sword as this is fit for a king above other kings and a lord above other lords. Now, as God hath seen fit for to intrust that sword into my keeping in so marvellous a manner as fell about, so must He mean that I am to be His servant for to do unusual things. Wherefore I will treasure this noble weapon not more for its excellent worth than because it shall be unto me as a sign of those great things that God, in His mercy, hath evidently ordained for me to perform for to do Him service."

So King Arthur had made for Excalibur a strong chest or coffer, bound around with many bands of wrought iron, studded all over with great nails of iron, and locked with three great padlocks. In this strong-box he kept Excalibur lying upon a cushion of crimson silk and wrapped in swathings of fine linen, and very few people ever beheld the sword in its glory excepting when it shone like a sudden flame in the uproar of battle.

For when the time came for King Arthur to defend his realm or his subjects from their enemies, then he would take out the sword, and fasten it upon the side of his body; and when he did so he was like unto a hero of God girt with a blade of shining lightning. Yea; at such times Excalibur shone with so terrible a brightness that the very sight thereof would shake the spirits of every wrong-doer with such great fear that he would, in a manner, suffer the pangs of death ere ever the edge of the blade had touched his flesh.

So King Arthur treasured Excalibur and the sword remained with him for all of his life, wherefore the name of Arthur and of Excalibur are one. So, I believe that that sword is the most famous of any that ever was seen or heard tell of in all the Courts of Chivalry.

As for the sheath of the blade, King Arthur lost that through the treachery of one who should, by rights, have been his dearest friend (as you shall hear of anon), and in the end the loss of that miraculous sheath brought it about that he suffered a very great deal of pain and sorrow.

All that also you shall read of, God willing, in due season.

So endeth the story of the winning of Excalibur, and may God give unto you in your life, that you may have His truth to aid you, like a shining sword, for to overcome your enemies; and may He give you Faith (for Faith containeth Truth as a scabbard containeth its sword), and may that Faith heal all your wounds of sorrow as the sheath of Excalibur healed all the wounds of him who wore that excellent weapon. For with Truth and Faith girded upon you, you shall be as well able to fight all your battles as did that noble hero of old, whom men called King Arthur.

PART III

The Winning of a Queen

Chapter First

How King Arthur Went to Tintagalon With Four of His Court, and How He Disguised Himself for a Certain Purpose.

Now, upon a certain day King Arthur proclaimed a high feast, which was held at Carleon upon Usk. Many noble guests were bidden, and an exceedingly splendid Court gathered at the King's castle. For at that feast there sat seven kings and five queens in royal state, and there were high lords and beautiful ladies of degree, to the number of three score and seven; and there were a multitude of those famous knights of the King's Court who were reckoned the most renowned in arms in all of Christendom. And of all this great gathering of kings, lords, and knights, not one man looked askance at his neighbor, but all were united in good fellowship. Wherefore, when the young King looked about him and beheld such peace and amity among all these noble lords where, aforetime, had been discord and ill-regard: "Certes," quoth he to himself, "it is wonderful how this reign of mine hath knit men together in kindness and good fellowship!" And because of such thoughts as these, his spirit took wings like unto a bird and sang within him.

Now while the King sat thus at feast, lo! there came an herald-messenger from the west-country. And the herald came and stood before the King, and said: "Greeting to thee, King Arthur!"

Then the King said: "Speak, and tell me, what is thy message?"

To which the herald made reply: "I come from King Leodegrance of Cameliard, who is in sore trouble. For thus it is: His enemy and thine enemy, King Ryence of North Wales (he who at one time in contempt of thee commanded thee to send him thy beard for to trim his mantle), doth make sundry demands of my master, King Leodegrance, which demands King Leodegrance is altogether loath to fulfil. And King Ryence of North Wales threateneth to bring war into Cameliard because King Leodegrance doth not immediately fulfil those demands. Now King Leodegrance hath no such array of knights and armed men as he one time had gathered about him for to defend his kingdom against assault. For, since thou in thy majesty hath brought peace to this realm and hath reduced the power of all those kings under thee, those knights who once made the Court of King Leodegrance so famous have gone elsewhither for to seek better opportunities for their great valor and prowess at arms than his peaceful Court may afford. Wherefore my master, King Leodegrance, doth beseech aid of thee, who art his King and Overlord."

To these things that the herald-messenger said, King Arthur, and all that Court that feasted with him, listened in entire silence. And the King's countenance, which erstwhiles had been expanded with cheerfulness, became overcast and dark with anger. "Ha!" he cried, "this is, verily, no good news that thou hast brought hither to our feast. Now I will give what aid I am able to thy master, King Leodegrance, in this extremity, and that right speedily. But tell me, sir herald, what things are they that King Ryence demandeth of thy master?"

"That I will tell you, Lord," quoth the herald-messenger. "Firstly, King Ryence maketh demand upon my master of a great part of those lands of Cameliard that march upon the borders of North Wales. Secondly, he maketh demand that the Lady Guinevere, the King's daughter, be delivered in marriage unto Duke Mordaunt of North Umber, who is of kin unto King Ryence, and that Duke, though a mighty warrior, is so evil of appearance, and so violent of temper, that I believe that there is not his like for ugliness or for madness of humor in all of the world."

Now when King Arthur heard this that the messenger said he was immediately seized with an extraordinary passion of anger. For his eyes appeared, an it were, to shoot forth sparks of pure light, his face flamed like fire, and he ground his teeth together like the stones of a quern. Then he immediately rose from the chair where he sat and went forth from that place, and all those who beheld his anger shuddered thereat and turned their eyes away from his countenance.

Then King Arthur went into an inner room of the castle by himself, and there he walked up and down for a great while, and in that time no one of his household dared to come nigh to him. And the reason of the King's wrath was this: that ever since he had lain wounded and sick nigh unto death in the forest, he bare in mind how the Lady Guinevere had suddenly appeared before him like some tall, straight, shining angel who had descended unto him out of Paradise—all full of pity, and exceedingly beautiful. Wherefore, at thought of that wicked, mad Duke Mordaunt of North Umber making demand unto marriage with her, he was seized with a rage so violent that it shook his spirit like a mighty wind.

So, for a long while, he walked up and down in his wrath as aforesaid, and no one durst come nigh unto him, but all stood afar off, watching him from a distance.

Then, after a while, he gave command that Merlin, and Sir Ulfius, and Sir Kay should come to him at that place where he was. And when they had come thither he talked to them for a considerable time, bidding Merlin for to make ready to go upon a journey with him, and bidding Sir Ulfius and Sir Kay for to gather together a large army of chosen knights and armed men, and to bring that army straightway into those parts coadjacent to the royal castle of Tintagalon, which same standeth close to the borders of North Wales and of Cameliard.

So Sir Ulfius and Sir Kay went about to do as King Arthur commanded, and Merlin also went about to do as he commanded; and the next day King Arthur and Merlin, together with certain famous knights of the King's Court who were the most approved at arms of all those about him—to wit, Sir Gawaine, and Sir Ewaine (who were nephews unto the King), and Sir Pellias and Sir Geraint, the son of Erbin—set forth for Tintagalon across the forest-land of Usk.

So they travelled for all that day and a part of the next, and that without adventure or misadventure of any sort. So they came, at last, to that large and noble castle, hight Tintagalon, which guards the country bordering upon Cameliard and North Wales. Here King Arthur was received with great rejoicing; for whithersoever the King went the people loved him very dearly. Wherefore the folk of Tintagalon were very glad when he came unto them.

Now the morning after King Arthur had come unto Tintagalon (the summer night having been very warm), he and Merlin were glad to arise betimes to go abroad for to enjoy the dewy freshness of the early daytime. So, in the cool of the day, they walked together in the garden (which was a very pleasant place), and beneath the shadow of a tall, straight tower. And all around about were many trees with a good shade, where the little birds sang sweetly in the cheerfulness of the summer weather.

And here King Arthur opened his mind very freely to Merlin, and he said: "Merlin, I do believe that the Lady Guinevere is the fairest lady in all of the world; wherefore my heart seems ever to be entirely filled with love for her, and that to such a degree that I think of her continually by day (whether I be eating, or drinking, or walking, or sitting still, or going about my business), and likewise I dream of her many times at night. And this has been the case with me, Merlin, ever since a month ago, when I lay sick in that hermit's cell in the forest, what time she came and stood beside me like a shining angel out of Paradise. So I am not willing that any other man than I should have her for his wife.

"Now I know very well that thou art wonderfully cunning

in those arts of magic that may change a man in his appearance so that even those who know him best may not recognize him. Wherefore I very greatly desire it of thee that thou wilt so disguise me that I may go, unknown of any man, into Cameliard, and that I may dwell there in such a way that I may see the Lady Guinevere every day. For I tell thee very truly that I greatly desire to behold her in such a wise that she may not be in any way witting of my regard. Likewise I would fain see for myself how great may be the perils that encompass King Leodegrance—the King being my right good friend."

"My Lord King," said Merlin, "it shall be as thou desirest, and this morning I will cause thee to be so disguised that no one in all the world shall be able to know thee who thou art."

So that morning, a little before the prime, Merlin came unto the King where he was and gave him a little cap. And the cap was of such a sort that when the King set it upon his head he assumed, upon the instant, the appearance of a rude and rustic fellow from the country-side. Then the King commanded that a jerkin of rough frieze should be brought to him, and with this he covered his royal and knightly vestments, and with it he hid that golden collar and its jewel, pendent, which he continually wore about his neck. Then, setting the cap upon his head, he assumed at once the guise of that peasant hind.

Whereupon, being thus entirely disguised, he quitted Tintagalon unknown of any man, and took his way a-foot unto the town of Cameliard.

Now toward the slanting of the day he drew nigh to that place, and lo! he beheld before him a large and considerable town of many comely houses with red walls and shining windows. And the houses of the town sat all upon a high, steep hill, the one overlooking the other, and the town itself was encompassed around about by a great wall, high and strong. And a great castle guarded the town, and the castle had very many towers and roofs. And all round about the tower were many fair gardens and lawns and meadows, and several orchards and groves of trees with thick and pleasing shade. Now at that time of the day the sky behind the tower was all, as it were, an entire flame of fire, so that the towers and the battlements of the castle and the roofs and the chimneys thereof stood altogether black against the brightness of the light. And, behold! great flocks of pigeons encircled the towers of the castle in a continual flight against that fiery sky. So, because King Arthur was a-weary with walking for all that day, it appeared to him that he had hardly ever beheld in all of his life so fair and pleasing a place as that excellent castle with its gardens and lawns and groves of trees.

Thus came King Arthur unto the castle of Cameliard, in the guise of a poor peasant from the country-side, and no man in all of the world knew him who he was.

So, having reached the castle, he made inquiries for the head gardener thereof; and when he had speech with the gardener he besought him that he might be taken into service into that part of the garden that appertained to the dwelling-place of the Lady Guinevere. Then the gardener looked upon him and saw that he was tall and strong and well framed, wherefore he liked him very well and took him into service even as he desired.

And thus it was that King Arthur of Britain became a gardener's boy at Cameliard.

Now the King was very glad to be in that garden; for in this pleasant summer season the Lady Guinevere came every day to walk with her damsels among the flowers, and King Arthur, all disguised as a peasant gardener boy, beheld her very many times when she came thither.

So King Arthur abode at that place for above a week, and he took no care that in all that time he enjoyed none of his kingly estate, but was only gardener's boy in the castle garden of Cameliard.

Now it happened upon a day when the weather was very warm, that one of the damsels who was in attendance upon the Lady Guinevere, arose all in the early morning whiles the air was still cool and refreshing. So, leaving the Lady Guinevere still sleeping, this damsel, whose name was Mellicene of the White Hand, went into the ante-room and, opening the casement thereof, looked forth into that garden of roses which adjoined the Lady Guinevere's bower.

Now there was at that place a carven marble figure of a

youth, holding in his arms a marble ewer, and a fountain of water, as clear as crystal, flowed out from the ewer into a basin of marble. And the figure, and the fountain, and the marble basin into which the fountain flowed lay beneath the shadow of a linden-tree. And all around was a thick growth of roses, so that the place was entirely hidden, saving only from those windows of the castle that were above.

So it befell that as the damsel looked down thitherward out of the window, she beheld a very wonderful sight. For, lo! a strange knight kneeled beside the fountain and bathed his face and his bosom in the crystal water thereof. And the damsel saw that the sunlight fell down through the leaves of the linden-tree and lay upon that strange knight. And she perceived that his hair and his beard were of the color of red gold—shining surpassingly in the brightness of the morning. And she beheld that his brow and his throat and his bosom were white like alabaster. And she beheld that around his neck and shoulders there hung a golden collar of marvellous beauty, so that when the sunlight shone upon it it flashed like lightning.

So, beholding this strange appearance—as it were a vision— the damsel Mellicine stood for a long while, all entranced with wonder and with pleasure, and wist not whether that which she saw was a dream or no dream, nor whether he who sat there was a spirit, or whether he was a man of flesh and blood.

Then, by and by, recovering somewhat from her astonishment, she withdrew herself softly from the casement, and, turning about, ran fleetly down the turret stairs, and so came out thence into that fair and blooming garden at the foot of the tower. So she ran through the garden with all speed and silence, and thus came down an alley-way and to the marble fountain and the linden-trees and the rose-trees around about where she had anon beheld that strange knight bathing himself in the crystal waters.

But King Arthur had heard the coming of that damsel, and had speedily set the cap upon his head again. So that when the damsel Mellicene came thither, she found no one by the fountain but the gardener's boy. Of him she demanded: "Who art thou, fellow? And why sittest thou here by the fountain?"

And unto her he replied: "I am the gardener's lad who came a short time ago to take service at this place."

"Then tell me, fellow," quoth she, "and tell me truly. Who was that young knight who was here beside the fountain but now, and whither hath he gone?" "Lady, whereunto," he said, "there has been no one at this fountain this day, but only I."

"Nay, fellow," she cried, "thou art deceiving me, for I do assure thee that with mine own eyes I beheld but now, where a strange young knight sat bathing himself in the waters of this fountain." And the gardener's boy said, "Lady, that which I have told you is the very truth, for indeed there hath no one been here this morn but only I. Wherefore, an thou deemest thou hast seen anyone else, thou art certainly mistaken."

At this the damsel set her look upon him, in great perplexity. Likewise, she marvelled very greatly, for she could not altogether disbelieve him. Nor yet could she entirely believe him either, because her eyes had beheld that which she had beheld, and she wotted that she had not been mistaken. Therefore she knew not what to think, and, because of her perplexity, she felt a very great displeasure at that gardener's boy. "Truly, wherefore," she said, "if thou art deceiving me, I shall certainly cause thee to suffer a great deal of pain, for I shall have thee whipped with cords." Thereupon she turned and went away from that place, much marvelling at that strange thing, and wondering what it all signified.

That morning she told unto the Lady Guinevere all that she had seen, but the Lady Guinevere only laughed at her and mocked her, telling her that she had been asleep and dreaming, when she beheld that vision. And, indeed, the damsel herself had begun to think this must be the case. Nevertheless, she thereafter looked out every morning from her casement window, albeit she beheld nothing for a great while, for King Arthur came not soon to that place again.

So, by and by, there befell another certain morning when she looked out of the casement and, lo! there sat that strange knight by the fountain once more as he had aforetime sat. And he bathed his face and his bosom in the water as he had aforetime done. And he appeared as comely and as noble as he had appeared before; and his hair and his young beard shone like gold as they had shone before in the sun. And this time she beheld that his collar of gold lay upon the brink of the fountain beside him, and it sparkled with great splendor in the sunlight the whiles he bathed his bosom. Then, after that damsel had regarded him for a considerable time, she ran with all speed to the chamber where the Lady Guinevere still lay, and she cried in a loud voice, "Lady! lady! arouse thee and come with me! For, lo! that same young knight whom I beheld before, is even now bathing himself at the fountain under the linden-tree."

Then the Lady Guinevere, greatly marvelling, aroused herself right quickly, and, dighting herself with all speed, went with the damsel unto that casement window which looked out into that part of the garden.

And there she herself beheld the young knight where he laved himself at the fountain. And she saw that his hair and his beard shone like gold in the sunlight; and she saw that his undervestment was of purple linen threaded with gold; and she saw that beside him lay that cunningly wrought color of gold inset with many jewels of various colors, and the collar shone with great splendor where it lay upon the marble verge of the fountain.

Somewhiles she gazed, exceedingly astonished; then she commanded the damsel Mellicene for to come with her, and therewith she turned and descended the turret stairs, and went quickly out into the garden, as her damsel had done aforetime. Then, as that damsel had done, she straightway hastened with all speed down the alley-way toward the fountain.

But, behold! when she had come there, she found no young knight, but only the gardener boy, exactly as had happened with the damsel Mellicene aforetime. For King Arthur had heard her coming, and had immediately put that enchanted cap upon his head. Then the Lady Guinevere marvelled very greatly to find there only the gardener's boy, and she wist not what to think of so strange a thing. Wherefore she demanded of him, even as Mellicene had done, whither had gone the young knight whom she had beheld anon there at the fountain. And unto her the gardener lad made answer as aforetime: "Lady! there hath been no one at this place at any time this morning, but only I."

Now when King Arthur had donned his cap at the coming of the Lady, he had, in his great haste, forgotten his golden collar, and this Guinevere beheld where it lay shining very brightly, beside the margin of the fountain. "How now!" quoth she. "Wouldst thou dare to make a mock of me! Now tell me, thou fellow, do gardeners' boys in the land whence thou didst come wear golden collars about their necks like unto that collar that lieth yonder beside the fountain? Now, an I had thee well whipped, it would be thy rightful due. But take thou that bauble yonder and give it unto him to whom it doth rightfully belong, and tell him from me that it doth ill become a true belted knight for to hide himself away in the privy gardens of a lady." Then turned she with the damsel Mellicene, and left she that place and went back again into her bower.

Yet, indeed for all that day, as she sat over her 'broidery, she did never cease to marvel and to wonder how it was possible that that strange young knight should so suddenly have vanished away and left only the poor gardener's boy in his stead. Nor, for a long time, might she unriddle that strange thing."

Then, of a sudden, at that time when the heat of the day was sloping toward the cooler part of the afternoon, she aroused herself because of a thought that had come in an instant unto her. So she called the damsel Mellicene to come to her, and she bade her to go and tell the gardener's lad for to fetch her straightway a basket of fresh roses for to adorn her tower chamber.

So Mellicene went and did as she bade, and after considerable time the gardener's lad came bearing a great basket of roses. And, lo! he wore his cap upon his head. And all the damsels in waiting upon the Lady Guinevere, when they saw how he wore his cap in her presence, cried out upon him, and Mellicene of the White Hand demanded of him: "What! How now, Sir boor! Dost thou know so little of what is due unto a king's daughter that thou dost wear thy cap even in the presence of the Lady Guinevere? Now I bid thee straightway to take thy cap off thy head."

And to her King Arthur made answer: "Lady, I cannot take off my cap."

Quoth the Lady Guinevere: "And why canst thou not take off thy cap, thou surly fellow?"

"Lady," said he, "I cannot take off my cap, because I have an ugly place upon my head."

"Then wear thy cap," quoth the Lady Guinevere. "Only fetch thou the roses unto me."

And so at her bidding, he brought the roses to her. But when he had come nigh unto the lady, she, of a sudden, snatched at the cap and plucked it off from his head. Then, lo! he was upon the instant transformed; for instead of the gardener's boy there stood before the Lady Guinevere and her damsel the appearance of a noble young knight with hair and beard like threads of gold. Then he let fall his basket of roses so that the flowers were scattered all over the floor, and he stood and looked at all who were there. And some of those damsels in attendance upon the Lady Guinevere shrieked, and others stood still from pure amazement and wist not how to believe what their eyes beheld. But not one of those ladies knew that he whom she beheld was King Arthur. Nevertheless the Lady Guinevere remembered that this was the knight whom she had found so sorely wounded, lying in the hermit's cell in the forest.

Then she laughed and flung him back his cap again. "Take thy cap," quoth she, "and go thy ways, thou gardener's boy who hath an ugly place upon his head." Thus she said because she was minded to mock him.

But King Arthur did not reply to her, but straightway, with great sobriety of aspect, set his cap upon his head again. So resuming his humble guise once more, he turned and quitted that place, leaving those roses scattered all over the floor even as they had fallen.

And after that time, whenever the Lady Guinevere would come upon the gardener's lad in the garden, she would say unto her damsel in such a voice that he might hear her speech: "Lo! yonder is the gardener's lad who hath an ugly place upon his head so that he must always wear his cap for to hide it."

Thus she spake openly, mocking at him; but privily she bade her damsels to say naught concerning these things, but to keep unto themselves all those things which had befallen.

Chapter Second

*How King Ryence Came to Cameliard and
How King Arthur Fought With the
Duke of North Umber.*

𝔑ow, upon a certain day at this time there came a messenger to the Court of King Leodegrance, with news that King Ryence of North Wales and Duke Mordaunt of North Umber were coming thither and that they brought with them a very noble and considerable Court of knights and lords. At this news King Leodegrance was much troubled in spirit, for he wist not what such a visit might betoken; and yet he greatly feared that it boded ill for him. So on that day when King Ryence and the Duke of North Umber appeared before the castle, King Leodegrance went forth to greet them and they three met together in the meadows that lie beneath the castle walls of Cameliard.

There King Leodegrance bade those others welcome in such manner as was fitting, desiring them that they should come into the castle with him so that he might entertain them according to their degree.

But to this courtesy upon the part of King Leodegrance, King Ryence deigned no pleasing reply. "Nay," quoth he, "we go not with thee into thy castle, King Leodegrance, until we learn whether thou art our friend or our enemy. For just now we are, certes, no such good friends with thee that we care to sit down at thy table and eat of thy salt. Nor may we be aught but enemies of thine until thou hast first satisfied our demands; to wit, that thou givest to me those lands which I demand of thee and that thou givest unto my cousin, Duke Mordaunt of North Umber, the Lady Guinevere to be his wife. In these matters thou hast it in thy power to make us either thy friends or thine enemies. Wherefore we shall abide here, outside of thy castle, for five days, in the which time thou mayst frame thine answer, and so we may know whether we shall be friends or enemies."

"And in the meantime," quoth Duke Mordaunt of North Umber, "I do hold myself ready for to contest my right unto the hand of the Lady Guinevere with any knight of thy Court who hath a mind to deny my just title thereto; and if thou hast no knight in all thy Court who can successfully assay a bout of arms with me, thou thyself canst hardly hope to succeed in defending thyself against that great army of knights whom King Ryence hath gathered together to bring against thee in case thou denyest us that which we ask."

Then was King Leodegrance exceedingly cast down in his spirits, for he feared those proud lords and he wist not what to say in answer to them. Wherefore he turned and walked back into his castle again, beset with great anxiety and sorrow of spirit. And King Ryence, and Duke Mordaunt and their Court of lords and knights pitched their pavilions in those meadows over against the castle, so that the plain was entirely covered with those pavilions. And there they took up their inn with great rejoicing and with the sound of feasting and singing and merry-making, for it was an exceeding noble Court King Ryence had gathered about him.

And when the next morning had come, Duke Mordaunt of North Umber went forth clad all in armor of proof. And he rode up and down the field before the castle and gave great challenge to those within; daring any knight to come forth for to meet him in knightly encounter. "Ho!" he cried, "how now, ye Knights of Cameliard! Is there no one to come forth to meet me? How then may ye hope to contend with the Knights of North Wales, an ye fear to meet with one single

Knight from North Umber?" So he scoffed at them in his pride, and none dared to come forth from Cameliard against him. For the Duke of North Umber was one of the most famous knights of his day, and one of exceeding strength and success at arms, and there was now, in these times of peace, no one of King Leodegrance's Court who was at all able to face a warrior of his approved skill and valor. Wherefore, no one took up that challenge which the Duke of North Umber gave to the Court of Cameliard. Meantime many people gathered upon the walls of Cameliard and gazed down therefrom upon that proud and haughty duke, all bedight in his splendid armor, and all were grieved and ashamed that there was no one in that peaceful town to go out against him. And all the lords and knights of King Ryence's Court came and stood in front of the King's pavilion and laughed and clapped their hands together, and cheered Duke Mordaunt, as he so rode up and down before them. And the greater they were expanded with mirth, the more abashed were the people of Cameliard. "Ho! Ho!" cried that proud Duke. "How now! Will no one come forth to meet me? How then may ye of Cameliard hope to face the King of North Wales and all his knightly array of which I am but one man?" And the people of Cameliard, gathered upon the walls, listened to him with shame and sorrow.

Now all this while King Arthur digged in the garden; but, nevertheless, he was well aware of everything that passed and of how that the Duke of North Umber rode up and down so proudly before the castle walls. So, of a sudden, it came to him that he could not abide this any longer. Wherefore he laid aside his spade and went out secretly by a postern way, and so up into the town.

Now there was in Cameliard an exceedingly rich merchant, by name Ralph of Cardiff, and the renown of his possessions and his high estate had reached even unto King Arthur's ears at Carleon. Accordingly it was unto his house that King Arthur directed his steps.

And while he was in a narrow way, not far from the merchant's house, he took off his magic cap of disguise and assumed somewhat of his noble appearance once more, for he was now of a mind to show his knightliness unto those who looked upon him. Accordingly, when he stood before the rich merchant in his closet, and when the merchant looked up into his face, he wist not what to think to behold so noble a lord clad all in frieze. For though King Arthur was a stranger to the good man, so that he knew not his countenance, yet that merchant wist that he was no ordinary knight, but that he must assuredly be one of high degree and in authority, even though he was clad in frieze.

Then King Arthur opened the breast of his jerkin and showed the merchant the gold collar that hung around his neck. And also he showed beneath the rough coat of frieze how that there was an undergarment of fine purple silk embroidered with gold. And then he showed to the good man his own signet ring, and when the merchant saw it, he knew it to be the ring of the King of Britain. Wherefore, beholding these tokens of high and lordly authority, the merchant arose and stood before the King and doffed his cap.

"Sir Merchant," quoth the King, "know that I am a stranger knight in disguise in this place. Ne'theless, I may tell thee that I am a very good friend to King Leodegrance and wish him exceeding well. Thou art surely aware of how the Duke of North Umber rides continually up and down before the Kings' castle, and challenges anyone within to come forth for to fight against him in behalf of the Lady Guinevere. Now I am of a mind to assay that combat mine own self, and I hope a very great deal that I shall succeed in upholding the honor of Cameliard and of bringing shame upon its enemies.

"Sir Merchant, I know very well that thou hast several suits of noble armor in thy treasury, for the fame of them hath reached unto mine ears though I dwell a considerable distance from this place. Wherefore I desire that thou shalt provide me in the best manner that thou art able to do, so that I may straightway assay a bout of arms with that Duke of North Umber. Moreover, I do pledge thee my knightly word that thou shalt be fully recompensed for the best suit of armor that thou canst let me have, and that in a very little while."

"My Lord," said Master Ralph, "I perceive that thou art no ordinary errant knight, but rather someone of extraordinary estate; wherefore it is a very great pleasure to fulfil all thy behests. But even an thou wert other than thou art, I would be altogether willing to equip thee with armor, seeing that thou hast a mind to ride forth against yonder duke."

Upon this he rang a little silver bell that stood nigh to him, and in answer to its sound several attendants immediately appeared. Into their hands he intrusted the person of the King, bidding them to do him extraordinary honor. Accordingly, certain of those attendants prepared for the King a bath of tepid water perfumed with ambergris, very grateful to the person. And after he was bathed in this bath and was wiped with soft linen towels, other attendants conducted him to a hall all hung with tapestries and 'broideries, and at this place a noble feast had been spread ready for his refreshment. Here that lordly merchant himself ministered to the King's wants, serving him with various meats—very dainty, and of several sorts—and likewise with fine white bread. And he poured him wine of various countries—some as red as ruby, others as yellow as gold; and indeed the King had hardly ever enjoyed a better feast than that which the merchant, Ralph of Cardiff, had thus spread for him.

And after he had entirely refreshed himself with eating, there came six pages richly clad in sarsanet of azure, and these, taking the King to an apartment of great state, they there clad him in a suit of Spanish armor, very cunningly wrought and all inlaid with gold. And the like of that armor was hardly to be found in all of the land. The juppon and the several trappings of the armor were all of satin and as white as milk. And the shield was white, and altogether without emblazonment or device of any sort. Then these attendants conducted the King into the courtyard, and there stood a noble war-horse, as white as milk, and all the trappings of the horse were of milk-white cloth without emblazonment or adornment of any sort; and the bridle and the bridle rein were all studded over with bosses of silver.

Then after the attendants had aided King Arthur to mount this steed, the lordly merchant came forward and gave him many words of good cheer, and so the king bade him adieu and rode away, all shining in white and glittering in fine armor, wherefore he resembled the full moon in harvest season.

And as he drave down the stony streets of the town, the people turned and gazed after him, for he made a very noble appearance as he passed along the narrow way between the houses of the town.

So King Arthur directed his way to the postern gate of the castle, and, having reached that place, he dismounted and tied his horse. Then he straightway entered the garden, and there, finding an attendant, he made demand that he should have present speech with the Lady Guinevere. So the attendant, all amazed at his lordly presence, went and delivered the message, and by and by the Lady Guinevere came, much wondering, and passed along a gallery with several of her damsels, until she had come over above where King Arthur was. And when King Arthur looked up and saw her above him, he loved her exceeding well. And he said to her: "Lady, I have great will to do thee such honor as I am able. For I go forth now to do combat with that Duke of North Umber who rides up and down before this castle. Moreover, I hope and verily believe that I shall encompass his downfall; accordingly, I do beseech of thee some token, such as a lady may give unto a knight for to wear when that knight rides forth to do her honor."

Then the Lady Guinevere said: "Certes, Sir Knight, I would that I knew who thou art. Yet, though I know not, nevertheless I am altogether willing for to take thee for my champion as thou offerest. So, touching that token thou speakest of, if thou wilt tell me what thing it is that thou desirest, I will gladly give it to thee."

"An that be so, Lady," said King Arthur, "I would fain have that necklace that thou wearest about thy throat. For, meseems that if I had that tied about my arm, I would find my valor greatly increased thereby."

"Pardee, Sir Knight," said the Lady, "what thou desirest of me thou shalt assuredly have." Thereupon speaking, she took from her long, smooth neck the necklace of pearls which she wore, and dropped the same down to King Arthur where he stood.

And King Arthur took the necklace and tied it about his arm, and he gave great thanks for it. Then he saluted the Lady Guinevere with very knightly grace, and she saluted him, and then, straightway, he went forth from that place, greatly expanded with joy that the Lady Guinevere had shown him such favor.

Now the report had gone about Cameliard that a knight was to go forth to fight the Duke of North Umber. Wherefore great crowds gathered upon the walls, and King Leodegrance and the Lady Guinevere and all the Court of the King came to that part of the castle walls overlooking the meadow where the Duke of North Umber defended. Wherefore, so great a concourse was presently assembled, that any knight might be encouraged to do his utmost before such a multitude as that which looked down upon the field.

Then of a sudden the portcullis of the castle was lifted, and the bridge let fall, and the White Champion rode forth to that encounter which he had undertaken. And, as he drave across that narrow bridge, the hoofs of his war-horse smote the boards with a noise like to thunder, and when he came out into the sunlight, lo! his armor flamed of a sudden like unto lightning, and when the people saw him they shouted aloud.

Then when the Duke of North Umber beheld a knight all clad in white, he rode straightway to him and spoke to him with words of knightly greeting. "Messire," he said, "I perceive that thou bearest no crest upon thy helm, nor hast thou a device of any sort upon thy shield, wherefore I know not who thou art. Ne'theless, I do believe that thou art a knight of good quality and of approved courage, or else thou wouldst not have thus come to this place."

"Certes, Sir Knight," said King Arthur, "I am of a quality equal to thine own. And as for my courage, I do believe that it hath been approved in as many encounters as even thine own hath been."

"Sir Knight," quoth the Duke of Umber, "thou speakest with a very large spirit. Ne'theless, thou mayst make such prayers as thou art able, for I shall now presently so cast thee down from thy seat, so that thou shalt never rise again; for so have I served better men than ever thou mayst hope to be."

To this King Arthur made answer with great calmness of demeanor: "That shall be according to the will of Heaven, Sir Knight, and not according to thy will."

So each knight saluted the other and rode to his assigned station, and there each dressed his spear and his shield, and made him ready for the encounter. Then a silence fell upon all so great that a man might hear his own heart beat in the stillness. So, for a small space, each knight sat like a statue made of iron. Then, of a sudden, each shouted to his war-horse, and drave spurs into his flank, and launched forth from his station. And so they met in the midst of the course with a noise like unto a violent thunder-clap. And lo! the spear of the Duke of North Umber burst into splinters unto the very truncheon thereof; but the spear of King Arthur broke not, but held, so that the Duke was cast out of his saddle like a windmill—whirling in the air and smiting the earth so that the ground shuddered beneath him. And indeed he rolled full three times over and over ere he ceased to fall.

Then all the people upon the wall shouted with might and main, so that the noise thereof was altogether astonishing; for they had hardly hoped that their champion should have proved so extraordinarily strong and skilful.

Meanwhile, those of King Ryence's Court ran immediately to the Duke of Umber where he lay upon the earth, and they straightway unlaced his helm for to give him air. And first they thought that he was dead, and then they thought that he was like to die; for, behold! he lay without any life or motion. Nor did he recover from that swoon wherein he lay for the space of full two hours and more.

Now whilst the attendants were thus busied about Duke Mordaunt of North Umber, King Arthur sat his horse, very quietly, observing all that they did. Then, perceiving that his enemy was not dead, he turned him about and rode away from that place.

Nor did he return unto Cameliard at that time, for he deemed that he had not yet entirely done with these enemies to the peace of his realm, wherefore he was minded not yet to return the horse and the armor to the merchant, but to keep them for a while for another occasion.

So he bethought him of how, coming to Cameliard, he had passed through an arm of the forest where certain wood-choppers were at work felling the trees. Wherefore, remembering that place, he thought that he would betake him thither and leave his horse and armor in the care of those rude folk until he would need those things once more. So now he rode away into the country-side, leaving behind him the town and the castle and all the noise of shouting and rejoicing; nor did he once so much as turn his head to look back toward that place where he had so violently overthrown his enemy.

And now you shall presently hear of certain pleasant adventures of a very joyous sort that befell him ere he had accomplished all his purposes. For when a man is a king among men, as was King Arthur, then is he of such a calm and equal temper that neither victory nor defeat may cause him to become either unduly exalted in his own opinion or so troubled in spirit as to be altogether cast down into despair. So if you would become like to King Arthur, then you shall take all your triumphs as he took this victory, for you will not be turned aside from your final purposes by the great applause that many men may give you, but you will first finish your work that you have set yourself to perform, ere you give yourself ease to sit you down and to enjoy the fruits of your victory.

Yea, he who is a true king of men, will not say to himself, "Lo! I am worthy to be crowned with laurels;" but rather will he say to himself, "What more is there that I may do to make the world the better because of my endeavors?"

Chapter Third

How King Arthur Encountered Four Knights and of What Befell Thereby.

Now, the day was extraordinarily sweet and pleasant unto one so lusty of frame and so lithe of heart as was good King Arthur. For the bright clouds swam smoothly across the blue sky in prodigious volumes of vapor, and the wind blew across the long grass of the meadow lands, and across the fields of growing wheat, so that a multitude of waves travelled over the hills and valleys like an it were across an entire sea of green. And now all the earth would be darkened with wide shadows from those clouds, and, anon, everything would burst out, of a sudden, into a wonderful radiance of sunlight once more. And the little birds they sang all gayly in the hedge-rows and the leafy thickets as though they would burst their tiny throats with singing, and the cock crowed, strong and lusty, from the farm croft, and all was so blithe and comely that the young King, with the visor of his helmet uplifted to the refreshment of the gentle breeze, would sometimes carol very joyously in his journeying. So travelled King Arthur in all that gay and tender summer season, when the earth was young and the time was of long-gone-by.

Now, you are to remember that when King Arthur had

come from Carleon unto the castle of Tintagalon, he had brought with him four young knights for to bear him company. And those knights aforesaid were as follows: There was Sir Gawaine, the son of King Lot and of Queen Margaise, and there was Sir Ewaine, the son of King Uriens and of Queen Morgana la Fay (and these two were nephews, half in blood, unto the King), and there was Sir Pellias, and there was Sir Geraint, the son of Erbin. These were the four noble young knights who had come with King Arthur from Camelot unto Tintagalon.

Now it befell, as King Arthur rode all gayly in the summer time as aforesaid, that he came to a certain part of the road where he beheld before him a tall and comely tower that stood upon a green hillock immediately by the roadside. And lo! there stood upon the balcony of that tower three fair damoiselles, clad all in green taffeta. And on the high road in front of the castle there was a knight clad all in very fine armor. And the knight sat upon a noble war-horse, and in his hands he held a lute, and he played upon the lute and sang in a voice of extraordinary sweetness. Whiles he sang those three ladies in green taffeta listened to him with great cheerfulness of mien. And whenever that knight would stint his singing, then those three ladies would clap their hands together with great acclaim, and would bid him to sing to them again; and so he would do with great readiness of spirit.

All this King Arthur beheld, and it appeared to him to be a very pleasant sight, wherefore he rejoiced at it exceedingly.

And as he drew nigh, lo! he beheld that the knight who thus sat upon his horse and played upon the lute and sang unto the accompaniment thereof, was none other than Sir Geraint, the son of Erbin. For that knight wore upon his crest the figure of a gryphon, and the device upon his shield was two gryphons rampant facing one another upon a field azure, and King Arthur knew that this was the crest and the device of Sir Geraint. And when the King perceived who was the knight who sat there and sang, he laughed unto himself and straightway closed his visor and made him ready for such encounter as might, perchance, befall. So he drew nigh to where the knight sang and the ladies listened.

Now when Sir Geraint perceived King Arthur approach, he ceased singing and hung up his lute behind him across his shoulder. Then, casting upward his look to those three fair ladies above him, quoth he: "Mesdames, ye have been pleased to listen to that singing which I have assayed altogether in your honor. Now, likewise, in your honor, I will perform a deed of knightly prowess which I very much hope shall bring great glory to you. For, if ye will be pleased to lend me that encouragement which your very great beauty can so easily afford, ye shall behold me, I doubt not, overthrow yonder knight completely, and that to your great credit and renown."

"Sir Knight," said that lady who spoke for the others, "you are, truly, a lord of noble bearing and exceedingly pleasing of address, wherefore we do wish you great success in this undertaking; and we do believe that you will succeed in that which you assay to do."

Upon these Sir Geraint gave those three damoiselles great thanks for their words, and thereupon he closed the visor of his helmet. So, dressing his spear and shield, and saluting those three ladies with great humility of demeanor, he went forth to meet King Arthur where he now sat at a little distance, very quietly and soberly awaiting his pleasure.

Now Sir Geraint knew not King Arthur because he wore no crest upon his helm and no device upon his shield, wherefore as he saluted him he made speech to him in this wise: "Ha! Messire, I know not who thou art, seeing that thou bearest neither crest nor device. Ne'theless, I am minded to do thee such honor as I may in running atilt with thee upon the behalf of those three damoiselles whom thou beholdest yonder upon that balcony. For I do affirm, and am ready to maintain the same with my knightly person, that those ladies are fairer than thy lady, whomsoever she may be."

"Sir Knight," quoth King Arthur, "I will gladly run a course with thee in honor of my lady; for, I may tell thee, she is a princess, and is held by many to be the most beautiful dame in all of the world. But I will only contend with thee upon one condition, and the condition is this—that he who is overthrown shall yield himself as servant unto the other for seven days, and in that time he shall do all that may be required of him."

"I will accept thy gage, Sir Unknown Knight," quoth Sir Geraint, "and when I have overthrown thee, I will yield thee unto those fair ladies yonder for to be their servant for seven days. And I do tell thee that there are a great many knights who would certainly regard that as being both a pleasant and an honorable task."

"And should I so chance as to overthrow thee," said King Arthur, "I will send thee for to serve my lady for that same period of time, and that will be even a pleasanter and a more honorable task than that which thou hast a mind for me to perform."

So each knight saluted the other, and thereupon each took such a stand as should cast the encounter immediately beneath where those three fair damoiselles looked down from the balcony. Then each knight dressed his spear and his shield, and, having made ready for the encounter, each sat for a small space entirely prepared. Then each shouted to his war-horse, and drave spur into its flank, and launched forth with wonderful speed to the assault. So they met in the very midst of the course with a force so vehement that the noise thereof was wonderfully appalling for to hear. And each knight smote the other in the very centre of his defences. And, lo! the spear of Sir Geraint burst into small pieces, even to the truncheon thereof; but the spear of King Arthur held, and Sir Geraint was cast so violently backward that both he and his horse were overthrown into the dust with a tumult like to a monstrous roaring of thunder.

And when Sir Geraint had recovered his footing, he was, for a while, so astonished that he wist not where he stood, for never had he been so overthrown in all of his life before. Then, coming quickly unto himself again, he straightway drew forth his sword and called upon King Arthur with exceeding vehemence for to come down from out of his saddle, and to fight him afoot.

"Nay, not so, Sir Knight," said King Arthur, "I will not have to do with thee in that way. Moreover, thou art not to forget that thou hast promised to give thyself unto me as my servant for seven days, for, assuredly, I have entirely overcome thee in this encounter, and now thou art pledged unto me."

Then Sir Geraint knew not what to say, being altogether abashed with shame and vexation at his overthrow. Ne'theless, he perceived that he must uphold his knightly word unto that which he had pledged himself to do; wherefore, he put up his sword again, though with exceeding discontent. "Sir Knight," said he, "I do acknowledge myself to have been overcome in this encounter, wherefore I yield myself now unto thy commands, according to my plighted word."

"Then I do place my commands upon thee in this wise," quoth King Arthur. "My command is, that thou goest straightway unto the Lady Guinevere at Cameliard, and that thou tellest her that thou hast been overthrown by that knight to whom she gave her necklace as a token. Moreover, I do desire that thou shalt obey her in everything that she may command thee to do, and that for the space of seven days to come."

"Sir Knight," quoth Sir Geraint, "that which thou biddest me to do, I will perform according to thy commands."

Thereupon he mounted his horse and went his way. And King Arthur went his way. And those three ladies who stood upon the balcony of the castle were exceedingly glad that they had beheld so noble an assay-at-arms as that which they had looked down upon.

Now, after King Arthur had travelled forward for the distance of two or three leagues or more, he came to a certain place of moorlands, where were many ditches of water, and where the heron and the marsh-hen sought harborage in the sedge. And here, at sundry points, were several windmills, with their sails all turning slowly in the sunlight before a wind which blew across the level plains of ooze. And at this place there was a long, straight causeway, with two long rows of pollard willows, one upon either hand. Now, when he had come nigh the middle of this causeway, King Arthur perceived two knights, who sat their horses in the shade of a great wind-mill that stood upon one side of the roadway. And a large shadow of the sails moved ever and anon across the roadway as the wheel of the mill turned slowly afore the wind. And all about the mill, and everywhere about, were great quantities of swallows that darted hither and thither like bees about a hive in midsummer. And King Arthur saw that those two knights, as they sat in the shadow of the mill, were eating of a great loaf of rye bread, fresh baked and of brittle crust; and they ate fair white cheese, which things the miller, all white with dust, served to them. But when these two knights perceived King Arthur, they immediately ceased eating that bread and cheese, and straightway closed their helmets. As for the miller, when he saw them thus prepare themselves, he went quickly back into the mill and shut the door thereof, and then went and looked out of a window which was over above where the knights were standing.

But King Arthur made very merry unto himself when he perceived that those two knights were Sir Gawaine and Sir Ewaine. For he knew that the one was Sir Gawaine because that the crest of his helmet was a leopard rampant, and because he bore upon his shield the device of a leopard rampant upon a field gules; and he knew that the other was Sir Ewaine, because he bore upon his crest an unicorn, and because the device upon his shield was that of a lady holding a naked sword in her hand, which same was upon a field or. Accordingly, whiles he was yet at some distance, King Arthur closed his helmet so that those two young knights might not know who he was.

So, when he had come anear to the two knights, Sir Gawaine rode forward for a little distance for to meet him. "Sir Knight," quoth he, "thou must know that this is soothly parlous ground whereon thou hast ventured; for there is no byway hence across the morass, and thou mayst not go forward without trying a tilt with me."

"Sir Knight," said King Arthur, "and I am very willing to run a tilt with thee. Ne'theless, I will only encounter thee upon one condition, and that is this: that he who is overthrown shall serve the other entirely for the space of seven full days."

"I do accept thy gage, "Sir Knight," quoth Sir Gawaine. For he said unto himself, "Of a surety, so exceedingly strong and skilful a knight as I shall easily encompass the overthrow of this unknown knight."

So each knight immediately took his appointed station, and having dressed his spear and his shield, and having fully prepared himself in every manner, and having rested for a little space, each suddenly shouted to his horse, and drave spur into the flanks thereof, and so rushed to the encounter. And each knight smote the other in the midst of his defence, and lo! the spear of Sir Gawaine burst into fragments. But the spear of King Arthur held, so that Sir Gawaine was lifted entirely out of his saddle and over the crupper of his horse. And indeed he fell with wonderful violence into the dust. Nor could he immediately rise from that fall, but lay all bedazed for a little while. And when he did arise, he perceived that the white knight who had overthrown him sat nigh to him upon his horse.

Then King Arthur spake and said: "Sir Knight, I have altogether overthrown thee, and so thou must now serve me according to thy knightly word."

Then up spake Sir Ewaine, who sat nearby upon his horse. "Not so, Sir Knight," he said; "not so, nor until thou hast had to do with me. For I do make demand of thee that thou shalt straightway joust with me. And if I overthrow thee I will claim of thee that thou shalt release my cousin from that servitude unto which he hath pledged himself. But if thou overthrowst me, then will I serve thee even as he hath pledged himself to serve thee."

"Sir Knight," said King Arthur, "I do accept thy gage with all readiness of spirit!"

So each knight took his assigned place and dressed himself for the encounter. Then they shouted, and drave together, rushing the one upon the other like unto two rams upon the hillside. And the spear of Sir Ewaine was also shivered into pieces. But King Arthur's spear held, so that the girths of Sir Ewaine's saddle were burst apart, and both the saddle and the knight were swept off the horse's back with such violence that a tower falling could not have made a greater noise than did Sir Ewaine when he smote the dust of that causeway.

Then Sir Ewaine arose to his feet and gazed upon him, all filled with entire amazement. To him came King Arthur, and bespake him thus: "Ha, Sir Knight, meseems that thou hast been fairly overcome this day. And so, according to your promises, both thou and yonder other knight must fulfil all my commands for the space of full seven days to come. Now this is the command that I set upon ye both: that ye shall straightway go unto the Lady Guinevere at Cameliard and shall take her greeting from her knight. And ye shall say to her that her knight unto whom she gave her necklace, hath sent ye, who are King's sons, for to do obedience unto her. And all that she shall command ye to do in the space of these seven days that are to come, that shall ye perform even unto the smallest grain."

"Sir Knight," said Sir Gawaine, "so we will do according to thy commands, having pledged ourselves thereunto. But when these seven days are passed, I do make my vow that I shall seek thee out and shall carry this combat unto its entire extremity. For it may happen to any knight to be unhorsed as I have been, yet I do believe that I may have a better success with thee an I battle with thee to the extremity of my endeavor."

"Sir Knight," said King Arthur, "it shall be even as thou desirest. Yet I do verily believe that when these seven days are passed thou wilt not have such a great desire for to fight with me as thou now hast."

Having so spoken, King Arthur saluted those two knights and they saluted him. And then he turned his horse and went his way. And whenever he bethought him of how those two good knights had fallen before his assault, and when he thought of how astonished and abashed they had been at their overthrow, he laughed aloud for pure mirth, and vowed unto himself that he had never in all of his life engaged in so joyous an adventure as this.

So when Sir Ewaine had mended the girths of his saddle then he and Sir Gawaine mounted their horses and betook their way toward Cameliard much cast down in spirits.

Then the miller came forth from the mill once more, greatly rejoiced at having beheld such a wonderfully knightly encounter from so safe a place as that from which he had beheld it.

And so King Arthur rode onward with great content of mind until the slanting of the afternoon had come, and by that time he had come nigh to that arm of the forest-land which he had in mind as the proper place where he might leave his horse and his armor.

Now as he drew nigh to this part of the forest skirts, he perceived before him at the roadside a gnarled and stunted oak-tree. And he perceived that upon the oak-tree there hung a shield, and that underneath the shield were written these words in fair large letters:

> "Whoso smiteth upon this shield
> Doeth so at the peril of his body."

Then King Arthur was filled with a great spirit, and, uplifting his spear, he smote upon that shield so that it rang like thunder.

Then immediately King Arthur heard a voice issue out of the forest crying, "Who hath dared to assail my shield!" And straightway there came out thence a knight of large frame, riding upon a horse white, like that which King Arthur himself rode. And the trappings of the horse and of the knight were all white like unto the trappings of King Arthur and his horse. And the knight bore upon his helmet as his crest a swan with outspread wings, and upon his shield he bore the emblazonment of three swans upon a field argent. And because of the crest and the emblazonment of the shield, King Arthur knew that this knight was Sir Pellias, who had come with him from Camelot to Tintagalon.

So when Sir Pellias had come nigh to where King Arthur waited for him, he drew rein and bespake him with great sternness of voice: "Ho! Ho! Sir Knight," quoted he. "Why didst thou dare to smite upon my shield! Verily, that blow shall bring thee great peril and dole. Now, prepare to defend thyself straightway because of what thou hast done."

"Stay! Stay! Sir Knight," said King Arthur, "it shall be as thou wouldst have it; and I will do combat with thee. Yet will I not assay this adventure until thou hast agreed that the knight who is overcome in the encounter shall serve the other in whatsoever manner that other may desire, for the space of one se'night from this time."

"Sir Knight," said Sir Pellias, "I do accept that risk, wherefore I bid thee now presently to prepare thyself for the encounter."

Thereupon each knight took his station and dressed his spear and shield. And when they had prepared themselves, they immediately launched together with a violence like to two stones cast from a catapult. So they met in the midst of the course, and again King Arthur was entirely successful in that assault which he made. For the spear of Sir Pellias burst to pieces, and the spear of King Arthur held; and Sir Pellias was cast with passing violence out of his saddle for the distance of more than half a spear's length behind the crupper of his horse. Nor did he altogether recover from that fall for a long time, so that King Arthur had to wait beside him for a considerable while ere he was able to lift himself up from the ground whereon he lay.

"Ha! Sir Knight," said King Arthur, "assuredly it hath not gone well with thee this day, for thou hast been entirely overthrown and now thou must straightway redeem thy pledge to serve me for seven days hereafter. Wherefore, I now set it upon thee as my command, that thou shalt go straightway unto Cameliard, and that thou shalt greet the Lady Guinevere from me, telling her that her knight unto whom she gave her necklace hath been successful in battle with thee. Likewise I set it upon thee that thou shalt obey her for the space of seven days in whatsoever she may command thee to do."

"Sir Knight," said Sir Pellias, "it shall even be as thou dost ordain. Yet I would that I knew who thou art, for I do declare that I have never yet in all my life been overthrown as thou hast overthrown me. And, indeed, I think that there are very few men in the world who could serve me as thou hast served me."

"Sir Knight," said King Arthur, "some time thou shalt know who I am. But, as yet, I am bound to entire secrecy."

Thereupon he saluted Sir Pellias and turned and entered the forest and was gone.

And Sir Pellias mounted his horse and betook him to Cameliard, much cast down and disturbed in spirit, yet much marvelling who that knight could be who had served him as he had been served.

So that day there came to Cameliard, first Sir Geraint and then Sir Gawaine and Sir Ewaine, and last of all there came Sir Pellias. And when these four beheld one another they were all abashed so that one scarce dared to look the other in the face.

And when they came before the Lady Guinevere and made their condition known to her, and told her how that knight who wore her necklace had overthrown them all and had sent them thither to serve her for a se'night, and when she reckoned how great and famous were those four knights in deeds of chivalry, she was exceedingly exalted that her knight should have approved himself so great in those deeds of arms which he had undertaken to perform. But she greatly marvelled who that champion could be, and debated those things in her own mind. For it was a thing altogether unheard of that one knight, in one day, and with a single spear, should have overthrown five such well proved and famous knights as Duke Mordaunt of North Umber, Sir Geraint, Sir Gawaine, Sir Ewaine, and Sir Pellias. So she gave herself great joy that she had bestowed the gift of her necklace upon so worthy a knight, and she was exceedingly uplifted with extraordinary pleasure at the thought of the credit he had endowed her withal.

Now after King Arthur had entered the forest, he came by and by to where those wood-choppers, afore spoken of, plied their craft. And he abided with them for that night; and when the next morning had come, he intrusted them with his horse and armor, charging them to guard those things with all care, and that they should be wonderfully rewarded therefor. Then he took his departure from that place with intent to return unto Cameliard. And he was clad in that jerkin of frieze which he had worn ever since he had left Tintagalon.

And when he had reached the outskirts of the forest, he set his cap of disguise upon his head and so resumed his mean appearance once more. So, his knightliness being entirely hidden, he returned to Cameliard for to be gardener's boy as he had been before.

Chapter Fourth

How the Four Knights Served the Lady Guinevere.

Now, when King Arthur returned to Cameliard once more (which fell upon the afternoon of a second day), he found the gardener waiting for him, exceedingly filled with wrath. And the gardener had a long birchen rod which he had fetched thither for to punish his boy withal, when that he should have returned to the garden again. So when he saw King Arthur he said: "Thou knave! wherefore didst thou quit thy work to go a-gadding?" And King Arthur laughed and said: "Touch me not." At this, the gardener waxed so exceeding wroth, that he catched the King by the collar of his jerkin with intent to beat him, saying: "Dost thou laugh at me, knave, and make a mock at me? Now I will beat thee well for the offence thou hast committed."

Then, when King Arthur felt that man's hand laid upon him, and when he heard the words that the gardener spake in his wrath, his royal spirit waxed very big within him and he cried out: "Ha, wretch! wouldst thou dare to lay thy hands upon my sacred person?" So saying, he seized the gardener by the wrists, and took the rod straight away from him, and struck him with it across the shoulders. And when that poor knave

felt himself thus in the powerful grasp of the angry King, and
when he felt the rod upon his shoulders, he straightway lifted
up a great outcry, albeit the blow hurt him not a whit. "Now
get thee gone!" quoth King Arthur, "and trouble me no more;
else will I serve thee in a way that will not at all belike thee."
Herewith he loosed that poor man and let him go; and the
gardener was so bemazed with terror, that both the earth and
the sky swam before him. For King Arthur's eyes had flashed
upon him like lightning, and those two hands had held his
wrists with wonderful power. Wherefore, when the King let
him go he gat him away as quickly as might be, all trembling
and sweating with a great fear.

So he went straight to the Lady Guinevere and complained
to her of the manner in which he had been treated. "Lady,"
quoth he, weeping with the memory of his terror, "my boy
goeth away for a day or more, I know not whither; and when I
would whip him for quitting his work he taketh the rod
straight away from me and beateth me with it. Wherefore,
now, I prithee, deal with him as is fitting, and let several strong
men drive him away from this place with rods."

Then the Lady Guinevere laughed. "Let be!" she said, "and
meddle with him no more; for, indeed, he appeareth to be a
very saucy fellow. As for thee! take thou no heed of his coming or his going, and haply I will deal with him in such a way as
shall be fitting."

Whereupon the gardener went his way, greatly marvelling
that the Lady Guinevere should be so mild in dealing with that
toward knave. And the Lady Guinevere went her way, very
merry. For she began to bethink her that there was soothly
some excellent reason why it should happen that when the
White Champion, who did such wonderful deeds, should come
thither, then that gardener's boy should go; and that when that
same Champion should go, then the gardener's boy should
come thitherward again. Wherefore she suspected many
things, and was wonderfully merry and cheerful of spirit.

Now, that day, in the afternoon, the Lady Guinevere
chanced to walk in the garden with her damsels, and with her
walked those four noble knights who had been sent thither by
her White Champion, to wit, Sir Gawaine, Sir Ewaine, Sir

Geraint, and Sir Pellias. And the gardener's lad was digging in the gardens; and as they passed by where he was the Lady Guinevere laughed aloud and cried out: "Look! Look! Messires and Ladies! Yonder is a very saucy fellow for to be a gardener's lad, for he continually weareth his cap, even when he standeth in the presence of lords and ladies."

Then Sir Gawaine up and spake, saying: "Is it even so? Now will I straightway go to yonder knave, and will take his hat off for him, and that in a way so greatly to his misliking, that I do not believe that he will ever offend by wearing it in our presence again."

At this the Lady Guinevere laughed a very great deal. "Let be!" she said, "let be! Sir Gawaine! it would ill beseem one so gentle as thou art to have to do with yonder saucy fellow. Moreover, he doth assure us all that he hath an ugly place upon his head, wherefore let him wear his cap in God's mercy."

Thus the Lady Guinevere, though she suspected a very great deal, was yet pleased to make a mock of him whom she suspected.

Now that day Duke Mordaunt of North Umber had entirely recovered from those sore hurts that he had suffered from his overthrow at the hands of the White Champion. Wherefore, the next morning having come, he appeared again before the castle as he had appeared aforetime—clad all in complete armor. So this time there rode before him two heralds, and when the duke and the two heralds had come to that part of the meadows that lay immediately before the castle of Cameliard, the heralds blew their trumpets exceedingly loud. So at the sound of the trumpets many people came and gathered upon the walls; and King Leodegrance came, and took stand upon a lesser tower that looked down upon the plain where were the Duke of North Umber and the two heralds. Then the Duke of North Umber lifted up his eyes and beheld King Leodegrance where he stood over above him upon the top of that tower, and he cried out in a loud voice: "What ho! King Leodegrance! Thou shalt not think because I suffered a fall from my horse through the mischance of an assault at arms, that thou art therefore quit of me. Yet, ne'theless, I do now make this fair proffer unto thee. To-morrow day I shall appear before this castle with six knights-companion. Now if thou hast any seven knights who are able to stand against me and my companions in an assault at arms—whether with spears or swords, or ahorse or afoot—then shall I engage myself for to give over all pretence whatsoever unto the hand of the Lady Guinevere. But if thou canst not provide such champions to contend successfully against me and my knights-companion, then shall I not only lay claim to Lady Guinevere, but I shall likewise seize upon and shall hold for mine own, three certain castles of thine that stand upon the borders of North Umber. And, likewise, I shall seize upon and shall hold for mine own all the lands and glebes appertaining unto those same castles. Moreover, this challenge of mine shall hold only until to-morrow at set of sun; after the which time it shall be null and void. Wherefore, King Leo-degrance, thou hadst best look to it straightway to provide thee with such champions as may defend thee from these demands aforesaid."

Hereupon those two heralds blew their trumpets once more, and Duke Mordaunt of North Umber turned his horse about and went away from that place. Then King Leodegrance also went his way, very sorrowful and downcast in his spirits. For he said to himself: "Is it at all likely that another champion shall come unto me like that wonderful White Champion who came two days since, I know not whence, for to defend me against mine enemies? And, touching that same White Champion; if I know not whence he came, so also I know not whither he hath departed; how then shall I know where to seek him to beseech his further aid in this time of mine extremity?" Wherefore he went his way, very sorrowful, and wist not what he was to do for to defend himself. So being thus exceedingly troubled in his spirit, he went straight unto his own room, and there shut himself therein; nor would he see any man nor speak unto anyone, but gave himself over entirely unto sorrow and despair.

Now in this extremity the Lady Guinevere bethought her of those four knights who had been pledged for to serve her for seven days. So she went unto them where they were and she bespoke them in this wise: "Messires, ye have been sent hither pledged for to serve me for seven days. Now I do ordain it of thee that you will take this challenge of Duke Mordaunt upon you at my behest, and I do much desire that you go forth to-morrow day for to meet this Duke of North Umber and his knights-companion in battle. For ye are terribly powerful knights, and I do believe you may easily defend us against our enemies."

But Sir Gawaine said, "Not so, Lady; not so! For though we are pledged unto thy service, yet are we not pledged unto the service of King Leodegrance, thy father. Nor have we quarrel of any sort with this Duke of North Umber, nor with his six knights-companion. For we are knights of King Arthur, his Court, nor may we, except at his command, take any foreign quarrel upon us in the service of another king."

Then was the Lady Guinevere exceedingly angry, wherefore she said with great heat: "Either thou art a wonderfully faithful lord unto thy King, Sir Gawaine, or else thou fearest to meet this Duke of North Umber and his knights-companion."

And at this speech of the Lady Guinevere's, Sir Gawaine was also exceedingly wroth, wherefore he made reply: "An thou wert a knight and not a lady, Dame Guinevere, thou wouldst think three or four time ere thou wouldst find courage to speak those words unto me." Whereupon he arose and went out from that place with a countenance all inflamed with wrath. And the Lady Guinevere went away also from that place and to her bower, where she wept a very great deal, both from sorrow and from anger.

Now all this while King Arthur had been very well aware of everything that passed; wherefore he by and by arose and went out and found the gardener. And he took the gardener strongly by the collar of his coat and held him where he was. And he said to him: "Sirrah! I have a command to set upon thee, and thou shalt perform that command to the letter, else, an thou perform it not, a very great deal of pain may befall thee." Herewith speaking, he thrust his hand into the bosom of his jerkin and brought forth thence that necklace of pearls which the Lady Guinevere had given him from about her neck. And he said further unto the gardener: "Thou shalt take this necklace to the Lady Guinevere and thou shalt say to her thus: that she is to send me forthwith bread and meat and wine and comfits from her own table. And thou shalt say unto her that I desire her to summon those four knights—to wit, Sir Gawaine, Sir Ewaine, Sir Geraint, and Sir Pellias—and that she is to bid those four for to come and serve me with those things for my refreshment. And thou art to say unto her that she is to lay her commands upon those knights that they are further to serve me according as I may command, and that they are henceforth to be my servants and not her servants. And these are the commands that I lay upon thee; that thou art to say these things unto the Lady Guinevere."

Now when the gardener heard those words he was so astonished that he wist not what to think, for he deemed that the gardener's lad had gone altogether mad. Wherefore he lifted up his voice and cried aloud, "How now! What is this thou sayest! Verily, should I do such a thing as this thou bidst me to do, either it will cost me my life or else it will cost thee thy life. For who would dare for to say such words unto the Lady Guinevere?"

But King Arthur said: "Ne'theless, thou shalt surely do as I command thee, sirrha. For if thou disobey in one single point, then I do assure thee it will go exceedingly ill with thee. For I have it in my power for to make thee suffer as thou hast never suffered before."

And upon this the gardener said, "I will go." For he said unto himself, "If I do as this fellow biddeth me, then will the Lady Guinevere have him punished in great measure, and so I shall be revenged upon him for what he did unto me yesterday. Moreover, it irks me exceedingly that I should have a lad for to work in the garden who behaves as this fellow does. Wherefore," he said, "I will go." So he took that necklace of pearls that King Arthur gave him, and he went forth and, after a while, he found the Lady Guinevere where she was. And when he had found her, he bespoke her in this wise:

"Lady, my garden boy hath assuredly gone entirely mad. For, under the threat of certain great harm he would do unto me an I performed not his errand, he hath sent me to offer a very grievous affront unto thee. For he hath sent me with this string of large beads for to give to thee; and he bids me to tell thee that thou art to send to him bread and meat and sweetmeats

and wine, such as thou usest at thine own table; and he bids me
to tell thee that these things are to be served to him by the four
noble knights who came hither the day before yesterday.   And
he saith that thou art to command those same knights that they
are to obey him in whatsoever he may command, for that they
are henceforth to be his servants and not thine.   And, indeed,
Lady, he would listen to naught that I might say to him
contrariwise, but he hath threatened me with dire injury an I
came not hither and delivered this message unto thee."

Now when the Lady Guinevere heard what the gardener
said, and when she beheld the necklace which she had given
unto that White Champion, and when she wist that the White
Champion and the gardener's boy were indeed one, she was
uplifted with an exceeding joy; wherefore she knew not
whether to laugh or whether to weep for that pure joy.   So she
arose and took the necklace of pearls, and she bade the gardener
for to come with her.   Then she went forth until she found
those four knights, and when she had found them she spake
unto them thus:

"My lords, awhile sin when I commanded you for to take
my quarrel with Duke Mordaunt of North Umber upon you
for my sake, ye would not do so.   And thou, my lord Gawaine,
didst speak such angry words as are not fitting that one who
serveth should speak unto his mistress, far less that a knight
should speak unto the daughter of a king.   Accordingly I have
it in my mind that ye shall perform a certain thing by way of
a penance, which, an ye refuse to do, I will know very well that
ye do not intend to fulfil that word which ye plighted to my
knight when he overthrew you all four in fair combat.   Now
my command is this: that ye take certain food prepared for my
table—meats and white bread and sweetmeats and wine—and
that ye take that food unto my gardener's boy, whose cap, Sir
Gawaine, thou didst threaten so valorously for to take away
from him this very morning.   And ye four are to serve the food
unto him as though he were a royal knight.   And when ye have
so served him, ye are to obey him in whatsoever he may ordain.
And this I put upon ye as a penalty because ye took not my
quarrel upon ye as true knights should, for hereafter ye are to
be servants unto that gardener's boy and not unto me.   Where-

fore ye are now to go unto the buttery of the castle, and
ye are to bid the sewer for to give you meats such as are served
upon mine own table. And the food ye are to serve upon silver
plates, and the wine ye are to serve in silver cups and goblets.
And ye are to minister unto that gardener's boy as though he
were a great lord of exceeding fame and renown."

Thus spake the Lady Guinevere, and when she had spoken,
she turned and left those four knights, and she took with her
the gardener, who was so astonished at that which he had heard,
that he wist not whether he had gone mad or whether the Lady
Guinevere had gone mad. And the Lady Guinevere bade the
gardener to go to the gardener's boy and to tell him that all
things should be fulfilled according to his commands. And so
the gardener did as he was told.

Now turn we to those four knights whom the Lady
Guinevere had left. For they were bemazed and abashed at the
singular commands she had set upon them. And when they
recovered from their amazement, they were inflamed with
exceeding indignation that, for the time, they wist not whether
that which they saw with their eyes was the light of day, or
whether it was altogether darkness. Nor could one of them
look at another in the face, so overcome were they with shame
at the affront that had been put upon them. Then up and spake
Sir Gawaine, and his voice so trembled with his exceeding
anger that he could scarce contain it for to speak his words.
"Messires," quoth he, "do ye not see how that this lady hath
wantonly put a great affront upon us because we would not do
that which she this morning bade us to do, and because we
would not take up her quarrel against the Duke of North
Umber? Now we will indeed serve this gardener's boy even as
she hath ordained. For we will serve him with meat and drink
as she hath commanded; and we will render our service unto
him as she hath bidden us to do. But observe ye; we are no
longer her servants, but we are his servants; wherefore we may
serve him as we choose for to do. So, when we have fulfilled
her commands and have served him with meat and drink, and
when we have obeyed all the behests he layeth upon us; then do
I make my vow that I, with mine own hand, shall slay that
gardener's boy. And when I have slain him, I will put his

head into a bag, and I will send that bag unto the Lady Guinevere by the meanest carrier whom I can find for that purpose. And so this proud lady shall receive an affront as great as that affront which she hath put upon us." And they all said that that which Sir Gawaine had planned should be exactly as he had said.

So those four lords went unto the sewer of the castle, and they asked for the best of that food which was to be served unto the Lady Guinevere—meats and bread and sweetmeats and wine. Then they took them silver plates and platters and they placed the food upon them; and they took silver cups and silver goblets and they poured the wine into them; and they went forth with these things. And when they had come back of the castle nigh to the stables, they found the gardener's boy, and they bade him sit down and eat and to drink. And they waited upon him as though he had been some great lord. And not one of those four knights wist who he was, nor that he was the great King whose servant they, soothly, were. For he wore his cap of disguise upon his head, wherefore they deemed him to be only a poor peasant fellow.

Now when Sir Ewaine beheld that he still wore his cap before them, he spake unto him with great indignation, saying: "Ha, villain! Wouldst thou wear thy cap even in the presence of great princes and lords such as we be?"

Unto this Sir Gawaine said, "Let be, it matters not." And then he said very bitterly unto the gardener's boy: "Eat thou well, sirrah! For thou shalt hardly eat another meal of food upon this earth."

To this the gardener's boy made reply: "Sir Knight, that, haply, shall lie unto another will than thine for to determine. For maybe, I shall eat many other meals than this. And, maybe, ye shall serve at them as ye are serving me now." And those four lords were astonished beyond measure that he should bespeak them thus so calmly and without any appearance of fear.

Then, after he had eaten, the gardener's boy said unto those knights, "Behold, Messires, I have had enough and am done; and now I have other commands for you to fulfil. And my next command is that ye shall make ready straightway to go abroad with me, and to that end ye shall clothe yourselves with complete armor. And thou, Sir Gawaine, shalt go to the head stable-keeper of this castle, and thou shalt demand of him that he shall make ready the Lady Guinevere's palfrey so that I may straightway ride forth upon it. And when ye are all encased in your armor, and when everything is duly appointed according to my command, ye shall bring that palfrey unto the postern gate of the castle, and there I shall meet ye for to ride forth with you."

And Sir Gawaine said: "It shall be done in every way according as thou dost command. But when we ride forth from this castle it shall be a sorry journey for thee."

And the gardener's boy said: "I think not so, Sir Gawaine."

Then those four went away and did according as the gardener's boy commanded. And when they had made themselves ready in full array of armor, and when they had obtained the Lady Guinevere's palfrey, they went unto the postern gate and there the gardener's boy met them. And when he saw that they sat their horses and that they moved not at his coming, he said: "Ha, Messires! would ye so entreat him whom ye have been ordained to serve? Now I do bid ye, Sir Gawaine and Sir Ewaine, for to come down and to hold my stirrup for me; and I bid ye, Sir Geraint and Sir Pellias, for to come down and to hold my palfrey for me whiles I mount."

Then those four noble knights did as they were commanded. And Sir Gawaine said: "Thou mayst command as thou dost list, and I do bid thee to make the most of it whiles thou mayst do so; for thou shalt have but a little while longer for to enjoy the great honor that hath fallen upon thee. For that honor which hath fallen upon thee—lo! it shall presently crush thee unto death."

And the gardener's boy said: "Not so; I believe I shall not die yet whiles." And again those four lords were greatly astonished at the calmness of his demeanor.

And so they rode forth from that place; and the gardener's boy would not permit that they should ride either before him or beside him, but he commanded them that they should ride behind him whiles they were still servants unto him.

So they rode as he assigned them for a considerable way.

Then after they had gone forward a great distance, they drew nigh to a gloomy and dismal woodland that lay entirely beyond the country coadjacent to Cameliard. Then, when they had come nigh unto this woodland, Sir Gawaine rode a little forward, and he said: "Sir Gardener's Boy, seest thou yonder woodland? Now when we come into it thou shalt immediately die, and that by a sword that hath never yet been touched by any but noble or knightly blood."

And King Arthur turned him about in his saddle, and he said: "Ha! Sir Gawaine! Wouldst thou ride forward thus when I bid thee to ride behind me?"

And as he spake he took the cap from off his head, and, lo! they all beheld that it was King Arthur who rode with them.

Then a great silence of pure astonishment fell upon them all, and each man sat as though he were turned into an image of stone. And it was King Arthur who first spake. And he said: "Ha! how now, Sir Knights? Have ye no words of greeting for to pay to me? Certes, ye have served me with a very ill grace this day. Moreover, ye have threatened to slay me; and now, when I speak to you, ye say naught in reply."

Then those four knights immediately cried out aloud; and they leaped down from off their horses, and they kneeled down into the dust of the road. And when King Arthur beheld them kneeling there, he laughed with great joyfulness of spirit, and he bade them for to mount their horses again, for the time was passing by when there was much to do.

So they mounted their horses and rode away, and as they journeyed forward the King told them all that had befallen him, so that they were greatly amazed, and gave much acclaim unto the knightliness with which he had borne himself in those excellent adventures through which he had passed. And they rejoiced greatly that they had a king for to rule over them who was possessed of such a high and knightly spirit.

So they rode to that arm of the forest where King Arthur had left his horse and his armor.

Chapter Fifth

How King Arthur Overcame the Enemies of King Leodegrance, and How His Royalty Was Proclaimed.

Now, when the next day had come, the Duke of North Umber and six knights-companion appeared upon the field in front of the castle of Cameliard as he had duly declared that he and they would do. And those seven champions appeared in very great estate; for in front of them there rode seven heralds with trumpets and tabards, and behind them there rode seven esquires, each esquire bearing the spear, the shield, the crest, and the banneret of the knight who was his lord and master. And the seven heralds blew their trumpets so exceedingly loud that the sound thereof penetrated unto the utmost parts of Cameliard, so that the people came running from everywhere. And while the heralds blew their trumpets the seven esquires shouted, and waved the spears and the bannerets. So those seven knights rode in such proud estate that those who looked upon them had hardly ever beheld such a splendid presentment of chivalry.

So they paraded up and down that field three times for its entire length, and, meantime, a great crowd of people, called thither by the blowing of the herald's trumpets, stood upon the walls and gazed therefrom at that noble spectacle. And all the

Court of King Ryence came, and stood upon the plain in front of the King's pavilion, and they shouted and cheered the Duke of North Umber and his six knights-companion.

Meanwhile, King Leodegrance of Cameliard was so cast down with trouble and shame that he did not choose to show his face, but hid himself away from all his Court. Nor would he permit anyone for to come into his presence.

Nevertheless, the Lady Guinevere, with sundry of her damsels, went unto the King's closet where he was, and knocked upon the door thereof, and when the King denied her to come in to him, she spake to him through the door, giving him words of good cheer, saying: "My lord King and father, I prithee for to look up and to take good cheer unto thyself. For I do assure thee that there is one who hath our cause in his hands, and that one is, certes, a very glorious champion. And he shall assuredly come by and by ere this day is done, and when he cometh, he shall certainly overthrow our enemies."

But King Leodegrance opened not the door, but he said: "My daughter, that which thou sayest thou sayest for to comfort me. For there is no other help for me in this time of trouble only God, His good strong help and grace." And she said: "Nay, I say that which is the truth; and the help that God shall send unto thee he shall certainly send through a worthy champion who at this moment hath our cause in his hand."

So spake the Lady Guinevere, so that whilst King Leodegrance came not forth, yet he was greatly comforted at that which she said to him.

Thus passed all that morning and a part of the afternoon, and yet no one appeared for to take up that challenge which the seven knights had declared. But, whilst the sun was yet three or four hours high, there suddenly appeared at a great distance a cloud of dust. And in that cloud of dust there presently appeared five knights, riding at great speed, thitherward. And when these had come nigh unto the walls, lo! the people beheld that he who rode foremost of all was that same White Champion who had aforetime overthrown the Duke of North Umber. Moreover, they perceived that the four knights who rode with that White Champion were very famous knights and of great prowess and glory of arms. For the one was Sir

Gawaine, and the other was Sir Ewaine, and the other was Sir Geraint, and the other was Sir Pellias. For the people of the castle and the town knew those four knights, because they had dwelt for two days at Cameliard, and they were of such exceeding renown that folk crowded from far and near for to look upon them whensoever they appeared.

So when the people upon the walls beheld who those knights were, and when they perceived that White Champion who had aforetime brought them such exceeding honor, they shouted aloud for the second time with a voice mightier than that with which they had the first time shouted.

Now King Leodegrance heard the people shouting, where-upon hope awoke of a sudden within him. So he straightway came forth with all speed for to see what was ado, and there he beheld those five noble champions about to enter into the field.

And the Lady Guinevere also heard the shouting and she came forth likewise and, behold! there was that White Champion and those four other knights. So when she beheld that White Knight and his four companions-at-arms, her heart was like to break within her for pure joy and gladness, wherefore she wept for the passion thereof, and laughed the whiles she wept. And she waved her kerchief unto those five noble lords and kissed her hand unto them, and the five knights saluted her as they rode past her and into the field.

Now, when the Duke of North Umber was made aware that those five knights had come against him and his knights-companion for to take up his challenge, he straightway came forth from his pavilion and mounted his horse. And his knights-companion came forth and mounted their horses, and he and they went forth for to meet those who had come against them.

And when the Duke of North Umber had come nigh enough, he perceived that the chiefest of those five knights was the White Champion who had aforetime overthrown him. Wherefore he said unto that White Champion: "Sir Knight, I have once before condescended unto thee who art altogether unknown to me or to anybody else that is here. For without inquiring concerning thy quality, I ran a course with thee, and, lo! by the chance of arms thou didst overthrow me. Now this quarrel is more serious than that, wherefore I and my companions-at-arms will not run a course with thee and they companions; nor will we fight with thee until I first know what is the quality of him against whom I contend. Wherefore, I bid thee declare thyself, who thou art and what is thy condition."

Then Sir Gawaine opened the umbril of his helmet, and he said: "Sir Knight, behold my face, and know that I am Gawaine, the son of King Lot. Wherefore thou mayst perceive that my condition and estate are even better than thine own. Now I do declare unto thee that yonder White Knight is of such a quality that he condescends unto thee when he doeth combat with thee."

"Ho, Sir Gawaine!" quoth the Duke of Umber. "What thou sayest is a very strange thing, for, indeed, there are few in this world who are so exalted that they may condescend unto me. Ne'theless, since thou dost avouch for him, I may not gainsay that which thou sayest. Yet, there is still another reason why we may not fight with ye. For, behold! we are seven well-approved and famous knights, and ye are but five; so, consider how unequal are our forces, and that you stand in great peril in undertaking so dangerous an encounter."

Then Sir Gawaine smiled right grimly upon that Duke of North Umber. "Gramercy for thy compassion, and for the tenderness which thou showeth concerning our safety, Sir Duke," quoth he. "But ne'theless, thou mayst leave that matter unto us with entire content of spirit upon thy part. For I consider that the peril in which ye seven stand is fully equal to our peril. Moreover, wert thou other than a belted knight, a simple man might suppose that thou wert more careful of thine own safety in this matter, than thou art of ours."

Now at these words the countenance of the Duke of North Umber became altogether covered with red, for he wist that he had, indeed, no great desire for this battle, wherefore he was ashamed because of the words which Sir Gawaine spake to him. So, each knight closed his helmet, and all turned their horses, and the one party rode unto one end of the field, and the other party rode to the other end of the field, and there each took stand in the place assigned unto them.

And they arranged themselves thus: In the middle was King

Arthur, and upon either hand were two knights; and in the middle was the Duke of North Umber, and upon either hand were three knights. So, when they had thus arrayed themselves they dressed their spears and their shields, and made them altogether ready for the onset. Then King Arthur and Duke Mordaunt each shouted aloud, and the one party hurled upon the other party with such violence that the ground shook and thundered beneath the hoofs of the horses, and the clouds of dust rose up against the heavens.

And so they met in the middle of the field with an uproar of such dreadful violence that one might have heard the crashing thereof for the distance of more than a mile away.

And when the one party had passed the other, and the dust of the encounter had arisen, lo! three of the seven had been overthrown, and not one of the five had lost his seat.

And one of those who had been overthrown was Duke Mordaunt of North Umber. And, behold! he never more arose again from the ground whereon he lay. For King Arthur had directed his spear into the very midst of his defences, and the spear had held, wherefore the point thereof had pierced the shield of the Duke of North Umber, and had pierced his body armor, and so violent was the stroke, that the Duke of North Umber had been lifted entirely out of his saddle, and had been cast a full spear's length behind the crupper of his horse. Thus died that wicked man, for as King Arthur drave past him, the evil soul of him quitted his body with a weak noise like to the squeaking of a bat, and the world was well rid of him.

Now when King Arthur turned him about at the end of the course and beheld that there were but four knights left upon their horses of all those seven against whom he and his companions had driven, he uplifted his spear, and drew rein upon his horse, and bespake his knights in this wise: "Messires, I am aweary of all this coil and quarrelling, and do not care to fight any more to-day, so go ye straightway and engage those knights in battle. As for me, I will abide here, and witness your adventure."

"Lord," said they, "we will do our endeavor as thou dost command."

So those four good knights did as he commanded, and they

went forth straightway against those other four, much encouraged that their King looked upon their endeavor. And King Arthur sat with the butt of his spear resting upon his instep, and looked upon the field with great content of spirit, and a steadfast countenance.

As for those four knights-companion that remained of the Duke of North Umber's party, they came not forth to this second encounter with so much readiness of spirit as they had done aforetime. For they were now well aware of how great was the excellent prowess of those other knights, and they beheld that their enemies came forth to this second encounter very fiercely, and with great valor and readiness of spirit. Wherefore their hearts melted away within them with doubt and anxiety as to the outcome of this second encounter.

Nevertheless, they prepared themselves with such resolve as might be, and came forth as they were called upon to do.

Then Sir Gawaine drave straight up to the foremost knight, who was a very well-known champion, hight Sir Dinador of Montcalm. And when he had come sufficiently nigh to him, he lifted himself up in his stirrups and he smote Sir Dinador so fierce a blow that he cleft the shield of that knight asunder, and he cleft his helmet, and a part of the blade of his sword brake away and remained therein.

And when Sir Dinador felt that blow, his brains swam like water, and he was fain to catch the horn of his saddle for to save himself from falling therefrom. Then a great terror straightway fell upon him, so that he drew rein violently to one side. So he fled away from that place with the terror of death hanging above him like to a black cloud of smoke. And when his companions beheld that stroke that Sir Gawaine delivered, and when they beheld Sir Dinador flee away from before him, they also drew rein to one side and fled away with all speed, pursued with an entire terror of their enemies. And Sir Gawaine and Sir Ewaine and Sir Geraint and Sir Pellias pursued them as they fled. And they chased them straight through the Court of King Ryence, so that the knights and nobles of that Court scattered hither and thither like chaff at their coming. And they chased those fleeing knights in among the pavilions of King Ryence's Court, and no man stayed them; and when they had chased those knights entirely away, they returned to that place where King Arthur still held his station, steadfastly awaiting them.

Now when the people of Cameliard beheld the overthrow of their enemies, and when they beheld how those enemies fled away from before the faces of their champions, they shouted with might and main, and made great acclaim. Nor did they stint their loud shouting when those four knights returned from pursuing their enemies and came back unto the White Champion again. And still more did they give acclaim when those five knights rode across the drawbridge and into the gateway of the town and into the town.

Thus ended the great bout-at-arms, which was one of the most famous in all the history of King Arthur's Court.

Now when King Arthur had thus accomplished his purposes, and when he had come into the town again, he went unto that merchant of whom he had obtained the armor that he wore, and he delivered that armor back to him again. And he said, "Tomorrow-day, Sir Merchant, I shall send thee two bags of gold for the rent of that armor which thou didst let me have."

To this the merchant said: "Lord, it is not needed that thou shouldst recompense me for that armor, for thou hast done great honor unto Cameliard by thy prowess."

But King Arthur said: "Have done, Sir Merchant, nor must thou forbid what I say. Wherefore take thou that which I shall send unto thee."

Thereupon he went his way, and, having set his cap of disguise upon his head, he came back into the Lady Guinevere's gardens again.

Now when the next morning had come the people of Cameliard looked forth and, lo! King Ryence had departed entirely away from before the castle. For that night he had struck his pavilions, and had withdrawn his Court, and had gone away from that place where he and his people had sat down for five days past. And with him he had taken the body of the Duke of North Umber, conveying it away in a litter surrounded by many lighted candles and uplifted by a peculiar pomp of ceremony. But when the people of Cameliard beheld that he was gone, they were exceedingly rejoiced, and made merry, and shouted and sang and laughed. For they wist not how deeply enraged King Ryence was against them; for his enmity aforetime toward King Leodegrance was but as a small flame when compared unto the anger that now possessed him.

Now that morning Lady Guinevere walked into her garden, and with her walked Sir Gawaine and Sir Ewaine, and lo! there she beheld the gardener's boy again.

Then she laughed aloud, and she said unto those two knights, "Messires behold! Yonder is the gardener's boy, who weareth his cap continually because he hath an ugly place upon his head."

Then those two knights, knowing who that gardener's boy was, were exceedingly abashed at her speech, and wist not what to say or whither to look. And Sir Gawaine spake, aside unto Sir Ewaine, and quoth he: " 'Fore Heaven, that lady knoweth not what manner of man is yonder gardener's boy; for, an she did, she would be more sparing of her speech."

And the Lady Guinevere heard Sir Gawaine that he spoke, but she did not hear his words. So she turned unto Sir Gawaine, and she said: "Sir Gawaine, haply it doth affront thee that that gardener's boy should wear his cap before us, and maybe thou wilt go and take it off from his head as thou didst offer to do two or three days since."

And Sir Gawaine said: "Peace, Lady! Thou knowest not what thou sayest. Yonder gardener's boy could more easily take my head from off my shoulders than I could take his cap from off his head."

At this the Lady Guinevere made open laughter; but in her heart she secretly pondered that saying and greatly marvelled what Sir Gawaine meant thereby.

Now about noon of that day there came an herald from King Ryence of North Wales, and he appeared boldly before King Leodegrance where the King sat in his hall with a number of his people about him. And the herald said: "My lord King: my master, King Ryence of North Wales, is greatly displeased with thee. For thou didst set certain knights upon Duke Mordaunt of North Umber, and those knights have slain that excellent nobleman, who was close kin unto King Ryence. Moreover, thou hast made no reply to those demands that my master, King Ryence, hath made touching the delivery unto him of certain lands and castles bordering upon North Wales. Wherefore my master is affronted with thee beyond measure. So my master, King Ryence, bids me to set forth to thee two conditions, and the conditions are these: Firstly, that thou dost immediately deliver into his hands that White Knight who slew the Duke of North Umber; secondly, that thou makest immediate promise that those lands in question shall be presently delivered unto King Ryence."

Then King Leodegrance arose from where he sat and spake to that herald with great dignity of demeanor. "Sir Herald," quoth he, "the demands that King Ryence maketh upon me pass all bounds for insolence. That death which the Duke of North Umber suffered, he suffered because of his own pride and folly. Nor would I deliver that White Knight into thy master's hands, even an I were able to do so. As for those lands that thy master demandeth of me, thou mayst tell King Ryence that I will not deliver unto him of those lands so much as a single blade of grass, or a single grain of corn that groweth thereon."

And the herald said: "If, so be, that is thine answer, King Leodegrance, then am I bidden for to tell thee that my master, King Ryence of North Wales, will presently come hither with an array of a great force of arms, and will take from thee by force those things which thou wilt not deliver unto him peacefully." Whereupon, so saying, he departed thence and went his way.

Now after the herald had departed, King Leodegrance went into his closet, and when he had come there he sent, privily, for the Lady Guinevere. So the Lady Guinevere came to him where he was. And King Leodegrance said to her: "My daughter, it hath happened that a knight clad all in white, and bearing no crest or device of any sort, hath twice come to our rescue and hath overthrown our enemies. Now it is said by everybody that that knight is thine own particular champion, and I hear say that he wore thy necklace as a favor when he first went out against the Duke of North Umber. Now I prithee, daughter, tell me who that White Champion is, and where he may be found."

Then the Lady Guinevere was overwhelmed with a confusion, wherefore she looked away from her father's countenance; and she said: "Verily, my Lord, I know not who that knight may be."

Then King Leodegrance spake very seriously to the Lady Guinevere, and he took her by the hand and said: "My daughter, thou art now of an age when thou must consider being mated unto a man who may duly cherish thee and protect thee from thine enemies. For, lo! I grow apace in years, and may not hope to defend thee always from those perils that encompass one of our estate. Moreover, since King Arthur (who is a very great King indeed) hath brought peace unto this realm, all that noble court of chivalry which one time gathered about me has been scattered elsewhither where greater adventures may be found than in my peaceful realm. Wherefore (as in the world hath seen this week past) I have now not one single knight whom I may depend upon to defend us in such times of peril as these which now overshadow us. Now, my daughter, it doth appear to me that thou couldst not hope to find anyone who could so well safeguard thee as this White Knight; for he doth indeed appear to be a champion of extraordinary prowess and strength. Wherefore it would be well if thou didst feel thyself to incline unto him as he appeareth to incline unto thee."

Then the Lady Guinevere became all rosy red as with a fire even unto her throat. And she laughed, albeit the tears overflowed her eyes and ran down upon her cheeks. So she wept, yet laughed in weeping. And she said unto King Leodegrance: "My Lord and father, an I give my liking unto any one in the manner thou speaketh of, I will give it only unto the poor gardener's boy who digs in my garden."

Then, at these words, the countenance of King Leodegrance became contracted with violent anger, and he cried out: "Ha, Lady! Wouldst thou make a mock and a jest of my words?"

Then the Lady Guinevere said: "Indeed, my Lord! I jest not and I mock not. Moreover, I tell thee for verity that that same gardener's boy knoweth more concerning the White Champion than anybody else in all of the world." Then King Leodegrance said: "What is this that thou tellest me?" And the Lady Guinevere said: "Send for that gardener's boy and thou shalt know." And King Leodegrance said: "Verily, there is more in this than I may at present understand."

So he called to him the chief of his pages, hight Dorisand, and he said to him: "Go, Dorisand, and bring hither the gardener's boy from the Lady Guinevere's garden."

So Dorisand, the page, went as King Leodegrance commanded, and in a little while he returned, bringing with him that gardener's boy. And with them came Sir Gawaine, and Sir Ewaine, and Sir Pellias and Sir Geraint. And those four lords stood over against the door, where they entered; but the gardener's boy came and stood beside the table where King Leodegrance sat. And the King lifted up his eyes and looked upon the gardener's boy, and he said: "Ha! Wouldst thou wear thy cap in our presence?"

The gardener's boy said: "I cannot take off my cap."

But the Lady Guinevere, who stood beside the chair of King Leodegrance, spake and said: "I do beseech thee, Messire, for to take off thy cap unto my father."

Whereupon the gardener's boy said: "At they bidding I will take it off."

So he took the cap from off his head, and King Leodegrance beheld his face and knew him. And when he saw who it was who stood before him, he made a great outcry from pure amazement. And he said: "My Lord and my King! What is this!" Thereupon he arose from where he sat, and he went and kneeled down upon the ground before King Arthur. And he set the palms of his hands together and he put his hands within the hands of King Arthur, and King Arthur took the hands of King Leodegrance within his own. And King Leodegrance said: "My Lord! My Lord! Is it then thou who hast done all these wonderful things?"

Then King Arthur said: "Yea; such as those things were, I have done them." And he stooped and kissed King Leodegrance upon the cheek and lifted him up unto his feet and gave him words of good cheer.

Now the Lady Guinevere, when she beheld those things that passed, was astonished beyond measure. And lo! she understood of a sudden all these things with amazing clearness. Wherefore a great fear fell upon her so that she trembled exceedingly, and said unto herself: "What things have I said unto this great King, and how have I made a mock of him and a jest of him before all those who were about me!" And at the thought thereof, she set her hand upon her side for to still the extreme disturbance of her heart. So, whilst King Arthur and King Leodegrance gave to one another words of royal greeting and of compliment, she withdrew herself and went and stood over against the window nigh to the corner of the wall.

Then, by and by, King Arthur lifted up his eyes and beheld her where she stood afar off. So he went straightway unto her and he took her by the hand, and he said: "Lady, what cheer?"

And she said: "Lord, I am afeard of thy greatness." And he said: "Nay, Lady. Rather it is I who am afeard of thee. For thy kind regard is dearer unto me than anything else in all the world, else had I not served for these twelve days as gardener's boy in thy garden all for the sake of thy good will." And she said: "Thou hast my good will, Lord." And he said: "Have I thy good will in great measure?" And she said: "Yea, thou hast it in great measure."

Then he stooped his head and kissed her before all those who were there, and thus their troth was plighted.

Then King Leodegrance was filled with such an exceeding joy that he wist not how to contain himself therefore.

Now, after these things, there followed a war with King Ryence of North Wales. For Sir Kay and Sir Ulfius had gathered together a great army as King Arthur had bidden them to do, so that when King Ryence came against Cameliard he was altogether routed, and his army dispersed, and he himself chased, an outcast, into his mountains.

Then there was great rejoicing in Cameliard. For, after his victory, King Arthur remained there for a while with an exceedingly splendid Court of noble lords and of beautiful ladies. And there was feasting and jousting and many famous bouts at arms, the like of which those parts had never before beheld. And King Arthur and the Lady Guinevere were altogether happy together.

Now, one day, whiles King Arthur sat at feast with King Leodegrance—they two being exceedingly expanded with cheerfulness—King Leodegrance said unto King Arthur: "My Lord, what shall I offer thee for a dowery with my daughter when thou takest her away from me for to be thy Queen?"

Then King Arthur turned to Merlin, who stood nigh to him, and he said: "Ha, Merlin! What shall I demand of my friend by way of that dowery?"

Unto him Merlin said: "My lord King, thy friend King Leodegrance hath one thing, the which, should he bestow it upon thee, will singularly increase the glory and renown of thy reign, so that the fame thereof shall never be forgotten."

And King Arthur said: "I bid thee, Merlin, tell me what is that thing."

So Merlin said: "My lord King, I will tell thee a story:

"In the days of thy father, Uther-Pendragon, I caused to be made for him a certain table in the shape of a ring, wherefore men called it the ROUND TABLE. Now, at this table were seats for fifty men, and these seats were designed for the fifty knights who were the most worthy knights in all the world. These seats were of such a sort, that whenever a worthy knight appeared, then his name appeared in letters of gold upon that seat that appertained unto him; and when that knight died, then would his name suddenly vanish from that seat which he had aforetime occupied.

"Now, forty-and-nine of these seats, except one seat, were altogether alike (saving only one that was set aside for the King himself, which same was elevated above the other seats, and was cunningly carved and inlaid with ivory and with gold), and the one seat was different from all the others, and it was called the SEAT PERILOUS. For this seat was unlike the others both in its structure and its significance; for it was all cunningly inset with gold and silver of curious device, and it was covered with a canopy of satin embroidered with gold and silver; and it was altogether of a wonderful magnificence of appearance. And no name ever appeared upon this seat, for only one knight in all of the world could hope to sit therein with safety unto himself.

For, if any other dared to sit therein, either he would die a sudden and violent death within three days' time, or else a great misfortune would befall him. Hence that seat was called the SEAT PERILOUS.

"Now, in the days of King Uther-Pendragon, there sat seven-and-thirty knights at the ROUND TABLE. And when King Uther-Pendragon died, he gave the ROUND TABLE unto his friend, King Leodegrance of Cameliard.

"And in the beginning of King Leodegrance's reign, there sat four-and-twenty knights at the ROUND TABLE.

"But times have changed since then, and the glory of King Leodegrance's reign hath paled before the glory of thy reign, so that his noble Court of knights have altogether quitted him. Wherefore there remaineth now not one name, saving only the name of King Leodegrance, upon all those fifty seats that surround the ROUND TABLE. So now that ROUND TABLE lieth beneath its pavilion altogether unused.

"Yet if King Leodegrance will give unto thee, my lord King, that ROUND TABLE for a dower with the Lady Guinevere, then will it lend unto thy reign its greatest glory. For in thy day every seat of that TABLE shall be filled, even unto the SEAT PERILOUS, and the fame of the knights who sit at it shall never be forgotten."

"Ha!" quoth King Arthur. "That would indeed be a dower worthy for any king to have with his queen."

"Then," King Leodegrance said, "that dower shalt thou have with my daughter; and if it bring thee great glory, then shall thy glory be my glory, and thy renown shall be my renown. For if my glory shall wane, and thy glory shall increase, behold! is not my child thy wife?"

And King Arthur said: "Thou sayest well and wisely."

Thus King Arthur became the master of that famous ROUND TABLE. And the ROUND TABLE was set up at Camelot (which some men now call Winchester). And by and by there gathered about it such an array of knights as the world had never beheld before that time, and which it shall never behold again.

Such was the history of the beginning of the ROUND TABLE in King Arthur's reign.

Chapter Sixth

How King Arthur Was Wedded in Royal State and How the Round Table Was Established.

AND now was come the early fall of the year; that pleasant season when the meadow-land and the wold were still green with summer that had only just passed; when the sky likewise was as of summer-time—extraordinarily blue and full of large floating clouds; when a bird might sing here and another there, a short song in memory of spring-time, when all the air was tempered with warmth and yet the leaves were everywhere turning brown and red and gold, so that when the sun shone through them it was as though a cloth of gold, broidered with brown and crimson and green, hung above the head. At this season of the year it is exceedingly pleasant to be a-field among the nut-trees with hawk and hound, or to travel abroad in the yellow world, whether it be a-horse or a-foot.

Now this was the time of year in which had been set the marriage of King Arthur and the Lady Guinevere at Camelot, and at that place was extraordinary pomp and glory of circumstance. All the world was astir and in a great ferment of joy, for everybody was exceedingly glad that King Arthur was to have him a Queen.

In preparation for that great occasion the town of Camelot was bedight very magnificently, for the stony street along which the Lady Guinevere must come to the royal castle of the King was strewn thick with fresh-cut rushes smoothly laid. Moreover it was in many places spread with carpets of excellent pattern such as might be fit to lay upon the floor of some goodly hall. Likewise all the houses along the way were hung with fine hangings of woven texture interwoven with threads of azure and crimson, and everywhere were flags and banners afloat in the warm and gentle breeze against the blue sky, wherefore that all the world appeared to be alive with bright colors, so that when one looked adown that street, it was as though one beheld a crooked path of exceeding beauty and gayety stretched before him.

Thus came the wedding-day of the King—bright and clear and exceedingly radiant.

King Arthur sat in his hall surrounded by his Court awaiting news that the Lady Guinevere was coming thitherward. And it was about the middle of the morning when there came a messenger in haste riding upon a milk-white steed. And the raiment of that messenger and the trappings of his horse were all of cloth of gold embroidered with scarlet and white, and the tabard of the messenger was set with many jewels of various sorts so that he glistened from afar as he rode, with a singular splendor of appearance.

So this herald-messenger came straight into the castle where the King abided waiting, and he said: "Arise, my lord King, for the Lady Guinevere and her Court draweth nigh."

Upon this the King immediately arose with great joy, and straightway he went forth with his Court of Knights, riding in great state. And as he went down that marvellously adorned street, all the people shouted aloud as he passed by, wherefore he smiled and bent his head from side to side; for that day he was passing happy and loved his people with wonderful friendliness.

Thus he rode forward unto the town gate, and out therefrom, and so came thence into the country beyond where the broad and well-beaten highway ran winding down beside the shining river betwixt the willows and the osiers.

And, behold! King Arthur and those with him perceived the Court of the Princess where it appeared at a distance, wherefore they made great rejoicing and hastened forward with all speed. And as they came nigh, the sun falling upon the apparels of silk and cloth of gold, and upon golden chains and the jewels that hung therefrom, all of that noble company that surrounded the Lady Guinevere her litter flashed and sparkled with surpassing radiance.

For seventeen of the noblest knights of the King's Court, clad in complete armor, and sent by him as an escort unto the lady, rode in great splendor, surrounding the litter wherein the Princess lay. And the framework of that litter was of richly gilded wood, and its curtains and its cushions were of crimson silk embroidered with threads of gold. And behind the litter there rode in gay and joyous array, all shining with many colors, the Court of the Princess—her damsels in waiting, gentlemen, ladies, pages, and attendants.

So those parties of the King and the Lady Guinevere drew nigh together until they met and mingled the one with the other.

Then straightway King Arthur dismounted from his noble horse and, all clothed with royalty, he went afoot unto the Lady Guinevere's litter, whiles Sir Gawaine and Sir Ewaine held the bridle of his horse. Thereupon one of her pages drew aside the silken curtains of the Lady Guinevere's litter, and King Leodegrance gave her his hand and she straightway descended therefrom, all embalmed, as it were, in exceeding beauty. So King Leodegrance led her to King Arthur, and King Arthur came to her and placed one hand beneath her chin and the other upon her head and inclined his countenance and kissed her upon her smooth cheek—all warm and fragrant like velvet for softness, and without any blemish whatsoever. And when he had thus kissed her upon the cheek, all those who were there lifted up their voices in great acclaim, giving loud voice of joy that those two noble souls had thus met together.

Thus did King Arthur give welcome unto the Lady Guinevere and unto King Leodegrance her father upon the highway beneath the walls of the town of Camelot, at the distance of half a league from that place. And no one who was there ever forgot that meeting, for it was full of extraordinary grace and noble courtliness.

Then King Arthur and his Court of Knights and nobles brought King Leodegrance and the Lady Guinevere with great ceremony unto Camelot and unto the royal castle, where

apartments were assigned to all, so that the entire place was alive with joyousness and beauty.

And when high noon had come, the entire Court went with great state and ceremony unto the cathedral, and there, surrounded with wonderful magnificence, those two noble souls were married by the Archbishop.

And all the bells rang right joyfully, and all the people who stood without the cathedral shouted with loud acclaim, and lo! the King and the Queen came forth all shining, like unto the sun for splendor and like unto the moon for beauty.

In the castle a great noontide feast was spread, and there sat thereat four hundred, eighty and six lordly and noble folk— kings, knights, and nobles—with queens and ladies in magnificent array. And near to the King and the Queen there sat King Leodegrance and Merlin, and Sir Ulfius, and Sir Ector the trustworthy, and Sir Gawaine, and Sir Ewaine, and Sir Kay, and King Ban, and King Pellinore and many other famous and exalted folk, so that no man had ever beheld such magnificent courtliness as he beheld at that famous wedding-feast of King Arthur and Queen Guinevere.

And that day was likewise very famous in the history of chivalry, for in the afternoon the famous Round Table was established, and that Round Table was at once the very flower and the chiefest glory of King Arthur's reign.

For about mid of the afternoon the King and Queen, preceded by Merlin and followed by all that splendid Court of kings, lords, nobles and knights in full array, made progression to that place where Merlin, partly by magic and partly by skill, had caused to be builded a very wonderful pavilion above the Round Table where it stood.

And when the King and the Queen and the Court had entered in thereat they were amazed at the beauty of that pavilion, for they perceived, an it were, a great space that appeared to be a marvellous land of Fay. For the walls were all richly gilded and were painted with very wonderful figures of saints and of angels, clad in ultramarine and crimson, and all those saints and angels were depicted playing upon various musical instruments that appeared to be made of gold. And overhead the roof of the pavilion was made to represent the sky, being all of cerulean blue sprinkled over with stars. And in the midst of that painted sky was an image, an it were, of the sun in his glory. And under foot was a pavement all of marble stone, set in squares of black and white, and blue and red, and sundry other colors.

In the midst of the pavilion was a Round Table with seats thereat exactly sufficient for fifty persons, and at each of the fifty places was a chalice of gold filled with fragrant wine, and at each place was a paten of gold bearing a manchet of fair white bread. And when the King and his Court entered into the pavilion, lo! music began of a sudden for to play with a wonderful sweetness.

Then Merlin came and took King Arthur by the hand and led him away from Queen Guinevere. And he said unto the King, "Lo! this is the Round Table."

Then King Arthur said, "Merlin, that which I see is wonderful beyond the telling."

After that Merlin discovered unto the King the various marvels of the Round Table, for first he pointed to a high seat, very wonderfully wrought in precious woods and gilded so that it was exceedingly beautiful, and he said, "Behold, lord King, yonder seat is hight the 'Seat Royal,' and that seat is thine for to sit in." And as Merlin spake, lo! there suddenly appeared sundry letters of gold upon the back of that seat, and the letters of gold read the name,

ARTHUR, KING

And Merlin said, "Lord, yonder seat may well be called the centre seat of the Round Table, for, in sooth, thou art indeed the very centre of all that is most worthy of true knightliness. Wherefore that seat shall be called the centre seat of all the other seats."

Then Merlin pointed to the seat that stood opposite to the Seat Royal, and that seat also was of a very wonderful appearance as afore told in this history. And Merlin said unto the King: "My lord King, that seat is called the Seat Perilous, for no man but one in all this world shall sit therein, and that man is not yet born upon the earth. And if any other man shall dare to sit therein that man shall either suffer death or a sudden and terrible misfortune for his temerity. Wherefore that seat is called the Seat Perilous."

"Merlin," quoth the King, "all that thou tellest me passeth the bound of understanding for marvellousness. Now I do beseech thee in all haste for to find forthwith a sufficient number of knights to fill this Round Table so that my glory shall be entirely complete."

Then Merlin smiled upon the King, though not with cheerfulness, and said, "Lord, why art thou in such haste? Know that when this Round Table shall be entirely filled in all its seats, then shall thy glory be entirely achieved and then forthwith shall thy day begin for to decline. For when any man hath reached the crowning of his glory, then his work is done and God breaketh him as a man might break a chalice from which such perfect ichor hath been drunk that no baser wine may be allowed to defile it. So when thy work is done and ended shall God shatter the chalice of thy life."

Then did the King look very steadfastly into Merlin's face, and said, "Old man, that which thou sayest is ever of great wonder, for thou speakest words of wisdom. Ne'theless, seeing that I am in God His hands, I do wish for my glory and for His good will to be accomplished even though He shall then entirely break me when I have served His purposes."

"Lord," said Merlin, "thou speakest like a worthy king and with a very large and noble heart. Ne'theless, I may not fill the Round Table for thee at this time. For, though thou hast gathered about thee the very noblest Court of Chivalry in all of Christendom, yet are there but two and thirty knights here present who may be considered worthy to sit at the Round Table."

"Then, Merlin," quoth King Arthur, "I do desire of thee that thou shalt straightway choose me those two and thirty."

"So will I do, lord King," said Merlin.

Then Merlin cast his eyes around and lo! he saw where King Pellinore stood at a little distance. Unto him went Merlin and took him by the hand. "Behold, my lord King," quoth he. "Here is the knight in all the world next to thyself who at this time is most worthy for to sit at this Round Table. For he is both exceedingly gentle of demeanor unto the poor and needy and at the same time is so terribly strong and skilful that I know not whether thou or he is the more to be feared in an encounter of knight against knight."

Then Merlin led King Pellinore forward and behold! upon the high seat that stood upon the left hand of the Royal Seat there appeared of a sudden the name,

PELLINORE

And the name was emblazoned in letters of gold that shone with extraordinary lustre. And when King Pellinore took his seat, great and loud acclaim long continued was given him by all those who stood round about.

Then after that Merlin had thus chosen King Arthur and King Pellinore he chose out of the Court of King Arthur the following knights, two and thirty in all, and these were the knights of great renown in chivalry who did first establish the Round Table. Wherefore they were surnamed "The Ancient and Honorable Companions of the Round Table."

To begin, there was Sir Gawaine and Sir Ewaine, who were nephews unto the King, and they sat nigh to him upon the right hand; there was Sir Ulfius (who held his seat but four years and

eight months unto the time of his death, after which Sir
Geheris—who was esquire unto his brother, Sir Gawaine—held
that seat); and there was Sir Kay the Seneschal, who was foster
brother unto the King; and there was Sir Baudwain of Britain
(who held his seat but three years and two months until his
death, after the which Sir Agravaine held that seat); and there
was Sir Pellias and Sir Geraint and Sir Constantine, son of Sir
Caderes the Seneschal of Cornwall (which same was king after
King Arthur); and there was Sir Caradoc and Sir Sagramore,
surnamed the Desirous, and Sir Dinadan and Sir Dodinas,
surnamed the Savage, and Sir Bruin, surnamed the Black, and
Sir Meliot of Logres, and Sir Aglaval and Sir Durnure, and Sir
Lamorac (which three young knights were sons of King
Pellinore), and there was Sir Griflet and Sir Ladinas and Sir
Brandiles and Sir Persavant of Ironside, and Sir Dinas of
Cornwall, and Sir Brian of Listinoise, and Sir Palomides and Sir
Degraine and Sir Epinogres, the son of the King of North
Umberland and brother unto the enchantress Vivien, and Sir
Lamiel of Cardiff, and Sir Lucan the Bottler and Sir Bedevere
his brother (which same bare King Arthur unto the ship of
Fairies when he lay so sorely wounded nigh unto death after
the last battle which he fought). These two and thirty knights
were the Ancient Companions of the Round Table, and unto
them were added others until there were nine and forty in all,
and then was added Sir Galahad, and with him the Round
Table was made entirely complete.

Now as each of these knights was chosen by Merlin, lo! as
he took that knight by the hand, the name of that knight
suddenly appeared in golden letters, very bright and shining,
upon the seat that appertained to him.

But when all had been chosen, behold! King Arthur saw that
the seat upon the right hand of the Seat Royal had not been
filled, and that it bare no name upon it. And he said unto
Merlin: "Merlin, how is this, that the seat upon my right hand
hath not been filled, and beareth no name?"

And Merlin said: "Lord, there shall be a name thereon in a
very little while, and he who shall sit therein shall be the
greatest knight in all the world until that the knight cometh
who shall occupy the Seat Perilous. For he who cometh shall

exceed all other men in beauty, strength, and knightly grace."

And King Arthur said: "I would that he were with us now."
And Merlin said: "He cometh anon."

Thus was the Round Table established with great pomp and great ceremony of estate. For first the Archbishop of Canterbury blessed each and every seat, progressing from place to place surrounded by his Holy Court, the choir whereof singing most musically in accord, whiles others swung censers from which there ascended an exceedingly fragrant vapor of frankincense, filling that entire pavilion with an odor of Heavenly blessedness.

And when the Archbishop had thus blessed every one of those seats, the chosen knight took each his stall at the Round Table, and his esquire came and stood behind him, holding the banneret with his coat-of-arms upon the spear-point above the knight's head. And all those who stood about that place, both knights and ladies, lifted up their voices in loud acclaim.

Then all the knights arose, and each knight held up before him the cross of the hilt of his sword, and each knight spake word for word as King Arthur spake. And this was the covenant of their Knighthood of the Round Table: That they would be gentle unto the weak; that they would be courageous unto the strong; that they would be terrible unto the wicked and the evil-doer; that they would defend the helpless who should call upon them for aid; that all women should be held unto them sacred; that they would stand unto the defence of one another whensoever such defence should be required; that they would be merciful unto all men; that they would be gentle of deed, true in friendship, and faithful in love. This was their covenant, and unto it each knight sware upon the cross of his sword, and in witness thereof did kiss the hilt thereof. Thereupon all who stood thereabouts once more gave loud acclaim.

Then all the knights of the Round Table seated themselves, and each knight brake bread from the golden patten, and quaffed wine from the golden chalice that stood before him, giving thanks unto God for that which he ate and drank.

Thus was King Arthur wedded unto Queen Guinevere, and thus was the Round Table established.

Conclusion

So endeth this Book of King Arthur which hath been told by me with such joyousness of spirit that I find it to be a very great pleasure, in closing this first volume of my work, to look forward to writing a second volume, which now presently followeth.

In that volume there shall be told the history of several very noble worthies who were of the Court of the King, and it seems to me to be a good thing to have to do with the history of such noble and honorable knights and gentlemen. For, indeed, it might well please anyone to read such an history, and to hear those worthies speak, and to behold in what manner they behaved in times of trial and tribulation. For their example will doubtless help us all to behave in a like manner in a like case.

THE BOOK OF

Three Worthies

Foreword

ERE beginneth the Second Book of the History of King
Arthur, called *The Book of Three Worthies*, because
it has to do with three very excellent, honorable Lords of
the Court of King Arthur.

Of these three, the first is Merlin the Wise, the second is
Sir Pellias, surnamed the Gentle Knight, and the third is
Sir Gawaine, the son of King Lot of Orkney and the Isles.

So now presently follows the story of the passing of
Merlin the Wise; in the which you shall see how the very
wisdom that Merlin possessed in such great measure was the
cause of his own undoing. Wherefore I do hope that you
yourselves may take that story unto heart so that you shall
see that those gifts of mind or person which God assigns
unto you may not be misused by you or others that they
shall become the means of compassing your own downfall.

For it shall not excuse you in any wise that, as you journey forward in your life, you shall find many men who,
like Merlin, have been endowed by the grace of God with

very great gifts of talent which they might very easily use to the great benefit of mankind, but which they do so misuse as to bring the greater ruin upon themselves and the greater harm unto other men.   For, if you shall prove so weak or so wicked as to misuse your talents in that manner unto the harm of others and of yourself, it shall not make your fault the less that others shall have done greater evil than yourself.

Wherefore, let this story of Merlin be a warning unto you, I pray you all.   For, though I do not believe that Merlin intended that his talents of magic should do harm unto others, yet, because of his folly, they did as great harm as though he himself had designed to do evil by means of them.   Yea, it is hard to tell whether the wickedness or the follies of men do the greater harm in the world; therefore seek to guard yourself well, not only against sin, but against folly and weakness likewise.

Prologue

PON a certain day King Arthur sat in the Royal Hall of Camelot with the Queen and all of his Court and all of her Court. And there was great joy and mirth at that place.

Whiles they sat there, there suddenly came an armed knight into the Hall, and his armor was all covered with blood and dust, and he had a great many wounds upon his body. Then all they who were at that place were astonished and affrighted at the aspect of that knight, for his appearance boded no good news to King Arthur. The knight-messenger came to where the King was, and he was nearly fainting with weakness and with the many wounds he had received, and he brought news unto those who were there present that five kings, enemies to King Arthur, had suddenly come into that land and that they were burning and harrying the country upon every side.

And the knight-messenger said that these five kings were the King of Denmark, the King of Ireland, the King of Soleyse, the King of the Vale, and the King of Longtinaise. These had brought with them a great host and were laying waste the land all around about, so that all the realm was in sore travail and sorrow because of their devastations.

Upon this news, King Arthur smote his palms together with great vehemence and cried out, "Alas! who would be a king! Will the time never come when these wars and disturbances shall cease and we shall have entire peace in this land!" Therewith he arose in great agitation and went out from that place, and all who were there were in sore trouble.

So King Arthur immediately sent messengers to two friendly kings who were nearest to him—to wit, to King Pellinore and to King Uriens of Gore—and he bade them to come to his aid without any loss of time. Meantime he himself gathered together a large army with intent to go forth to meet his enemies forthwith.

So he went forth and upon the third day he came with his army unto the forest of Tintagalon and there he stayed with intent to rest for a little until King Pellinore and King Uriens should have joined him.

But the five kings, his enemies, had news that King Arthur was at that place, and thereupon they made a forced march through North Wales with intent to strike him ere those other two kings could come to his aid. So they came by night to where King Arthur was, and they fell upon him so unexpectedly that there was great danger of his army being put to rout before that assault.

But King Arthur drew his army together by his own courage and large-heartedness, and so they defended themselves with a great spirit until King Pellinore appeared with his army and joined in that battle.

So in the end King Arthur won a great victory over his enemies; for they were put to rout and scattered in every direction. Likewise by means of that war, and because of the submissions of these five kings, King Arthur recovered all that realm that had once been his father's, and more besides.

Now in that war eight of the knights of the Round Table lost their lives, and King Arthur mourned their loss with great dolor; for these were the first knights of the Round Table who had lost their lives in doing battle in his defence.

Whilst King Arthur was grieving very sorely for these eight knights, Merlin came unto him, and said, "Be not downcast, lord, for lo! thou hast many excellent knights still left about thee and thou canst certainly not have a very great deal of trouble in filling those eight places that have been thus made empty by death. Now if thou followest my counsel, thou must choose some very worthy adviser from the knights-companion of thy Round Table, and thou wilt consult with him in this matter (for the counsel of two is better than the counsel of one), and between ye ye may fill those places made vacant by war."

This counsel appeared very good to King Arthur, so he did as Merlin advised. For that morning he summoned King Pellinore to his privy closet and laid the matter before him and they two communed together thereupon. In that consultation King Pellinore advised King Arthur in this wise: That there should be four old and worthy knights chosen to fill four of those empty seats, and that there should be four young and ardent knights chosen to fill the other four seats, and in that manner all those eight seats should be filled.

Now that advice appeared to King Arthur to be good, wherefore he said, "Let it be that way." So first they two chose the four old knights as follows: There was King Uriens of Gore, and King Lac, and Sir Hervise de Reuel, and Sir Galliar of Rouge. And from the younger knights of the Court they chose Sir Marvaise of Leisle, and Sir Lionel, the son of King Ban of Benwick, and Sir Cadar of Cornwall. So that there was one place yet to be filled.

Now it was a very hard thing to determine who should fill that place, for there were at that time two very honorable young knights at the Court. One of these was Sir Baudemagus, a young knight, brother of Sir Ewaine and son of King Uriens of Gore and Queen Morgana le Fay (which lady was half-sister unto King Arthur as hath been aforetold). And the other young knight was Sir Tor who, though late come to the Court, had performed several very famous adventures. And Sir Tor was a son of King Pellinore (though not of his Queen), and King Pellinore loved him a very great deal.

Then King Pellinore said to King Arthur, "Lord, there are certainly but two knights in all thy Court to choose from for to fill this eighth seat at the Round Table: one of these is thy sister's son, Sir Baudemagus, and the other is my son, Sir Tor.

Now I may not advise thee in this matter, wherefore do thou, Lord, choose the one or the other of these young knights to fill that place. But this I may say, that it will please me very greatly if thy favor should fall upon Sir Baudemagus, for then will all the world believe that I have been above reproach in my dealings in this affair, whereas should Sir Tor be chosen all men would say that I favored mine own son."

Then King Arthur meditated upon this matter for a long while and by and by he spoke and said, "Sir, I have weighed this whole affair, and it is my belief that Sir Tor is the better knight of those twain. For he hath performed several very excellent adventures, whilst Sir Baudemagus, though a worthy knight, hath not yet made manifest any very great achievement in the fields of chivalry. So, in God's name, let Sir Tor be seated as companion of the Round Table."

Then King Pellinore said, "So be it," and thereupon they both arose and went forth from that place.

And, lo! that very moment the names of those eight worthies so chosen appeared each upon the back of the seat at the Round Table that appertained unto him, and so the decision of those two knights was confirmed in the sight of all the world in that manner.

Now when the word of all this reached the ears of Queen Morgana le Fay she was greatly affronted that Sir Baudemagus, her son, should have been passed by and that another should have been chosen in his stead. Wherefore she cried out against King Arthur in the hearing of several people, saying: "Ha! how is this! is blood and kinship of no account in the eyes of this King that he passes by so worthy a knight as his own nephew to choose one who is not of lawful birth in his stead? Now, my husband's house has suffered many grievous ills at the hands of King Arthur, for, lo! he hath taken away our royal power and hath made us all little better than captives in his own Court. This in itself is as great an affront as though we were his bitter enemies instead of his nigh of kin. But this that he hath now done to my son in thus passing him by is a greater affront than that other."

And Queen Morgana le Fay spake in this wise not only to King Uriens, who was her husband, but to Sir Ewaine and to

Sir Baudemagus, who were her sons. But King Uriens of Gore rebuked her for her speech, for he had grown to love King Arthur very much because of the high nobility of his nature, and likewise Sir Ewaine rebuked her saying that he would listen to no ill thing said of King Arthur, for that not only did he love King Arthur better than anyone else in all the world, but that the King was at once the looking-glass of all knighthood and likewise the very fountain-head of honor.

So spake these two; but Sir Baudemagus hearkened to what his mother, Queen Morgana said, for he was very angry with King Arthur because the King had passed him by. Wherefore he took his departure from the Court without asking leave of King Arthur and went errant in quest of adventure, and at this King Arthur was very sorry.

Now, as aforesaid, Queen Morgana le Fay spake her indignation to several other people of the Court, so that word thereof came at last to the ears of King Arthur and grieved him a very great deal. So when Queen Morgana came to him one day and besought his leave for to quit the Court, he spake to her with great sadness of spirit, saying, "My sister, I am very sorry that you are not pleased with what I have done in this matter, for God knows that I have endeavored to do to the best of my power. And though I would rather a great deal that Sir Baudemagus were fellow of the Round Table, yet it was my very honest belief that, for several reasons, Sir Tor had the best right to a seat at that Table. Now if I chose otherwise than according to my right judgment, what virtue would the Round Table have, seeing that I should have shown favor unto a man because of his kinship to me?"

Then Queen Morgana le Fay said with great heat, "Sir, all that you say only adds to the affront that our house hath sustained at your hands. For now you not only deny my son that seat, but you belittle him by comparing him to his disadvantage with this low-born knight whom you have chosen. Now, the only pleasure that I can have in talking to you is to beseech you to let me go away from this place."

Then King Arthur, speaking with great dignity, said, "Lady, it shall be as you would have it, and you shall go whithersoever it pleases you. For God forbid that I should stay you in your wishes. Moreover, I shall see to it that you shall not depart from this place without such a Court for company as may very well befit one who is the wife of one king and the sister of another."

And so he did as he said he would do, for he sent Queen Morgana le Fay away from his Court with great honor and in high estate of circumstance. But the more patient King Arthur was with her and the more he showed her favor, the more angry Queen Morgana le Fay was with him and the more she hated him.

So she betook her way to an estuary of the sea and there she dismissed those whom the King had sent with her and embarked with her own Court in several ships, betaking her way to that enchanted isle, hight Avalon, which was her home.

This island of Avalon was a very strange, wonderful land, such as was not to be seen anywhere else in all the world. For it was like a Paradise for beauty, being covered all over with divers gardens of flowers, intermingled with plantations of fair trees, some bearing fruit and others all a-bloom with blossoms. And besides these were many terraces of lawns, and smooth slopes of grass lying all about the borders of the island, and overlooking the sea from tall white walls of pure marble. And in the midst of these gardens and orchards and plantations and lawns and terraces, were a multitude of castles and towers built up the one above the other—some as white as snow and others very gay with many colors.

And the greatest marvel of that wonderful island was this: that in the midst of all those castles and towers was a single tower built entirely of loadstone. And in that lay the great mystery of that place.

For the island floated upon the surface of the water, and that tower of loadstone possessed such a potency that Avalon would float from place to place according to the will of Queen Morgana le Fay, so that sometimes it would be here, and sometimes it would be there, as that royal lady willed it to be.

Nor was there a very many people who had seen that island, for somewhiles it would be all covered over with a mist of enchantment like to silver, so that no eyes could behold it unless they were fay. But sometimes it had been seen, as it were a vision of Paradise. What time he who beheld it would hear gay voices sounding from its lawns and plantations—very thin and clear because of the great distance (for no one ever came nigh to Avalon unless by authority of Queen Morgana le Fay), and he would hear music of so sweet a sort that it was likely that his soul would grow all faint because of the music. Then Avalon would suddenly disappear very marvellously, and he who had seen it would be aware that it was not likely that he would ever see it again.

Such was the island of Avalon, and if you would read of it more particularly you shall find much about it in a certain book written in French and called "Ogier le Danois."

Queen Morgana le Fay loved this island a very great deal, and it is said by many that King Arthur is yet alive in that place, lying there very peacefully and tranquilly whiles he awaits that certain time when he shall return unto the world to make right all that is wrong therein. So it is I have told you of it with these particulars at this place.

PART I

The Story of Merlin

Chapter First

How Queen Morgana le Fay Meditated Evil Against King Arthur and How She Sent a Damsel to Beguile the Enchanter Merlin.

Now Morgana le Fay was a very cunning enchantress, and was so much mistress of magic that she could, by means of potent spells, work her will upon all things, whether quick or dead. For Merlin himself had been her master in times past, and had taught her his arts whilst she was still a young damsel at the Court of Uther-Pendragon. So it was that, next to Merlin, she was, at that time, the most potent enchanter in all the world. Nevertheless she lacked Merlin's foreknowledge of things to happen and his gift of prophecy thereupon, for these things he could not impart unto anyone, wherefore she had not learned them of him.

Now, after Queen Morgana le Fay had come to the Island of Avalon as aforetold, she brooded a great deal over that affront which she deemed King Arthur had placed upon her house; and the more she brooded upon it the more big did it become in her mind. Wherefore, at last, it seemed to her that she could have no pleasure in life unless she could punish King Arthur for that which he had done. Yea; she would have been glad to see him dead at her feet because of the anger that she felt against him.

But Queen Morgana was very well aware that she could never do the King, her brother, an injury so long as Merlin was there to safeguard him, for Merlin would certainly foresee any danger that might threaten the King, and would counteract it, wherefore she was aware that if she would destroy the King, she must first destroy Merlin.

Now, there was at the Court of Queen Morgana le Fay, a certain damsel of such marvellous and bewitching beauty that her like was hardly to be seen in all of the world. This damsel was fifteen years old and of royal blood, being the daughter of the King of Northumberland; and her name was Vivien. This damsel, Vivien, was both wise and cunning beyond all measure for one so young. Moreover, she was without any heart, being cold and cruel to all who were contrary-minded to her wishes. So, because she was so cunning and wise, Queen Morgana liked her and taught her many things of magic and sorcery which she knew. But, notwithstanding all that Queen Morgana did for her, this maiden did not feel any love for her mistress, being altogether devoid of heart.

One day this damsel and Queen Morgana le Fay sat together in a garden of that magic island of Avalon, and the garden was upon a very high terrace and overlooked the sea. And the day was very fair and the sea so wonderfully blue that it appeared to be as though the blue sky had melted into water and the water into the sky. As Vivien and the Queen sat in this beautiful place, the Queen said to the damsel, "Vivien, what wouldst thou rather have than anything else in all the world?" To which Vivien replied, "Lady, I would rather have such wisdom as thou hast, than anything else."

Then Queen Morgana laughed and said, "It is possible for thee to be as wise as I am, and wiser too, if so be thou wilt do according to my ordination. For I know a way in which thou mayst obtain wisdom."

"How may I obtain that wisdom, Lady?" said Vivien.

Then Queen Morgana le Fay said, "Hearken and I will tell thee. Thou must know that Merlin, whom thou hast several times seen at the Court of King Arthur, is the master of all the wisdom that it is possible for anyone to possess in this world. All that I know of magic Merlin hath taught me, and he knoweth many things that he did not teach me, but which he withheld from me. For Merlin taught me, when I was a young damsel at the Court of my mother's husband, because I was beautiful in his eyes. For Merlin loveth beauty above all things else in the world, and so he taught me many things of magic and was very patient with me.

"But Merlin hath a gift which belongeth to him and which he cannot communicate to anyone else, for it is instinct with him. That gift is the gift of foreseeing into the future and the power of prophesying thereupon.

"Yet though he may foresee the fate of others, still he is blind to his own fate. For so he confessed to me several times: that he could not tell what was to happen in his own life when that happening concerned himself alone.

"Now thou, Vivien, art far more beautiful than I was at thine age. Wherefore I believe that thou wilt easily attract the regard of Merlin unto thee. And if I give thee, besides, a certain charm which I possess, I may cause it to be that Merlin may love thee so much that he will impart to thee a great deal more of his wisdom than ever he taught me when I was his disciple.

"But thou art to know, Vivien, that in winning this gift of knowledge from Merlin thou wilt put thyself in great peril. For, by and by, when the charm of thy beauty shall have waned with him, then he may easily regret what he hath done in imparting his wisdom to thee; in the which case there will be great danger that he may lay some spell upon thee to deprive thee of thy powers; for it would be impossible that both thou and he could live in the same world and each of ye know so much cunning of magic."

Now unto all this Vivien listened with a great deal of attention, and when Queen Morgana had ended the damsel said, "Dear Lady, all that thou tellest me is very wonderful, and I find myself possessed with a vehement desire to attain such knowledge in magic as that. Wherefore, if thou wilt help me in this matter so that I may beguile his wisdom from Merlin, thou wilt make of me a debtor unto thee for as long as I may live. And touching the matter of any danger that may fall to me in this affair, I am altogether willing to assume that; for I have a great hope that I may be able so to protect myself from Merlin that no harm shall befall me. For when I have drawn all the knowledge that I am able to obtain from him, then I will use that same knowledge to cast such a spell upon him that he shall never be able to harm me or anyone else again. In this I shall play my wit against his wisdom and my beauty against his cunning, and I believe that I shall win at that game."

Then Queen Morgana fell a-laughing beyond all measure, and when she had stinted her laughter, she cried, "Hey, Vivien! certes thou art cunning beyond anything that I ever heard tell of, and I believe that thou art as wicked as thou art cunning. For whoever heard of a child of fifteen years old who would speak such words as thou has just now spoken; or whoever could suppose that so young a girl could conceive the thought of compassing the downfall of the wisest magician who hath ever lived."

Then Queen Morgana le Fay set to her lips a small whistle of ivory and gold and blew very shrilly upon it, and in reply there came running a young page of her Court. Queen Morgana commanded him to bring to her a certain casket of alabaster, cunningly carved and adorned with gold and set with several precious stones. And Queen Morgana opened the box and took from within it two rings of pure yellow gold, beautifully wrought and set, the one ring with a clear white stone of extraordinary brilliancy, and the other with a stone as red as blood. Then Queen Morgana said, "Vivien, behold these two rings! They possess each a spell of wonderful potency. For if thou wearest that ring with the white stone, whoever weareth the ring with the red stone shall love thee with such a passion of love that thou mayst do with him whatever thou hast a will to do. So take these rings and go to King Arthur's Court and use them as thy cunning may devise."

So Vivien took the two rings and gave Queen Morgana le Fay thanks beyond all measure for them.

Now King Arthur took much pleasure in holding a great

feast each Pentecost, at which time his Court was gathered about him with much mirth and rejoicing. At such times it delighted him to have some excellent entertainment for to amuse himself and his Court, wherefore it befell that nearly always something happened that gave much entertainment to the King. So came the Feast of Pentecost, and King Arthur sat at the table with a great many noble and lordly folk and several kings and queens. Now as they all sat at that feast, their spirits greatly expanded with mirth and good cheer, there suddenly came into the hall a very beautiful young damsel, and with her a dwarf, wonderfully misshapen and of a very hideous countenance. And the maiden was dressed all in flame-colored satin, very rich, and with beautiful embroidery of gold and embroidery of silver. And her hair, which was red like gold, was coiled into a net of gold. And her eyes were black as coals and extraordinarily bright and glistening. And she had about her throat a necklace of gold of three strands, so that with all that gold and those bright garments she shone with wonderful splendor as she entered the hall. Likewise, the dwarf who accompanied her was clad all in flame-colored raiment, and he bore in his hands a cushion of flame-colored silk with tassels of gold, and upon the cushion he bare a ring of exceeding beauty set with a red stone.

So when King Arthur beheld this beautiful maiden he supposed nothing else, than that there was some excellent entertainment, and at that he rejoiced a very great deal.

But when he looked well at the damsel it appeared to him that he knew her face, wherefore he said to her, "Damsel, who art thou?" "Sir," she said, "I am the daughter of the King of Northumberland, and my name is Vivien," and thereat King Arthur was satisfied.

Then King Arthur said to her, "Lady, what is that thou hast upon yonder cushion, and why hast thou honored us by coming hitherward?" To the which Vivien made reply, "Lord, I have here a very good entertainment for to give you pleasure at this Feast of Pentecost. For here is a ring of such a sort that only he who is the most wise and the most worthy of all men here present may wear it." And King Arthur said, "Let us see the ring."

So Vivien took the ring from the cushion which the dwarf held and she came and brought it unto King Arthur, and the King took the ring into his own hand. And he perceived that the ring was extraordinarily beautiful, wherefore he said, "Maiden, have I thy leave to try this ring upon my finger?" And Vivien said, "Yea, lord."

So King Arthur made attempt to place the ring upon his finger; but, lo! the ring shrank in size so that it would not pass beyond the first joint thereof. Wherefore King Arthur said, "It would appear that I am not worthy to wear this ring."

Then the damsel, Vivien, said, "Have I my lord's leave to offer this ring to others of his Court?" And King Arthur said, "Let the others try the ring." So Vivien took the ring to the various folk of the Court, both lords and ladies, but not one of these could wear the ring. Then last of all Vivien came to the place where Merlin sat, and she kneeled upon the ground before him and offered the ring to him; and Merlin, because this concerned himself, could not forecast into the future to know that harm was intended to him. Nevertheless he looked sourly upon the damsel and he said, "Child, what is this silly trick thou offerest me?" "Sir," quoth Vivien, "I beseech you for to try this ring upon your finger." Then Merlin regarded the damsel more closely, and he perceived that she was very beautiful, wherefore his heart softened toward her a great deal. So he spake more gently unto her and he said, "Wherefore should I take the ring?" To the which she made reply, "Because I believe that thou art the most wise and the most worthy of any man in all this place, wherefore the ring should belong to thee." Then Merlin smiled, and took the ring and placed it upon his finger, and, lo! it fitted the finger exactly. Thereupon Vivien cried out, "See! the ring hath fitted his finger and he is the most wise and the most worthy." And Merlin was greatly pleased that the ring which the beautiful damsel had given him had fitted his finger in that way.

Then, after a while, he would have withdrawn the ring again but, behold! he could not, for the ring had grown to his finger as though it were a part of the flesh and the bone thereof. At this Merlin became much troubled in spirit and very anxious, for he did not understand what might be meant by the magic of the ring. So he said, "Lady, whence came this ring?" And Vivien said, "Sir, thou knowest all things; dost thou then not know that this ring was sent hitherward from Morgana le Fay?" Then again Merlin was greatly a-doubt, and he said, "I hope there may be no evil in this ring." And Vivien smiled upon him and said, "What evil could there be in it?"

Now by this time the great magic that was in the ring began to work upon Merlin's spirit, wherefore he regarded Vivien very steadily, and suddenly he took great pleasure in her beauty. Then the magic of the ring gat entire hold upon him and, lo! a wonderful passion immediately seized upon his heart and wrung it so that it was pierced as with a violent agony.

And Vivien beheld what passed in Merlin's mind, and she laughed and turned away. And several others who were there also observed the very strange manner in which Merlin regarded her, wherefore they said among themselves, "Of a surety Merlin is bewitched by the beauty of that young damoiselle."

So, after that time the enchantment of the ring of Morgana le Fay so wrought upon Merlin's spirit that he could in no wise disentangle himself from Vivien's witchery; for from that day forth, whithersoever she went, there he might be found not far away; and if she was in the garden, he would be there; and if she was in the Hall, he also would be there; and if she went a-hawking he would also be a-horseback. And all the Court observed these things and many made themselves merry and jested upon it. But, Vivien hated Merlin with all her might, for she saw that they all made merry at that folly of Merlin's, and he wearied her with his regard. But she dissembled this disregard before his face and behaved to him in all ways as though she had a great friendship for him.

Now it happened upon a day that Vivien sat in the garden, and it was wonderfully pleasant summer weather, and Merlin came into the garden and beheld Vivien where she sat. But when Vivien perceived Merlin coming she suddenly felt so great a disregard for him that she could not bear for to be nigh him at that time, wherefore she arose in haste with intent to escape from him. But Merlin hurried and overtook her and he said to her, "Child, do you then hate me?" And Vivien said,

"Sir, I do not hate you." But Merlin said, "In very truth I believe that you do hate me." And Vivien was silent.

Then in a little Merlin said, "I would that I knew what I might do for you so that you would cease to hate me, for I find that I have a wonderful love for you." Upon this Vivien looked at Merlin very strangely, and by and by she said, "Sir, if you would only impart your wisdom and your cunning unto me, then I believe that I could love you a very great deal. For, behold! I am but as a young child in knowledge and thou art so old and so wise that I am afraid of thee. If thou wouldst teach me thy wisdom so that I might be thine equal, then haply I might grow to have such a regard for thee as thou wouldst have me feel."

Upon this Merlin looked very steadily at Vivien and he said, "Damsel, thou art, certes, no such foolish child as thou dost proclaim thyself to be; for I see that thine eyes are very bright with a cunning beyond thy years. Now I misdoubt that if I should teach thee the wisdom which thou dost desire to possess, either it would be to thy undoing or else it would be to my undoing."

Then Vivien cried out with a very loud and piercing voice, "Merlin, if thou dost love me, teach me thy wisdom and the cunning of thy magic and then I will love thee beyond anyone else in all the world!"

But Merlin sighed very deeply, for his heart misgave him. Then by and by he said, "Vivien, thou shalt have thy will and I will teach thee all those things of wisdom and magic that thou desirest to know."

Upon this Vivien was filled with such vehement agony of joy that she did not dare to let Merlin look into her countenance lest he should read what was therein written. Wherefore she cast down her eyes and turned her face away from him. Then in a little while she said, "Master, when wilt thou teach me that wisdom?"

To this Merlin made reply, "I shall not teach thee to-day nor to-morrow nor at this place; for I can only teach thee those knowledges in such solitude that there shall be nothing to disturb thy studies. But to-morrow thou shalt tell King Arthur that thou must return unto thy father's kingdom. Then we will depart together accompanied by thy Court; and when we have come to some secluded place, there I will build a habitation by the means of my magic and we shall abide therein until I have instructed thee in wisdom."

Then Vivien made great joy, and she caught Merlin's hand in hers and she kissed his hand with great passion.

So the next day Vivien besought King Arthur that he would give her leave to return unto her father's Court, and upon the third day she and Merlin and a number of attendants who were in service upon the damsel, quitted the Court of King Arthur and departed as though to go upon their way to the Kingdom of Northumberland.

But after they had gone some little distance from the Court of the King, they turned to the eastward and took their way toward a certain valley of which Merlin was acquainted, and which was so fair and pleasant a place that it was sometimes called the Valley of Delight, and sometimes the Valley of Joyousness.

Chapter Second

*How Merlin Journeyed With Vivien Unto
the Valley of Joyousness and How He
Builded for Her a Castle at That
Place. Also, How He Taught
Her the Wisdom of Magic
and of How She Compassed
His Downfall Thereby.*

So, Merlin and Vivien and those who were with them
travelled for three days to the eastward, until, toward the
end of the third day, they reached the confines of a very dark
and dismal forest. And there they beheld before them trees so
thickly interwoven together that the eyes could not see
anything at all of the sky because of the thickness of the foliage.
And they beheld the branches and the roots of the trees that
they appeared like serpents all twisted together. Wherefore
Vivien said, "Sir, this is a very dismal woodland." "Yea," said
Merlin, "so it appeareth to be. Ne'theless there lieth within
this forest that place which is called by some the Valley of
Joyousness, and by others the Valley of Delight, because of the
great beauty of that place. And there are several pathways
extending through this forest by the means of which that valley
may be reached by a man, whether a-horse or afoot."

And after a while they found it was as Merlin said, for they came by and by upon one of those pathways and entered it and penetrated into the forest. And, lo! within that doleful woodland it was so dark that it appeared as though night-time had fallen, although it was bright daylight beyond the borders thereof, wherefore many of that party were very much afraid. But Merlin ever gave them good cheer and so they went forward upon their way. So, by and by, they came out at last from that place and into the open again, whereat they were greatly rejoiced and took much comfort.

Now, by this time, the evening had come, very peaceful and tranquil, and they beheld beneath them a valley spread out in that light and it was wonderfully beautiful. And in the centre of the valley was a small lake so smooth and clear, like to crystal, that it appeared like an oval shield of pure silver laid down upon the ground. And all about the margin of the lake were level meadows covered over with an incredible multitude of flowers of divers colors and kinds, very beautiful to behold.

When Vivien saw this place she cried unto Merlin, "Master, this is, indeed, a very joyous valley, for I do not believe that the blessed meadows of Paradise are more beautiful than this." And Merlin said, "Very well; let us go down into it." So they went down and, as they descended, the night fell apace and the round moon arose into the sky and it was hard to tell whether that valley was the more beautiful in the daytime or whether it was the more beautiful when the moon shone down upon it in that wise.

So they all came at last unto the borders of the lake and they perceived that there was neither house nor castle at that place.

Now upon this the followers of Merlin murmured amongst themselves, saying, "This enchanter hath brought us hither-ward, but how will he now provide for us that we may find a resting-place that may shelter us from the inclement changes of the weather. For the beauty of this spot cannot alone shelter us from rain and storm." And Merlin overheard their murmur-ings and he said, "Peace! take ye no trouble upon that matter, for I will very soon provide ye a good resting-place." Then he said to them, "Stand ye a little distance aside till I show ye what I shall do." So they withdrew a little, as he commanded them, and he and Vivien remained where they were. And Vivien said, "Master, what wilt thou do?" And Merlin said, "Wait a little and thou shalt see."

Therewith he began a certain very powerful conjuration so that the earth began for to tremble and to shake and an appearance as of a great red dust arose into the air. And in this dust there began to appear sundry shapes and forms, and these shapes and forms arose very high into the air and by and by those who gazed thereon perceived that there was a great structure apparent in the midst of the cloud of red dust.

Then, after a while, all became quiet and the dust slowly disappeared from the air, and, behold! there was the appearance of a marvellous castle such as no one there had ever beheld before, even in a dream. For the walls thereof were of ultramarine and vermilion and they were embellished and adorned with figures of gold, wherefore that castle showed in the moonlight like as it were a pure vision of great glory.

Now Vivien beheld all that Merlin had accomplished and she went unto him and kneeled down upon the ground before him and took his hand and set it to her lips. And while she kneeled thus, she said, "Master, this is assuredly the most wonderful thing in the world. Wilt thou then teach me such magic that I may be able to build a castle like this castle out of the elements?" And Merlin said, "Yea; all this will I teach thee and more besides; for I will teach thee not only how thou mayst create such a structure as this out of invisible things, but will also teach thee how thou mayst, with a single touch of thy wand, dissipate that castle instantly into the air; even as a child, with a stroke of a straw, may dissipate a beautiful shining bubble, which, upon an instant is, and upon another instant is not. And I will teach thee more than that, for I will teach thee how to change and transform a thing into the semblance of a different thing; and I will teach thee spells and charms such as thou didst never hear tell of before."

Then Vivien cried out, "Master, thou art the most wonderful man in all of the world!" And Merlin looked upon Vivien and her face was very beautiful in the moonlight and he loved her a very great deal. Wherefore he smiled upon her and said, "Vivien, dost thou still hate me?" And she said, "Nay, master."

But she spake not the truth, for in her heart she was evil and the heart of Merlin was good, and that which is evil will always hate that which is good. Wherefore, though Vivien lusted for the knowledge of necromancy, and though she spake so lovingly with her lips, yet in her spirit she both feared and hated Merlin because of his wisdom. For she wist right well that, except for the enchantment of that ring which he wore, Merlin would not love her any longer in that wise. Wherefore she said in her heart, "If Merlin teaches me all of his wisdom, then the world cannot contain both him and me."

Now Merlin abided with Vivien in that place for a year and a little more, and in that time he taught her all of magic that he was able to impart. So at the end of that time he said unto her, "Vivien, I have now taught thee so much that I believe there is no one in all of the world who knoweth more than thou dost of these things of magic which thou hast studied in this time. For not only hast thou such power of sorcery that thou canst make the invisible elements take form at thy will, and not only canst thou transform at thy will one thing into the appearance of an altogether different thing, but thou hast such potent magic in thy possession that thou mayst entangle any living soul into the meshes thereof, unless that one hath some very good talisman to defend himself from thy wiles. Nor have I myself very much more power than this that I have given to thee."

So said Merlin, and Vivien was filled with great joy. And she said in her heart, "Now, Merlin, if I have the good fortune to entangle thee in my spells, then shalt thou never behold the world again."

Now, when the next day had come, Vivien caused a very noble feast to be prepared for herself and Merlin. And by means of the knowledge which Merlin had imparted to her she produced a certain very potent sleeping-potion which was altogether without taste. This potion she herself infused into a certain noble wine, and the wine she poured into a golden chalice of extraordinary beauty.

So when that feast was ended, and whiles she and Merlin sat together, Vivien said, "Master, I have a mind to do thee a great honor." And Merlin said, "What is it?" "Thou shalt see," said Vivien. Therewith she smote her hands together and there

immediately came a young page unto where they were, and he
bare that chalice of wine in his hand and gave it unto Vivien.
Then Vivien took the chalice and she went to where Merlin sat
and kneeled down before him and said, "Sir, I beseech thee to
take this chalice and to drink the wine that is within it. For as
that wine is both very noble and very precious, so is thy

wisdom both very noble and very precious; and as the wine is
contained within a chalice of priceless cost, so is thy wisdom
contained within a life that hath been beyond all value to the
world." Therewith she set her lips to the chalice and kissed the
wine that was in it.

Then Merlin suspected no evil, but he took the chalice and
quaffed of the wine with great cheerfulness.

After that, in a little, the fumes of that potent draught began
to arise into the brains of Merlin and it was as though a cloud
descended upon his sight, and when this came upon him he was
presently aware that he was betrayed, wherefore he cried out
thrice in a voice, very bitter and full of agony, "Woe! Woe!
Woe!" And then he cried out, "I am betrayed!" And therewith he strove to arise from where he sat but he could not.

That while Vivien sat with her chin upon her hands and regarded him very steadily, smiling strangely upon him. So presently Merlin ceased his struggles and sank into a sleep so deep that it was almost as though he had gone dead. And when that had happened Vivien arose and leaned over him and set a very powerful spell upon him. And she stretched out her forefinger and wove an enchantment all about him so that it was as though he was entirely encompassed with a silver web of enchantment. And when she had ended, Merlin could move neither hand nor foot nor even so much as a finger-tip, but was altogether like some great insect that a cunning and beautiful spider had enmeshed in a net-work of fine, strong web.

Now, when the next morning had come, Merlin awoke from his sleep and he beheld that Vivien sat over against him regarding him very narrowly. And they were in the same room in which he had fallen asleep. And when Vivien perceived that Merlin was awake, she laughed and said, "Merlin, how is it with thee?" And Merlin groaned with great passion, saying, "Vivien, thou hast betrayed me."

At this Vivien laughed again very shrilly and piercingly, and she said, "Behold! Merlin, thou art altogether in my power; for thou art utterly inwoven in those enchantments which thou, thyself, hast taught me. For lo! thou canst not move a single hair without my will. And when I leave thee, the world shall see thee no more and all thy wisdom shall be my wisdom and all thy power shall be my power, and there shall be no other in the whole world who shall possess the wisdom which I possess."

Then Merlin groaned with such fervor that it was as though his heart would burst asunder. And he said, "Vivien, thou hast brought me to such shame that even were I released from this spell I could not endure that any man should ever see my face again. For I grieve not for my undoings so much as I grieve at the folly that hath turned mine own wisdom against me to my destruction. So I forgive thee all things that thou hast done to me to betray me; yet there is one thing alone which I crave of thee."

And Vivien said, "Does it concern thee?" And Merlin said, "No, it concerns another." Then Vivien said, "What is it?"

Then Merlin said, "It is this: Now I have received my gift of foresight again, and I perceive that King Arthur is presently in great peril of his life. So I beseech thee, Vivien, that thou wilt straightway go to where he is in danger, and that thou wilt use thy powers of sorcery for to save him. Thus, by fulfilling this one good deed, thou shalt haply lessen the sin of this that thou hast done to betray me."

Now at that time Vivien was not altogether bad as she afterward became, for she still felt some small pity for Merlin and some small reverence for King Arthur. Wherefore now she laughed and said, "Very well, I will do thy desire in this matter. Whither shall I go to save that King?"

Then Merlin replied, "Go into the West country and unto the castle of a certain knight hight Sir Domas de Noir, and when thou comest there then thou shalt immediately see how thou mayst be of aid to the good King." Upon this Vivien said, "I will do this thing for thee, for it is the last favor that anyone may ever render unto thee in this world."

Therewith Vivien smote her hands together and summoned many of her attendants. And when these had come in she presented Merlin before them, and she said, "Behold how I have bewitched him. Go! See for yourselves! Feel of his hands and his face and see if there be any life in him." And they went to Merlin and felt of him; his hands and arms and his face, and even they plucked at his beard, and Merlin could not move in any wise but only groan with great dolor. So they all laughed and made them merry at his woful state.

Then Vivien caused it by means of her magic that there should be in that place a great coffer of stone. And she commanded those who were there that they should lift Merlin up and lay him therein and they did as she commanded. Then she caused it that, by means of her magic, there should be placed a huge slab of stone upon that coffer such as ten men could hardly lift, and Merlin lay beneath that stone like one who was dead.

Then Vivien caused it to be that the magic castle should instantly disappear and so it befell as she willed. Then she caused it that a mist should arise at that place, and the mist was of such a sort that no one could penetrate into it, or sever it asunder, nor could any human eye see what was within. Then, when she had done all this, she went her way with all of her Court from that valley, making great joy in that she had triumphed over Merlin.

Nevertheless she did not forget her promise, but went to the castle of Sir Domas de Noir, and after a while it shall all be told how it befell at that place.

Such was the passing of Merlin, and God grant it that you may not so misuse the wisdom He giveth you to have, that it may be turned against you to your undoing. For there can be no greater bitterness in the world than this: That a man shall be betrayed by one to whom he himself hath given the power of betraying him.

And now turn we unto King Arthur to learn how it fell with him after Merlin had thus been betrayed to his undoing.

Chapter Third

*How Queen Morgana le Fay Returned to
Camelot and to the Court With Intent to
Do Ill to King Arthur. Also How King
Arthur and Others Went a-Hunting
and of What Befell Thereby.*

Now, after Merlin had quitted the Court with Vivien in
that manner aforetold, Queen Morgana le Fay returned
again to Camelot. There she came unto King Arthur and
kneeled before him, bowing her face, with an appearance of
great humility. And she said, "Brother, I have meditated much
upon these matters that have passed and I perceive that I have
done very ill to talk against thee as I have done, and to be so
rebellious against thy royalty. Wherefore I crave of thee to
forgive me my evil words and thoughts against thee."

Then King Arthur was very much moved and he came to
Queen Morgana and took her by the hand and lifted her up
upon her feet and kissed her brow, and her eyes, saying, "My
sister, I have no ill-will against thee, but nothing but love for
thee in my heart." And so, Queen Morgana le Fay abode at the
Court in the same manner as she had aforetime done, for King
Arthur believed that they were reconciled.

Now one day, Queen Morgana and the King fell into a friendly talk concerning Excalibur, and Queen Morgana le Fay expressed a very great desire to see that noble weapon more closely than she had yet done, and King Arthur said he would sometime show it to her. So the next day he said, "Sister, come with me and I will show thee Excalibur." Therewith he took Queen Morgana by the hand and led her into another apartment where was a strong wooden coffer bound with bands of iron. Then the King opened the coffer and therein Queen Morgana le Fay beheld Excalibur where he lay in his sheath. Then King Arthur said to her, "Lady, take this sword and examine it as you please." Therewith Queen Morgana took Excalibur into her hands and lifted him out of the coffer. And she drew the sword out of the sheath and, lo! the blade flashed like lightning. Then she said, "Sir, this is a very beautiful sword and I would that I might take it hence and keep it for a little so that I might enjoy it in full measure."

Now King Arhtur was of a mind to show the Queen great courtesy at this time of their reconciliation, wherefore he said to her, "Take it, and be thou its keeper for as long as thou wilt." So Queen Morgana took Excalibur and his sheath and bare them away with her to her inn, and she hid the sword in the bed in which she slept.

Then Queen Morgana sent for sundry goldsmiths, eight in number, and for certain armorsmiths, eight in number, and for certain cunning jewellers, eight in number, and she said unto them, "Make me a sword in every particular like this sword that I have here." And thereupon she showed then Excalibur in his sheath. So these goldsmiths and armorsmiths and lapidaries labored with great diligence, and in a fortnight they had made a sword so exactly like Excalibur that no eye could have told the difference betwixt the one and the other. And Queen Morgana le Fay kept both swords by her until her purposes should have been fulfilled.

It befell upon a certain day that King Arthur proclaimed a hunt, and he and all of his Court were party thereunto.

Now the day before this hunt took place Queen Morgana le Fay came to King Arthur and said, "Brother, I have here for thee a very beautiful and noble horse which I intend to give thee as a gift of love." Therewith she called aloud and there came two grooms bringing a horse as black as jet and all beset with trappings and harness of silver. And the horse was of such extraordinary beauty that neither King Arthur nor anybody who was with him had ever before seen its like for beauty. So a wonderful delight possessed the King at sight of the horse and he said, "Sister, this is the noblest gift I have had given to me for this long time." "Ha! brother," quoth Queen Morgana, "doth that horse then belike thee?" "Yea," said King Arthur, "it belikes me more than any horse that I ever beheld before." "Then," quoth Queen Morgana, "consider it as a gift of reconciliation betwixt thee and me. And in sign of that reconciliation I beg of thee that thou wilt ride that horse forth upon the hunt to-morrow day." And King Arthur said, "I will do so."

So the next day he rode forth to the hunt upon that horse as he said that he would do.

Now it happened some time after noon that the hounds started a hart of extraordinary size, and the King and all of his Court followed the chase with great eagerness. But the horse of King Arthur soon outstripped all the other horses saving only that of a certain very honorable and worthy knight of the Court hight Sir Accalon of Gaul. So Sir Accalon and the King rode at a great pace through the forest, and they were so eager with the chase that they wist not whither they were riding. And at last they overtook the hart and found that it was embushed in a very thick and tangled part of the forest, and there King Arthur slew the stag, and so the chase was ended.

Now after this had come to pass, the King and Sir Accalon would have retraced their way whither they had come, but in a little they perceived that they were lost in the mazes of the woodland and wist not where they were. For they had followed the chase so far that they were in an altogether strange country. So they wandered hither and thither at great length until eventide, at which time they were oppressed with hunger and weariness. Then King Arthur said to Sir Accalon, "Messire, meseems we shall have nowhere to rest ourselves to-night unless it be beneath a tree in this forest."

To this Sir Accalon made reply, "Lord, if thou wilt follow my counsel thou wilt let our horses seek their own way through this wilderness, so, haply, because of the instinct of such creatures, they shall bring us unto some place of habitation."

Now this advice appeared to be very good to King Arthur, wherefore he did as Sir Accalon advised and let loose his bridle-rein and allowed his horse to travel as it listed. So King Arthur's horse went along a certain path, and Sir Accalon followed after the King. And they went a great pass in this wise, and the night was descending upon them in the forest.

But, before it was entirely dark, they emerged out of that forest and into an open place where they beheld before them a very wide estuary, as it were an inlet of the sea. And before them was a beach of sand, very smooth, and white, and they two went down to that beach and stood upon the shore, and they wist not what to do, for there was no habitation in sight in any direction.

Now, whiles they stood there a-doubt, they suddenly perceived a ship at a very great distance away. And this ship approached where they were, sailing very rapidly. As the ship drew nigh to that place they perceived that it was of a very strange and wonderful appearance, for it was painted in many divers colors, very gaudy and brilliant, and the sails were all of cloth of silk, woven in divers colors and embroidered with figures like to the figures of a tapestry; and King Arthur was very greatly amazed at the appearance of that ship.

Now, as they stood so watching the ship, they perceived that it drew nigher and nigher to that place where they were, and in a little it beached itself upon the shore of sand not very far away from them.

Then King Arthur said to Sir Accalon, "Sir, let us go forward to the shore where we may look into this ship, for never did I see its like before in all of my life, wherefore I have a thought that maybe it is fay."

So they two went to where the ship was and they stood upon the shore and looked down into it, and at first they thought that there was no one upon board of the ship, for it appeared to be altogether deserted. But as they stood there marvelling at the wonderfulness of that ship and at the manner in which it had come thither, they beheld, of a sudden, that certain curtains that hung before an apartment at the farther extremity of the ship were parted asunder and there came forth from that place twelve very beautiful damsels. Each of these was clad in a rich garment of scarlet satin very bright and shining, and each wore around her head a circlet of gold, and each had many bracelets of gold upon her arms. These damsels came forward unto where the two knights were and they said, "Welcome, King Arthur!" And they said, "Welcome, Sir Accalon!"

At this King Arthur was very much astonished that they should know him, and he said, "Fair ladies, how is this? Ye appear to know me very well, but I know ye not. Who are ye that know me and my companion and call us by name?"

Unto this the chiefest of those damsels made reply, "Sir, we are part fay and we know all about you; and we know how that ye have been following a very long chase; and we know that ye are aweary, anhungered, and athirst. Wherefore we beseech ye that ye come aboard of this ship and rest and refresh yourselves with food and drink."

Now, this appeared to King Arthur to be a very bel-adventure, wherefore he said to Sir Accalon, "Messire, I have a great mind for to go aboard this ship and to follow out this adventure." And Sir Accalon said, "Lord, if thou goest, I will go also."

So those ladies let fall a gangplank from the ship and King Arthur and Sir Accalon drave their horses up the gangplank and aboard the ship, and immediately they did so, the ship withdrew itself from the sands and sailed away as it had come—very swiftly—and it was now the early nighttime with the moon very round and full in the sky like to a disk of pure shining silver.

Then those twelve damoiselles aided King Arthur and Sir Accalon to dismount; and some took their horses away and others led them into a fair chamber at the end of the ship. And in this chamber King Arthur beheld that a table had been placed as though for their entertainment, spread with a linen cloth and set with divers savory meats, and with manchets of white bread and with several different sorts of excellent wines.

And at the sight King Arthur and Sir Accalon were very much rejoiced, for they were very greatly anhungered.

So they immediately sat themselves down at that table and they ate and drank with great heartiness, and whiles they did so some of those damsels served them with food, and others held them in pleasant discourse, and others made music upon lutes and citterns for their entertainment. So they feasted and made very merry.

But, after a while, a very great drowsiness of sleep began to descend upon King Arthur; albeit, he deemed that that drowsiness had come upon him because of the weariness of the chase. So presently he said, "Fair damsels, ye have refreshed us a very great deal and this hath been a very pleasant adventure. But I would now that ye had a place for us to sleep."

Unto this the chiefest of the damsels replied, "Lord, this boat hath been prepared for your refreshment, wherefore all things have been made ready for you with entire fulness."

Therewith some of those twelve damsels conducted King Arthur into a sleeping-chamber that had been prepared for him, and others led Sir Accalon into another chamber prepared for him. And King Arthur marvelled at the beauty of his chamber, for he thought that he had never beheld a more excellently bedight bed-chamber than that one into which he had now entered. So King Arthur laid himself down with much comfort to his body, and straightway he fell into a deep and gentle sleep, without dream or disturbance of any sort.

Now when King Arthur awoke from that sleep, he was astonished beyond all measure so that he wist not whether he was still asleep and dreaming, or whether he was awake. For, lo! he lay upon a pallet in a very dark and dismal chamber all of stone. And he perceived that this chamber was a dungeon, and all about him he heard the sound of many voices in woful complaint. Then King Arthur said to himself, "Where is that ship in which I was last night, and what hath become of those ladies with whom I spake?"

Upon this he looked about him and, behold! he saw that he was indeed in a dungeon and that there were many knights in very sad estate all about him. Wherefore he perceived that they also were captives and that it was they who had made that sound of woful lamentation which he had heard when awaking.

Then King Arthur aroused himself from where he lay and he saw that all those knights who were prisoners there were strangers unto him, and he knew not them and they knew not him. And of these knights there were two and twenty who were prisoners in that place.

Then King Arthur said, "Messires, who are you and where am I at these present?" To the which the chiefest of those knights who were prisoners made reply, "Sir, we are, like yourself, prisoners in a dungeon of this castle, and the castle belongs to a certain knight, hight Sir Domas, surnamed le Noir."

Then King Arthur made great marvel at what had befallen him, wherefore he said, "Messires, here is a very singular thing hath happened to me, for last night I was asleep in a very wonderful ship that I believe was fay, and with me was a knight-companion, and, lo! this morning I awake alone in this dungeon, and know not how I came hither."

"Sir," said the knight who spake for the others, "thou wert last night brought hither by two men clad in black, and thou wert laid down upon yonder pallet without awaking, wherefore it is very plain to me that thou art in the same case that we are in, and that thou art a prisoner unto this Sir Domas le Noir."

Then King Arthur said, "Tell me, who is this Sir Domas, for I declare that I never before heard of him." "I will tell you," said the captive knight, and therewith he did so as follows:

"I believe," said he, "that this Sir Domas is the falsest knight that liveth, for he is full of treason and leasing, and is altogether a coward in this heart. Yet he is a man of very great estate and very powerful in these parts.

"Now there are two brothers, and Sir Domas is one and the other is hight Sir Ontzlake, and Sir Domas is the elder and Sir Ontzlake is the younger. When the father of these two knights died, he left the one an equal patrimony with the other. But now it hath come about that Sir Domas hath nearly all of those estates and that Sir Ontzlake hath only one castle, which same he now holdeth by the force of arms and because of his own courage. For, though Sir Domas is altogether a coward in his heart, yet he hath cunning and guile beyond any man of whom I ever heard tell; wherefore it hath so come about that of his father's patrimony Sir Domas hath everything and Sir Ontzlake hath nothing saving only that one castle and the estate thereunto appertaining.

"Now it would appear to be very strange that Sir Domas is not satisfied with all this, yet he is not satisfied, but he covets that one castle and that small estate that is his brother's, so that he can hardly have any pleasure in life because of his covetousness. Yet he knoweth not how to obtain that estate from his brother, for Sir Ontzlake is a very excellent knight, and the only way that Sir Domas can lay hands upon that estate is by having to do with his brother as man to man in a contest at arms, and this he is afraid to attempt.

"So, for a long time, Sir Domas hath been in search of a knight who may take up his case for him, and do battle against Sir Ontzlake in his behalf. Wherefore all the knights whom he can arrest he bringeth to this castle and giveth them their choice, either to take up his case against his brother, or else to remain in this place as his prisoner without ransom. So he hath arrested all of us, and hath made demand of each that he should do battle in his behalf. But not one of us will take up the case of such an evil-conditioned knight as Sir Domas, so we all remain his prisoners."

"Well," quoth King Arthur, "this is a very wonderful case. But methinks that if Sir Domas maketh his appeal to me, I will take up his case. For I would rather do that than remain a prisoner here for all my life. But if I should take upon me this battle and be successful therein, then I will afterward have to do with Sir Domas himself in such a manner as I do not believe would be very much to his liking."

Now a little while after this the door of that prison-house was opened by the porter, and there entered a very fair young damsel. And this damsel came to King Arthur and she said to him, "What cheer?" "I cannot tell," quoth King Arthur, "but meseems I am in a very sorry pass in this place." "Sir," said the damsel, "I am grieved to see so noble-appearing a knight in so dolorous a case. But if you will undertake to defend the cause of the lord of this castle with your person against his enemy, then you shall have leave to go whithersoever you please." To this King Arthur made reply, "Lady, this is a very hard case, that either I must fight a battle I care not for, or else remain a prisoner here without ransom for all of my days. But I would liever fight than live here all my life, and so I will undertake that adventure as thou wouldst have me do. But if I do battle for the lord of this castle, and if I should have Grace of Heaven to win that battle, then it must be that all these, my companions in imprisonment, shall also go forth with me into freedom."

To this the damsel said, "Very well, be it so, for that shall content the master of this castle."

Then King Arthur looked more closely at the maiden, and he said, "Damsel, meseems I should know thy face, for I think I have seen thee somewhere before this." "Nay, sir," said she, "that can hardly be, for I am the daughter of the lord of this castle."

But in this she was false, for she was one of the damsels of Morgana le Fay; and she was one of those who had beguiled King Arthur into the ship the night before; and it was she who had brought him to that castle and had delivered him into the hands of Sir Domas. And all these things she had done upon command of Queen Morgana le Fay.

Then King Arthur said, "But if I do this battle, thou must carry a message for me unto the Court of King Arthur, and that message must be delivered unto Queen Morgana le Fay into her own hands. Then, when that is done, I will do this battle for the cause of Sir Domas." And the damsel said, "It shall be done so."

So King Arthur wrote a sealed letter to Queen Morgana le Fay that she should send to him his sword Excalibur; and he sent that message to her. And when Queen Morgana received that letter she laughed and said, "Very well, he shall have a sword that shall please his eye as well as Excalibur." And therewith she sent him that other sword that she had had made exactly like Excalibur.

So Sir Domas sent word unto his brother Sir Ontzlake, that he had now a champion for to do battle in his behalf to recover all that portion of their patrimony which Sir Ontzlake still withheld from him.

Now when Sir Ontzlake received this message he was thrown into great trouble of spirit, for a little while before he had been very sorely wounded in a tournament in the which a spear had been thrust through both his thighs, so that he was then abed with that wound and without power to arise therefrom. Wherefore he wist not what to do in this case, for he could not do battle upon his own behalf, and he had no one to do battle for him.

Chapter Fourth

*What Befell Sir Accalon, and How King
Arthur Fought an Affair-at-Arms
With Swords, and How He Came
Nigh to Losing His Life
Thereby.*

HERE followeth the account of what happened unto Sir Accalon the morning after he went aboard that magic ship with King Arthur as aforetold.

Now when Sir Accalon awoke from that same sleep it was with him as it had been with King Arthur; for, at first, he wist not whether he was still asleep and dreaming or whether he was awake. For, lo! he found himself to be lying beside a marble basin of clear water that gushed up very high from a silver tube. And he perceived that not far from this fountain was a large pavilion of parti-colored silk which stood upon the borders of a fair meadow of grass.

So Sir Accalon was altogether astonished to find himself in this place when he had fallen asleep on board that ship, wherefore he was afraid that all this was the fruit of some very evil spell. So he crossed himself and said, "God save King Arthur from any harm, for it seems to me that those damsels upon that ship have wrought some magic upon us for to separate us the one from the other." So saying, he arose from where he lay with intent to inquire further into that matter.

Now, as he made some noise in bestirring himself, there came forth from that pavilion aforementioned a very hideous dwarf, who saluted him with all civility and with high respect. Then Sir Accalon said to the dwarf, "Sirrah, who are you?" Unto which the dwarf made answer, "Messire, I belong unto the lady of yonder pavilion, and she hath sent me to bid you welcome to this place, and to invite you in for to partake of a repast with her." "Ha!" quoth Sir Accalon, "and how was it I came hither?" "Sir," said the dwarf, "I do not know, but when we looked forth this morning we saw you lying here by the fountain side."

Then Sir Accalon made great marvel at that which had happened to him, and by and by he said, "Who is thy lady?" To which the dwarf replied, "She is hight the Lady Gomyne of the Fair Hair, and she will be passingly glad of your company in her pavilion."

Upon this Sir Accalon arose, and, having laved himself at the fountain and so refreshed himself, he went with the dwarf unto the pavilion of that lady. And when he had come there he saw that in the centre of the pavilion was a table of silver spread with a fair white cloth and covered with very excellent food for a man to break his fast withal.

Now immediately Sir Accalon came into the pavilion, the curtains upon the further side thereof were parted and there entered from a further chamber a very beautiful lady and gave Sir Accalon welcome to that place. And Sir Accalon said to her, "Lady, methinks thou art very civil to invite me thus into thy pavilion." "Nay, sir," said the lady, "it took no great effort to be civil unto a knight so worthy as thou." Then she said to Sir Accalon, "Sir, wilt thou sit here at the table with me and break thy fast?"

At this Sir Accalon was very glad, for he was anhungered, and the beauty of the lady pleased him a very great deal, wherefore it afforded him great joy for to be in her company.

So they two sat at the table with a very cheerful and pleasant spirit and the dwarf waited upon them.

Now after Sir Accalon and the Lady of the Pavilion had

broken their fasts she spake to him in this wise, "Sir knight, thou appearest to be a very strong and worthy lord and one very well used to feats of arms and to prowess in battle."

To this Sir Accalon made reply, "Lady, it does not beseem me to bespeak of my own worth, but this much I may freely say; I have engaged in several affrays at arms in such measure as a knight with belt and spurs may do, and I believe that both my friends and mine enemies have had reason to say that I have at all times done my devoirs to the best of my powers."

Then the damoiselle said, "I believe you are a very brave and worthy knight, and being such you might be of service to a good worthy knight who is in sad need of such service as one knight may render unto another."

To this Sir Accalon said, "What is that service?" And the damoiselle replied, "I will tell thee: There is, dwelling not far from this place, a certain knight hight Sir Ontzlake, who hath an elder brother hight Sir Domas. This Sir Domas hath served Sir Ontzlake very ill in many ways, and hath deprived him of well nigh all of his patrimony, so that only a little is left to Sir Ontzlake of all the great possessions that were one time his father's. But even such a small holding as that Sir Domas begrudges Sir Ontzlake, so that Sir Ontzlake must needs hold what he hath by such force of arms as he may himself maintain. Now Sir Domas hath found himself a champion who is a man of a great deal of strength and prowess, and through this champion Sir Domas challenges Sir Ontzlake's right to hold even that small part of those lands which were one time his father's; wherefore if Sir Ontzlake would retain what is his he must presently do battle therefore.

"Now this is a very sad case for Sir Ontzlake, for a short time since he was wounded by a spear at a tournament and was pierced through both of his thighs, wherefore he is not now able to sit upon his horse and to defend his rights against assault. Wherefore meseems that a knight could have no better cause to show his prowess than in the defence of so sad a case as this."

So spake that lady, and to all she said Sir Accalon listened with great attention, and when she had ended he said, "Lady, I would be indeed right willing to defend Sir Ontzlake's right, but, lo! I have no armor nor have I any arms to do battle withal."

Then that damoiselle smiled very kindly upon Sir Accalon and she said to him, "Sir, Sir Ontzlake may easily fit thee with armor that shall be altogether to thy liking. And as for arms, I have in this pavilion a sword that hath but one other fellow in all the world."

Upon this she arose and went back into that curtained recess from which she had come, and thence she presently returned, bringing a certain thing wrapped in a scarlet cloth. And she opened the cloth before Sir Accalon's eyes, and lo! that which she had there was King Arthur's sword Excalibur in his sheath. Then the damoiselle said, "This sword shall be thine if thou wilt assume this quarrel upon behalf of Sir Ontzlake."

Now when Sir Accalon beheld that sword he wist not what to think, and he said to himself, "Certes, either this is Excalibur or else it is his twin brother." Therewith he drew the blade from out of its shield and it shined with extraordinary splendor. Then Sir Accalon said, "I know not what to think for pure wonder, for this sword is indeed the very image of another sword I wot of." When he so spake that damoiselle smiled upon him again, and she said, "I have heard tell that there is in the world another sword like to this."

Then Sir Accalon said, "Lady, to win this sword for myself I would be willing to fight in any battle whatsoever." And the damoiselle replied, "Then if thou wilt fight this battle for Sir Ontzlake thou art free to keep that sword for thine own," at the which Sir Accalon was rejoiced beyond all measure of gladness.

So it came about that, by the wiles of Queen Morgana le Fay, King Arthur was brought to fight a battle unknowingly with a knight very much beloved by him, and that that knight had Excalibur to use against his master. For all these things had come to pass through the cunning of Morgana le Fay.

Now a fair field was prepared for that battle in such a place as was convenient both to Sir Domas and to Sir Ontzlake, and thither they came upon the day assigned, each with his knight-champion and his attendants, Sir Ontzlake being brought thither in a litter because of the sore wound in his thighs. Also a great many other folk came to behold the combat, for the news thereof had gone forth to a great distance around about that place. So, all being in readiness, the two knights that were to do battle in that field were brought within the barriers of combat, each fully armed and each mounted upon a very good horse.

Now King Arthur was clad all in armor of Sir Domas, and Sir Accalon was clad in armor that belonged to Sir Ontzlake, and the head of each was covered by his helmet so that neither of those two knew the other.

Then the herald came forth and announced that the battle was toward, and each knight immediately put himself in readiness for the assault. Thereupon, the word for assault being given, the two rushed forth, each from his station, with such speed and fury that it was wonderful to behold. And so they met in the midst of the course with a roar as of thunder, and the spear of each knight was burst all into small pieces unto the truncheon which he held in his hand. Upon this each knight voided his horse with great skill and address, and allowed it to run at will in that field. And each threw aside the truncheon of his spear and drew his sword, and thereupon came, the one against the other, with the utmost fury of battle.

It was at this time that Vivien came to that place upon the behest of Merlin, and she brought with her such a Court and state of beauty that a great many people took notice of her with great pleasure. So Vivien and her Court took stand at the barriers whence they might behold all that was toward. And Vivien regarded those two knights and she could not tell which was King Arthur and which was his enemy, wherefore she said, "Well, I will do as Merlin desired me to do, but I must wait and see this battle for a while ere I shall be able to tell which is King Arthur, for it would be a pity to cast my spells upon the wrong knight."

So these two knights came together in battle afoot, and first they foined and then they both struck at the same time and, lo! the sword of King Arthur did not bite into the armor of Sir Accalon, but the sword of Sir Accalon bit very deeply into the armor of King Arthur and wounded him so sorely that the blood ran down in great quantities into his armor. And after that they struck very often and very powerfully, and as it was at first so it was afterward, for the sword of Sir Accalon ever bit into the armor of King Arthur, and the sword of King Arthur bit not at all into his enemy's armor. So in a little while it came that King Arthur's armor was stained all over red with the blood that flowed out from a great many wounds, and Sir Accalon bled not at all because of the sheath of Excalibur which he wore at his side. And the blood of King Arthur flowed down upon the ground so that all the grass around about was ensanguined with it. So when King Arthur beheld how all the ground was wet with his own blood, and how his enemy bled not at all, he began to fear that he would die in that battle: wherefore he said to himself, "How is this? Hath the virtue departed out of Excalibur and his sheath? Were it not otherwise I would think that that sword which cutteth me so sorely is Excalibur and that this sword is not Excalibur."

Upon this a great despair of death came upon him, and he ran at Sir Accalon and smote him so sore a blow upon the helm that Sir Accalon nigh fell down upon the ground.

But at that blow the sword of King Arthur broke short off at the cross of the handle and fell into the grass among the blood, and the pommel thereof and the cross thereof was all that King Arthur held in his hand.

Now at that blow Sir Accalon waxed very mad, so he ran at King Arthur with intent to strike him some dolorous blow. But when he saw that King Arthur was without weapon, he paused in his assault and he said, "Sir Knight, I see that thou art without weapon and that thou hast lost a great deal of blood. Wherefore I demand thee to yield thyself unto me."

Then King Arthur was again very much a-dread that his death was near to him; yet, because of his royalty, it was not possible for him to yield to any knight. So he said, "Nay, Sir Knight, I may not yield myself unto thee for I would liever die with honor than yield myself without honor. For though I lack a weapon, there are peculiar reasons why I may not lack worship. Wherefore thou mayst slay me as I am without weapon and that will be thy shame and not my shame."

"Well," said Sir Accalon, "as for the shame I will not spare thee unless thou dost yield to me." And King Arthur said, "I will not yield me." Thereupon Sir Accalon said, "Then stand thou away from me so that I may strike thee." And, when King Arthur had done as Sir Accalon bade him, Sir Accalon smote him such a woful blow that the King fell down upon his knees. Then Sir Accalon raised Excalibur with intent to strike King Arthur again, and with that all the people who were there cried out upon him to spare so worshipful a knight. But Sir Accalon would not spare him.

Then Vivien said unto herself, "Certes, that must be King Arthur who is so near to his death, and I do make my vow that it would be a great pity for him to die after he hath fought so fiercely." So when Sir Accalon raised his sword that second time with intent to strike his enemy, Vivien smote her hands with great force, and emitted at the same time a spell of such potency that it appeared to Sir Accalon upon the instant as though he had received some very powerful blow upon his arm. For with that spell his arm was benumbed all from the finger-tips unto the hollow of his armpit, and thereupon Excalibur fell out of Sir Accalon's hands and into the grass.

Then King Arthur beheld the sword and he perceived that it was Excalibur and therewith he knew that he had been betrayed. Wherefore he cried out thrice, in a very loud voice, "Treason! Treason! Treason!" and with that he set his knee upon the blade and before Sir Accalon could stay him he had seized it into his hands.

Then it appeared to King Arthur that a great virtue had come into him because of that sword. Wherefore he arose from his knees and ran at Sir Accalon and smote him so sorely that the blade penetrated his armor to the depth of half a palm's breadth. And he smote him again and again and Sir Accalon cried out in a loud voice, and fell down upon his hands and knees. Then King Arthur ran to him and catched the sheath of Excalibur and plucked it away from Sir Accalon and flung it away, and thereupon the wounds of Sir Accalon burst out bleeding in great measure. Then King Arthur catched the helmet of Sir Accalon and rushed it off his head with intent to slay him.

Now because King Arthur was blinded with his own blood he did not know Sir Accalon, wherefore he said, "Sir Knight, who art thou who hast betrayed me?" And Sir Accalon said, "I have not betrayed thee. I am Sir Accalon of Gaul and I am knight in good worship of King Arthur's Court."

But when King Arthur heard this he made great outcry and he said, "How is this? Know you who I am?" And Sir Accalon said, "Nay, I know you not." Then King Arthur said, "I am King Arthur who am thy master." And upon this he took off his helmet and Sir Accalon knew him.

And when Sir Accalon beheld King Arthur he swooned away and lay like one dead upon the ground, and King Arthur said, "Take him hence."

Then when those who were there were aware who King Arthur was, they burst over the barriers and ran toward him with great outcry of pity. And King Arthur would have left this place but upon that he also swooned away because of the great issue of blood that had come from him, wherefore all those who were round about took great sorrow, thinking that he was dying, wherefore they bewailed themselves without stint.

Then came Vivien out into that field and she said, "Let me have him, for I believe that I shall be able to cure his hurts." So she commanded that two litters should be brought and she placed King Arthur in one of the litters and she placed Sir Accalon in the other, and she bore them both away to a priory of nuns that was at no great distance from that place.

So when Vivien had come there she searched the wounds of King Arthur and bathed them with a very precious balsam, so that they immediately began to heal. As for Sir Accalon, she would not have to do with his wounds, but let one of her attendants bathe him and dress his hurts.

Now when the next morning had come, King Arthur was so much recovered that he was able to arise, though very weak and sick nigh unto death. So he got up from his couch and he would not permit anyone to stay him, and he wrapped a cloak about him and went to the place where Sir Accalon lay. When he had come there he questioned Sir Accalon very narrowly and Sir Accalon told him all that had happened to him after he had left that ship, and how the strange damsel had given him a sword for to fight with. So when King Arthur heard all that Sir Accalon had to tell him, he said, "Messire, I think that thou art not to be blamed in this matter, but I much do fear me that there is treachery here to compass my ruin."

Then he went out from that place and he found Vivien and he said to her, "Damsel, I beseech thee to dress the wounds of that knight with the same balsam that thou didst use to dress my wounds." "Lord," said Vivien, "I cannot do so, for I have no more of that balsam." But what she said was false, for she did have more of that balsam, but she did not choose to use it upon Sir Accalon.

So that afternoon Sir Accalon died of his wounds which he had received in his battle with King Arthur.

And that day King Arthur summoned Sir Domas and Sir Ontzlake into his presence and they came and stood before him, so filled with the terror of his majesty, that they had not the power to stand, but fell down upon their knees unto him.

Then King Arthur said, "I will pardon you, for ye knew not what ye did. But thou, Sir Domas, I believe, art a very false and treasonable knight, wherefore I shall deprive thee of all thy possessions but that one single castle which thy brother had and that I shall give unto thee, but all thy possessions I shall give unto Sir Ontzlake. And I shall further ordain that thou shalt never hereafter have the right to ride upon any horse but a palfrey, for thou art not worthy to ride upon a courser as a true knight hath a right to do. And I command it of thee that thou shalt presently liberate all those knights who were my companions in captivity, and thou shalt recompense them for all the injury that thou hast done to them according as it shall be decided by a Court of Chivalry."

Therewith he dismissed those two knights, and they were very glad that he had dealt so mercifully with them.

Conclusion

Now shortly after that combat betwixt King Arthur and Sir Accalon the news thereof was brought to Queen Morgana le Fay, and the next day thereafter she heard that Sir Accalon was dead, and she wist not how it could be that her designs could have so miscarried. Then she was a-doubt as to how much King Arthur might know of her treachery, so she said to herself, "I will go and see my brother, the King, and if he is aware of my treason I will beseech him to pardon my transgression." So, having made diligent inquiry as to where it was that King Arthur lay, she gathered together her Court of knights and esquires and went thitherward.

So she came to that place upon the fifth day after the battle, and when she had come there she asked of those who were in attendance what cheer the King had. They answered her, "He is asleep and he must not be disturbed." To the which Queen Morgana le Fay replied, "No matter, I am not to be forbidden, for I must presently see him and speak with him." So they did not dare to stay her because she was the King's sister.

So Queen Morgana went into the chamber where the King lay and he did not waken at her coming. Then Queen Morgana was filled full of hatred and a great desire for revenge, wherefore she said to herself, "I will take Excalibur and his shield and will carry them away with me to Avalon, and my brother shall never see them again." So she went very softly to where King Arthur lay, and she looked upon him as he slept and perceived that he had Excalibur beside him and that he held the handle of the sword in his hand while he slept. Then Queen Morgana said, "Alas, for this, for if I try to take

Excalibur away from him, haply he will awake and he will slay me for my treason." Then she looked and perceived where the sheath of Excalibur lay at the foot of the couch. So she took the sheath of Excalibur very softly and she wrapped it up in her mantle and she went out thence, and King Arthur did not awaken at her going.

So Queen Morgana came out from the King's chamber and she said to those in attendance, "Do not waken the King, for he sleepeth very soundly." Therewith she mounted her horse and went her way from that place.

Now, after a considerable while, King Arthur awoke and he looked for the sheath of Excalibur, but he perceived that it was gone, wherefore he said immediately, "Who hath been here?" They in attendance made answer, "Queen Morgana le Fay had been here and she came in and saw you and went her way without waking you." Then King Arthur's heart misgave him, and he said, I fear me that she hath dealt treacherously with me from the beginning to the end of these adventures."

Whereupon he arose and summoned all his knights and esquires and mounted his horse for pursuit of Queen Morgana, although he was still passing sick and faint from his sore wounds and loss of blood.

Now, as the King was about ready to depart, Vivien came to him where he was, and she said, "Lord, take me with thee, for if thou dost not do so thou wilt never recover Excalibur his sheath, nor wilt thou ever overtake Queen Morgana le Fay." And King Arthur said, "Come with me, damsel, in God's name." So Vivien went with him in pursuit of Queen Morgana.

Now, by and by, as she fled, Queen Morgana le Fay looked behind her and therewith she perceived that Vivien was with the party of King Arthur, wherefore her heart failed her and she said, "I fear me that I am now altogether ruined, for I have aided that damsel to acquire such knowledge of magic that I shall have no spells to save myself from her counter-spell. But at any rate it shall be that King Arthur shall never have the sheath of Excalibur again for to help him in his hour of need."

Now at that time they were passing beside the margin of a

lake of considerable size. So Queen Morgana le Fay took the sheath of Excalibur in both her hands and swung it by its belt above her head and she threw it a great distance out into the water.

Then, lo! a very singular miracle occurred, for there suddenly appeared a woman's arm out of the water and it was clad in white. And it was adorned with many bracelets. And the hand of the arm catched the sheath of Excalibur and drew it underneath the water and no one ever beheld that sheath again.

So the sheath of Excalibur was lost, and that was a grievous thing for King Arthur in after time, as you may some time read.

Now after Queen Morgana le Fay had thus thrown the sheath of Excalibur into the lake, she went on a little farther to where was a very lonely place with a great many rocks and stones lying about upon the ground. And when she had come to that place she exercised very potent spells of magic that Merlin had taught her. So, by means of those spells, she transformed herself and all of her Court and all of their horses into large round stones of divers sizes.

Then in a little while came King Arthur to that place with his knights and esquires, and he was exceedingly heavy of heart, for he had beheld from a great distance how Queen Morgana le Fay had thrown the sheath of Excalibur into that lake.

Now when the King and his Court had come to that spot the damsel Vivien called out upon him to stop and she said to him, "Lord, dost thou behold all those great round stones?" "Yea," said the King, "I do see them." Then Vivien said, "Lo! those stones are Queen Morgana le Fay and the Court who were with her. For this magic that she hath done to change herself and them into stones was a certain thing that Merlin had taught her. Now I myself know that magic, and I also know how to remove that magic at my will. Wherefore, if thou wilt promise to immediately punish that wicked woman for all her treason by depriving her of her life, then will I bring her back unto her true shape again so that thou mayst have her in thy power."

Then King Arthur looked upon Vivien with great displeasure, and he said, "Damsel, thou hast a cruel heart! Thou thyself hast suffered no injury at the hands of Queen Morgana; wherefore, then, wouldst thou have me slay her? Now, but for all thou hast done for me I would be very much affronted with thee. As for her, I forgive her all of this, and I shall forgive her again and again and yet again if she sin against me. For her mother was my mother, and the blood which flows in her veins and in my veins cometh from the same fountain-head, wherefore I will do no evil thing against her. Let us return again whence we came."

Then Vivien looked upon King Arthur very bitterly, and she laughed with great scorn, and said, "Thou art both a fool and a dotard," and therewith she vanished from the sight of all.

And after that, because King Arthur had rebuked her for her wickedness in the presence of others, she hated him even more than Morgana le Fay had hated him.

Some time after that, King Arthur heard how Merlin had been beguiled by Vivien, and he sorrowed with great bitterness that Merlin was lost unto the world in that wise.

So endeth the story of the passing of Merlin.

PART II

The Story of Sir Pellias

Chapter First

*How Queen Guinevere Went a-Maying
and of How Sir Pellias Took Upon
Him a Quest in Her Behalf.*

Now it befell upon a pleasant day in the spring-time, that Queen Guinevere went a-Maying with a goodly company of Knights and Ladies of her Court. And among those Knights were Sir Pellias, and Sir Geraint, and Sir Dinadan, and Sir Aglaval, and Sir Agravaine, and Sir Constantine of Cornwall, and sundry others, so that the like of that Court was hardly to be found in all of the world, either then or before or since.

The day was exceedingly pleasant with the sunlight all yellow, like to gold, and the breeze both soft and gentle. The small birds they sang with very great joy, and all about there bloomed so many flowers of divers sorts that the entire meadows were carpeted with their tender green. So it seemed to Queen Guinevere that it was very good to be abroad in the field and beneath the sky at such a season.

Now as the Queen and her Court walked in great joy among the blossoms, one of the damsels attendant upon the Lady

Guinevere cried out of a sudden, "Look! Look! Who is that cometh yonder?" Thereupon Queen Guinevere lifted up her eyes, and she beheld that there came across the meadows a damsel riding upon a milk-white palfrey, accompanied by three pages clad in sky-blue raiment. That damsel was also clad entirely in azure, and she wore a finely wrought chain of gold about her neck and a fillet of gold about her brows, and her hair, which was as yellow as gold, was wrapped all about with bands of blue ribbon embroidered with gold. And one of the pages that followed the damsel bare a square frame of no very great size, and that the frame was enveloped and covered with a curtain of crimson satin.

Now when the Queen beheld that goodly company approaching, she bade one of the knights attendant upon her for to go forth to meet the damsel. And the knight who went forth in obedience to her command was Sir Pellias.

So when Sir Pellias met the damsel and her three pages, he spake to her in this wise: "Fair damsel, I am commanded by yonder lady for to greet you and to crave of you the favor of your name and purpose."

"Sir Knight," said the damsel, "I do perceive from your countenance and address that you are some lord of very high estate and of great nobility, wherefore I will gladly tell to you that my name is Parcenet, and that I am a damsel belonging to the Court of a certain very high dame who dwelleth at a considerable distance from here, and who is called the Lady Ettard of Grantmesnle. Now I come hitherward desiring to be admitted into the presence of Queen Guinevere. Accordingly, if you can tell me whereabout I may find that noble lady, I shall assuredly be very greatly beholden unto you."

"Ha, Lady!" quoth Sir Pellias, "thou shalt not have very far to go to find Queen Guinevere; for, behold! yonder she walketh, surrounded by her Court of Lords and Ladies." Then the damsel said, "I prithee bring me unto her."

So Sir Pellias led Parcenet unto the Queen, and Queen Guinevere received her with great graciousness of demeanor, saying, "Damsel, what is it that ye seek of us?"

"Lady," quoth the damsel, "I will tell you that very readily. The Lady Ettard, my mistress, is considered by all in those parts where she dwelleth to be the most beautiful lady in the world. Now, of late, there hath come such a report of your exceeding beauty that the Lady Ettard hath seen fit for to send me hitherward to see with mine own eyes if that which is recorded of you is soothly true. And indeed, Lady, now that I stand before you, I may not say but that you are the fairest dame that ever mine eyes beheld unless it be the Lady Ettard aforesaid."

Then Queen Guinevere laughed with very great mirth. And she said, "It appears to me to be a very droll affair that thou shouldst have travelled so great a distance for so small a matter." Then she said, "Tell me, damsel, what is that thy page beareth so carefully wrapped up in that curtain of crimson satin?"

"Lady," quoth the damsel, "it is a true and perfect likeness of the Lady Ettard, who is my mistress."

Then Queen Guinevere said, "Show it to me."

Upon this the page who bore the picture dismounted from his palfrey and, coming to Queen Guinevere, he kneeled down upon one knee and uncovered the picture so that the Queen and her Court might look upon it. Thereupon they all beheld that that picture was painted very cunningly upon a panel of ivory framed with gold and inset with many jewels of divers colors. And they saw that it was the picture of a lady of such extraordinary beauty that all they who beheld it marvelled thereat. "Hey, damsel!" quoth Queen Guinevere, "thy lady is, indeed, graced with wonderful beauty. Now if she doth in sooth resemble that picture, then I believe that her like to loveliness is not to be found anywhere in the world."

Upon this Sir Pellias spake out and said, "Not so, Lady; for I do protest, and am willing to maintain my words with the peril of my body, that thou thyself art much more beautiful than that picture."

"Hey day, Sir Knight!" quoth the damsel Parcenet, "it is well that thou dost maintain that saying so far away from Grant-mesnle; for at that place is a certain knight, hight Sir Engamore of Malverat, who is a very strong knight indeed, and who maintaineth the contrary to thy saying in favor of the Lady Ettard against all comers who dare to encounter him."

Then Sir Pellias kneeled down before Queen Guinevere, and

set his palms together. "Lady," he said, "I do pray thee of thy grace that thou wilt so far honor me as to accept me for thy true knight in this matter. For I would fain assay an adventure in thy behalf if I have thy permission for to do so. Wherefore, if thou grantest me leave, I will straightway go forth to meet this knight of whom the damsel speaketh, and I greatly hope that when I find him I shall cause his overthrow to the increasing of thy glory and honor."

Then Queen Guinevere laughed again with pure merriment. "Sir," quoth she, "it pleases me beyond measure that thou shouldst take so small a quarrel as this upon thee in my behalf. For if, so be, thou dost assume so small a quarrel, then how much more wouldst thou take a serious quarrel of mine upon thee? Wherefore I do accept thee very joyfully for my champion in this affair. So go thou presently and arm thyself in such a way as may be fitting for this adventure."

"Lady," said Sir Pellias, "if I have thy leave, I will enter into this affair clad as I am. For I entertain hopes that I shall succeed in winning armor and accoutrements upon the way, in the which case this adventure will be still more to thy credit than it would otherwise be."

At this the Queen was very much pleased, that her knight should undertake so serious an adventure clad only in holiday attire; wherefore she said, "Let it be as thou wouldst have it." Thereupon she bade her page, Florian, for to go fetch the best horse that he might obtain for Sir Pellias; and Florian, running with all speed, presently returned with a noble steed, so black of hue that I believe there was not a single white hair upon him.

Then Sir Pellias gave adieu to Queen Guinevere, and her merry Maycourt, and they gave him adieu and great acclaim, and thereupon he mounted his horse and rode away with the damsel Parcenet and the three pages clad in blue.

Now when these had gone some distance the damsel Parcenet said, "Sir, I know not thy name or thy condition, or who thou art?"

Unto this Sir Pellias said, "Damsel, my name is Pellias and I am a knight of King Arthur's Round Table."

At that Parcenet was very much astonished, for Sir Pellias

was held by many to be the best knight-at-arms alive, saving only King Arthur and King Pellinore. Wherefore she cried out, "Messire, it will assuredly be a very great honor for Sir Engamore to have to do with so famous a knight as thou." Unto this Sir Pellias said, "Damsel, I think there are several knights of King Arthur's Round Table who are better knights than I." But Parcenet said, "I cannot believe that to be the case."

Then after awhile Parcenet said to Sir Pellias, "Messire, how wilt thou get thyself armor for to fight Sir Engamore?"

"Maiden," said Sir Pellias, "I do not know at these present where I shall provide me armor; but before the time cometh for me to have to do with Sir Engamore, I have faith that I shall find armor fit for my purpose. For thou must know that it is not always the defence that a man weareth upon his body that bringeth him success, but more often it is the spirit that uplifteth him unto his undertakings."

Then Parcenet said, "Sir Pellias, I do not believe that it is often the case that a lady hath so good a knight as thou for to do battle in her behalf." To which Sir Pellias said very cheerfully, "Damsel, when thy time cometh I wish that thou mayst have a very much better knight to serve thee than I." "Sir," quoth Parcenet, "such a thing as that is not likely to befall me." At the which Sir Pellias laughed with great lightness of heart. Then Parcenet said, "Heigh ho! I would that I had a good knight for to serve me."

To this Sir Pellias made very sober reply, "Maiden, the first one that I catch I will give unto thee for thy very own. Now wouldst thou have him fair or dark, or short or tall? For if thou wouldst rather have him short and fair I will let the tall, dark one go; but if thou wouldst have him tall and dark, I will let go the other sort."

Then Parcenet looked very steadily at Sir Pellias, and she said, "I would have him about as tall as thou art, and with the same color of hair and eyes, and with a straight nose like unto thine, and with a good wit such as thou hast."

"Alas!" said Sir Pellias, "I would that thou hadst told me this before we had come so far from Camelot; for I could easily have got thee such a knight at that place. For they have them there in such plenty that they keep them in wicker cages, and sell them two for a farthing." Whereat Parcenet laughed very cheerfully, and said, "Then Camelot must be a very wonderful place, Sir Pellias."

So, with very merry discourse they journeyed upon their way with great joy and good content, taking much pleasure in the spring-time and the pleasant meadows whereon they travelled, being without care of any sort, and heart-full of cheerfulness and good-will.

That night they abided at a very quaint, pleasant hostelry that stood at the outskirts of the Forest of Usk, and the next morning they departed betimes in the freshness of the early day, quitting that place and entering into the forest shadows.

Now, after they had travelled a considerable distance in that forest, the damsel Parcenet said to Sir Pellias, "Sir, do you know what part of the woods this is?" "Nay," said Sir Pellias. "Well," said Parcenet, "this part of the woodland is sometimes called Arroy, and is sometimes called the Forest of Adventure. For I must tell you it is a very wonderful place, full of magic of sundry sorts. For it is said that no knight may enter into this forest but some adventure shall befall him."

"Damsel," said Sir Pellias, "that which thou tellest me is very good news. For, maybe, if we should fall in with some adventure at this place I may then be able to obtain armor suitable for my purpose."

So they entered the Forest of Adventure forthwith, and then travelled therein for a long way, marvelling greatly at the aspect of that place into which they were come. For the Forest was very dark and silent and wonderfully strange and altogether different from any other place that they had ever seen. Wherefore it appeared to them that it would not be at all singular if some extraordinary adventure should befall them.

So after they had travelled in this wise for a considerable pass they came of a sudden out of those thicker parts of the woodland to where was an opening of considerable extent. And there they beheld before them a violent stream of water that flowed very turbulently and with great uproar of many noises. And they saw that by the side of the stream of water there was a thorn-tree, and that underneath the thorn-tree was a bank of green moss, and that upon the bank of moss there sat an aged woman of a very woful appearance. For that old woman was extraordinarily withered with age, and her eyes were all red as though with a continual weeping of rheum, and many bristles grew upon her cheeks and her chin, and her face was covered with such a multitude of wrinkles that there was not any place that was free from wrinkles.

Now when that old woman beheld Sir Pellias and Parcenet and the three pages approaching where she sat, she cried out in a loud voice, "Sir, wilt thou not bear me over this water upon thy horse? For, lo! I am very old and feeble and may not cross this river by myself."

Then Parcenet rebuked the old woman, saying, "Peace, be still! Who art thou to ask this noble knight for to do thee such a service as that?"

Then Sir Pellias was not pleased with Parcenet, wherefore he said, "Damsel, thou dost not speak properly in this matter, for that which beseemeth a true knight is to give succor unto anyone soever who needeth his aid. For King Arthur is the perfect looking-glass of knighthood, and he hath taught his knights to give succor unto all who ask succor of them, without regarding their condition. So saying Sir Pellias dismounted from his horse and lifted the old woman up upon the saddle thereof. Then he himself mounted once more and straightway rode into the ford of the river and so came across the torrent with the old woman in safety to the other side. And Parcenet followed him, marvelling very greatly at his knightliness, and the three pages followed her.

Now when they had reached the other side of the water, Sir Pellias dismounted with intent to aid the old woman to alight from the horse. But she waited not for his aid, but immediately leaped down very lightly from where she was. And, lo! Sir Pellias beheld that she whom he had thought to be only an aged and withered beldame was, in truth, a very strange, wonderful lady of extraordinary beauty. And, greatly marvelling, he beheld that she was clad in apparel of such a sort as neither he nor any who were there had ever beheld before. And because of her appearance he was aware that she was not like any ordinary mortal, but that she was doubtless of enchantment. For he perceived that her face was of a wonderful clearness, like to ivory for whiteness, and that her eyes were very black and extraordinarily bright, like unto two jewels set into ivory; and he perceived that she was clad all in green from head to foot and that her hair was long and perfectly black and like to fine silk for softness and for glossiness; and he perceived that she had about her neck a collar of opal stones and emeralds inset into gold, and that about her wrists were bracelets of finely wrought gold inset with opal stones and emeralds. Wherefore from all these circumstances he knew that she must be fay.

(For thus was the Lady Nymue of the Lake; and so had she appeared unto King Arthur, and so did she appear unto Sir Pellias and those who were with him.)

So, beholding the wonderful magical quality of that lady, Sir Pellias kneeled down before her and set his hands together, palm to palm. But the Lady of the Lake said, "Sir, why dost thou kneel to me?" "Lady," quoth Sir Pellias, "because thou art so wonderfully strange and beautiful." "Messire," said the Lady of the Lake, "thou hast done a very good service to me and art, assuredly, a very excellent knight. Wherefore, arise and kneel no longer!" So Sir Pellias arose from his knees and stood before her, and he said, "Lady, who art thou?" To the which she made reply, "I am one who holdeth an exceedingly kind regard toward King Arthur and all his knights. My name is Nymue and I am the chiefest of those Ladies of the Lake of whom thou mayst have heard tell. I took upon me that form of a sorry old woman for to test thy knightliness, and, lo! I have not found thee amiss in worthy service." Then Sir Pellias said, "Lady, thou hast assuredly done me great favor in these." Upon that the Lady of the Lake smiled upon Sir Pellias very kindly, and she said, "Sir, I have a mind to do thee a greater favor than that."

Therewith, so saying, she immediately took from about her neck that collar of opal stones, of emeralds and gold, and hung it about the shoulders of Sir Pellias, so that it hung down upon his breast with a very wonderful glory of variegated colors.

"Keep this," she said, "for it is of very potent magic."

"Keep this," she said, "for it is of very potent magic"

Upon that she vanished instantly from the sight of those who were there, leaving them astonished and amazed beyond measure at what had befallen.

And Sir Pellias was like one who was in a dream, for he wist not whether that which he had beheld was a vision, or whether he had seen it with his waking eyes. Wherefore he mounted upon his horse in entire silence, as though he knew not what he did. And likewise in entire silence he led the way from that place. Nor did any of those others speak at that time; only after they had gone a considerable distance Parcenet said, speaking in a manner of fear, "Messire, that was a very wonderful thing that befell us." To which Sir Pellias said, "Yea, maiden."

Now that necklace which the Lady of the Lake had hung about the neck of Sir Pellias possessed such a virtue that whosoever wore it was beloved of all those who looked upon him. For the collar was enchanted with that peculiar virtue; but Sir Pellias was altogether unaware of that circumstance, wherefore he only took joy to himself because of the singular beauty of the jewel which the Lady of the Lake had given him.

Chapter Second

*How Sir Pellias Overcame a Red Knight,
Hight Sir Adresack, and of How He
Liberated XXII Captives From That
Knight's Castle.*

ow, after that wonderful happening, they journeyed con-
tinuously for a great while. Nor did they pause at any
place until they came, about an hour after the prime of the day,
to a certain part of the forest where charcoal-burners were
plying their trade. Here Sir Pellias commanded that they
should draw rein and rest for a while, and so they dismounted
for to rest and to refresh themselves, as he had ordained that
they should do.

Now as they sat there refreshing themselves with meat and
drink, there came of a sudden from out of the forest a sound of
great lamentation and of loud outcry, and almost immediately
there appeared from the thickets, coming into that open place, a
lady in woful array, riding upon a pied palfrey. And behind
her rode a young esquire, clad in colors of green and white and
seated upon a sorrel horse. And he also appeared to be
possessed of great sorrow, being in much disarray and very
downcast of countenance. And the lady's face was all be-
swollen and inflamed with weeping, and her hair hung down

upon her shoulders with neither net nor band for to stay it in place, and her raiment was greatly torn by the brambles and much stained with forest travel. And the young esquire who rode behind her came with a drooping head and a like woful disarray of apparel, his cloak dragging behind him and made fast to his shoulder by only a single point.

Now when Sir Pellias beheld the lady and the esquire in such sad estate, he immediately arose from where he sat and went straightway to the lady and took her horse by the bridle and stayed it where it was. And the lady looked at him, yet saw him not, being altogether blinded by her grief and distraction. Then Sir Pellias said to her, "Lady, what ails thee that thou sorrowest so greatly?" Whereunto she made reply, "Sir, it matters not, for thou canst not help me." "How know ye that?" said Sir Pellias. "I have a very good intention for to aid thee if it be possible for me to do so."

Then the lady looked more narrowly at Sir Pellias, and she perceived him as though through a mist of sorrow. And she beheld that he was not clad in armor, but only in a holiday attire of fine crimson cloth. Wherefore she began sorrowing afresh, and that in great measure, for she deemed that here was one who could give her no aid in her trouble. Wherefore she said, "Sir, thy intentions are kind, but how canst thou look to give me aid when thou hast neither arms nor defences for to help thee in taking upon thee such a quarrel?" But Sir Pellias said, "Lady, I know not how I may aid thee until that thou tellest me of thy sorrow. Yet I have good hope that I may serve thee when I shall know what it is that causes thee such disorder of mind." Thereupon, still holding the horse by the bridle, he brought the lady forward to that place where Parcenet still sat beside the napkin spread with food with which they had been refreshing themselves. And when he had come to that place, he, with all gentleness, constrained the lady for to dismount from her horse. Then, with equal gentleness, he compelled her to sit down upon the grass and to partake of the food. And when she had done so, and had drunk some of the wine, she found herself to be greatly refreshed and began to take to herself more heart of grace. Thereupon, beholding her so far recovered, Sir Pellias again demanded of her what was her trouble and besought her that she would open her heart unto him.

So, being encouraged by his cheerful words, she told to Sir Pellias the trouble that had brought her to that pass.

"Sir Knight," she said, "the place where I dwell is a considerable distance from this. Thence I came this morning with a very good knight, hight Sir Brandemere, who is my husband. We have been married but for a little over four weeks, so that our happiness until this morning was as yet altogether fresh with us. Now this morning Sir Brandemere would take me out a-hunting at the break of day, and so we went forth with a brachet of which my knight was wonderfully fond. So, coming to a certain place in the forest, there started up of a sudden from before us a doe, which same the brachet immediately pursued with great vehemence of outcry. Thereupon, I and my lord and this esquire followed thereafter with very great spirit and enjoyment of the chase. Now, when we had followed the doe and the hound for a great distance—the hound pursuing the doe with a great passion of eagerness—we came to a certain place where we beheld before us a violent stream of water which was crossed by a long and narrow bridge. And we beheld that upon the other side of the stream there stood a strong castle with seven towers, and that the castle was built up upon the rocks in such a way that the rocks and the castle appeared to be altogether like one rock.

"Now, as we approached the bridge aforesaid, lo! the portcullis of the castle was lifted up and the drawbridge was let fall very suddenly and with a great noise, and there immediately issued forth from out of the castle a knight clad altogether in red. And all the trappings and the furniture of his horse were likewise of red; and the spear which he bore in his hand was of ash-wood painted red. And he came forth very terribly, and rode forward so that he presently stood at the other end of that narrow bridge. Thereupon he called out aloud to Sir Brandemere, my husband, saying: 'Whither wouldst thou go, Sir Knight?' And unto him Sir Brandemere made reply: 'Sir, I would cross this bridge, for my hound, which I love exceedingly, hath crossed here in pursuit of a doe.' Then that Red Knight cried out in a loud voice, 'Sir Knight, thou comest not upon this bridge but at thy peril; for this bridge belongeth unto me, and whosoever would cross it must first overthrow me or else he may not cross.'

"Now, my husband, Sir Brandemere, was clad at that time only in a light raiment such as one might wear for hunting or for hawking; only that he wore upon his head a light bascinet enwrapped with a scarf which I had given him. Ne'theless, he was so great of heart that he would not abide any challenge such as that Red Knight had given unto him; wherefore, bidding me and this esquire (whose name is Ponteferet) to remain upon the farther side of the bridge, he drew his sword and rode forward to the middle of the bridge with intent to force a way across if he was able so to do. Whereupon, seeing that to be his intent, that Red Knight, clad all in complete armor, cast aside his spear and drew his sword and rode forward to meet my knight. So they met in the middle of the bridge, and when they had thus met that Red Knight lifted himself in his stirrup and smote my husband, Sir Brandemere, upon the crown of his bascinet with his sword. And I beheld the blade of the Red Knight's sword that it cut through the bascinet of Sir Brandemere and deep into his brain-pan, so that the blood ran down upon the knight's face in great abundance. Then Sir Brandemere straightway fell down from his horse and lay as though he were gone dead.

"Having thus overthrown him, that Red Knight dismounted from his horse and lifted up Sir Brandemere upon the horse whence he had fallen so that he lay across the saddle. Then taking both horses by the bridles the Red Knight led them straight back across the bridge and so into his castle. And as soon as he had entered into the castle the portcullis thereof was immediately closed behind him and the drawbridge was raised. Nor did he pay any heed whatever either to me or to the esquire Ponteferet, but he departed leaving us without any word of cheer; nor do I now know whether my husband, Sir Brandemere, is living or dead, or what hath befallen him."

And as the lady spake these words, lo! the tears again fell down her face in great abundance.

Then Sir Pellias was very much moved with compassion, wherefore he said, "Lady, thy case is, indeed, one of exceeding sorrowfulness, and I am greatly grieved for thee. And, indeed, I would fain aid thee to all the extent that is in my power. So, if thou wilt lead me to where is this bridge and that grimly castle of which thou speakest, I make thee my vow that I will assay to the best of my endeavor to learn of the whereabouts of thy good knight, and as to what hath befallen him."

"Sir," said the lady, "I am much beholden unto thee for thy good will. Yet thou mayst not hope for success shouldst thou venture to undertake so grave an adventure as that without either arms or armor for to defend thyself. For consider how grievously that Red Knight hath served my husband, Sir Brandemere, taking no consideration as to his lack of arms or defence. Wherefore, it is not likely that he will serve thee any more courteously." And to the lady's words Parcenet also lifted up a great voice, bidding Sir Pellias not to be so unwise as to do this thing that he was minded to do. And so did Ponteferet, the esquire, also call out upon Sir Pellias, that he should not do this thing, but that he should at least take arms to himself ere he entered upon this adventure.

But to all that they said Sir Pellias replied, "Stay me not in that which I would do, for I do tell you all that I have several times undertaken adventures even more perilous than this and yet I have 'scaped with no great harm to myself." Nor would he listen to anything that the lady and the damsel might say, but, arising from that place, he aided the lady and the damsel to mount their palfreys. Then mounting his own steed, and the esquire and the pages having mounted their steeds, the whole party immediately departed from that place.

So they journeyed for a great distance through the forest, the esquire, Ponteferet, directing them how to proceed in such a way as should bring them by and by to the castle of the Red Knight. So, at last they came to a more open place in that wilderness where was a steep and naked hill before them. And when they had reached to the top of that hill they perceived beneath them a river, very turbulent and violent. Likewise they saw that the river was spanned by a bridge, exceedingly straight and narrow, and that upon the farther side of the bridge and of the river there stood a very strong castle with seven tall towers. Moreover the castle and the towers were built up upon the rocks, very lofty and high, so that it was hard to tell where the rocks ceased and the walls began, wherefore the towers and the walls appeared to be altogether one rock of stone.

Then the esquire, Ponteferet, pointed with his finger, and said, "Sir Knight, yonder is the castle of the Red Knight, and into it he bare Sir Brandemere after he had been so grievously wounded." Then Sir Pellias said unto the lady, "Lady, I will presently inquire as to thy husband's welfare."

Therewith he set spurs to his horse and rode down the hill toward the bridge with great boldness. And when he had come nigher to the bridge, lo! the portcullis of the castle was lifted and the drawbridge was let fall with a great noise and tumult, and straightway there issued forth from out of the castle a knight clad all in armor and accoutrements of red, and this knight came forward with great speed toward the bridge's head. Then, when Sir Pellias saw him approaching so threateningly, he said unto those who had followed him down the hill: "Stand fast where ye are and I will go forth to bespeak this knight, and inquire into the matter of that injury which he hath done unto Sir Brandemere." Upon this the esquire, Ponteferet, said unto him, "Stay, Sir Knight, thou wilt be hurt." But Sir Pellias said, "Not so, I shall not be hurt."

So he went forth very boldly upon the bridge, and when the Red Knight saw him approach, he said, "Ha! who art thou who darest to come thus upon my bridge?"

Unto him Sir Pellias made reply, "It matters not who I am, but thou art to know, thou discourteous knight, that I am come to inquire of thee where thou hast disposed of that good knight Sir Brandemere, and to ask of thee why thou didst entreat him so grievously a short time since."

At this the Red Knight fell very full of wrath. "Ha! ha!" he cried vehemently, "that thou shalt presently learn to thy great sorrow, for as I have served him, so shall I quickly serve thee, so that in a little while I shall bring thee unto him; then thou mayst ask him whatsoever thou dost list. But seeing that thou art unarmed and without defence, I would not do thee any bodily ill, wherefore I demand of thee that thou shalt presently surrender thyself unto me, otherwise it will be very greatly to thy pain and sorrow if thou compellest me to use force for to constrain thy surrender."

Then Sir Pellias said, "What! what! Wouldst thou thus assail a knight who is altogether without arms or defence as I am?" And the Red Knight said, "Assuredly shall I do so if thou dost not immediately yield thyself unto me."

"Then," quoth Pellias, "thou art not fit for to be dealt with as beseemeth a tried knight. Wherefore, should I encounter thee, thy overthrow must be of such a sort as may shame any belted knight who weareth golden spurs."

Thereupon he cast about his eyes for a weapon to fit his purpose, and he beheld how that a certain huge stone was loose upon the coping of the bridge. Now this stone was of such a size that five men of usual strength could hardly lift it. But Sir Pellias lifted it forth from its place with great ease, and, raising it with both hands, he ran quickly toward that Red Knight and flung the rock at him with much force. And the stone smote the Red Knight upon the middle of the shield and drave it back upon his breast, with great violence. And the force of the blow drave the knight backward from his saddle, so that he fell down to the earth from his horse with a terrible tumult and lay upon the bridgeway like one who was altogether dead.

And when they within the castle who looked forth therefrom, saw that blow, and when they beheld the overthrow of the Red Knight, they lifted up their voices in great lamentation so that the outcry thereof was terrible to hear.

But Sir Pellias ran with all speed to the fallen knight and set his knee upon his breast. And he unlaced his helmet and lifted it. And he beheld that the face of the knight was strong and comely and that he was not altogether dead.

So when Sir Pellias saw that the Red Knight was not dead, and when he perceived that he was about to recover his breath from the blow that he had suffered, he drew that knight's misericordia from its sheath and set the point to his throat, so that when the Red Knight awoke from his swoon he beheld death, in the countenance of Sir Pellias and in the point of the dagger.

So when the Red Knight perceived how near death was to him he besought Sir Pellias for mercy, saying, "Spare my life unto me!" Whereunto Sir Pellias said, "Who art thou?" And the knight said, "I am hight Sir Adresack, surnamed of the Seven Towers." Then Sir Pellias said to him, "What hast thou done unto Sir Brandemere and how doth it fare with that good knight?" And the Red Knight replied, "He is not so seriously wounded as you suppose."

Now when Sir Brandemere's lady heard this speech she was greatly exalted with joy, so that she smote her hands together, making great cry of thanksgiving.

But Sir Pellias said, "Now tell me, Sir Adresack, hast thou other captives beside that knight, Sir Brandemere, at thy castle?" To which Sir Adresack replied, "Sir Knight, I will tell thee truly; there are in my castle one and twenty other captives besides him: to wit, eighteen knights and esquires of degree and three ladies. For I have defended this bridge for a long time and all who have undertaken to cross it, those have I taken captive and held for ransom. Wherefore I have taken great wealth and gained great estate thereby."

Then Sir Pellias said, "Thou art soothly a wicked and discourteous knight so to serve travellers that come thy way, and I would do well for to slay thee where thou liest. But since thou hast besought mercy of me I will grant it unto thee, though I will do so only with great shame unto thy knighthood. Moreover, if I spare to thee thy life there are several things which thou must perform. First thou must go unto Queen Guinevere at Camelot, and there must thou say unto her that the knight who left her unarmed hath taken thine armor from thee and hath armed himself therewith for to defend her honor. Secondly, thou must confess thy faults unto King Arthur as thou hast confessed them unto me and thou must beg his pardon for the same, craving that he, in his mercy, shall spare thy life unto thee. These are the things thou must perform."

To this Sir Adresack said, "Very well, these things do I promise to perform if thou wilt spare my life."

Then Sir Pellias permitted him to arise and he came and stood before Sir Pellias. And Sir Pellias summoned the esquire, Ponteferet, unto him, and he said, "Take thou this knight's armor from off of his body and put it upon my body as thou knowest how to do." And Ponteferet did as Sir Pellias bade him. For he unarmed Sir Adresack and he clothed Sir Pellias in Sir Adresack's armor, and Sir Adresack stood ashamed before them all. Then Sir Pellias said unto him, "Now take me into thy castle that I may there liberate those captives that thou so wickedly holdest as prisoners." And Sir Adresack said, "It shall be done as thou dost command."

Thereupon they all went together unto the castle and into the castle, which was an exceedingly stately place. And there they beheld a great many servants and attendants, and these came at the command of Sir Adresack and bowed themselves down before Sir Pellias. Then Sir Pellias bade Sir Adresack for to summon the keeper of the dungeon, and Sir Adresack did so. And Sir Pellias commanded the keeper that he should conduct them unto the dungeon, and the keeper bowed down before him in obedience.

Now when they had come to that dungeon they beheld it to be a very lofty place and exceedingly strong. And there they found Sir Brandemere and those others of whom Sir Adresack had spoken.

But when that sorrowful lady perceived Sir Brandemere, she ran unto him with great voice of rejoicing and embraced him and wept over him. And he embraced her and wept and altogether forgot his hurt in the joy of beholding her again.

And in the several apartments of that part of the castle, there were in all eighteen knights and esquires, and three ladies besides Sir Brandemere. Moreover, amongst those knights were two from King Arthur's Court: to wit, Sir Brandiles and Sir Mador de la Porte. Whereupon these beholding that it was Sir Pellias who had liberated them, came to him and embraced him with great joy and kissed him upon either cheek.

And all those who were liberated made great rejoicing and gave Sir Pellias such praise and acclaim that he was greatly contented therewith.

Then when Sir Pellias beheld all those captives who were in the dungeon he was very wroth with Sir Adresack, wherefore he turned unto him and said, "Begone, Sir Knight, for to do that penance which I imposed upon thee to perform, for I am very greatly displeased with thee, and fear me lest I should repent me of my mercy to thee."

Thereupon Sir Adresack turned him away and he immediately departed from that place. And he called to him his esquire and he took him and rode away to Camelot for to do that penance which he had promised Sir Pellias to do.

Then, after he was gone, Sir Pellias and those captives whom he had liberated, went through the divers parts of the castle. And there they found thirteen chests of gold and silver money and four caskets of jewels—very fine and of great brilliancy—all of which treasure had been paid in ransom by those captives who had aforetime been violently held prisoners at that place.

And Sir Pellias ordained that all those chests and caskets should be opened, and when those who were there looked therein, the hearts of all were wonderfully exalted with joy at the sight of that great treasure.

Then Sir Pellias commanded that all that treasure of gold and silver should be divided into nineteen equal parts, and when it had been so divided, he said, "Now let each of you who have been held captive in this place, take for his own one part of that treasure as a recompense for those sorrows which he hath endured." Moreover, to each of the ladies who had been held as captives in that place, he gave a casket of jewels, saying unto her, "Take thou this casket of jewels as a recompense for that sorrow which thou hast suffered. And unto Sir Brandemere's lady he gave a casket of the jewels for that which she had endured.

But when those who were there beheld that Sir Pellias reserved no part of that great treasure for himself, they all cried out upon him: "Sir Knight! Sir Knight! How is this? Behold, thou hast set aside no part of this treasure for thyself."

Then Sir Pellias made answer: "You are right, I have not so. For it needs not that I take any of this gold and silver, or any of these jewels, for myself. For, behold! ye have suffered much at the hands of Sir Adresack, wherefore ye should receive recompense therefore, but I have suffered naught at his hands, wherefore I need no such recompense."

Then were they all astonished at his generosity and gave him great praise for his largeness of heart.   And all those knights vowed unto him fidelity unto death.

Then, when all these things were accomplished, Sir Brandemere implored all who were there that they would come with him unto his castle, so that they might refresh themselves with a season of mirth and good faring.   And they all said that they would go with him, and they did go.   And at the castle of Sir Brandemere there was great rejoicing with feasting and jousting for three days.

And all who were there loved Sir Pellias with an astonishing love because of that collar of emeralds and opals and of gold. Yet no one knew of the virtue of that collar, nor did Sir Pellias know of it.

So Sir Pellias abided at that place for three days.   And when the fourth day was come he arose betimes in the morning and bade saddle his horse, and the palfrey of the damsel Parcenet, and the horses of their pages.

Then when all those who were there saw that he was minded to depart, they besought him not to go, but Sir Pellias said, "Stay me not, for I must go."

Then came to him those two knights of Arthur's Court, Sir Brandiles and Sir Mador de la Porte, and they besought him that he would let them go with him upon that adventure.   And at first Sir Pellias forbade them, but they besought him the more, so that at last he was fain to say, "Ye shall go with me."

So he departed from that place with his company, and all those who remained gave great sorrow that he had gone away.

Chapter Third

How Sir Pellias Did Battle With Sir Engamore, Otherwise the Knight of the Green Sleeves, and of What Befell the Lady Ettard.

Now, Sir Pellias and his party and the damsel Parcenet and her party travelled onward until after a while in the afternoon they came unto the utmost boundaries of the forest, where the woodlands ceased altogether and many fields and meadows, with farms and crofts and plantations of trees all a-bloom with tender leaves and fragrant blossoms, lay spread out beneath the sky.

And Sir Pellias said, "This is indeed a very beautiful land into which we have come." Whereat the damsel Parcenet was right well pleased, for she said, "Sir, I am very glad that that which thou seest belikes thee; for all this region belongeth unto the Lady Ettard, and it is my home. Moreover, from the top of yonder hill one mayst behold the castle of Grantmesnle which lieth in the valley beneath." Then Sir Pellias said, "Let us make haste! For I am wonderfully desirous of beholding that place."

So they set spurs to their horses and rode up that hill at a hand gallop. And when they had reached the top thereof, lo! beneath them lay the Castle of Grantmesnle in such a wise that it was as though upon the palm of a hand. And Sir Pellias beheld that it was an exceedingly fair castle, built altogether without of a red stone, and containing many buildings of red brick within the wall. And behind the walls there lay a little town, and from where they stood they could behold the streets thereof, and the people coming and going upon their businesses. So Sir Pellias, beholding the excellence of that castle, said, "Certes, maiden, yonder is a very fair estate."

"Yea," said Parcenet; "we who dwell there do hold it to be a very excellent estate."

Then Sir Pellias said to Parcenet: "Maiden, yonder glade of young trees nigh unto the castle appeareth to be a very cheerful spot. Wherefore at that place I and my companions in arms will take up our inn. There, likewise, we will cause to be set up three pavilions for to shelter us by day and by night. Meantime, I beseech of thee, that thou wilt go unto the lady, thy mistress, and say unto her that a knight hath come unto this place, who, albeit he knoweth her not, holdeth that the Lady Guinevere of Camelot is the fairest lady in all of the world. And I beseech thee to tell the lady that I am here to maintain that saying against all comers at the peril of my body. Wherefore, if the lady have any champion for to undertake battle in her behalf, him will I meet in yonder field to-morrow at mid-day a little before I eat my mid-day meal. For at that time I do propose for to enter into yonder field, and to make parade therein until my friends bid me for to come in to my dinner; and I shall take my stand in that place in honor of the Lady Guinevere of Camelot."

"Sir Pellias," said the damsel, "I will even do as thou desirest of me. And, though I may not wish that thou mayst be the victor in that encounter, yet am I soothly sorry for to depart from thee. For thou art both a very valiant and a very gentle knight, and I find that I have a great friendship for thee."

Then Sir Pellias laughed, and he said, "Parcenet, thou art minded to give me praise that is far beyond my deserving." And Parcenet said, "Sir, not so, for thou dost deserve all that I may say to thy credit."

Thereupon they twain took leave of one another with very good will and much kindness of intention, and the maiden and the three pages went the one way, and Sir Pellias and his two companions and the several attendants they had brought with them went into the glade of young trees as Sir Pellias had ordained.

And there they set up three pavilions in the shade of the trees; the one pavilion of fair white cloth, the second of green cloth, and the third of scarlet cloth. And over each pavilion they had set a banner emblazoned with the device of that knight unto whom the pavilion appertained: above the white pavilion was the device of Sir Pellias: to wit, three swans displayed upon a field argent; above the red pavilion, which was the pavilion of Sir Brandiles, was a red banner emblazoned with his device: to wit, a mailed hand holding in its grasp a hammer; above the green pavilion, which was that of Sir Mador de la Porte, was a green banner bearing his device, which was that of a carrion crow holding in one hand a white lily flower and in the other a sword.

So when the next day had come, and when mid-day was nigh at hand, Sir Pellias went forth into that field before the castle as he had promised to do, and he was clad all from head to foot in the red armor which he had taken from the body of Sir Adresack, so that in that armor he presented a very terrible appearance. So he rode up and down before the castle walls for a considerable while crying in a loud voice, "What ho! What ho! Here stands a knight of King Arthur's Court and of his Round Table who doth affirm, and is ready to maintain the same with his body, that the Lady Guinevere, King Arthur's Queen of Camelot, is the most beautiful lady in all of the world, barring none whomsoever. Wherefore, if any knight maintaineth otherwise, let him straightway come forth for to defend his opinion with his body."

Now after Sir Pellias had thus appeared in that meadow there fell a great commotion within the castle, and many people came upon the walls thereof and gazed down upon Sir Pellias where he paraded that field. And after a time had passed, the drawbridge of the castle was let fall, and there issued forth a knight, very huge of frame and exceedingly haughty of demeanor. This knight was clad altogether from head to foot in green armor, and upon either arm he wore a green sleeve, whence he was sometimes entitled the Knight of the Green Sleeves.

So that Green Knight rode forward toward Sir Pellias, and Sir Pellias rode forward unto the Green Knight, and when they had come together they gave salute with a great deal of civility and knightly courtesy. Then the Green Knight said unto Sir Pellias, "Sir Knight, wilt thou allow unto me the great favor for to know thy name?"

Whereunto Sir Pellias made reply, "That will I so. I am Sir Pellias, a knight of King Arthur's Court and of his Round Table."

Then the Green Knight made reply, "Ha, Sir Pellias, it is a great honor for me to have to do with so famous a knight, for who is there in Courts of Chivalry who hath not heard of thee? Now, if I have the good fortune for to overthrow thee, then will all thy honor become my honor. Now, in return for thy courtesy for making proclamation of thy name, I give unto thee my name and title, which is Sir Engamore of Malverat, further known as the Knight of the Green Sleeves. And I may furthermore tell thee that I am the champion unto the Lady Ettard of Grantmesnle, and that I have defended her credit unto peerless beauty for eleven months, and that against all comers, wherefore if I do successfully defend it for one month longer, then do I become lord of her hand and of all this fair estate. So I am prepared to do the uttermost in my power in her honor."

Then Sir Pellias said, "Sir Knight, I give thee gramercy for thy words of greeting, and I too will do my uttermost in this encounter." Thereupon each knight saluted each other with his lance, and each rode to his appointed station.

Now a great concourse of people had come down to the lower walls of the castle and of the town for to behold the contest of arms that was toward, wherefore it would be hard to imagine a more worthy occasion where knights might meet in a glorious contest of friendly jousting, wherefore each knight prepared himself in all ways, and dressed him his spear and his lance with great care and circumspection. So when all had been prepared for that encounter, an herald, who had come forth from the castle into the field, give the signal for assault.

Thereupon in an instant, each knight drave spurs into his horse and rushed the one against the other, with such terrible speed that the ground shook and trembled beneath the beating of their horses' feet. So they met exactly in the centre of the field of battle, the one knight smiting the other in the midst of his defences with a violence that was very terrible to behold. And the spear of Sir Engamore burst into as many as thirty pieces, but the spear of Sir Pellias held so that the Green Knight was hurtled so violently from out of his saddle that he smote the earth above a spear's length behind the crupper of his horse.

Now when those who had stood upon the walls beheld how entirely the Green Knight was overthrown in the encounter, they lifted up their voices in great outcry; for there was no other such knight as Sir Engamore in all those parts. And more especially did the Lady Ettard make great outcry; for Sir Engamore was very much beloved by her; wherefore, seeing him so violently flung down upon the ground, she deemed that perhaps he had been slain.

Then three esquires ran to Sir Engamore and lifted him up and unlaced his helm for to give him air. And they beheld that he was not slain, but only in a deep swoon. So by and by he opened his eyes, and at that Sir Pellias was right glad, for it would have grieved him had he slain that knight. Now when Sir Engamore came back unto his senses once more, he demanded with great vehemence that he might continue that contest with Sir Pellias afoot and with swords. But Sir Pellias would not have it so. "Nay, Sir Engamore," quoth he, "I will not fight thee so serious a quarrel as that, for I have no such despite against thee." And at that denial Sir Engamore fell a-weeping from pure vexation and shame of his entire overthrow.

Then came Sir Brandiles and Sir Mador de la Porte and gave Sir Pellias great acclaim for the excellent manner in which he had borne himself in the encounter, and at the same time they offered consolation unto Sir Engamore and comforted him for the misfortune that had befallen him. But Sir Engamore would take but little comfort in their words.

Now whiles they thus stood all together, there issued out from the castle the Lady Ettard and an exceedingly gay and comely Court of esquires and ladies, and these came across the meadow toward where Sir Pellias and the others stood.

Then when Sir Pellias beheld that lady approach, he drew his misericordia and cut the thongs of his helmet, and took the helmet off of his head, and thus he went forward, bareheaded, for to meet her.

But when he had come nigh to her he beheld that she was many times more beautiful than that image of her painted upon the ivory panel which he had aforetime beheld, wherefore his heart went forth unto her with a very great strength of liking. So therewith he kneeled down upon the grass and set his hands together palm to palm, before her, and he said: "Lady, I do very greatly crave thy forgiveness that I should thus have done battle against thy credit. For, excepting that I did that endeavor for my Queen, I would rather, in another case, have been thy champion than that of any lady whom I have ever beheld."

Now at that time Sir Pellias wore about his neck the collar of emeralds and opal stones and gold which the Lady of the Lake had given to him. Wherefore, when the Lady Ettard looked upon him, that necklace drew her heart unto him with very great enchantment. Wherefore she smiled upon Sir Pellias very cheerfully and gave him her hand and caused him to arise from that place where he kneeled. And she said to him, "Sir Knight, thou art a very famous warrior; for I suppose there is not anybody who knoweth aught of chivalry but hath heard of the fame of Sir Pellias, the Gentle Knight. Wherefore, though my champion Sir Engamore of Malverat hath heretofore overthrown all comers, yet he need not feel very much ashamed to have been overthrown by so terribly strong a knight."

Then Sir Pellias was very glad of the kind words which the Lady Ettard spake unto him, and therewith he made her known unto Sir Brandiles and Sir Mador de la Porte. Unto these knights also, the Lady Ettard spake very graciously, being moved thereto by the extraordinary regard she felt toward Sir Pellias. So she besought those knights that they would come into the castle and refresh themselves, with good cheer, and with that, the knights said that they would presently do so. Wherefore they returned each knight unto his pavilion, and

there each bedight himself with fine raiment and with ornaments of gold and silver in such a fashion that he was noble
company for any Court. Then those three knights betook
themselves unto the castle of Grantmesnle, and when they had
come thither everybody was astonished at the nobility of their
aspect.

But Sir Engamore, who had by now recovered from his fall,
was greatly cast down, for he said unto himself, "Who am I
in the presence of these noble lords?" So he stood aside and
was very downcast of heart and oppressed in his spirits.

Then the Lady Ettard set a very fine feast and Sir Pellias and
Sir Brandiles and Sir Mador de la Porte were exceedingly glad
thereof. And upon her right hand she placed Sir Pellias, and
upon her left hand she placed Sir Engamore. And Sir
Engamore was still more cast down, for, until now, he had
always sat upon the right hand of the Lady Ettard.

Now because Sir Pellias wore that wonderful collar which
the Lady of the Lake had given unto him, the Lady Ettard
could not keep her regard from him. So after they had
refreshed themselves and had gone forth into the castle
pleasaunce for to walk in the warm sunshine, the lady would
have Sir Pellias continually beside her. And when it came time
for those foreign knights to quit the castle, she besought Sir
Pellias that he would stay a while longer. Now Sir Pellias was
very glad to do that, for he was pleased beyond measure with
the graciousness and the beauty of the Lady Ettard.

So by and by Sir Brandiles and Sir Mador de la Porte went
back unto their pavilions, and Sir Pellias remained in the castle
of Grantmesnle for a while longer.

Now that night the Lady Ettard let to be made a supper for
herself and Sir Pellias, and at that supper she and Sir Pellias
alone sat at the table, and the damsel Parcenet waited in
attendance upon the lady. Whiles they ate, certain young
pages and esquires played very sweetly upon harps, and certain
maidens who were attendant upon the Court of the lady sang so
sweetly that it expanded the heart of the listener to hear them.
And Sir Pellias was so enchanted with the sweetness of the
music, and with the beauty of the Lady Ettard, that he wist not
whether he were indeed upon the earth or in Paradise,

wherefore, because of his great pleasure, he said unto the Lady Ettard, "Lady, I would that I might do somewhat for thee to show unto thee how high is the regard and the honor in which I hold thee."

Now as Sir Pellias sat beside her, the Lady Ettard had continually held in observation that wonderful collar of gold and of emerald and of opal stones which hung about his neck; and she coveted that collar exceedingly. Wherefore, she now said unto Sir Pellias, "Sir Knight, thou mayst indeed do me great favor if thou hast a mind for to do so." "What favor may I do thee, Lady?" said Sir Pellias. "Sir," said the Lady Ettard, "thou mayst give unto me that collar which hangeth about thy neck."

At this the countenance of Sir Pellias fell, and he said, "Lady, I may not do that; for that collar came unto me in such an extraordinary fashion that I may not part it from me."

Then the Lady Ettard said, "Why mayst thou not part it from thee, Sir Pellias?"

Thereupon Sir Pellias told her all of that extraordinary adventure with the Lady of the Lake, and of how that fairy lady had given the collar unto him.

At this the Lady Ettard was greatly astonished, and she said, "Sir Pellias, that is a very wonderful story. Ne'theless, though thou mayst not give that collar unto me, yet thou mayst let me wear it for a little while. For indeed I am charmed by the beauty of that collar beyond all manner of liking, wherefore I do beseech thee for to let me wear it for a little."

Then Sir Pellias could refuse her no longer, so he said, "Lady, thou shalt have it to wear for a while." Thereupon he took the collar from off of his neck, and he hung it about the neck of the Lady Ettard.

Then, after a little time the virtue of that jewel departed from Sir Pellias and entered into the Lady Ettard, and the Lady Ettard looked upon Sir Pellias with altogether different eyes than those with which she had before regarded him. Wherefore she said unto herself: "Hah! what ailed me that I should have been so enchanted with that knight to the discredit of my champion who hath served me so faithfully? Hath not this knight done me grievous discredit? Hath he not come hitherward for no other reason than for that purpose? Hath he not overthrown mine own true knight in scorn of me? What then hath ailed me that I should have given him such regard as I have bestowed upon him?" But though she thought all this, yet she made no sign thereof unto Sir Pellias, but appeared to laugh and talk very cheerfully. Nevertheless, she immediately began to cast about in her mind for some means whereby she might be revenged upon Sir Pellias; for she said unto herself, "Lo! is he not mine enemy and is not mine enemy now in my power? Wherefore should I not take full measure of revenge upon him for all that which he hath done unto us of Grantmesnle?"

So by and by she made an excuse and arose and left Sir Pellias. And she took Parcenet aside, and she said unto the damsel Parcenet, "Go and fetch me hither presently a powerful sleeping-draught." Then Parcenet said, "Lady, what would you do?" And the Lady Ettard said, "No matter." And Parcenet said, "Would you give unto that noble knight a sleeping-draught?" And the lady said, "I would." Then Parcenet said, "Lady, that would surely be an ill thing to do unto one who sitteth in peace at your table and eateth of your salt." Whereunto the Lady Ettard said, "Take thou no care as to that, girl, but go thou straightway and do as I bid thee."

Then Parcenet saw that it was not wise for her to disobey the lady. Wherefore she went straightway and did as she was bidden. So she brought the sleeping-draught to the lady in a chalice of pure wine, and the Lady Ettard took the chalice and said to Sir Pellias, "Take thou this chalice of wine, Sir Knight, and drink it unto me according to the measure of that good will thou hast unto me." Now Parcenet stood behind her lady's chair, and when Sir Pellias took the chalice she frowned and shook her head at him. But Sir Pellias saw it not, for he was intoxicated with the beauty of the Lady Ettard, and with the enchantment of the collar of emeralds and opal stones and gold which she now wore. Wherefore he said unto her, "Lady, if there were poison in that chalice, yet would I drink of the wine that is in it at thy command."

At that the Lady Ettard fell a-laughing beyond measure, and

she said, "Sir Knight, there is no poison in that cup."

So Sir Pellias took the chalice and drank the wine, and he said, "Lady, how is this? The wine is bitter." To which the Lady Ettard made reply, "Sir, that cannot be."

Then in a little while Sir Pellias his head waxed exceedingly heavy as if it were of lead, wherefore he bowed his head upon the table where he sat. That while the Lady Ettard remained watching him very strangely, and by and by she said, "Sir Knight, dost thou sleep?" To the which Sir Pellias replied not, for the fumes of the sleeping-draught had ascended into his brains and he slept.

Then the Lady Ettard arose laughing, and she smote her hands together and summoned her attendants. And she said to them, "Take this knight away, and convey him into an inner apartment, and when ye have brought him thither, strip him of his gay clothes and of his ornaments so that only his under-garments shall remain upon him. And when ye have done that, lay him upon a pallet and convey him out of the castle and into that meadow beneath the walls where he overthrew Sir Engamore, so that when the morning shall arise he shall become a mock and a jest unto all who shall behold him. Thus shall we humiliate him in that same field wherein he overthrew Sir Engamore, and his humiliation shall be greater than the humiliation of Sir Engamore hath been."

Now when the damsel Parcenet heard this she was greatly afflicted, so that she withdrew herself apart and wept for Sir Pellias. But the others took Sir Pellias and did unto him as the Lady Ettard had commanded.

Now when the next morning had come, Sir Pellias awoke with the sun shining into his face. And he wist not at all where he was, for his brains were befogged by the sleeping-draught which he had taken. So he said unto himself, "Am I dreaming, or am I awake? for certes, the last that I remember was that I sat at supper with the Lady Ettard, yet here I am now in an open field with the sun shining upon me."

So he raised himself upon his elbow, and behold! he lay beneath the castle walls nigh to the postern gate. And above him, upon the top of the wall, was a great concourse of people, who, when they beheld that he was awake, laughed at him and mocked at him. And the Lady Ettard also gazed down at him from a window and he saw that she laughed at him and made herself merry. And lo! he beheld that he lay there clad only in his linen undervestment, and that he was in his bare feet as though he were prepared to sleep at night. So he sat upon the cot, saying unto himself, "Certainly this must be some shameful dream that oppresses me." Nor was he at all able to recover from his bewilderment.

Now, as he sat thus, the postern gate was opened of a sudden, and the damsel Parcenet came out thence. And her face was all be-wet with tears, and she bare in her hand a flame-colored mantle. Straightway she ran to Sir Pellias, and said, "Thou good and gentle knight, take thou this and wrap thyself in it."

Upon this Sir Pellias wist that this was no dream, but a truth of great shame; wherefore he was possessed with an extreme agony of shame, so that he fell to trembling, whilst his teeth chattered as though with an ague. Then he said to Parcenet, "Maiden, I thank thee." And he could find no more words to say. So he took the mantle and wrapped himself in it.

Now when the people upon the walls beheld what Parcenet had done, they hooted her and reviled her with many words of ill-regard. So the maiden ran back again into the castle, but Sir Pellias arose and went his way toward his pavilion wrapped in that mantle. And as he went he staggered and tottered like a drunken man, for a great burden of shame lay upon him almost more than he could carry.

So when Sir Pellias had reached his pavilion, he entered it and threw himself on his face upon his couch and lay there without saying anything. And by and by Sir Brandiles and Mador de la Porte heard of that plight into which Sir Pellias had fallen, and thereupon they hastened to where he lay and made much sorrow over him. Likewise, they were exceedingly wroth at the shame that had been put upon him; wherefore they said, "We will get us aid from Camelot, and we will burst open yonder castle and we will fetch the Lady Ettard hither to crave thy pardon for this affront. This we will do even if we have to drag her hither by the hair of her head."

But Sir Pellias lifted not his head, only he groaned and he

said, "Let be, Messires; for under no circumstance shall ye do that thing, she being a woman. As it is, I would defend her honor even though I died in that defence. For I know not whether I am bewitched or what it is that ails me, but I love her with a very great passion and I cannot tear my heart away from her."

At this Sir Brandiles and Sir Mador de la Porte were greatly astonished, wherefore they said the one to the other, "Certes, that lady hath laid some powerful spell upon him."

Then after a while Sir Pellias bade them go away and leave him, and they did so, though not with any very good will.

So Sir Pellias lay there for all that day until the afternoon had come. Then he aroused himself and bade his esquire for to bring him his armor. Now when Sir Brandiles and Sir Mador de la Porte heard news of this they went to where he was and said, "Sir, what have ye a mind to do?" To this Sir Pellias said, "I am going to try to win me unto the Lady Ettard's presence." Then they said, "What madness is this?" "I know not," said Sir Pellias, "but, meseems, that if I do not behold the Lady Ettard and talk with her I shall surely die of longing to see her." And they say, "Certes, this is madness." Whereunto he replied, "I know not whether it is madness or whether I am caught in some enchantment."

So the esquire fetched unto Sir Pellias his armor as he had commanded, and he clad Sir Pellias in it so that he was altogether armed from head to foot. Thereupon straightway Sir Pellias mounted his horse and rode out toward the castle of Grantmesnle.

Now when the Lady Ettard beheld Sir Pellias again parading the meadow below the castle, she called unto her six of her best knights, and she said unto them, "Behold, Messires, yonder is that knight who brought so much shame upon us yesterday. Now I bid ye for to go forth against him and to punish him as he deserveth."

So those six knights went and armed themselves, and when they had done so they straightway rode forth against Sir Pellias.

Now, when Sir Pellias beheld these approach, his heart overflowed with fury and he shouted in a great voice and drave forward against them. And for a while they withstood him, but he was not to be withstood, but fought with surpassing fury, wherefore they presently brake from before him and fled. So he pursued them with great fury about that field and smote four of them down from their horses. Then, when there were but two of those knights remaining, Sir Pellias of a sudden ceased to fight, and he cried out unto those two knights, "Messires, I surrender myself unto ye."

Now at that those two knights were greatly astonished, for they were entirely filled with the fear of his strength, and wist not why he should yield to them. Nevertheless they came and laid hands upon him and took him toward the castle. Upon this Sir Pellias said unto himself, "Now they will bring me unto the Lady Ettard, and I shall have speech with her." For it was for this that he had suffered himself to be taken by those two knights.

But it was not to be as Sir Pellias willed it. For when they had brought him close under the castle, the Lady Ettard called unto them from a window in the wall. And she said, "What do you with that knight?" They say, "We bring him to you, Lady." Upon this she cried out very vehemently, "Bring him not to me, but take him and tie his hands behind his back and tie his feet beneath his horse's belly, and send him back unto his companions."

Then Sir Pellias lifted up his eyes unto that window and he cried out in a great passion of despair, "Lady, it was unto thee I surrendered, and not unto these unworthy knights."

But the Lady Ettard cried out all the more vehemently, "Drive him hence, for I do hate the sight of him."

So those two knights did as the Lady Ettard said; they took Sir Pellias and bound him hand and foot upon his horse. And when they had done so they allowed his horse for to bear him back again unto his companions in that wise.

Now when Sir Brandiles and Sir Mador de la Porte beheld how Sir Pellias came unto them with his hands bound behind his back and his feet tied beneath his horse's belly, they were altogether filled with grief and despair. So they loosed those cords from about his hands and feet, and they cried out upon Sir Pellias, "Sir Knight, Sir Knight, art thou not ashamed to permit such infamy as this?" And Sir Pellias shook and trembled as though with an ague, and he cried out in great despair, "I care not what happens unto me!" They said, "Not unto thyself, Sir Knight; but what shame dost thou bring upon King Arthur and his Round Table!" Upon this Sir Pellias cried aloud, with a great and terrible voice, "I care not for them, either."

All of this befell because of the powerful enchantment of the collar of emeralds and opal stones and of gold which Sir Pellias had given unto the Lady Ettard, and which she continually wore. For it was beyond the power of any man to withstand the enchantment of that collar. So it was that Sir Pellias was bewitched and brought to that great pass of shame.

Chapter Fourth

How Queen Guinevere Quarrelled With Sir Gawaine, and How Sir Gawaine Left the Court of King Arthur for a While.

Now, in the same measure that Queen Guinevere felt high regard for Sir Pellias, in that same degree she felt misliking for Sir Gawaine. For, though Sir Gawaine was said of many to have a silver tongue, and whiles he could upon occasion talk in such a manner as to beguile others unto his will, yet he was of a proud temper and very stern and haughty. Wherefore he would not always brook that the Lady Guinevere should command him unto her will as she did other knights of that Court. Moreover, she could not ever forget how Sir Gawaine did deny her that time at Cameliard when she besought him and his companions for aid, in her time of trouble, nor how discourteous his speech had been to her upon that occasion. So there was no great liking between these two proud souls, for Queen Guinevere held to her way and Sir Gawaine held to his way under all circumstances.

Now it happened upon an occasion that Sir Gawaine and Sir Griflet and Sir Constantine of Cornwall sat talking with five ladies of the Queen's Court in a pleached garden that lay beneath the tower of the Lady Guinevere, and they made very pleasant discourse together. For some whiles they would talk and make them merry with jests and contes, and other whiles one or another would take a lute that they had with them and would play upon it and would sing.

Now while these lords and ladies sat thus enjoying pleasant discourse and singing in that manner, Queen Guinevere sat at a window that overlooked the garden, and which was not very high from the ground, wherefore she could overhear all that they said. But these lords and ladies were altogether unaware that the Queen could overhear them, so that they talked and laughed very freely, and the Queen greatly enjoyed their discourse and the music that they made.

That day was extraordinarily balmy, and it being well toward the sloping of the afternoon, those lords and ladies were clad in very gay attire. And of all who were there Sir Gawaine was the most gayly clad, for he was dressed in sky-blue silk embroidered with threads of silver. And Sir Gawaine was playing upon the lute and singing a ballad in an exceedingly pleasing voice so that Queen Guinevere, as she sat at the window beside the open casement, was very well content for to listen to him.

Now there was a certain greyhound of which Queen Guinevere was wonderfully fond; so much so that she had adorned its neck with a collar of gold inset with carbuncles. At that moment the hound came running into that garden and his feet were wet and soiled with earth. So, hearing Sir Gawaine singing and playing upon the lute, that hound ran unto him and leaped upon him. At this Sir Gawaine was very wroth, wherefore he clinched his hand and smote the hound upon the head with the knuckles thereof, so that the hound lifted up his voice with great outcry.

But when Queen Guinevere beheld that blow she was greatly offended, wherefore she called out from her window, "Why dost thou smite my dog, Messire?" And those lords and ladies who were below in the garden were very much surprised and were greatly abashed to find that the Queen was so nigh unto them as to overhear all that they had said and to behold all that they did.

But Sir Gawaine spake up boldly, saying, "Thy dog affronted me, Lady and whosoever affronteth me, I strike."

Then Queen Guinevere grew very angry with Sir Gawaine, wherefore she said, "Thy speech is over-bold, Messire," and Sir Gawaine said, "Not over-bold, Lady; but only bold enough for to maintain my rights."

At this speech the Lady Guinevere's face flamed like fire and her eyes shone very bright and she said, "I am sure that thou dost forget unto whom thou speakest, Sir Knight," at the which Sir Gawaine smiled very bitterly and said, "And thou, Lady, dost not remember that I am the son of a king so powerful that he needs no help from any other king for to maintain his rights."

At these words all those who were there fell as silent as though they were turned into stones, for that speech was exceedingly bold and haughty. Wherefore all looked upon the ground, for they durst not look either upon Queen Guinevere nor upon Sir Gawaine. And the Lady Guinevere, also, was silent for a long time, endeavoring to recover herself from that speech, and when she spake, it was as though she was half smothered by her anger. And she said, "Sir Knight, thou art proud and arrogant beyond measure, for I did never hear of anyone who dared to give reply unto his Queen as thou hast spoken unto me. But this is my Court, and I may command in it as I choose; wherefore I do now bid thee for to begone and to show thy face no more, either here nor in Hall nor any of the places where I hold my Court. For thou art an offence unto me, wherefore in none of these places shalt thou have leave to show thy face until thou dost ask my pardon for the affront which thou hast put upon me." Then Sir Gawaine arose and bowed very low to the Queen Guinevere and he said, "Lady, I go. Nor will I return thitherward until thou art willing for to tell me that thou art sorry for the discourteous way in which thou hast entreated me now and at other times before my peers."

So saying, Sir Gawaine took his leave from that place, nor did he turn his head to look behind him. And Queen Guinevere went into her chamber and wept in secret for anger and for shame. For indeed she was greatly grieved at what had befallen; yet was she so proud that she would in no wise have recalled the words that she had spoken, even had she been able.

Now when the news of that quarrel had gone about the castle it came unto the ears of Sir Ewaine, wherefore Sir Ewaine went straightway unto Sir Gawaine, and asked him what was ado, and Sir Gawaine, who was like one distraught and in great despair, told him everything. Then Sir Ewaine said: "Thou wert certainly wrong for to speak unto the Queen as thou didst. Nevertheless, if thou art banished from this Court, I will go with thee, for thou art my cousin-german and my companion, and my heart cleaveth unto thee." So Sir Ewaine went unto King Arthur, and he said, "Lord, my cousin, Sir Gawaine, hath been banished from this Court by the Queen. And though I may not say that he hath not deserved that punishment, yet I would fain crave thy leave for to go along with him."

At this King Arthur was very grieved, but he maintained a steadfast countenance, and said, "Messire, I will not stay thee from going where it pleases thee. As for thy kinsman, I daresay he gave the Queen such great offence that she could not do otherwise than as she did."

So both Sir Ewaine and Sir Gawaine went unto their inns and commanded their esquires for to arm them. Then they, with their esquires, went forth from Camelot, betaking their way toward the forest lands.

There those two knights and their esquires travelled for all that day until the gray of the eventide, what time the birds were singing their last songs ere closing their eyes for the night. So, finding the evening drawing on apace, those knights were afraid that they would not be able to find kindly lodging ere the night should descend upon them, and they talked together a great deal concerning that thing. But as they came to the top of a certain hill, they beheld below them a valley, very fair and well tilled, with many cottages and farm-crofts. And in the midst of that valley was a goodly abbey very fair to look upon; wherefore Sir Gawaine said unto Sir Ewaine: "If yonder abbey is an abbey of monks, I believe we shall find excellent lodging there for to-night."

So they rode down into that valley and to the abbey, and they found a porter at the wicket of whom they learned that it was indeed an abbey of monks. Wherefore they were very glad and made great rejoicing.

But when the abbot of that abbey learned who they were and of what quality and high estate, he was exceedingly pleased for to welcome them, wherefore he brought them into that part of the abbey where he himself dwelt. There he bade them welcome and had set before them a good supper, whereat they were very much rejoiced. Now the abbot was merry of soul, and took great pleasure in discourse with strangers, so he diligently inquired of those two knights concerning the reason why they were errant. But they told him naught concerning that quarrel at Court, but only that they were in search of adventure. Upon this the abbot said, "Ha, Messires, if ye are in search of adventures, ye may find one not very far from this place."

So Sir Gawaine said, "What adventure is that?" And the abbot replied, "I will tell ye; if ye will travel to the eastward from this place, ye will come, after a while, to a spot where ye shall find a very fair castle of gray stone. In front of that castle ye will find a good level meadow, and in the midst of the meadow a sycamore-tree, and upon the sycamore-tree a shield to which certain ladies offer affront that shield you will discover a very good adventure."

Then Sir Gawaine said, "That is a very strange matter. Now, to-morrow morning we will go to that place and will endeavor to discover of what sort that adventure may be." And the abbot said, "Do so," and laughed in great measure.

So when the next morning had come, Sir Gawaine and Sir Ewaine gave adieu unto the abbot, and took their leave of that place, riding away unto the eastward, as the abbot had advised. And after they had ridden in that direction for two or three hours or more they beheld before them the borders of a forest all green and shady with foliage, and very cheerful in the warmth of the early summer day. And, lo! immediately at the edge of the woodland there stood a fair, strong castle of gray stone, with windows of glass shining very bright against the sky.

Then Sir Gawaine and Sir Ewaine beheld that everything was as the abbot had said; for in front of the castle was a smooth, level meadow with a sycamore-tree in the midst thereof. And as they drew near they perceived that a sable shield hung in the branches of the tree, and in a little they could see that it bore the device of three white goshawks displayed. But that which was very extraordinary was that in front of that shield there stood seven young damsels, exceedingly fair of face, and that these seven damsels continually offered a great deal of insult to that shield. For some of those damsels smote it ever and anon with peeled rods of osier, and others flung lumps of clay upon it, so that the shield was greatly defaced therewith. Now nigh to the shield was a very noble-appearing knight clad all in black armor, and seated upon a black war-horse, and it was very plain to be seen that the shield belonged unto that knight, for otherwise he had no shield. Yet, though that was very likely his shield, yet the knight offered no protest either by word or by act to stay those damoiselles from offering affront thereunto.

Then Sir Ewaine said unto Sir Gawaine, "Yonder is a very strange thing that I behold; belike one of us is to encounter yonder knight." And Sir Gawaine said, "Maybe so." Then Sir Ewaine said, "If it be so then I will undertake the adventure." "Not so," said Sir Gawaine, "for I will undertake it myself, I being the elder of us twain, and the better seasoned in knighthood." So Sir Ewaine said, "Very well. Let it be that way, for thou art a very much more powerful knight than I, and it would be a pity for one of us to fail in this undertaking." Thereupon Sir Gawaine said, "Let be, then, and I will undertake it."

So he set spurs to his horse and he rode rapidly to where those damsels offered affront in that way to the sable shield. And he set his spear in rest and shouted in a loud voice, "Get ye away! Gey ye away!" So when those damsels beheld the armed knight riding at them in that wise they fled away shrieking from before him.

Then the Sable Knight, who sat not a great distance away, rode forward in a very stately manner unto Sir Gawaine, and he said, "Sir Knight, why dost thou interfere with those ladies?" Whereunto Sir Gawaine replied, "Because they offered insult unto what appeared to me to be a noble and knightly shield." At this the Sable Knight spake very haughtily, saying, "Sir Knight, that shield belongeth unto me and I do assure thee that

I am very well able for to take care of it without the interference of any other defender." To which Sir Gawaine said, "It would appear not, Sir Knight."

Then the Sable Knight said, "Messire, an thou thinkest that thou art better able to take care of that shield than I, I think that thou wouldst do very well to make thy words good with thy body." To this Sir Gawaine said, "I will do my endeavor to show thee that I am better able to guard that shield than thou art who ownest it."

Upon this the Sable Knight, without further ado, rode unto the sycamore-tree, and took down from thence the shield that hung there. And he dressed the shield upon his arm and took his spear in hand and made him ready for defence. And Sir Gawaine likewise made him ready for defence, and then each knight took such station upon the field as appeared unto him to be fitting.

Now, when the people of that castle perceived that a combat of arms was toward, they crowded in great numbers to the walls, so that there were as many as twoscore ladies and esquires and folk of different degrees looking down upon that field of battle from the walls.

So when those knights were altogether prepared, Sir Ewaine gave the signal for encounter and each knight shouted aloud and drave spurs into his charger and rushed forward to the assault with a noise like thunder for loudness.

Now, Sir Gawaine thought that he should easily overcome his adversary in this assault and that he would be able to cast him down from out of his saddle without much pains, for there was hardly any knight in that realm equal to Sir Gawaine for prowess. And, indeed, he had never yet been unhorsed in combat excepting by King Arthur. So when those two rode to the assault, the one against the other, Sir Gawaine thought of a surety that his adversary would fall before him. But it was not so, for in that attack Sir Gawaine's spear was broken into many pieces, but the spear of the Sable Knight held, so that Sir Gawaine was cast with great violence out of the saddle, smiting the dust with a terrible noise of falling. And so astonished was he at that fall that it appeared unto him not as though he fell from his saddle, but as though the earth rose up and smote him. Wherefore he lay for a while all stunned with the blow and with the astonishment thereof.

But when he heard the shouts of the people upon the castle wall, he immediately aroused himself from where he lay in the dust, and he was so filled with rage and shame that he was like one altogether intoxicated. Wherefore he drew his sword and rushed with great fury upon his enemy with intent to hew him down by main strength. Then that other knight, seeing him come thus at him, immediately voided his own saddle and drew his sword and put himself in posture either for assault or for defence. So they lashed together, tracing this way and that, and smiting with such fury that the blows they gave were most terrible for to behold. But when Sir Ewaine beheld how fierce was that assault, he set spurs unto his horse and pushed him between the knights-contestant, crying out aloud, "Sir Knights! Sir Knights! what is this? Here is no cause for such desperate battle." But Sir Gawaine cried out very furiously, "Let be! let be! and stand aside! for this quarrel concerns thee not." And the Sable Knight said, "A-horse or afoot, I am ready to meet that knight at any time."

But Sir Ewaine said, "Not so; ye shall fight no more in this quarrel. For shame, Gawaine! For shame to seek such desperate quarrel with a knight that did but meet thee in a friendly fashion in a fair contest!"

Then Sir Gawaine was aware that Sir Ewaine was both just and right; wherefore he put up his sword in silence, albeit he was like to weep for vexation at the shame of his overthrow. And the Sable Knight put up his sword also, and so peace was made betwixt those two.

Then the Sable Knight said, "I am glad that this quarrel is ended, for I perceive, Messires, that ye are assuredly knights of great nobility and gentleness of breeding; wherefore I would that we might henceforth be friends and companions instead of enemies. Wherefore I do beseech ye for to come with me a little ways from here where I have taken up my inn, so that we may rest and refresh ourselves in my pavilion."

Unto this Sir Ewaine said, "I give thee gramercy for thy courtesy, Sir Knight; and we will go with thee with all the pleasure that it is possible to feel." And Sir Gawaine said, "I am content." So these three knights straightway left the field of battle.

And when they had come to the edge of the forest Sir Gawaine and Sir Ewaine perceived a very fine pavilion of green silk set up beneath the tree. And about that pavilion were many attendants of divers sorts all clad in colors of green and white. So Sir Gawaine perceived that the knight who had overthrown him was certainly someone of very high estate, wherefore he was very greatly comforted. Then the esquires of those three knights came and removed the helmet, each esquire from his knight, so that the knight might be made comfortable thereby. And when this was done Sir Gawaine and Sir Ewaine perceived that the Sable Knight was very comely of countenance, being ruddy of face and with hair like to copper for redness. Then Sir Ewaine said unto the knight, "Sir Unknown Knight, this knight, my companion, is Sir Gawaine, son of King Urien of Gore, and I am Ewaine, the son of King Lot of Orkney. Now, I crave of thee that wilt make thyself known unto us in like manner."

"Ha," said the other; "I am glad that ye are such very famous and royal knights, for I am also of royal blood, being Sir Marhaus, the son of the King of Ireland."

Then Sir Gawaine was very glad to discover how exalted was the quality of that knight who overthrew him and he said unto Sir Marhaus, "Messire, I make my vow, that thou art one of the most terrible knights in the world. For thou hast done unto me this day what only one knight in all the world hath ever done, and that is King Arthur, who is my uncle and my lord. Now thou must certainly come unto the Court of King Arthur, for he will be wonderfully glad for to see thee, and maybe he will make thee a Knight of his Round Table—and there is no honor in all of the world that can be so great as that." Thus he spoke unthinkingly; and then he remembered. Wherefore he smote his fist against his forehead, crying out, "Aha! aha! who am I for to bid thee to come unto the Court of King Arthur, who only yesterday was disgraced and banished therefrom?"

Then Sir Marhaus was very sorry for Sir Gawaine, and he inquired concerning the trouble that lay upon him, and Sir Ewaine told Sir Marhaus all about that quarrel; at that Sir

Marhaus was still more sorry for Sir Gawaine, wherefore he said, "Messires, I like ye both wonderfully well, and I would fain become your companion in the adventures ye are to undertake. For now I need remain here no longer. Ye must know that I was obliged to defend those ladies who assailed my shield until I had overthrown seven knights in their behalf. And I must tell ye that Sir Gawaine was the seventh knight I have overthrown. Wherefore, since I have now overthrown him, I am now released from my obligation and may go with ye."

Then Sir Gawaine and Sir Ewaine were very much astonished that any knight should lie beneath so strange an obligation as that—to defend those who assailed his shield—and they besought Sir Marhaus to tell them why he should have been obliged to fulfil such a pledge. So Sir Marhaus said, "I will tell ye. The case was this: Some whiles ago I was travelling in these parts with a hawk upon my wrist. At that time I was clad very lightly in holiday attire, to wit: I wore a tunic of green silk, and hosen one of green and one of white. And I had nothing upon me by way of defence but a light buckler and a short sword. Now, coming unto a certain stream of water, very deep and rapid, I perceived before me a bridge of stone crossing that stream, but so narrow that only one horseman might cross the bridge at a time. So I entered upon that bridge and was part way across it, when I perceived a knight in armor coming the other way. And behind the knight there sat upon a pillion a very fair lady with golden hair and very proud of demeanor. Now, when that knight perceived me upon the bridge, he cried aloud, 'Get back! get back! and suffer me to pass!' But this I would not do, but said, 'Not so, Sir Knight, for, having advanced so far upon this bridge, I have certes the right of way to complete my passage, and it is for you to wait and to permit me to cross.' But the knight would not do so, but immediately put himself in posture of offence and straightway came against me upon the bridge with intent either to slay me or to drive me back unto the other extremity of the bridge. But this he was not able to do, for I defended myself very well with my light weapons. And I so pushed my horse against his horse that I drave him backward from off the bridge and into the water, whereinto the horse and the knight and the lady all of them fell with a terrible uproar.

"At this the lady shrieked in great measure and both she and the knight were like to drown in the water, the knight being altogether clad in armor, so that he could not uplift himself above the flood. Wherefore, beholding their extremity, I leaped from off my horse and into the water, and with great ado and with much danger unto myself, I was able to bring them both unto the land.

"But that lady was very greatly offended with me, for her fair raiment was altogether wet and spoiled by the water, wherefore she upbraided me with great vehemence. So I kneeled down before her and besought her pardon with all humility, but she still continued to upbraid me. Then I offered unto her for to perform any penance that she might set upon me. At this the lady appeared to be greatly mollified, for she said, 'Very well, I will set thee a penance,' and when her knight had recovered she said, 'Come with us,' and so I mounted my horse and followed them. So after we had gone a considerable distance we came to this place and here she commanded me as follows: 'Sir Knight,' quoth she, 'this castle belongeth unto me and unto this knight who is my lord. Now, this shall be the penance for the affront thou hast given me: thou shalt take thy shield and hang it up in yonder sycamore-tree and every day I will send certain damsels of mine own out from the castle. And they shall offend against that shield and thou shalt not only suffer whatever offence they may offer, but thou shalt defend them against all comers until thou hast overcome seven knights.'

"So I have done until this morning, when thou, Sir Gawaine, camest hither. Thou art the seventh knight against whom I have contended, and as I have overcome thee, my penance is now ended and I am free."

Then Sir Gawaine and Sir Ewaine gave Sir Marhaus great joy that his penance was completed, and they were very well satisfied each party with the others. So Sir Gawaine and Sir Ewaine abided that night in the pavilion of Sir Marhaus and the next morning they arose and, having laved themselves in a forest stream, they departed from that place.

So they entered the forest land once more and made their way by certain paths, they knew not witherward; and they travelled all that morning and until the afternoon was come.

Now, as they travelled thus Sir Marhaus said of a sudden, "Messires, know ye where we are come to?" "Nay," they said, "we know not." Then Sir Marhaus said, "This part of the forest is called Arroy and it is further called 'The Forest of Adventure.' For it is very well known that when a knight, or a party of knights enter this forest, they will assuredly meet with an adventure of some sort, from which some come forth with credit while others fail therein." And Sir Ewaine said, "I am glad that we have come hither. Now let us go forward into this forest."

So those three knights and their esquires continued onward in that woodland where was silence so deep that even the tread of their horses upon the earth was scarcely to be heard. And there was no note of bird and no sound of voice and hardly did any light penetrate into the gloom of that woodland. Wherefore those knights said unto one another, "This is soothly a very strange place and one, maybe, of enchantment."

Now when they had come into the very midst of these dark woodlands, they perceived of a sudden, in the pathway before them, a fawn as white as milk. And round the neck of the fawn was a collar of pure gold. And the fawn stood and looked at them, but when they had come nigh to it, it turned and ran along a very narrow path. Then Sir Gawaine said, "Let us follow that fawn and see where it goeth." And the others said, "We are content." So they followed that narrow path until of a sudden they came to where was a little open lawn very bright with sunlight. In the midst of the lawn was a fountain of water, and there was no fawn to be seen, but, lo! beside the fountain there sat a wonderfully beautiful lady, clad all in garments of green. And the lady combed her hair with golden comb, and her hair was like to the wing of a raven for blackness. And upon her arms she wore very wonderful bracelets of emeralds and of opal stones inset into cunningly wrought gold. Moreover, the face of the lady was like ivory for whiteness and her eyes were bright like jewels set in ivory. Now, when this lady perceived the knights she arose and laid aside her golden comb and bound up the locks of her hair with ribbons of scarlet silk, and thereupon, she came to those knights and gave them greeting.

Then those three knights gat them down straightway from off their horses, and Sir Gawaine said, "Lady, I believe that thou art not of mortal sort, but that thou art of faërie." Unto this the lady said, "Sir Gawaine, thou art right," and Sir Gawaine marvelled that she should know his name so well. Then he said to her, "Lady, who art thou?" and she made answer, "My name is Nymue and I am the chiefest of those Ladies of the Lake of whom thou mayst have heard. For it was I who gave unto King Arthur his sword Excalibur; for I am very friendly unto King Arthur and to all the noble Knights of his Court. So it is that I know ye all. And I know that thou, Sir Marhaus, shall become one of the most famous Knights of the Round Table." And all they three marvelled at the lady's words. Then she said, "I prithee tell me what it is that ye seek in these parts?" And they say, "We seek adventure." "Well," said she, "I will bring you unto adventure, but it is Sir Gawaine who must undertake it." And Sir Gawaine said, "That is very glad news." Then the lady said, "Take me behind you upon your saddle, Sir Gawaine, and I will show unto you that adventure." So Sir Gawaine took the lady up behind him upon the saddle, and lo! she brought with her a fragrance such as he had never known before; for that fragrance was so subtle that it seemed to Sir Gawaine that the forest gave forth that perfume which the Lady of the Lake brought with her.

So the Lady of the Lake brought them by many devious ways out from that part of the forest; and she brought them by sundry roads and paths until they came out into an open country, very fruitful and pleasant to behold; and she brought them up a very high hill, and from the top of the hill they looked down upon a fruitful and level plain as upon a table spread out before them. And they beheld that in the midst of the plain was a noble castle built all of red stone and of red bricks; and they beheld that there was a small town built also of red bricks.

Now as they sat their horses there on top of the hill they perceived of a sudden a knight clad all in red armor who came forth from a glade of trees. And they saw that the knight paraded the meadow that lay in front of the castle, and they saw that he gave challenge to those within the castle. Then they perceived that the drawbridge of the castle was let fall of a sudden and that there issued from thence ten knights clad in complete armor. And they beheld those ten knights assail the one knight in red armor, and they beheld the one knight assail the ten. And they beheld that for a while those ten withstood the one, but that he assailed them so terribly that he smote down four of them very quickly. Then they beheld that the rest brake and fled from before that one, and that the Red Knight pursued the others about the meadow with great fury. And they saw that he smote down one from out his saddle and another and another until but two of those knights were left.

Then Sir Gawaine said, "That is certainly a very wonderful sight for to see." But the Lady of the Lake only smiled and said, "Wait a little."

So they waited and they saw that when the Red Knight had smitten down all of his enemies but those two, and that when he had put those two in great peril of their lives, he of a sudden sheathed his sword and surrendered himself unto them. And they saw that those two knights brought the Red Knight to the castle, and that when they had brought him there a lady upon the wall thereof bespake that Red Knight as with great violence of language. And they beheld that those two knights took the Red Knight and bound his hands behind his back, and that they bound his feet beneath his horse's belly, and that they drave him away from that place.

All this they beheld from the top of that hill, and the Lady of the Lake said unto Sir Gawaine, "There thou shalt find thy adventure, Sir Gawaine." And Sir Gawaine said, "I will go," and the Lady of the Lake said, "Do so."

Thereupon, lo! she vanished from their sight and they were greatly amazed.

Chapter Fifth

How Sir Gawaine Met Sir Pellias and How He Promised to Aid Him With the Lady Ettard.

---

ow, after that wonderful lady had disappeared from their sight in that manner, those three knights stood for a little while altogether astonished, for they wist not how to believe what their eyes had beheld. Then, by and by, Sir Gawine spake, saying, "Certes, that was a very wonderful thing that happened to us, for in all my life I never knew so strange a miracle to befall. Now, it is very plain that some excellent adventure lieth in what we have seen, wherefore let us descend into yonder valley, for there we shall doubtless discover what that signifies which we have just now beheld. For I make my vow that I have hardly ever seen so terribly powerful a knight as he who has just now fought yonder battle, wherefore I can in no wise understand why, when he should so nearly have obtained a victory over his enemies, he should have surrendered himself to them as he did."

And Sir Ewaine and Sir Marhaus agreed that it would be well to go down and inquire what was the meaning of that which they had beheld.

So they three and their attendants rode down into the valley. And they rode forward until they had come to a certain glade of trees and there they beheld three goodly pavilions that stood there: the one pavilion of white cloth, the second pavilion of green cloth, and the third pavilion of scarlet cloth.

Now, as the three knights-companion drew nigh to the pavilions, there came forth two knights to meet them. And when Sir Gawaine and Sir Ewaine saw the shields of the two, they immediately knew that they were Sir Brandiles and Sir Mador de la Porte. And in the same manner Sir Brandiles and Sir Mador de la Porte knew Sir Gawaine and Sir Ewaine, and each party was very much astonished at thus meeting the other in so strange a place. So when they came together they gave one another very joyful greeting and clasped hands with strong love and good fellowship.

Then Sir Gawaine made Sir Marhaus acquainted with Sir Brandiles and Sir Mador de la Porte and thereupon the five knights all went together into those three pavilions, discoursing the while with great amity and pleasure. And when they had come into the pavilion of Sir Brandiles they found there spread a good refreshment of white bread and wine of excellent savor.

Then after a while Sir Gawaine said to Sir Brandiles and Sir Mador de la Porte, "Messires, we observed a little while ago a very singular thing; for, as we stood together at the top of yonder hill and looked down into this plain we beheld a single knight clad all in red armor who did battle with ten knights. And that one knight in red armor combated the ten with such fury that he drave them all from before him, though they were so many and he but one. And truly I make my vow that I have hardly ever seen a knight show such great prowess in arms as he. Yet, when he had overcome all but two of those knights, and was in fair way to win a clear victory, he suddenly yielded himself unto the two and suffered them to take him and bind him and drive him with great indignity from the field. Now, I pray ye, tell me what was the meaning of that which we beheld, and who was that knight who fought so great a battle and yet yielded himself so shamefully."

At this Sir Brandiles and Sir Mador de la Porte made no answer, but directed their looks another way, for they knew not what to say. But when Sir Gawaine beheld that they were abashed he began more than ever to wonder what that thing meant; wherefore he said, "What is this? Why do ye not answer me? I bid ye tell me what is the meaning of your looks, and who is that red knight!"

Then after a while Sir Mador de la Porte said, "I shall not tell you, but you may come and see."

Then Sir Gawaine began to think maybe there was something in this that it would be better not to publish, and that, haply, he had best examine further into the matter alone. So he said unto the other knights, "Bide ye here a little, Messires, and I will go with Sir Mador de la Porte."

So Sir Gawaine went with Sir Mador de la Porte, and Sir Mador led him unto the white pavilion. And when they had come there Sir Mador drew aside the curtains of the pavilion, and he said, "Enter!" and Sir Gawaine entered.

Now, when he had come into the pavilion he perceived that a man sat upon a couch of rushes covered with an azure cloth, and in a little he perceived that man was Sir Pellias. But Sir Pellias saw not him immediately, but sat with his head bowed, like one altogether overwhelmed by a great despair.

But when Sir Gawaine beheld who it was that sat upon the couch, he was greatly amazed and cried out, "Ha! is it thou, Sir Pellias? is it thou?"

But when Sir Pellias heard Sir Gawaine's voice, and when he perceived who it was that spake to him, he emitted an exceedingly bitter cry. And sprang to his feet and ran as far away as the walls of the pavilion would let him, and turned his face unto the walls thereof.

Then, after a while, Sir Gawaine spoke very sternly to Sir Pellias, saying, "Messire, I am astonished and very greatly ashamed that a Knight of King Arthur's Royal Court and of his Round Table should behave in so dishonorable a manner as I saw thee behave this day. For it is hardly to be believed that a knight of such repute and nobility as thou would suffer himself to be taken and bound by two obscure knights as thou didst suffer thyself this day. How couldst thou bring thyself to submit to such indignity and insult? Now, I do demand of thee that thou wilt explain this matter unto me."

But Sir Pellias was silent and would not make any reply.

Then Sir Gawaine cried out very fiercely, "Ha! wilt thou not answer me?" and Sir Pellias shook his head.

Then Sir Gawaine said, still speaking very fiercely, "Messire! thou shalt answer me one way or another! For either thou shalt tell me the meaning of thy shameful conduct, or else thou shalt do extreme battle with me. For I will not suffer it that thou shalt bring such shame upon King Arthur and his Round Table without myself defending the honor and the credit of him and of it. One while thou and I were dear friends, but unless thou dost immediately exculpate thyself I shall hold thee in contempt, and shall regard thee as an enemy."

Upon this Sir Pellias spake like unto one that was nigh distracted, and he said, "I will tell thee all." Then he confessed everything unto Sir Gawaine, telling all that had befallen since that time when he had left the May Court of Queen Guinevere to enter upon this adventure, and Sir Gawaine listened unto him with great amazement. And when Sir Pellias had made an end of telling all that had befallen him, Sir Gawaine said, "Certes, this is very wonderful. Indeed, I cannot understand how thou camest to be so entangled in the charms of this lady unless she hath bewitched thee with some great enchantment."

Unto this Sir Pellias said, "Yea, I believe that I have been bewitched, for I am altogether beside myself in this, and am entirely unable to contain my passion."

Then Sir Gawaine bethought him for a long while, considering that matter very seriously; and by and by he said, "I have a plan, and it is this: I will go unto the Lady Ettard myself, and will inquire diligently into this affair. And if I find that anyone hath entangled thee in enchantments, it will go hard with me but I will punish that one with great dolor. For I shall not have it that another enchanter shall beguile thee as one hath already beguiled Merlin the Wise."

Then Sir Pellias said unto Sir Gawaine, "How wilt thou accomplish this matter so as to gain into the presence of the Lady Ettard?"

Thereupon Sir Gawaine replied, "That I will tell thee. We twain shall exchange armor, and I will go unto the castle in thy armor. When I have come there I shall say that I have overcome thee in an encounter, and have taken thine armor away from thee. Then they will haply admit me into the castle to hear my story, and I shall have speech with her."

Then Sir Pellias said, "Very well; it shall be as thou dost ordain."

So Sir Pellias summoned an esquire, and Sir Gawaine summoned his esquire, and those two removed the armor from Sir Pellias, and clad Sir Gawaine therein. After they had done that Sir Gawaine mounted upon the horse of Sir Pellias, and rode openly into that field wherein Sir Pellias had aforetime paraded.

Now, it happened that the Lady Ettard was at that time walking upon a platform within the castle walls, from which place she looked down into that meadow. So when she beheld a red knight parading in the meadow, she thought it was Sir Pellias come thither again, and at that she was vexed and affronted beyond all measure. Wherefore she said unto those nigh her, "That knight vexes me so wofully that I fear me I shall fall ill of vexation if he cometh here many more times. I would that I knew how to rid myself of him; for already, and only an hour ago, I sent ten good knights against him, and he overcame them all with great despatch and with much dishonor unto them and unto me."

So she beckoned to the Red Knight, and when he had come nigh to the walls of the castle, she said to him, "Sir Knight, why dost thou come hitherward to afflict me and to affront me thus? Canst thou not understand that the more often thou comest to tease me in this manner, the more do I hate thee?"

Then Sir Gawaine opened the umbril of his helmet and showed his face, and the Lady Ettard saw that the Red Knight was not Sir Pellias. And Sir Gawaine said, "Lady, I am not that one whom thou supposest me to be, but another. For, behold! I have thine enemy's armor upon my body, wherefore thou mayst see that I have overcome him. For thou mayst suppose that it is hardly to be thought that I could wear his armor unless I took it from him by force of arms. Wherefore thou needst trouble thyself no more about him."

Then the Lady Ettard could not think otherwise than this knight (whom she knew not) had indeed overthrown Sir Pellias in a bout of arms, and had taken his armor away from him. And indeed she was exceedingly astonished that such a thing could have happened; for it appeared to her that Sir Pellias was one of the greatest knights in the world; wherefore she marvelled who this knight could be who had overthrown him in battle. So she gave command to sundry of those in attendance upon her that they should go forth and bring that red knight into the castle and that they should pay him great honor; for that he must assuredly be one of the very greatest champions in the world.

Thus Sir Gawaine came into the castle and was brought before the Lady Ettard where she stood in a wonderfully large and noble hall. For that hall was illuminated by seven tall windows of colored glass, and it was hung around with tapestries and hangings, very rich and of a most excellent quality, wherefore Sir Gawaine was greatly astonished at the magnificence of all that he beheld in that place.

Now, Sir Gawaine had taken the helmet from off his head, and he bore it under his arm and against his hip, and his head was bare so that all who were there could see his face very plainly. Wherefore they all perceived that he was exceedingly comely, that his eyes were as blue as steel, his nose high and curved, and his hair and beard very dark and rich in color. Moreover, his bearing was exceedingly steadfast and haughty, so that those who beheld him were awed by the great knightliness of his aspect.

Then the Lady Ettard came to Sir Gawaine and gave him her hand, and he kneeled down and set it to his lips. And the lady bespoke him very graciously, saying, "Sir Knight, it would give me a great deal of pleasure if thou wouldst make us acquainted with thy name, and if thou wouldst proclaim thy degree of estate unto us."

Unto this Sir Gawaine made reply, "Lady, I cannot inform you of these things at these present, being just now vowed unto secrecy upon those points, wherefore I do crave your patience for a little."

Then the Lady Ettard said, "Sir Knight, it is a great pity that we may not know thy name and degree; ne'theless, though we are as yet in ignorance as to thy quality, I yet hope that thou wilt give us the pleasure of thy company awhile, and that thou wilt condescend to remain within this poor place for two days or three, whiles we offer thee such refreshment as we are able to do."

Now here a very untoward thing befell. To wit, it was this: The Lady Ettard had come to love that necklace of emeralds and of opal stones and of gold that she had borrowed from Sir Pellias, and that to such a degree that she never let it depart from her whether by day or by night. Wherefore she wore it at that moment hanging about her neck and her throat. So, as she talked to Sir Gawaine, he looked upon that necklace, and the enchantment thereof began to take a very great hold upon him. For he presently began to feel as though his heart was drawn with exceeding ardency out of his bosom and unto the Lady Ettard; so much so that, in a little while, he could not at all keep his regard withdrawn from her. And the more that he looked upon the necklace and the lady the more did the enchantment of the jewel take hold upon his spirits. Accordingly, when the Lady Ettard spake so graciously unto him, he was very glad to accept of her kindness; wherefore he said, gazing very ardently at her the whiles, "Lady, thou art exceedingly gentle to extend so great a courtesy unto me; wherefore I shall be glad beyond measure for to stay with thee for a short while."

At these words the Lady Ettard was very greatly pleased, for she said to herself, "Certes, this knight (albeit I know not who he may be) must be a champion of extraordinary prowess and of exalted achievement. Now, if I can persuade him to remain in this castle as my champion, then shall I doubtless gain very great credit thereby; for I shall have one for to defend my rights who must assuredly be the greatest knight in all the world." Wherefore she set forth every charm and grace of demeanor to please Sir Gawaine, and Sir Gawaine was altogether delighted by the kindness of her manner.

Now, Sir Engamore was there present at that time, wherefore he was very greatly troubled in spirit. For in the same degree that Sir Gawaine received courtesy from the Lady Ettard, in that same degree Sir Engamore was cast down into great sorrow and distress—so much so that it was a pity for to see him. For Sir Engamore said to himself, "Aforetime, ere these foreign knights came hitherward, the Lady Ettard was very kind to me, and was willing to take me for her champion and lord. But first came Sir Pellias and overthrew me, and now cometh this strange knight and overthroweth him, wherefore, in the presence of such a great champion as this, I am come to be as nothing in her sight." So Sir Engamore withdrew himself from that place and went unto his closet, where he sat himself down alone in great sorrow.

Now the Lady Ettard had given command that a very noble and splendid feast should be prepared for Sir Gawaine and for herself, and whilst it was preparing she and Sir Gawaine walked together in the pleasaunce of the castle. For there was a very pleasant shade in the place, and flowers grew there in great abundance, and many birds sang very sweetly in among the blossoms of the trees. And as Sir Gawaine and the lady walked thus together, the attendants stood at a little distance and regarded them. And they said to one another, "Assuredly it would be a very good thing if the Lady Ettard would take this knight for her champion, and if he should stay here in Grantmesnle forever."

So Sir Gawaine and the lady walked together, talking very cheerfully, until sunset, and at that time the supper was prepared and they went in and sat down to it. And as they supped, a number of pages, very fair of face, played upon harps before them; and sundry damsels sang very sweetly in accord to that music, so that the bosom of Sir Gawaine was greatly expanded with joy. Wherefore he said to himself, "Why should I ever leave this place? Lo! I have been banished from King Arthur's Court; why then should I not establish here a Court of mine own that might, in time, prove to be like to his for glory?" And the Lady Ettard was so beautiful in his eyes that this seemed to him to be a wonderfully pleasant thought.

Now turn we unto Sir Pellias:

For after Sir Gawaine had left him, the heart of Sir Pellias began to misgive him that he had not been wise; and at last he said to himself, "Suppose that Sir Gawaine should forget his duty to me when he meeteth the Lady Ettard. For it seems that haply she possesses some potent charm that might well draw the heart of Sir Gawaine unto her. Wherefore if Sir Gawaine should come within the circle of such enchantment as that, he may forget his duty unto me and may transgress against the honor of his knighthood."

And the more that Sir Pellias thought of this the more troubled he grew in his mind. So at last, when evening had fallen, he called an esquire unto him and he said, "Go, and fetch me hither the garb of a black friar, for I would fain go unto the castle of Grantmesnle in disguise." So the esquire went as he commanded and brought him such a garb, and Sir Pellias clad himself therein.

Now, by that time, the darkness had come entirely over the face of the earth so that it would not have been possible for anyone to know Sir Pellias, even if they had seen his face. So he went unto the castle, and they who were there, thinking that he was a black friar, as he appeared to be, admitted him into the castle by the postern gate.

So, as soon as Sir Pellias had come into the castle, he began to make diligent inquiry concerning where he might find that knight who had come thither in the afternoon, and those within the castle, still thinking him to be a friar of black orders, said unto him, "What would ye with that knight?" To the which Sir Pellias said, "I have a message for him." They of the castle said, "Ye cannot come at that knight just now, for he is at supper with the Lady Ettard, and he holds her in pleasant discourse."

At this Sir Pellias began to wax very angry, for he greatly misliked the thought that Sir Gawaine should then make merry with the Lady Ettard. So he said, speaking very sternly, "I must presently have speech with that knight, wherefore I bid ye to bring me unto him without delay." Then they of the castle said, "Wait and we will see if that knight is willing to have you come to him."

So one of the attendants went unto that place where Sir Gawaine sat at supper with the Lady Ettard, and he said, "Sir Knight, there hath come hither a black friar who demandeth to have present speech with thee, and he will not be denied, but continually maketh that demand."

At this Sir Gawaine was greatly troubled in his conscience,

for he knew that he was not dealing honorably by Sir Pellias, and he pondered whether or not this black friar might be a messenger from his friend. But yet he could not see how he might deny such a messenger speech with him. So, after a while of thought, he said, "Fetch the black friar hither and let him deliver his message to me."

So Sir Pellias, in the garb of a black friar, was brought by the attendants into the outer room of that place where Sir Gawaine sat at supper with the lady. But for a little time Sir Pellias did not enter the room, but stood behind the curtain of the ante-room and looked upon them, for he desired to make sure as to whether or no Sir Gawaine was true to him.

Now everything in that room where the knight and the lady sat was bedight with extraordinary splendor, and it was illuminated by a light of several score of waxen tapers that sent forth a most delightful perfume as they burned. And as Sir Pellias stood behind the curtains, he beheld Sir Gawaine and the Lady Ettard as they sat at the table together, and he saw that they were filled with pleasure in the company of one another. And he saw that Sir Gawaine and the lady quaffed wine out of the same chalice and that the cup was of gold. And as he saw those two making merry with one another, he was filled with great anger and indignation, for he now perceived that Sir Gawaine had betrayed him.

So, by and by, he could contain himself no longer, wherefore he took five steps into that room and stood before Sir Gawaine and the Lady Ettard. And, when they looked upon him in great surprise, he cast back the hood from his face and they knew him. Then the Lady Ettard shrieked with great vehemence, crying out, "I have been betrayed!" and Sir Gawaine sat altogether silent, for he had not a single word to say either to the lady or to Sir Pellias.

Then Sir Pellias came close to the Lady Ettard with such a fell countenance that she could not move for fear. And when he had come nigh to her he catched that necklace of emeralds and opal stones and gold with such violence that he brake the clasp thereof and so plucked it from her neck. Then he said, "This is mine and thou hast no right to it!" And therewith he thrust it into his bosom. Then he turned upon Sir Gawaine where he sat, and he said, "Thou art false both unto thy knighthood and unto thy friendship, for thou hast betrayed me utterly." Thereupon he raised his arm and smote Sir Gawaine

upon the face with the back of his hand so violently that the mark of his fingers was left in red all across the cheek of Sir Gawaine.

Then Sir Gawaine fell as pale as ashes and he cried out, "Sir, I have in sooth betrayed thee, but thou hast offered such affront to me that our injury is equal." To the which Sir Pellias made reply, "Not so; for the injury I gave to thee is only upon thy cheek, but the injury thou gavest to me is upon my heart. Ne'theless, I will answer unto thee for the affront I have done thee. But thou also shalt answer unto me for the offence thou hast done unto me, in that thou hast betrayed me."

Then Sir Gawaine said, "I am willing to answer unto thee in full measure." And Sir Pellias said, "Thou shalt indeed do so." Thereupon he turned and left that place, nor did he so much as look again either at Sir Gawaine or at the Lady Ettard.

But, now that the Lady Ettard no longer had the magic collar about her neck, Sir Gawaine felt nothing of the great enchantment that had aforetime drawn him so vehemently unto her. Accordingly, he now suffered a misliking for her as great as that liking which had aforetime drawn him unto her. Wherefore he said to himself, "How was it possible that for this lady I could have so betrayed my knighthood and have done so much harm unto my friend!" So he pushed back his chair very violently and arose from that table with intent to leave her.

But when the Lady Ettard saw his intent she spake to him with very great anger, for she was very much affronted in that he had deceived her when he said that he had overcome Sir Pellias. Wherefore she said with great heat, "Thou mayst go, and I am very willing for to have thee do so, for thou didst say false when thou didst tell me that thou hadst overcome Sir Pellias. For now I perceive that he is both a stronger and a nobler knight than thou. For he smote thee as though thou wert his servant, and thou yet bearest the marks of his fingers upon thy cheek."

At this Sir Gawaine was exceedingly wroth and entirely filled with the shame of that which had befallen him, wherefore he said, "Lady, I think thou hast bewitched me to bring me to such a pass of dishonor. As for Sir Pellias, look forth into that meadow to-morrow and see if I do not put a deeper mark upon him than ever he hath put upon me." Thereupon he left that place and went down into the court-yard and called upon the attendants who were there for to fetch him his horse. So they did as he commanded and he straightway rode forth into the night.

And he was very glad of the darkness of the night, for it appeared to him that it was easier to bear his shame in the darkness, wherefore when he had come to the glade of trees he would not enter the pavilion where his friends were. And also, when Sir Ewaine and Sir Marhaus came out unto him and bade him to come in, he would not do so, but stayed without in the darkness; for he said unto himself, "If I go in where is a light, haply they will behold the mark of Sir Pellias his hand upon my face."

So he stayed without in the darkness and bade them to go away and leave him alone.

But when they had gone he called his esquire unto him and he said, "Take this red armor off me and carry it into the pavilion of Sir Pellias, for I hate it." So the esquire did as Sir Gawaine commanded, and Sir Gawaine walked up and down for the entire night, greatly troubled in spirit and in heart.

Chapter Sixth

How the Lady of the Lake Took Back Her Necklace From Sir Pellias.

Now, when the next morning had come, Sir Gawaine summoned his esquire unto him and said, "Fetch hither my armour and case me in it." And the esquire did so. Then Sir Gawaine said, "Help me unto my horse," and the esquire did so. And the morning was still very early, with the grass all lustrous and sparkling with dew, and the little birds singing with such vehemence that it might have caused anyone great joy to be alive. Wherefore, when Sir Gawaine was seated a-horseback and in armor, he began to take more courage unto himself, and the dark vapors that had whilom overshadowed him lifted themselves a little. So he bespoke his esquire with stronger voice, saying, "Take this glove of mine and bear it to Sir Pellias and tell him that Sir Gawaine parades in the meadow in front of the castle and that he there challenges Sir Pellias for to meet him a-horse or afoot, howsoever that knight may choose."

At these that esquire was very much astonished, for Sir Gawaine and Sir Pellias had always been such close friends that there was hardly their like for friendship in all that land, wherefore their love for one another had become a byword with all men. But he held his peace concerning his thoughts

and only said, "Wilt thou not eat food ere thou goest to battle?"
And Sir Gawaine said, "Nay, I will not eat until I have fought.
Wherefore do thou go and do as I have bid thee."

So Sir Gawaine's esquire went to Sir Pellias in his pavilion and
he gave unto that knight the glove of Sir Gawaine, and he
delivered Sir Gawaine's message to him. And Sir Pellias said,
"Tell thy master that I will come forth to meet him as soon as
I have broken my fast."

Now, when the news of that challenge had come to the ears
of Sir Brandiles and Sir Mador de la Porte and Sir Ewaine and
Sir Marhaus, those knights were greatly disturbed thereat, and
Sir Ewaine said to the others, "Messires, let us go and make
inquiries concerning this business." So the four knights went to
the white pavilion where Sir Pellias was breaking his fast.

And when they had come into the presence of Sir Pellias, Sir
Ewaine said to him, "What is this quarrel betwixt my kinsman
and thee?" And Sir Pellias made reply, "I will not tell thee, so,
let be and meddle not with it."

Then Sir Ewaine said, "Wouldst thou do serious battle with
thy friend?" To which Sir Pellias said, "He is a friend to me
no longer."

Then Sir Brandiles cried out, "It is a great pity that a quarrel
should lie betwixt such friends as thou and Sir Gawaine. Wilt
thou not let us make peace betwixt you?" But Sir Pellias
replied, "Ye cannot make peace, for this quarrel cannot be
stayed until it is ended."

Then those knights saw that their words could be of no avail
and they went away and left Sir Pellias.

So when Sir Pellias had broken his fast he summoned an
esquire named Montenoir, and he bade him case him in that red
armor that he had worn for all this time, and Montenoir did so.
Then, when Sir Pellias was clad in that armor, he rode forth into
the meadow before the castle where Sir Gawaine paraded. And
when he had come thither those four other knights came to him
again and besought him that he would let peace be made
betwixt him and Sir Gawaine, but Sir Pellias would not listen
to them, and so they went away again and left him, and he rode
forth into the field before the castle of Grantmesnle.

Now a great concourse of people had come down upon the

castle walls for to behold that assault-at-arms, for news thereof had gone all about that place. And it had also come to be known that the knight that would do combat with Sir Pellias was that very famous royal knight hight Sir Gawaine, the son of King Lot of Orkney, and a nephew of King Arthur; wherefore all the people were very desirous to behold so famous a knight do battle.

Likewise the Lady Ettard came down to the walls and took her stand in a lesser tower that overlooked the field of battle. And when she had taken her stand at that place she beheld that Sir Pellias wore that necklace of emeralds and opal stones and gold above his body armor, and her heart went out to him because of it, wherefore she hoped that he might be the victor in that encounter.

Then each knight took his station in such place as seemed to him to be fitting, and they dressed each his spear and his shield and made him ready for the assault. Then, when they were in all ways prepared, Sir Marhaus gave the signal for the assault. Thereupon each knight instantly quitted that station which he held, dashing against the other with the speed of lightning, and with such fury that the earth thundered and shook beneath their horses' hoofs. So they met fairly in the centre of the course, each knight striking the other in the very midst of his defences. And in that encounter the spear of Sir Gawaine burst even to the hand-guard, but the spear of Sir Pellias held, so that Sir Gawaine was cast out of his saddle with terrible violence, smiting the earth with such force that he rolled thrice over in the dust and then lay altogether motionless as though bereft of life.

At this, all those people upon the walls shouted with a great voice, for it was an exceedingly noble assault-at arms.

Then the four knights who stood watching that encounter made all haste unto Sir Gawaine where he lay; and Sir Pellias also rode back and sat his horse nigh at hand. Then Sir Ewaine and Sir Gawaine's esquire unlaced the helmet of Sir Gawaine with all speed, and, behold! his face was the color of ashes and they could not see that he breathed.

Thereupon Sir Marhaus said, "I believe that thou hast slain this knight, Sir Pellias," and Sir Pellias said, "Dost thou think so?" "Yea," quoth Sir Marhaus, "and I deem it a great pity." Unto which Sir Pellias made reply, "He hath not suffered more than he deserved."

At these words Sir Ewaine was filled with great indignation, wherefore he cried out, "Sir Knight, I think that thou forgettest the quality of this knight. For not only is he a fellow-companion of the Round Table, to whom thou hast vowed entire brotherhood, but he is also the son of a king and the nephew of King Arthur himself."

But to this Sir Pellias maintained a very steadfast countenance and replied, "I would not repent me of this were that knight a king in his own right instead of the son of a king."

Then Sir Ewaine lifted up his voice with great indignation, crying out upon Sir Pellias, "Begone! or a great ill may befall thee." "Well," said Sir Pellias, "I will go."

Upon this he turned his horse and rode away from that place and entered the woodland and so was gone from their sight.

Then those others present lifted up Sir Gawaine and bare him away unto the pavilion late of Sir Pellias, and there they laid him upon the couch of Sir Pellias. But it was above an hour ere he recovered himself again; and for a great part of that while those nigh unto him believed him to have been dead.

But not one of those knights wist what was the case; to wit, that Sir Pellius had been so sorely wounded in the side in that encounter that it was not to be hoped that he could live for more than that day. For, though the spear of Sir Gawaine had burst, and though Sir Pellias had overthrown him entirely, yet the head of Sir Gawaine's spear had pierced the armor of Sir Pellias, and had entered his side and had there broken off, so that of the iron of the spear, the length of the breadth of a palm had remained in the body of Sir Pellias a little above the midriff. Wherefore, while Sir Pellias sat there talking so steadfastly unto those four knights, he was yet whiles in a great passion of pain, and the blood ran down into his armor in abundance. So, what with the loss of the blood, and of the great agony which he suffered, the brain of Sir Pellias swam as light as a feather all the time that he held talk with those others. But he said not a word concerning the grievous wound he had received, but rode away very proudly into the forest.

But when he had come into the forest he could not forbear him any longer, but fell to groaning very sorely, crying out, "Alas! alas! I have certes got my death-wound in this battle!"

Now it chanced that morn that the damsel Parcenet had ridden forth to fly a young gerfalcon, and a dwarf belonging to the Lady Ettard had ridden with her for company. So, as the damsel and the dwarf rode through a certain part of the forest skirt, not a very great distance from Grantmesnle, where the thicker part of the woodland began and the thinner part thereof ceased, the damsel heard a voice in the woodlands, lamenting with very great dolor. So she stopped and harkened, and by and by she heard that voice again making a great moan. Then Parcenet said to the dwarf, "What is that I hear? Certes, it is the voice of someone in lamentation. Now let us go and see who it is that maketh such woful moan." And the dwarf said, "It shall be as thou sayest."

So the damsel and the dwarf went a little way farther and there they beheld a knight sitting upon a black horse beneath an oak-tree. And that knight was clad altogether in red armor, wherefore, Parcenet knew that it must be Sir Pellias. And she saw that Sir Pellias leaned with the butt of his spear upon the ground and so upheld himself upon his horse from which he would otherwise have fallen because of his great weakness, and all the while he made that great moan that Parcenet had heard. So, seeing him in this sorry condition, Parcenet was overcome with great pity, and she made haste to him crying out, "Alas! Sir Pellias, what ails thee?"

Then Sir Pellias looked at her as though she were a great way removed from him, and, because of the faintness of his soul, he beheld her, as it were, through thin water. And he said, very faintly, "Maiden, I am sore hurt." Thereupon she said, "How art thou hurt, Sir Pellias?" And he replied, "I have a grievous wound in my side, for a spear's point standeth therein nigh a palm's breadth deep so that it reaches nearly to my heart, wherefore, meseems that I shall not live for very long."

Upon this the maiden cried out, "Alas! alas! what is this!" and she made great lament and smote her hands together with sorrow that that noble knight should have come to so grievous an extremity.

Then the dwarf that was with Parcenet, seeing how greatly she was distracted by sorrow, said, "Damsel, I know of a certain place in this forest (albeit it is a considerable distance from this) where there dwelleth a certain very holy hermit who is an extraordinarily skilful leech. Now, an we may bring this knight unto the chapel where that hermit dwelleth, I believe that he may be greatly holpen unto health and ease again."

Upon this Parcenet said, "Gansaret"—for Gansaret was the dwarf's name—"Gansaret, let us take this knight unto that place as quickly as we are able. For I tell thee sooth when I say that I have a very great deal of love for him." "Well," said the dwarf, "I will show thee where that chapel is."

So the dwarf took the horse of Sir Pellias by the bridle-rein and led the way through that forest, and Parcenet rode beside Sir Pellias and upheld him upon his saddle. For some whiles Sir Pellias fainted with sickness and with pain so that he would else have fallen had she not upheld him. Thus they went forward very sorrowfully and at so slow a pace that it was noontide ere they came to that certain very dense and lonely part of the forest where the hermit abided.

And when they had come unto that place the dwarf said, "Yonder, damsel, is the chapel whereof I spake."

Then Parcenet lifted up her eyes and she beheld where was a little woodland chapel built in among the leafy trees of the forest. And around this chapel was a little open lawn bedight with flowers, and nigh to the door of the hermitage was a fountain of water as clear as crystal. And this was a very secret and lonely place and withal very silent and peaceful, for in front of the chapel they beheld a wild doe and her fawn browsing upon the tender grass and herbs without any fear of harm. And when the dwarf and the maiden and the wounded knight drew nigh, the doe and the fawn looked up with great wide eyes and spread their large ears with wonder, yet fled not, fearing no harm, but by and by began their browsing again. Likewise all about the chapel in the branches of the trees were great quantities of birds, singing and chirping very cheerfully. And those birds were waiting for their mid-day meal that the hermit was used to cast unto them.

(Now this was that same forest sanctuary whereunto King

Arthur had come that time when he had been so sorely wounded by Sir Pellinore as hath been aforetold in this history.)

As the maiden and the dwarf and the wounded knight drew nigh to this chapel, a little bell began ringing very sweetly so that the sound thereof echoed all through those quiet woodlands, for it was now the hour of noon. And Sir Pellias heard that bell as it were a great way off, and first he said, "Whither am I come?" and then he made shift to cross himself. And Parcenet crossed herself and the dwarf kneeled down and crossed himself. Then when the bell had ceased ringing, the dwarf cried out in a loud voice, "What ho! what ho! here is one needing help!"

Then the door of the sanctuary was opened and there came forth from that place a very venerable man with a long white beard as it were of finely carded wool. And lo! as he came forth, all those birds that waited there flew about him in great quantities, for they thought that he had come forth for to feed them; wherefore the hermit was compelled to brush those small fowls away with his hands as he came unto where the three were stationed.

And when he had come unto them he demanded of them who they were and why they had come thither with that wounded knight. So Parcenet told him how it was with them, and of how they had found Sir Pellias so sorely wounded in the forest that morning and had brought him hitherward.

Then, when the hermit had heard all of her story, he said, "It is well and I will take him in." So he took Sir Pellias into his cell, and when they had helped lay him upon the couch, Parcenet and the dwarf went their way homeward again.

After they had gone, the hermit examined the hurt of Sir Pellias, and Sir Pellias lay in a deep swoon. And the swoon was so deep that the hermit beheld that it was the death-swoon, and that the knight was nigh to his end. So he said, "This knight must assuredly die in a very little while, for I can do naught to save him." Wherefore he immediately quitted the side of Sir Pellius and set about in haste to prepare the last sacrament such as might be administered unto a noble knight who was dying.

Now whiles the hermit was about this business the door opened of a sudden and there came into that place a very strange lady clad all in green and bedight around the arms with armlets of emeralds and opal stones inset into gold. And her hair, which was very soft, was entirely black and was tied about with a cord of crimson ribbon. And the hermit beheld that her face was like to ivory for whiteness and that her eyes were bright, like unto jewels set into ivory, wherefore he knew that she was no ordinary mortal.

And this lady went straight to Sir Pellias and leaned over him so that her breath touched his forehead. And she said, "Alas! Sir Pellias, that thou shouldst lie so." "Lady," said the hermit, "thou mayst well say 'Alas,' for this knight hath only a few minutes to live." To this the lady said, "Not so, thou holy man, for I tell thee that this knight shall have a long while yet to live." And when she had said this she stooped and took from about his neck that necklace of emeralds and opal stones and gold that encircled it and she hung it about her own neck.

Now when the hermit beheld what she did, he said, "Lady, what is this that thou doest, and why dost thou take that ornament from a dying man?"

But the lady made reply very tranquilly, "I gave it unto him, wherefore I do but take back again what is mine own. But now I prithee let me be with this knight for a little while, for I have great hope that I may bring back life unto him again."

Then the hermit was a-doubt and he said, "Wilt thou endeavor to heal him by magic?" And the lady said, "If I do, it will not be by magic that is black."

So the hermit was satisfied and went away, and left the lady alone with Sir Pellias.

Now when the lady was thus alone with the wounded knight she immediately set about doing sundry very strange things. For first she brought forth a loadstone of great power and potency and this she set to the wound. And, lo! the iron of the spear-head came forth from the wound; and as it came Sir Pellias groaned with great passion. And when the spear-point came forth there burst out a great issue of blood like to a fountain of crimson. But the lady immediately pressed a fragrant napkin of fine cambric linen to the wound and stanched the blood, and it bled no more, for she held it within the veins by very potent spells of magic. So, the blood being stanched in this wise, the lady brought forth from her bosom a small crystal phial filled with an elixir of blue color and of a very singular fragrance. And she poured some of this elixir between the cold and leaden lips of the knight; and when the elixir touched his lips the life began to enter into his body once more; for, in a little while, he opened his eyes and gazed about him with a very strange look, and the first thing that he beheld was that lady clad in green who stood beside him, and she was so beautiful that he thought that haply he had died and was in Paradise, wherefore he said, "Am I then dead?"

"Nay, thou art not dead," said the lady, "yet hast thou been parlously nigh to death." "Where then am I?" said Sir Pellias. And she replied, "Thou art in a deep part of the forest, and this is the cell of a saint-like hermit of the forest." At this Sir Pellias said, "Who is it that hath brought me back to life?" Upon this the lady smiled and said, "It was I."

Now for a little while Sir Pellias lay very silent, then by and by he spake and said, "Lady, I feel very strangely." "Yea," said the lady, "that is because thou hast now a different life." Then Sir Pellias said, "How is it with me?" And the lady said, "It is thus: that to bring thee back to life I gave thee to drink of a certain draught of an *elixir vitae* so that thou art now only half as thou wert before; for if by the one half thou art mortal, by the other half thou art fay."

Then Sir Pellias looked up and beheld that the lady had about her neck the collar of emeralds and opal stones and gold which he had aforetime worn. And, lo! his heart went out to her with exceeding ardor, and he said, "Lady, thou sayest that I am half fay, and I do perceive that thou art altogether fay. Now, I pray thee to let it be that henceforth I may abide nigh unto where thou art." And the lady said, "It shall be as thou dost ask, for it was to that end I have suffered thee nearly to die, and then have brought thee back unto life again."

Then Sir Pellias said, "When may I go with thee?" And she said, "In a little when thou hast had to drink." "How may that be?" said Sir Pellias, "seeing that I am but yet like unto a little child for weakness." To the which the lady made reply,

"When thou hast drunk of water thy strength shall return unto thee, and thou shalt be altogether well and whole again."

So the Lady of the Lake went out, and presently returned, bearing in her hand an earthen crock filled with water from the fountain near at hand. And when Sir Pellias had drunk that water he felt, of a sudden, his strength come altogether back to him.

Yet he was not at all as he had been before, for now his body felt as light as air, and his soul was dilated with a pure joy such as he had never felt in his life before that time. Wherefore he immediately uprose from his couch of pain, and he said, "Thou hast given life unto me again, now do I give that life unto thee forever."

Then the lady looked upon him and smiled with great loving-kindness. And she said, "Sir Pellias, I have held thee in tender regard ever since I beheld thee one day in thy young knighthood drink a draught of milk at a cottager's hut in this forest. For the day was warm and thou hadst set aside thy helmet, and a young milkmaid, brown of face and with bare feet, came and brought thee a bowl of milk, which same thou didst drink of with great appetite. That was the first time that I beheld thee—although thou didst not see me. Since that time I have had great friendship for all thy fellowship of King Arthur's Court and for King Arthur himself, all for thy sake."

Then Sir Pellias said, "Lady, wilt thou accept me for thy knight?" and she said, "Aye." Then Sir Pellias said, "May I salute thee?" And she said, "Yea, if it pleasures thee." So Sir Pellias kissed her upon the lips, and so their troth was plighted.

Now return we unto Parcenet and the dwarf:

After those two had left that hermitage in the woodland, they betook their way again toward Grantmesnle, and when they had come nigh out of the forest at a place not far from the glade of trees wherein those knights-companion had taken up their inn, they met one of those knights clad in half-armor, and that knight was Sir Mador de la Porte. Then Parcenet called upon him by name, saying, "Alas! Sir Mador, I have but this short time quitted a hermit's cell in the forest where I left Sir Pellias sorely wounded to death, so I fear me he hath only a little while to live."

Then Sir Mador de la Porte cried out, "Ha! maiden, what is this thou tellest me? That is a very hard thing to believe; for when Sir Pellias quitted us this morn he gave no sign of wound or disease of any sort."

But Parcenet replied, "Ne'theless, I myself beheld him lying in great pain and dole, and, ere he swooned his death-swoon, he himself told me that he had the iron of a spear in his side."

Then Sir Mador de la Porte said, "Alas! alas! that is sorry news! Now, damsel, by thy leave and grace, I will leave thee and hasten to my companions to tell them this news." And Parcenet said, "I prithee do so."

So Sir Mador de la Porte made haste to the pavilion where were his companions, and he told them the news that he had heard.

Now at this time Sir Gawaine was altogether recovered from the violent overthrow he had suffered that morning, wherefore when he heard the news that Sir Mador de la Porte brought to him, he smote his hands together and cried out aloud, "Woe is me! what have I done! For first I betrayed my friend, and now I have slain him. Now I will go forth straightway to find him and to crave his forgiveness ere he die."

But Sir Ewaine said, "What is this that thou wouldst do? Thou art not yet fit to undertake any journey."

Sir Gawaine said, "I care not, for I am determined to go and find my friend." Nor would he suffer any of his companions to accompany him; but when he had summoned his esquire to bring him his horse, he mounted thereon and rode away into the forest alone, betaking his way to the westward, and lamenting with great sorrow as he journeyed forward.

Now when the afternoon had fallen very late, so that the sun was sloping to its setting, and the light fell as red as fire through the forest leaves, Sir Gawaine came to that hermit's cell where it stood in the silent and solitary part of the forest woodland. And he beheld that the hermit was outside of his cell digging in a little garden of lentils. So when the hermit saw the armed knight come into that lawn all in the red light of the setting sun, he stopped digging and leaned upon his trowel. Then Sir Gawaine drew nigh, and, as he sat upon his horse, he told the holy man of the business whereon he had come.

To this the hermit said, "There came a lady hither several hours ago, and she was clad all in green, and was of a very singular appearance, so that it was easy to see that she was fay. And by means of certain charms of magic that lady cured thy friend, and after she had healed him, the two rode away into the forest together."

Then Sir Gawaine was very much amazed, and he said, "This is a very strange thing that thou tellest me, that a knight who is dying should be brought back to life again in so short a time, and should so suddenly ride forth from a bed of pain. Now, I prithee tell me whither they went." The hermit said, "They went to the westward." Whereupon, when Sir Gawaine heard this, he said, "I will follow them."

So he rode away and left the hermit gazing after him. And as he rode forward upon his way, the twilight began to fall apace, so that the woodlands after a while grew very dark and strange all around him. But as the darkness descended a very singular miracle happened, for, lo! there appeared before Sir Gawaine, a light of a pale blue color, and it went before him and showed him the way, and he followed it, much marvelling.

Now after he had followed the light for a very long time he came at last, of a sudden, to where the woodland ceased, and where there was a wide, open plain of very great extent. And this plain was all illuminated by a singular radiance which was like that of a clear full moonlight, albeit no moon was shining at that time. And in that pale and silver light Sir Gawaine could see everything with wonderful distinctness; wherefore he beheld that he was in a plain covered all over with flowers of divers sorts, the odors whereof so filled the night that it appeared to press upon the bosom with a great pleasure. And he beheld that in front of him lay a great lake, very wide and still. And all those things appeared so strange in that light that Sir Gawaine wotted that he had come into a land of faëry. So he rode among tall flowers toward that lake in a sort of fear, for he wist not what was to befall him.

Now as he drew near the lake he perceived a knight and a lady approaching him; and when they had come nigh he beheld that the knight was Sir Pellias, and that his countenance was exceedingly strange. And he beheld that the lady was she whom he had aforetime seen all clad in green apparel when he had travelled in the Forest of Adventure with Sir Ewaine and Sir Marhaus.

Now when Sir Gawaine first beheld Sir Pellias he was filled with a great fear, for he thought it was a spirit that he saw. But when he perceived that Sir Pellias was alive, there came into his bosom a joy as great as that fear had been; wherefore he made haste toward Sir Pellias. And when he had come near to Sir Pellias, he leaped from off of his horse, crying out, "Forgive! Forgive!" with great vehemence of passion. Then he would have taken Sir Pellias into his arms, but Sir Pellias withdrew himself from the contact of Sir Gawaine, though not with any violence of anger. And Sir Pellias spake in a voice very thin and of a silvery clearness as though it came from a considerable distance, and he said, "Touch me not, for I am not as I was aforetime, being not all human, but part fay. But concerning my forgiveness: I do forgive thee whatsoever injury I may have suffered at thy hands. And more than this I give unto thee my love, and I greatly hope for thy joy and happiness. But now I go away to leave thee, dear friend, and haply I shall not behold thee again, wherefore I do leave this with thee as my last behest; to wit, that thou dost go back to King Arthur's Court and make thy peace with the Queen. So thou mayst bring them news of all that hath happened unto me."

Then Sir Gawaine cried out in great sorrow, "Whither wouldst thou go?"

And Sir Pellias said, "I shall go to yonder wonderful city of gold and azure which lieth in yonder valley of flowers."

Then Sir Gawaine said, "I see no city but only a lake of water."

Whereupon Sir Pellias replied, "Ne'theless, there is a city yonder and thither I go, wherefore I do now bid thee farewell."

Then Sir Gawaine looked into the face of Sir Pellias and beheld again that strange light that it was of a very singular appearance, for, lo! it was white like to ivory and his eyes shone like jewels set in ivory, and a smile lay upon his lips and grew neither more nor less, but always remained the same. (For those who were of that sort had always that singular appearance and smiled in that manner—to wit, the Lady of the Lake, and Sir Pellias, and Sir Launcelot of the Lake.)

Then Sir Pellias and the Lady of the Lake turned and left Sir Gawaine where he stood, and they went toward the lake, and they entered the lake, and when the feet of the horse of Sir Pellias had touched the water of the lake, lo! Sir Pellias was gone and Sir Gawaine beheld him no more, although he stood there for a long time weeping with great passion.

So endeth the story of Sir Pellias.

But Sir Gawaine returned unto the Court of King Arthur as he had promised Sir Pellias to do, and he made his peace with Queen Guinevere and, thereafter, though the Queen loved him not, yet there was a peace betwixt them. And Sir Gawaine published these things to the Court of King Arthur and all men marvelled at what he told.

And only twice thereafter was Sir Pellias ever seen of any of his aforetime companions.

And Sir Marhaus was made a Companion of the Round Table and became one of the foremost knights thereof.

And the Lady Ettard took Sir Engamore into favor again, and that summer they were wedded and Sir Engamore became lord of Grantmesnle.

So endeth this story.

PART III

The Story of Sir Gawaine

Chapter First

*How a White Hart Appeared Before King
Arthur, and How Sir Gawaine and
Gaheris, His Brother, Went in
Pursuit Thereof, and of What
Befell Them in That Quest.*

UPON a certain time King Arthur, together with Queen
Guinevere and all of his Court, were making progression
through that part of his kingdom which was not very near to
Camelot. At this time the King journeyed in very great state,
and Queen Guinevere had her Court about her, so there were
many esquires and pages; wherefore, what with knights, lords,
and ladies in attendance, more than six score of people were
with the King and Queen.

Now it chanced that at this time the season of the year was
very warm, so that when the middle of the day had come the
King commanded that a number of pavilions should be spread
for their accommodation, wherein that they might rest there

until the heat of the day had passed. So the attendants spread three pavilions in a pleasant glade upon the outskirts of the forest.

When this had been done, the King gave command that the tables, whereat they were to eat their mid-day meal, should be spread beneath the shadow of that glade of trees; for there was a gentle wind blowing and there were many birds singing, so that it was very pleasant to sit in the open air.

Accordingly the attendants of the Court did as the King commanded, and the tables were set upon the grass beneath the shade, and the King and Queen and all the lords and ladies of their Courts sat down to that cheerful repast.

Now whiles they sat there feasting with great content of spirit, and with much mirth and goodly talk among themselves, there came of a sudden a great outcry from the woodland that was near by, and therewith there burst forth from the cover of that leafy wilderness a very beautiful white hart pursued by a white brachet of equal beauty. And there was not a hair upon either of these animals that was not as white as milk, and each wore about its neck a collar of gold very beautiful to behold.

The hound pursued the white hart with a very great outcry and bellowing, and the hart fled in the utmost terror. In this wise they ran thrice around the table where King Arthur and his Court sat at meat, and twice in that chase the hound caught the hart and pinched it on its haunch, and therewith the hart leaped away, and all they who sat there observed that there was blood at two places upon its haunch where the hound had pinched it. But each time the hart escaped from the hound, and the hound followed after it with much outcry of yelling so that King Arthur and Queen Guinevere and all their Court were annoyed at the noise and tumult that those two creatures made. Then the hart fled away into the forest again by another path, and the hound pursued it and both were gone, and the baying of the hound sounded more and more distant as it ran away into the woodland.

Now, ere the King and Queen and their Court had recovered from their astonishment at these things, there suddenly appeared at that part of the forest whence the hart and the hound had emerged, a knight and a lady, and the knight was of very lordly presence and the lady was exceedingly beautiful. The knight was clad in half-armor, and the lady was clad in green as though for the chase; and the knight rode upon a charger of dapple gray, and the lady upon a piebald palfrey. With them were two esquires, also clad for the chase.

These, seeing the considerable company gathered there, paused as though in surprise, and whilst they stood so, there suddenly appeared another knight upon a black horse, clad in complete armor, and he seemed to be very angry. For he ran upon the half-armed knight and smote him so sorry a blow with his sword, that the first knight fell down from his horse and lay upon the ground as though dead; whereat the lady who was with him shrieked with great dolor.

Then the full-armed knight upon the black horse ran to the lady and catched her, and he lifted her from her palfrey and laid her across the horn of his saddle, and thereupon he rode back into the forest again. The lady screamed with such vehemence of violent outcry, that it was a great pity to hear her, but the knight paid no attention to her shrieking, but bore her away by main force into the forest.

Then, after he and the lady had gone, the two esquires came and lifted up the wounded knight upon his horse, and then they also went away into the forest and were gone.

All this King Arthur and his Court beheld from a distance, and they were so far away that they could not stay that knight upon the black horse from doing what he did to carry away the lady into the forest; nor could they bring succor to that other knight in half-armor whom they had beheld struck down in that wise. So they were very greatly grieved at what they had beheld and knew not what to think of it. Then King Arthur said to his Court, "Messires, is there not some one of you who will follow up this adventure and discover what is the significance of that which we have seen, and compel that knight to tell why he behaved as he did?"

Upon this Sir Gawaine said, "Lord, I shall be very glad indeed to take upon me this adventure if I have thy leave to do so." And King Arthur said, "Thou hast my leave." Then Sir Gawaine said, "Lord, I would that thou would also let me take my younger brother, Gaheris, with me as mine esquire in this undertaking, for he groweth apace unto manhood, and yet he hath never beheld any considerable adventure at arms." So King Arthur said, "Thou hast my leave to take thy brother."

At this Gaheris was very glad, for he was of an adventurous spirit, wherefore the thought of going with his brother upon this quest gave him great pleasure.

So they two went to the pavilion of Sir Gawaine, and there Gaheris aided Sir Gawaine as his esquire to don his armor. Then they rode forth upon that quest which Sir Gawaine had undertaken.

Now they journeyed onward for a very considerable distance, following that direction which they had seen the hart take when it had sped away from before the hound, and when, from time to time, they would meet some of the forest folk, they would inquire of them whither had fled that white brachet and the white hart, and whither had fled the knight and the lady, and so they followed that adventure apace.

By and by, after a long pass—it being far advanced in the afternoon—they were suddenly aware of a great uproar of conflict, as of a fierce battle in progress. So they followed this sound, and after a while they came to an open meadow-land with very fair and level sward. Here they beheld two knights fighting with great vehemence of passion, and with a very deadly purpose. Then Sir Gawaine said, "What is this? Let us go see." So he and Gaheris rode forward to where those two knights were engaged, and as they approached, the two knights paused in their encounter, and rested upon their weapons. Then Sir Gawaine said, "Ha! Messires, what is to do and why do ye fight with such passion, the one against the other, in that wise?" Then one of the knights said to Sir Gawaine, "Sir, this does not concern you;" and the other said, "Meddle not with us, for this battle is of our own choosing."

"Messires," said Sir Gawaine, "I would be very sorry to interfere in your quarrel, but I am in pursuit of a white hart and a white brachet that came this way, and also of a knight who hath carried off a lady upon the same pass. Now I would be greatly beholden to ye if you would tell me if ye have seen aught of one or the other."

Then that knight who had first spoken said, "Sir, this is a very strange matter, for it was upon account of that very white hart and that brachet, and of the knight and the lady that we two were just now engaged in that battle as thou didst behold. For the case is this: We two are two brothers, and we were riding together in great amity when that hart and that hound came hitherward. Then my brother said he very greatly hoped that the white hart would escape from the hound, and I said that I hoped that the hound would overtake the hart and bring it to earth. Then came that knight with that lady, his captive, and I said that I would follow that knight and rescue the lady, and my brother said that he would undertake that adventure.

"Upon these points we fell into dispute; for it appeared to me that I felt great affection for that hound, and my brother felt as extraordinary regard for the white hart, and that as I had first spoken I should have the right to follow that adventure; but my brother felt affection for the hart, and he considered that as he was the elder of us twain, he had the best right to the adventure. So we quarrelled, and by and by we fell to upon that fight in which thou did see us engaged."

At this Sir Gawaine was very greatly astonished, and he said, "Messires, I cannot understand how so great a quarrel should have arisen from so small a dispute; and, certes, it is a great pity for two brothers to quarrel as ye have done, and to give one another such sore cuts and wounds as I perceive you have both received."

"Messires," said the second knight, "I think thou art right, and I now find myself to be very much ashamed of that quarrel." And the other said, "I too am sorry for what I have done."

Then Sir Gawaine said, "Sirs, I would be very glad indeed if you would tell me your names." And the one knight said, "I am called Sir Sorloise of the Forest." And the other said, "I am called Sir Brian of the Forest."

Then Sir Sorloise said, "Sir Knight, I would deem it a very great courtesy if thou wouldst tell me who thou art."

"I would be very glad to do that," said Sir Gawaine, and therewith he told them his name and condition. Now, when they heard who Sir Gawaine was, those two knights were very greatly astonished and pleased; for no one in all the courts of chivalry was more famous than Sir Gawaine, the son of King Lot of Orkney. Wherefore those two brothers said, "It is certainly a great joy to us to meet so famous a knight as thou art, Sir Gawaine."

Then Sir Gawaine said, "Sir Knights, that hart and that hound came only a short while ago to where King Arthur and Queen Guinevere and their Courts of lords and ladies were at feast, and there, likewise, all we beheld that knight seize upon the lady and make her captive. Wherefore, I and my brother have come forth upon command of King Arthur for to discover what is the meaning of that which we beheld. Now I shall deem it a very great courtesy upon your part if you will cease from this adventure and will go in amity unto the Court of the King, and will tell him of what ye beheld and of how you quarrelled and of how we met. For otherwise I myself will have to engage ye both, and that would be a great pity; for ye are weary with battle and I am fresh."

Then these two knights said, "Sir, we will do as you desire, for we have no wish to have to do with so powerful a knight as you."

Thereupon those two knights departed and went to the Court of King Arthur as Sir Gawaine ordained, and Sir Gawaine and his brother rode forward upon their adventure.

Now, by and by they came nigh to a great river, and there they beheld before them a single knight in full armor, who carried a spear in his hand and a shield hanging to his saddle-bow. Thereupon Sir Gawaine made haste forward and he called aloud to the knight, and the knight paused and waited until Sir Gawaine had overtaken him. And when Sir Gawaine came up to that knight he said, "Sir Knight, hast thou seen a white hart and a white hound pass by this way? And hast thou seen a knight bearing off a captive lady?"

Unto this the knight said, "Yea, I beheld them both, and I am even now following after them with intent to discover whither they are bound." Then Sir Gawaine said, "Sir Knight, I bid thee not to follow this adventure farther, for I myself am set upon it. Wherefore I desire thee for to give it over so that

I may undertake it in thy stead." "Sir," said the other knight, speaking with a very great deal of heat, "I know not who thou art, nor do I care a very great deal. But touching the pursuance of this adventure, I do tell thee that I myself intend to follow it to the end and so will I do, let who will undertake to stay me."

Thereupon Sir Gawaine said, "Messire, thou shalt not go forward upon this adventure unless thou hast first to do with me." And the knight said, "Sir, I am very willing for that."

So each knight took such stand upon that field as appeared to him to be best, and each put himself into a posture of defence and dressed his shield and his spear. Then, when they were thus prepared in all ways, they immediately launched forth, the one against the other, rushing together with great speed and with such an uproar that the ground trembled and shook beneath them. So they met together in the midst of the course and the spear of the strange knight burst all into small pieces, but the spear of Sir Gawaine held; wherefore he hurled that knight out of his saddle with such violence that he smote the ground with a blow like an earthquake.

Then Sir Gawaine rode back to where his enemy was (for that knight was unable to arise), and he removed the helmet from the head of the fallen knight and beheld that he was very young and comely.

Now, when the fresh air smote upon the knight's face, he presently awoke from his swoon and came back unto his senses again, whereupon Sir Gawaine said, "Dost thou yield unto me?" And the knight said, "I do so." Then Sir Gawaine said, "Who art thou?" And the knight said, "I am called Sir Alardin of the Isles," "Very well," said Sir Gawaine; "then I lay my command upon thee in this wise: that thou shalt go to the Court of King Arthur and deliver thyself to him as a captive of my prowess. And thou art to tell him all that thou knowest of the hart and the hound and the knight and the lady. And thou shalt tell him all that hath befallen thee in this assault."

So the knight said that he would do that, and thereupon they parted, the one party going the one way and the other party going the other way.

After that Sir Gawaine and his brother, Gaheris, rode a considerable distance until they came, by and by, through a woodland into an open plain, and it was now about the time of sunset. And they beheld in the midst of the plain a very stately and noble castle with five towers and of very great strength.

And right here they saw a sight that filled them with great sorrow, for they beheld the dead body of that white brachet lying beside the road like any carrion. And they saw that the hound was pierced through with three arrows, wherefore they wist that it had been slain very violently.

Now when Sir Gawaine beheld that beautiful hound lying dead in that wise, he was filled with great sorrow. "What a pity it is," he cried, "that this noble hound should be slain in this wise; for I think that it was the most beautiful hound that ever I saw in all my life. Here hath assuredly been great treachery against it; for it hath been foully dealt with because of that white hart which it pursued. Now, I make my vow that if I can find that hart I will slay it with mine own hands, because it was in that chase that this hound met its death."

After that they rode forward toward that castle, and as they drew nigh, lo! they beheld that white hart with the golden collar browsing upon the meadows before the castle.

Now, as soon as the white hart beheld those two strangers, it fled with great speed toward the castle, and it ran into the court-yard of the castle. And when Sir Gawaine beheld the stag, he gave chase in pursuit of it with great speed, and Gaheris followed after his brother.

So Sir Gawaine pursued the white hart into the court-yard of the castle and from thence it could not escape. Then Sir Gawaine leaped him down from his horse and drew his sword and slew the hart with a single blow of his weapon.

This he did in great haste, but when he had done that and it was too late to mend it, he repented him of what he had done very sorely.

Now with all this tumult, there came out the lord and the lady of that castle; and the lord was one of very haughty and noble aspect, and the lady was extraordinarily graceful and very beautiful of appearance. And Sir Gawaine looked upon the lady and he thought he had hardly ever seen so beautiful a dame, wherefore he was more sorry than ever that, in his haste, he had slain that white hart.

But when the lady of the castle beheld the white hart, that it lay dead upon the stone pavement of the court-yard, she smote her hands together and shrieked with such shrillness and strength, that it pierced the ears to hear her. And she cried out, "Oh, my white hart, art thou then dead?" And therewith she fell to weeping with great passion. Then Sir Gawaine said, "Lady, I am very sorry for what I have done, and I would that I could undo it." Then the lord of that castle said to Sir Gawaine, "Sir, didst thou slay that stag?" "Yea," said Sir Gawaine. "Sir," said the lord of the castle, "thou hast done very ill in this matter, and if thou wilt wait a little I will take full vengeance upon thee." Unto which Sir Gawaine said, "I will wait for thee as long as it shall please thee."

Then the lord of the castle went into his chamber and clad himself in his armor, and in a little while he came out very fiercely. "Sir," said Sir Gawaine, "what is thy quarrel with me?" And the lord of the castle said, "Because thou hast slain the white hart that was so dear to my lady." To the which Sir Gawaine said, "I would not have slain the white hart only that because of it the white brachet was so treacherously slain." Upon this the lord of the castle was more wroth than ever, and he ran at Sir Gawaine and smote him unawares, so that he clave through the epaulier of his armor and cut through the flesh and unto the bone of the shoulder, so that Sir Gawaine was put to a great agony of pain at the stroke. Then Sir Gawaine was filled with rage at the pain of the wound, wherefore he smote the knight so woful a blow that he cut through his helmet and into the bone beneath, and thereupon the knight fell down upon his knees because of the fierceness of the blow, and he could not rise up again. Then Sir Gawaine catched his helmet and rushed it off from his head.

Upon this the knight said in a weak voice, "Sir Knight, I crave mercy of you, and yield myself to you."

But Sir Gawaine was very furious with anger because of that unexpected blow which he had received and because of the great agony of the wound, he would not have mercy, but lifted up his sword with intent to slay that knight.

Then the lady of the castle beheld what Sir Gawaine was intent to do, and she brake away from her damsels and ran and flung herself upon the knight so as to shield him with her own body. And in that moment Sir Gawaine was striking and could not stay his blow; nevertheless, he was able to turn his sword in his hand so that the edge thereof did not smite the lady. But the flat of the sword struck her upon the neck a very grievous blow, and the blade cut her a little, so that the blood ran down her smooth white neck and over her kerchief; and with the violence of the blow the lady fell down and lay upon the ground as though she were dead.

Now when Sir Gawaine beheld that, he thought that he had slain that lady in his haste, and he was all a-dread at what he had done, wherefore he cried, "Woe is me! what have I done?"

"Alas!" said Gaheris, "that was a very shameful blow that thou didst strike; and the shame of it is mine also because thou art my brother. Now I wish I had not come with thee to this place."

Then Sir Gawaine said to the lord of that castle, "Sir, I will spare thy life, for I am very sorry for what I have done in my haste."

But the knight of the castle was filled with great bitterness, because he thought that his lady was dead, wherefore he cried out as in despair, "I will not now have thy mercy, for thou art a knight without mercy and without pity. And since thou hast slain my lady, who is dearer to me than my life, thou mayst slay me also. For that is the only service which thou canst now render me."

But by now the damsels of the lady had come to her where she lay, and the chiefest of these cried out to the lord of the castle, "Ha, sir, thy lady is not dead, but only in a swoon from which she will presently recover."

Then when the lord of the castle heard that, he fell to weeping in great measure from pure joy; for now that he knew his lady was alive he could not contain himself for joy. Therewith Sir Gawaine came to him and lifted him up from the ground where he was, and kissed him upon the cheek. Then certain others came and bare the lady away into her chamber, and there in a little while she recovered from that swoon and was but little the worse for the blow she had received.

That night Sir Gawaine, and his brother, Gaheris, abided with the knight and the lady, and when the knight learned who Sir Gawaine was, he felt it great honor to have so famous a knight in that place. So they feasted together that evening in great amity.

Now, after they had refreshed themselves, Sir Gawaine said, "I beseech you, sir, to tell me what was the meaning of the white hart and the white brachet which led me into this adventure."

To this the lord of the castle (whose name was Sir Ablamor of the Marise) said, "I will do so." And therewith he spake as follows:

"You must know, sir, that I have a brother who hath always been very dear to me, and when I took this, my lady, unto wife, he took her sister as his wife.

"Now, my brother dwelt in a castle nigh to this, and we held commerce together in great amity. But it befell upon a day that my lady and my brother's lady were riding through this forest together discoursing very pleasantly. What time there appeared a lady unto them, exceedingly beautiful, and of very strange appearance, for I do not think that either my lady or her sister ever beheld her like before.

"This strange lady brought unto those two ladies a white hart and a white brachet, and the hart and the hound she held each by a silver chain attached to a golden collar that encircled its neck. And the white hart she gave unto my lady and the white brachet she gave unto my lady's sister. And then she went away leaving them very glad.

"But their gladness did not last for very long, for ever since that time there hath been nothing else but discord between my brother and myself, and between my lady and her sister, for the white hound hath ever sought the white hart for to destroy it, wherefore I and my lady have entertained very great offence against my brother and his lady because they did not keep the white brachet at home. So it has come to pass that a number of times we have sought to destroy the hound, so that my brother and his lady have held equal offence against us.

"Now this day it chanced I was toward the outskirts of the

forest to the east of us, when I heard a great outcry in the woodland, and by and by the white hart that belonged to my lady came fleeing through the woodland, and the white brachet that belonged to my brother's lady was in pursuit of it; and my brother and his lady and two esquires followed rapidly after the hart and the brachet.

"Then I was very greatly angered, for it seemed to me that they were chasing that white hart out of despite of my lady and myself, wherefore I followed after them with all speed.

"So I came upon them at the outskirts of the woodland, nigh to where there were a number of pavilions pitched in the shade of a glade of trees in the midst of the meadow, and there, in mine anger, I struck my brother a great blow so that I smote him down from his horse. And I catched his lady and I threw her across the horn of my saddle and I bore her here away to this castle, and here I have held her out of revenge because they pursued the white hart which belonged to my lady. For my lady loved that hart as she loved nothing else in the world, excepting myself."

"Sir," said Sir Gawaine, "this is a very strange matter. Now I beseech thee to tell me of what appearance was that lady who gave the white hart and the white hound unto those two ladies?" "Messire," said the knight, "she was clad all in crimson, and about her throat and arms were a great many ornaments of gold beset with stones of divers colors, and her hair was red like gold and was enmeshed in a net of gold, and her eyes were very black and shone with exceeding brightness, and her lips were like coral, so that she possessed a very strange appearance."

"Ha!" said Sir Gawaine, "from this description methinks that lady could have been none other than the sorceress Vivien. For now she spendeth all of her time in doing such mischief as this by means of her enchantment, out of pure despite. And, indeed, I think it would be a very good thing if she were put out of this world so that she could do no more such mischief. But tell me, Messire, where now is that lady, thy wife's sister?" "Sir," said the knight, "she is in this castle and is a prisoner of honor." "Well," quoth Sir Gawaine, "since now both the hart and the hound are dead, ye can assuredly bear no more enmity toward her and your brother, wherefore I do beseech you that you will let her go free, and will enter again into a condition of amity and good-will the one with the other, in such a manner as hath afore obtained between you." And the lord of the castle said, "Sir, it shall be so."

And so he set the lady free at that time, and thereafter there was amity between them as Sir Gawaine had ordained.

And the next day Sir Gawaine and his brother, Gaheris, returned unto this Court of the King and he told King Arthur and his Court all that had befallen, hiding nothing from them.

Now, Queen Guinevere was very much displeased when she heard how Sir Gawaine would show no mercy to that knight and how he had struck the lady with his sword. Wherefore she said aside to one of those who stood nigh to her, "It seems to me to be a very strange thing for a belted knight to do, to refuse to give mercy unto a fallen enemy and to strike a lady with his sword; for I should think that any sword that had drawn blood from a lady in such wise would be dishonored for aye; and I cannot think that anyone who would strike a lady in that wise would hold himself guiltless unto his vow of knighthood."

This Sir Gawaine overheard and he was exceedingly wroth thereat. But he concealed his anger at that time. Only after he had gone away he said to Gaheris, his brother, "I believe that lady hateth me with all her heart; but some time I will show to her that I have in me more courtesy and am more gentle than she believes me to be. As for my sword, since she deemeth it to be dishonored by that blow, I will not use it any more." So he took the sword out of its sheath and brake it across his knee and flung it away.

Now all this hath been told to set forth that which follows; for there ye shall learn what great things of nobility Sir Gawaine could do when it behooved him to do them. For, haply, ye who have read this story may feel as Queen Guinevere did, that Sir Gawaine was not rightwise courteous as a belted knight should have been in that adventure aforetold.

Chapter Second

How King Arthur Became Lost in the Forest, and How He Fell Into a Very Singular Adventure in a Castle Unto Which He Came.

Now, it befell upon a time some while after this, that King Arthur was at Tintagalon upon certain affairs of state. And Queen Guinevere and her Court and the King's Court made progression from Camelot unto Carleon, and there they abided until the King should be through his business at Tintagalon and should join them at Carleon.

Now that time was the spring of the year, and all things were very jolly and gay, wherefore King Arthur became possessed with a great desire for adventure. So he called unto him a certain favorite esquire, hight Boisenard, and he said to him, "Boisenard, this day is so pleasant that I hardly know how I may contain myself because of the joy I take in it, for it seems to be that my heart is nigh ready to burst with great pleasure of desiring. So I am of a mind to go a-gadding with only thee for companion."

To this Boisenard said, "Lord, I know of nothing that would give to me a greater pleasure than that."

So King Arthur said, "Very well, let us then go away from this place in such a manner that no one will be aware of our departure. And so we will go to Carleon and surprise the Queen by coming unexpectedly to that place."

So Boisenard brought armor, without device, and he clad the King in that armor; and then they two rode forth together, and no one wist that they had left the castle.

And when they came forth into the fields, King Arthur whistled and sang and jested and laughed and made himself merry; for he was as a war-horse turned forth upon the grass that taketh glory in the sunshine and the warm air and becometh like unto a colt again.

So by and by they came into the forest and rode that way with great content of spirit; and they took this path and they took that path for no reason but because the day was so gay and jolly. So, by and by, they lost their way in the mazes of the woodland and knew not where they were.

Now when they found themselves to be lost in that wise they journeyed with more circumspection, going first by this way and then by that, but in no manner could they find their way out from their entanglement. And so fell night-time and they knew not where they were; but all became very dark and obscure, with the woodland full of strange and unusual sounds around about them.

Then King Arthur said, "Boisenard, this is a very perplexing pass and I do not know how we shall find lodging for this night."

To this Boisenard said, "Lord, if I have thy permission to do so, I will climb one of these trees and see if I can discover any sign of habitation in this wilderness." And King Arthur said, "Do so, I pray thee."

So Boisenard climbed a very tall tree and from the top of the tree he beheld a light a great distance away, and he said, "Lord, I see a light in that direction." And therewith he came down from the tree again.

So King Arthur and Boisenard went in the direction that Boisenard had beheld the light, and by and by they came out of the forest and into an open place where they beheld a very great castle with several tall towers, very grim and forbidding of appearance. And it was from this castle that the light had appeared that Boisenard had seen. So they two rode up to the castle and Boisenard called aloud and smote upon the gate of the castle. Then immediately there came a porter and demanded of them what they would have. Unto him Boisenard said, "Sirrah, we would come in to lodge for to-night, for we are a-weary." So the porter said, "Who are you?"—speaking very roughly and rudely to them, for he could not see of what condition they were because of the darkness. Then Boisenard said, "This is a knight of very good quality and I am his esquire, and we have lost our way in the forest and now we come hither seeking shelter."

"Sir," said the porter, "if ye know what is good for you, ye will sleep in the forest rather than come into this place, for this is no very good retreat for errant knights to shelter themselves."

Upon this King Arthur bespake the porter, for that which the porter said aroused great curiosity within him. So he said, "Nay, we will not go away from here and we demand to lodge here for this night."

Then the porter said, "Very well; ye may come in." And thereupon he opened the gate and they rode into the courtyard of that castle.

Now at the noise of their coming, there appeared a great many lights within the castle, and there came running forth divers attendants. Some of these aided King Arthur and Boisenard to dismount, and others took the horses, and others again brought basins of water for them to wash withal. And after they had washed their faces and hands, other attendants brought them into the castle.

Now as they came into the castle, they were aware of a great noise of very many people talking and laughing together, with the sound of singing and of harping. And so they came into the hall of the castle and beheld that it was lighted with a great number of candles and tapers and torches. Here they found a multitude of people gathered at a table spread for a feast, and at the head of the table there sat a knight, well advanced in years and with hair and beard white as milk. Yet he was exceedingly strong and sturdy of frame, having shoulders of wonderful broadness and a great girth of chest. This knight was of a very stern and forbidding appearance, and was clad altogether in black, and he wore around his neck a chain of gold, with a locket of gold hanging pendant from it.

Now when this knight beheld King Arthur and Boisenard come into the hall, he called aloud to them in a very great voice bidding them to come and sit with him at the head of the table; and they did so, and those at the head of the table made place for them, and thus they sat there beside the knight.

Now King Arthur and Boisenard were exceedingly hungry, wherefore they ate with great appetite and made joy of the entertainment which they received, and meantime the knight held them in very pleasant discourse, talking to them of such things as would give them the most entertainment. So after a while the feast was ended and they ceased from eating.

Then, of a sudden, the knight said to King Arthur, "Messire, thou art young and lusty of spirit and I doubt not but thou hath a great heart within thee. What say you now to a little sport betwixt us two?" Upon this King Arthur regarded that knight very steadily and he believed that his face was not so old as it looked; for his eyes were exceedingly bright and shone like sparks of light; wherefore he was a-doubt and he said, "Sir, what sport would you have?" Upon this the knight fell a-laughing in great measure and he said, "This is a very strange sport that I have in mind, for it is this: That thou and I shall prove the one unto the other what courage each of us may have." And King Arthur said, "How shall we prove that?" Whereunto the knight made reply, "This is what we shall do: Thou and I shall stand forth in the middle of this hall, and thou shalt have leave to try to strike off my head; and if I can receive that blow without dying therefrom, then I shall have leave to strike thy head off in a like manner."

Upon this speech King Arthur was greatly a-dread and he said, "That is very strange sport for two men to engage upon."

Now when King Arthur said this, all those who were in the hall burst out laughing beyond all measure and as though they would never stint from their mirth. Then, when they had become in a measure quiet again, the knight of that castle said, "Sir, art thou afraid of that sport?" Upon which King Arthur fell very angry and he said, "Nay, I am not afeared, for no man hath ever yet had reason to say that I showed myself afeared of anyone." "Very well," said the knight of the castle; "then let us try that sport of which I spake." And King Arthur said, "I am willing."

Then Boisenard came to King Arthur where he was, and he said, "Lord, do not thou enter into this thing, but rather let me undertake this venture in thy stead, for I am assured that some great treachery is meditated against thee." But King Arthur said, "Nay; no man shall take my danger upon himself, but I will assume mine own danger without calling upon any man to take it." So he said to the knight of the castle, "Sir, I am ready for that sport of which thou didst speak, but who is to strike that first blow and how shall we draw lots therefor?" "Messire," said the knight of the castle, "there shall be no lots drawn. For, as thou art the guest of this place, so shall thou have first assay at that sport."

Therewith that knight arose and laid aside his black robe, and he was clad beneath in a shirt of fine linen very cunningly worked. And he wore hosen of crimson. Then he opened that linen undergarment at the throat and he turned down the collar thereof so as to lay his neck bare to the blow. Thereupon he said, "Now, Sir Knight, thou shalt have to strike well if thou wouldst win at this sport."

But King Arthur showed no dread of that undertaking, for he arose and drew Excalibur so that the blade of the sword flashed with exceeding brightness. Then he measured his distance, and lifted the sword, and he smote the knight of the castle with all his might upon the neck. And, lo! the blade cut through the neck of the knight of the castle with wonderful ease, so that the head flew from the body to a great distance away.

But the trunk of the body of that knight did not fall, but instead of that it stood, and it walked to where the head lay, and the hands of the trunk picked up the head and they set the head back upon the body, and, lo! that knight was as sound and whole as ever he had been in all his life.

Upon this all those of the castle shouted and made great mirth, and they called upon King Arthur that it was now his turn to try that sport. So the King prepared himself, laying

aside his surcoat and opening his undergarment at the throat, as
the knight of the castle had done. And at that Boisenard made
great lamentation. Then the knight of the castle said, "Sir, art
thou afeared?" And King Arthur said, "No, I am not afeared,
for every man must come to his death some time, and it appears
that my time hath now come, and that I am to lay down my life
in this foolish fashion for no fault of mine own."

Then the knight of the castle said, "Well, stand thou away a
little distance so that I may not strike thee too close, and so lose
the virtue of my blow."

So King Arthur stood forth in the midst of the hall, and the
knight of the castle swung his sword several times, but did not
strike. Likewise, he several times laid the blade of the sword
upon King Arthur's neck, and it was very cold. Then King
Arthur cried out in great passion, "Sir, it is thy right to strike,
but I beseech thee not to torment me in this manner." "Nay,"
said the knight of the castle, "it is my right to strike when it
pleases me, and I will not strike any before that time. For if
it please me I will torment thee for a great while ere I slay
thee." So he laid his sword several times more upon King

Arthur's neck, and King Arthur said no more, but bore that torment with a very steadfast spirit.

Then the knight of the castle said, "Thou appearest to be a very courageous and honorable knight, and I have a mind to make a covenant with thee." And King Arthur said, "What is that covenant?" "It is this," said the knight of the castle, "I will spare thee thy life for a year and a day if thou wilt pledge me thy knightly word to return hither at the end of that time."

Then King Arthur said, "Very well; it shall be so." And therewith he pledged his knightly word to return at the end of that time, swearing to that pledge upon the cross of the hilt of Excalibur.

Then the knight of the castle said, "I will make another covenant with thee." "What is it?" said King Arthur. "My second covenant is this," quoth the knight of the castle, "I will give to thee a riddle, and if thou wilt answer that riddle when thou returnest hither, and if thou makest no mistake in that answer, then will I spare thy life and set thee free." And King Arthur said, "What is that riddle?" To which the knight made reply, "The riddle is this: What is it that a woman desires most of all in the world?"

"Sir," said King Arthur, "I will seek to find the answer to that riddle, and I give thee gramercy for sparing my life for so long a time as thou hast done, and for giving me the chance to escape my death." Upon this the knight of the castle smiled very sourly, and he said, "I do not offer this to thee because of mercy to thee, but because I find pleasure in tormenting thee. For what delight canst thou have in living thy life when thou knowest that thou must, for a surety, die at the end of one short year? And what pleasure canst thou have in living even that year when thou shalt be tormented with anxiety to discover the answer to my riddle?"

Then King Arthur said, "I think thou art very cruel." And the knight said, "I am not denying that."

So that night King Arthur and Boisenard lay at the castle, and the next day they took their way thence. And King Arthur was very heavy and troubled in spirit; ne'theless he charged Boisenard that he should say nothing concerning that which had befallen, but that he should keep it in secret. And

Boisenard did as the King commanded, and said nothing concerning that adventure.

Now in that year which followed, King Arthur settled his affairs. Also he sought everywhere to find the answer to that riddle. Many there were who gave him answers in plenty, for one said that a woman most desired wealth, and another said she most desired beauty, and one said she desired power to please, and another said that she most desired fine raiment; and one said this, and another said that; but no answer appeared to King Arthur to be good and fitting for his purpose.

So the year passed by, until only a fortnight remained; and then King Arthur could not abide to stay where he was any longer, for it seemed to him his time was very near to hand, and he was filled with a very bitter anxiety of soul, wherefore he was very restless to be away.

So he called Boisenard to him, and he said, "Boisenard, help me to arm, for I am going away."

Then Boisenard fell a-weeping in very great measure, and he said, "Lord, do not go."

At this King Arthur looked very sternly at his esquire, and said, "Boisenard, how is this? Wouldst thou tempt me to violate mine honor? It is not very hard to die, but it would be very bitter to live my life in dishonor; wherefore tempt me no more, but do my bidding and hold thy peace. And if I do not return in a month from this time, then mayst thou tell all that hath befallen. And thou mayst tell Sir Constantine of Cornwall that he is to search the papers in my cabinet, and that there he will find all that is to be done should death overtake me."

So Boisenard put a plain suit of armor upon King Arthur, though he could hardly see what he was about for the tears that flowed down out of his eyes in great abundance. And he laced upon the armor of the King a surcoat without device, and he gave the King a shield without device. Thereupon King Arthur rode away without considering whither his way took him. And of everyone whom he met he inquired what that thing was that a woman most desired, and no one could give him an answer that appeared to him to be what it should be, wherefore he was in great doubt and torment of spirit.

Now the day before King Arthur was to keep his covenant at

that castle, he was wandering through the adjacent forest in great travail of soul, for he wist not what he should do to save his life. As he wandered so, he came of a sudden upon a small hut built up under an overhanging oak-tree so that it was very hard to tell where the oak-tree ended and the hut began. And there were a great many large rocks all about covered with moss, so that the King might very easily have passed by the hut only that he beheld a smoke to arise therefrom as from a fire that burned within. So he went to the hut and opened the door and entered. At first he thought there was no one there, but when he looked again he beheld an old woman sitting bent over a small fire that burned upon the hearth. And King Arthur had never beheld such an ugly beldame as that one who sat there bending over that fire, for her ears were very huge and flapped, and her hair hung down over her head like to snakes, and her face was covered all over with wrinkles so that there were not any places at all where there was not a wrinkle; and her eyes were bleared and covered over with a film, and the eyelids were red as with the continual weeping of her eyes, and she had but one tooth in her mouth, and her hands, which she spread out to the fire, were like claws of bone.

Then King Arthur gave her greeting and she gave the King greeting, and she said to him, "My lord King, whence come ye? and why do ye come to this place?"

Then King Arthur was greatly astonished that that old woman should know him, who he was, and he said, "Who are you that appeareth to know me?" "No matter," said she, "I am one who meaneth you well; so tell me what is the trouble that brings you here at this time." So the King confessed all his trouble to that old woman, and he asked her if she knew the answer to that riddle, "What is it that a woman most desires?" "Yea," said the old woman, "I know the answer to that riddle very well, but I will not tell it to thee unless thou wilt promise me something in return."

At this King Arthur was filled with very great joy that the old woman should know the answer to that riddle, and he was filled with doubt of what she would demand of him, wherefore he said, "What is it thou must have in return for that answer?"

Then the old woman said, "If I aid thee to guess thy riddle aright, thou must promise that I shall become wife unto one of the knights of thy Court, whom I may choose when thou returnest homeward again."

"Ha!" said King Arthur, "how may I promise that upon the behalf of anyone?" Upon this the old woman said, "Are not the knights of thy Court of such nobility that they will do that to save thee from death?" "I believe they are," said King Arthur. And with that he meditated a long while, saying unto himself, "What will my kingdom do if I die at this time? I have no right to die." So he said to the old woman, "Very well, I will make that promise."

Then she said unto the King, "This is the answer to that riddle: That which a woman most desires is to have her will." And the answer seemed to King Arthur to be altogether right.

Then the old woman said, "My lord King, thou hast been played upon by that knight who hath led thee into this trouble, for he is a great conjurer and a magician of a very evil sort. He carrieth his life not within his body, but in a crystal globe which he weareth in a locket hanging about his neck; wherefore it was that when thou didst cut the head from off his body, his life remained in that locket and he did not die. But if thou hadst destroyed that locket, then he would immediately have died."

"I will mind me of that," said King Arthur.

So King Arthur abided with that old woman for that night, and she refreshed him with meat and drink and served him very well. And the next morning he set forth unto that castle where he had made his covenant, and his heart was more cheerful than it had been for a whole year.

Chapter Third

*How King Arthur Overcame the Knight-
Enchanter, and How Sir Gawaine
Manifested the High Nobility of
His Knighthood.*

Now, when King Arthur came to the castle, the gateway thereof was immediately opened to him and he entered. And when he had entered, sundry attendants came and conducted him into the hall where he had aforetime been. There he beheld the knight of that castle and a great many people who had come to witness the conclusion of the adventure. And when the knight beheld King Arthur he said to him, "Sir, hast thou come to redeem thy pledge?" "Yea," said King Arthur, "for so I made my vow to thee." Then the knight of the castle said, "Sir, hast thou guessed that riddle?" And King Arthur said, "I believe that I have." The knight of the castle said, "Then let me hear thy answer thereto. But if thou makest any mistake, or if thou dost not guess aright, then is thy life forfeit." "Very well," said King Arthur, "let it be that way. Now this is the answer to thy riddle: That which a woman most desires is to have her will."

Now when the lord of the castle heard King Arthur guess aright he wist not what to say or where to look, and those who were there also perceived that the King had guessed aright.

Then King Arthur came very close to that knight with great

sternness of demeanor, and he said, "Now, thou traitor knight! thou didst ask me to enter into thy sport with thee a year ago, so at these present it is my turn to ask thee to have sport with me. And this is the sport I will have, that thou shalt give me that chain and locket that hang about thy neck, and that I shall give thee the collar which hangeth about my neck."

At this, the face of that knight fell all pale, like to ashes, and he emitted a sound similar to the sound made by a hare when the hound lays hold upon it. Then King Arthur catched him very violently by the arm, and he catched the locket and brake it away from about the knight's neck, and upon that the knight shrieked very loud, and fell down upon his knees and besought mercy of the King, and there was great uproar in that place. Then King Arthur opened the locket and lo! there was a ball as of crystal, very clear and shining. And King Arthur said, "I will have no mercy," and therewith he flung the ball violently down upon the stone of the pavement so that it brake with a loud noise. Then, upon that instant, the knight-conjurer gave a piercing bitter cry and fell down upon the ground; and when they ran to raise him up, behold! he was entirely dead.

Now when the people of that castle beheld their knight thus suddenly dead, and when they beheld King Arthur how he stood in the fury of his kingly majesty, they were greatly afeared so that they shrunk away from the King where he stood. Then the King turned and went out from that castle and no one stayed him, and he mounted his horse and rode away, and no one gave him let or hindrance in his going.

Now when the King had left the castle in that wise, he went straight to the hut where was the old beldame and he said to her, "Thou hast holpen me a very great deal in mine hour of need, so now will I fulfil that pledge which I made unto thee, for I will take thee unto my Court and thou shalt choose one of my knights for thy husband. For I think there is not one knight in all my Court but would be very glad to do anything that lieth in his power to reward one who hath saved me as thou hast done this day."

Therewith he took that old woman and he lifted her up upon the crupper of his horse; then he himself mounted upon his horse, and so they rode away from that place. And the King comported himself to that aged beldame in all ways with the utmost consideration as though she had been a beautiful dame of the highest degree in the land. Likewise he showed her such respect that had she been a lady of royal blood, he could not have shown greater respect to her.

So in due time they reached the Court, which was then at Carleon. And they came there nigh about mid-day.

Now about that time it chanced that the Queen and a number of the lords of the Court, and a number of the ladies of the Court, were out in the fields enjoying the pleasantness of the Maytime; for no one in all the world, excepting the esquire, Boisenard, knew anything of the danger that beset King Arthur; hence all were very glad of the pleasantness of the season. Now as King Arthur drew nigh to that place, these lifted up their eyes and beheld him come, and they were astonished beyond all measure to see King Arthur come to them across that field with that old beldame behind him upon the saddle, wherefore they stood still to wait until King Arthur reached them.

But when King Arthur had come to them, he did not dismount from his horse, but sat thereon and regarded them all very steadfastly; and Queen Guinevere said, "Sir, what is this? Hast thou a mind to play some merry jest this day that thou hast brought hither that old woman?"

"Lady," said King Arthur, "excepting for this old woman it were like to have been a very sorry jest for thee and for me; for had she not aided me I would now have been a dead man and in a few days you would doubtless all have been in great passion of sorrow."

Then all they who were there marvelled very greatly at the King's words. And the Queen said, "Sir, what is it that hath befallen thee?"

Thereupon King Arthur told them all that had happened to him from the very beginning when he and Boisenard had left the castle of Tintagalon. And when he had ended his story, they were greatly amazed.

Now there were seventeen lords of the Court there present. So when King Arthur had ended his story, he said unto these, "Messires, I have given my pledge unto this aged woman that any one of you whom she may choose, shall take her unto him as his wife, and shall treat her with all the regard that it is possible for him to do; for this was the condition that she laid upon me. Now tell me, did I do right in making unto her my pledge that I would fulfil that which she desired?" And all of those who were present said, "Yea, lord, thou didst right, for we would do all in the world for to save thee from such peril as that from which thou hast escaped."

Then King Arthur said to that old woman, "Lady, is there any of these knights here whom you would choose for to be your husband?" Upon this, the old woman pointed with her very long, bony finger unto Sir Gawaine, saying, "Yea, I would marry that lord, for I see by the chain that is around his neck and by the golden circlet upon his hair and by the haughty nobility of his aspect, that he must be the son of a king."

Then King Arthur said unto Sir Gawaine, "Sir, art thou willing to fulfil my pledge unto this old woman?" And Sir Gawaine said, "Yea, lord, whatsoever thou requirest of me, that will I do." So Sir Gawaine came to the old woman and took her hand into his and set it to his lips; and not one of all those present so much as smiled. Then they all turned their faces and returned unto the King's castle; and they were very silent and downcast, for this was sore trouble that had come upon that Court.

Now after they had returned unto the Court, they assigned certain apartments therein to that old woman, and they clad her in rich raiment such as a queen might wear, and they assigned unto her a Court such as was fit for a queen; and it seemed to all the Court that, in the rich robes which she wore, she was ten times more ugly than she was before. So when eleven days had passed, Sir Gawaine was wedded to that old woman in the chapel of the King's Court with great ceremony and pomp of circumstance, and all of those who were there were as sad and as sorrowful as though Sir Gawaine had been called upon to suffer his death.

Afterward that they were married, Sir Gawaine and the old woman went to Sir Gawaine's house and there Sir Gawaine shut himself off from all the world and suffered no one to come nigh him; for he was proud beyond all measure, and in this great humiliation he suffered in such a wise that words cannot tell how great was that humiliation. Wherefore he shut himself away from the world that no one might behold his grief and his shame.

And all the rest of that day he walked continually up and down his chamber, for he was altogether in such despair that it came unto his mind that it would be well if he took his own life; for it seemed to him impossible for to suffer such shame as that which had come upon him. So after a while it fell the dark of the early night and therewith a certain strength came to Sir Gawaine and he said, "This is a shame for me for to behave in this way; for since I have married that lady she is my true wedded wife and I do not treat her with that regard unto which she hath the right." So he went out of that place and sought the apartment of that old woman who was his wife, and by that time it was altogether dark. But when Sir Gawaine had come into that place where she was, that old woman upbraided him, crying out upon him, "So, Sir! You have treated me but ill upon this our wedding-day, for you have stayed all the afternoon away from me and now only come to me when it is dark night." And Sir Gawaine said, "Lady, I could not help it, for I was very sore oppressed with many cares. But if I have disregarded thee this day, I do beseech thy forgiveness therefore, and I will hold myself willing to do all that is in my power to recompense thee for any neglect that I have placed upon thee." Then the lady said, "Sir, it is very dark in this place; let us then have a light." "It shall be as thou dost desire," said Sir Gawaine, "and I, myself, will go and fetch a light for thee."

So Sir Gawaine went forth from that place and he brought two waxen tapers, one in either hand, and he bore them in candlesticks of gold; for he was minded to show all respect unto that old woman. And when he came into the room he perceived that she was at the farther end of the apartment and he went toward her, and she arose and stood before him as he approached.

But when the circle of light fell upon that old woman, and when Sir Gawaine beheld her who stood before him, he cried out aloud in a very great voice because of the great marvel and wonder of that which he saw. For, instead of that old woman whom he had left, he beheld a lady of extraordinary beauty and in the very flower of her youth. And he beheld that her hair was long and glossy and very black, and that her eyes were likewise black like to black jewels, and that her lips were like coral, and her teeth were like pearls. So, for a while, Sir Gawaine could not speak, and then he cried out, "Lady! lady! who art thou?"

Then that lady smiled upon Sir Gawaine with such loving-kindness that he wist not what to think, other than that this was an angel who had descended to that place out of paradise. Wherefore he stood before her for a long time and could find no more words to say, and she continued to smile upon him very kindly in that wise. Then by and by Sir Gawaine said to her, "Lady, where is that dame who is my wife?" And the lady said, "Sir Gawaine, I am she." "It is not possible," cried out Sir Gawaine, "for she was old and extraordinarily ugly, but I believe that thou art beautiful beyond any lady whom I have beheld." And the lady said, "Nevertheless, I am she and because thou hast taken me for thy wife with thine own free will and with great courtesy, so is a part of that enchantment that lay upon me removed from me. For I will now be able to appear before thee in mine own true shape. For whiles I was a little while ago so ugly and foul as thou didst behold me to be, now am I to be as thou seest me, for one-half the day— and the other half thereof I must be ugly as I was before."

Then Sir Gawaine was filled beyond all words with great joy. And with that joy there came an extreme passion of loving regard for that lady. So he cried out aloud several times, "This is surely the most wonderful thing that ever befell any man in all the world." Therewith he fell down upon his knees and took that lady's hands into his own hands, and kissed her hands with great fervor, and all the while she smiled upon him as she had done at first.

Then again the lady said, "Come, sit thee down beside me and let us consider what part of the day I shall be in the one guise, and what part of the day I shall be in the other guise; for all day I may have the one appearance, and all night I may have the other appearance."

Then Sir Gawaine said, "I would have thee in this guise

during the night time, for then we are together at our own inn; and since thou art of this sort that I now see thee, I do not at all reckon how the world may regard thee."

Upon this the lady spake with great animation, saying, "No, sir, I would not have it in that wise, for every woman loveth the regard of the world, and I would fain enjoy such beauty as is

mine before the world, and not endure the scorn and contempt of men and women."

To this Sir Gawaine said, "Lady, I would have it the other way."

And she said, "Nay, I would have it my way."

Then Sir Gawaine said, "So be it. For since I have taken thee for my wife, so must I show thee respect in all matters; wherefore thou shalt have thy will in this and in all other things."

Then that lady fell a-laughing beyond all measure and she said, "Sir, I did but put this as a last trial upon thee, for as I am now, so shall I always be."

Upon this Sir Gawaine was so filled with joy that he knew not how to contain himself.

So they sat together for a long time, hand in hand. Then after a while Sir Gawaine said, "Lady, who art thou?" Unto which she made reply, "I am one of the Ladies of the Lake; but for thy sake I have become mortal like to other women and have quit that very beautiful home where I one time dwelt. I have kept thee in my heart for a considerable while, for I was not very far distant at that time when thou didst bid adieu to Sir

Pellias beside the lake. There I beheld how thou didst weep and bewail thyself when Sir Pellias left thee, wherefore my heart went out to thee with great pity. So, after a while, I quitted that lake and became mortal for thy sake. Now, when I found the trouble into which King Arthur had fallen I took that occasion to have him fetch me unto thee so that I might test the entire nobility of thy knighthood; and, lo! I have found it all that I deemed it possible to be. For though I appeared to thee so aged, so ugly, and so foul, yet hast thou treated me with such kind regard that I do not believe that thou couldst have behaved with more courtesy to me had I been the daughter of a king. Wherefore it doth now afford me such pleasure for to possess thee for my knight and my true lord, that I cannot very well tell thee how great is my joy therein."

Then Sir Gawaine said, "Lady, I do not think it can be so great as my joy in possessing thee." And thereupon he came to her and laid his hand upon her shoulder and kissed her upon the lips.

Then, after that, he went forth and called with a great voice all through that house, and the people of the house came running from everywhere. And he commanded that the people should bring lights and refreshments, and they brought the lights, and when they had brought them and beheld that beautiful lady instead of the aged dame, they were filled with great wonder and joy; wherefore they cried out aloud and clapped their hands together and made much sound of rejoicing. And they set a great feast for Sir Gawaine and his lady, and in place of the sorrow and darkness that had been, there was joy and light, and music and singing; wherefore those of the King's Court, beholding this from a distance, said, "It is very strange that Sir Gawaine should have taken so much joy of having wedded that old beldame."

But when the next morning had come, that lady clad herself in raiment of yellow silk, and she hung about her many strands of precious stones of several colors, and she set a golden crown upon her head. And Sir Gawaine let call his horse, and he let call a snow-white palfrey for the lady, and thereupon they rode out from that place and entered the Court of the King. But when the King and the Queen and their several Courts beheld that lady, they were filled with such great astonishment that they wist not what to say for pure wonder. And when they heard all that had happened, they gave great joy and loud acclaim so that all their mourning was changed into rejoicing. And, indeed, there was not one knight there of all that Court who would not have given half his life to have been so fortunate in that matter as was Sir Gawaine, the son of King Lot of Orkney.

Such is the story of Sir Gawaine, and from it I draw this significance: as that poor ugly beldame appeared unto the eyes of Sir Gawaine, so doth a man's duty sometimes appear to him to be ugly and exceedingly ill-favored unto his desires. But when he shall have wedded himself unto that duty so that he hath made it one with him as a bridegroom maketh himself one with his bride, then doth that duty become of a sudden very beautiful unto him and unto others.

So may it be with ye that you shall take duty unto yourselves no matter how much it may mislike ye to do so. For indeed a man shall hardly have any real pleasure in his life unless his inclination becometh wedded unto his duty and cleaveth unto it as a husband cleaveth unto his wife. For when inclination is thus wedded unto duty, then doth the soul take great joy unto itself as though a wedding had taken place betwixt a bridegroom and a bride within its tabernacle.

Likewise, when you shall have become entirely wedded unto your duty, then shall you become equally worthy with that good knight and gentleman Sir Gawaine; for it needs not that a man shall wear armor for to be a true knight, but only that he shall do his best endeavor with all patience and humility as it hath been ordained for him to do. Wherefore, when your time cometh unto you to display your knightness by assuming your duty, I do pray that you also may approve yourself as worthy as Sir Gawaine approved himself in this story which I have told you of as above written.

Conclusion

So endeth this volume wherein hath been told, with every circumstance of narration, the history of those Three Worthies who were of the Court of King Arthur.

And now, if God will give me the grace to do so, I will some time, at no very great time from this, write the further history of sundry other knights and worthies of whom I have not yet spoken.

And among the first of these shall be Sir Launcelot, whom all the world knoweth to have been the greatest knight in prowess of arms of any who has lived, excepting Sir Galahad, who was his son. And I shall tell you the story of Sir Ewaine and Sir Geraint, and of Sir Percival and of sundry others.

But of this another time. For now, with great regret I bid you adieu and bring this history unto a close.

So may God grant us to come together at another time with such happiness and prosperity that you may have a free and untroubled heart to enjoy the narrated history of those excellent men which I shall then set before you. Amen.